SERAMPORE MISSION

Perspectives in Contexts

SERAMPORE MISSION

Perspectives in Contexts

EDITOR
Johnson Thomaskutty

2019

Serampore Mission: Perspectives in Contexts —Jointly published by the Rev. Dr. Ashish Amos of the Indian Society for Promoting Christian Knowledge (ISPCK), Post Box 1585, Kashmere Gate, Delhi-110006 and Union Biblical Seminary (UBS), Pune, Maharashtra-411037.

ISBN: 978-93-88945-06-6

Laser typeset by

ISPCK, Post Box 1585, 1654, Madarsa Road, Kashmere Gate, Delhi-110006 • *Tel:* 23866323

e-mail: ashish@ispck.org.in • ella@ispck.org.in
website: www.ispck.org.in

Contents

Contributors

Rev. Dr. Santanu K. Patro is the Registrar of the Senate of Serampore College (University), West Bengal, India. Formerly, he served the Eastern Theological College, Jorhat, Assam, and Gurukul Lutheran Theological College and Research Institute, Chennai, India, in the capacity of a Faculty Member, Bursar, Church Relations Officer, Faculty Secretary, Head of the Department of Religious Studies, and Dean of Graduate and Post-Graduate Studies. He is the author of *A Feminist Reading of Womanhood in Dark Kali Tradition* (Delhi: ISPCK, 2006).

Dr. Roger E. Hedlund served as Editor, *Oxford Encyclopedia of South Asian Christianity* (New Delhi: Oxford University Press, 2012); Director Emeritus, Mylapore Institute for Religious Studies, Chennai, India; Retired Managing Editor, *Dharma Deepika: A South Asian Journal of Missiological Research*; Associate Professor of Missiology at Union Biblical Seminary, Yavatmal/ Pune (1974-1978); Professor of Mission Research at Serampore College and Carey Library (1994-1997).

Rev. Dr. Songram Basumatary is Professor and HOD of Theology and Ethics at Gurukul Lutheran Theological College and Research Institute, Chennai, India. He is the author of *Ethnicity and Tribal Theology: Problem and Prospect for Peaceful Co-existence in North East India* (Bern/Oxford: Peter Lang, 2014) and the editor of *Transforming Reformation: Reformation in Perspectives* (Chennai: Gurukul Publications, 2017); and *Migration in Perspectives: Towards Theology of Migration from the Margins* (Chennai: Gurukul Publications, 2018).

Rev. Dr. Subhro Sekhar Sircar is Professor of New Testament in the Faculty of Theology, Serampore College, and North India Institute of Post Graduate Theological Studies (NIIPGTS), Serampore, Hooghly, West Bengal, India.

Formerly, he served as the Vice-Principal (Theology) of the Serampore College. He is the author of *Paul's Theology of Mission to the Nations in Romans* (Biblical Hermeneutics Rediscovered 8; New Delhi: Christian World Imprints, 2018).

Dr. Prakash Abraham Mathew teaches in the Department of Old Testament Studies at Union Biblical Seminary, Pune, India. Previously, he taught OT subjects in Jubilee Memorial Bible College and Indian Theological Seminary, both in Chennai. His doctoral dissertation was titled *Role of Holiness Laws for the Formation and Legitimization of Collective Identity in Leviticus 17-26.* He has also authored five academic articles and published them in some of the theological journals in India.

Dr. J. Stanly Jones teaches New Testament at Union Biblical Seminary, Pune, India. He is also the Registrar of the Seminary. He earned his doctorate under the Senate of Serampore College and the dissertation was titled *The Healing Narratives as a Mode of Resistance to Oppressive Institutions in the World of Jesus Movement with Special Reference to Mark's Gospel.*

Rev. Dr. Johnson Thomaskutty teaches New Testament at Union Biblical Seminary, Pune, India. Formerly, he served the Serampore College, Hooghly, West Bengal, as Lecturer of New Testament and as the College Chaplain. He is the author of *Dialogue in the Book of Signs: A Polyvalent Analysis of John 1:19-12:50* (Biblical Interpretation Series 136; Leiden/Boston: E. J. Brill, 2015) and *Saint Thomas the Apostle: New Testament, Apocrypha, and Historical Traditions* (T&T Clark Jewish and Christian Texts Series 25; New York/London: Bloomsbury T&T Clark, 2018). He has also authored over forty academic articles and published them in the leading national and international journals and monographs.

Dr. Annie George serves in the Department of Christian Ministry at Faith Theological Seminary, Manakala, Kerala, India. Besides she is part of the pastoral team of Adoor Vineyard Church, Kerala, India. She is the author of *Children's Perceptions of the Role of Biblical Narratives in Their Spiritual Formation.* Her vision is to see children and youths equipped at home and church to passionately serve Jesus and his creation.

Rev. Dr. Woba James is Associate Professor and HOD of History of Christianity at Eastern Theological College, Jorhat, Assam. Currently, he also serves as the President of CHAI-NEI. He is the author of *Revisiting*

Ecumenical Theological Education in India: With Special Reference to the Senate of Serampore College (Christian Heritage Discovered 34; Delhi: Christian World Imprints, 2016) and *Major Issues in the History of Christianity in India: A Postcolonial Reading* (Mokokchung: Tribal Development and Communication Center, 2013).

Rev. Dr. Shiju Mathew is Associate Professor and HOD of Old Testament Studies at Union Biblical Seminary, Pune, India. He is the author of *Biblical Law Codes in Creative Tension: A Postcolonial Womanist Reading* (2016). He also published several of his articles in some of the leading academic journals published in India.

Rev. Dr. George Philip teaches New Testament and Greek language at Bethel Bible College, Guntur, Andhra Pradesh, India. He is the author of *Paul and Common Meal: Re-socialization of the Christian Community* (Biblical Hermeneutics Rediscovered 7; New Delhi: Christian World Imprints, 2017).

Rev. Dr. Jangkholam Haokip teaches Theology and Eco-Justice at Union Biblical Seminary, Pune, India. Currently, he is Dean of Theology and Ethics in the Seminary. He authored *Can God Save My Village?* (Carlisle: Langham Monographs, 2014); co-edited *Becoming a Missional Congregation in the Twenty-First Century Indian Context* (Delhi: ISPCK, 2016); and articles in the leading theological journals and monographs in India and abroad.

Rev. Dr. Viju Wilson teaches Christian Theology at Union Biblical Seminary, Pune, India. Apart from several articles, he has authored a book, *Ecclesiology of Prophetic Participation*; co-edited a book, *Among the People*; and completed a research work, *Dalit Heritage and Liberative Traditions in India.*

Dr. Mayang Longkumer is Academic Dean and teaches New Testament at the South India Biblical Seminary, Bangarapet, India. He is the author of *The New World: A Sociological Approach to Revelation* (Mokokchung: TTDC Publication, 2010) and *Apular: A Biography of Rev. K. Longri* (Jorhat: Penuel Ministry Publication, 2006).

Rev. (Dr.) James Patole is an ordained Minister of Christian and Missionary Alliance, based in Pune, India. He serves as an Associate Director for North India Urban Ministry at Evangelical Fellowship of India's NCUT. His PhD specialization is in Urban Missions and Globalization Studies. He is the author of *Principles of Biblical Economics* (Hyderabad/London: Authentic

Books, 2007) and *Offerings; Principles and Promises* (Bombay: Gospel Literature Service, 2011).

Dr. Kaholi Zhimomi teaches History of Christianity at the United Theological College, Bangalore, India. She holds the Fredrick S. Downs Associate Professor of History of Christianity. She was formerly the Assistant Editor of the *Baptist News of the Council of Baptist Churches in North East India*, Guwahati, and is currently the Editor of *Masihi Sevak: Journal of Christian Ministry* of the United Theological College.

Dr. Giri Krishnan is Associate Professor of Religions at Union Biblical Seminary, Pune, India. Formerly he served as the Principal of Kerala Theological Seminary (KTS), Kottarakara, Kerala. Moreover, he served as teaching faculty in the Theology Department of Serampore College, North India Institute of Post-Graduate Theological Studies (NIIPGTS), West Bengal, and Gospel For Asia Biblical Seminary (GFABS), Kerala. He is the author of *Brahmajijñāsā of Śaṅkara as Theology: A Post Colonial Appraisal* (2013), and *Śabda Pramāṇa and Indian Biblical Hermeneutics* (2015).

Foreword

Santanu K. Patro

It is impossible to separate the Serampore Mission from the Serampore College, and further the Serampore College from the Serampore Trio/ Quartet, namely William Carey, Joshua and Hannah Marshman, and William Ward. They were the pioneer missionaries of the late 18th and early 19th century who had evolved a holistic approach to Christian missions. Looking back after 200 years (1818-2018), we get the impression that their approach was truly revolutionary and radical to their times. The Serampore missionaries addressed the issues of religion, politics, economics, and socio-cultural life situations of the natives. More importantly, they were inclusive and ecumenical in their approach. For them, the Gospel of Jesus Christ has no boundaries by which it should be operated. They unravelled the myth that the Gospel is not limited to Christian religious traditions; rather they recognized the Gospel as Jesus' movement to transform human society. It is both humanitarian and spiritual at the same time. Therefore, it is personal and societal.

William Carey arrived in Kolkata, India, on 11th November 1792, after a voyage of five long months. After two weeks in India, Carey compared his feeling with what Paul felt when he was in Athens. He went out to describe India as one of the finest countries in the world, full of industrious inhabitants. Three-fifths of the land were uncultivated and jungles with wild beasts and serpents. His goal was to make the Gospel saturate in all spheres, so that the uncultivated lands would be harvested with plenty, fruits would be planted in the jungles, and people would be liberated from all bondages of 'wilderness.' Being a naturalist and Botanist, he did not intend to destroy the wilderness that houses animals and reptiles; rather he made them to be cultivable to grow flora and fauna. This radical understanding of the Gospel makes William Carey truly the "Father [Mother] of Modern Missions."

William Carey served forty long years as a missionary. His life and work were inspirations to millions of missionaries to receive a similar vision and venture across the globe. He pioneered the Protestant Missionary Movement. J. Herbert Kane rightly remarked, "What Luther was to the Protestant Reformation, Carey was to the Christian Missionary Movement." Simultaneously, new political power, new spiritual values, western science, and English education in the 19th century paved the way for 'Indian Renaissance' that engaged religious leaders to reform their own religious traditions.

In 1818, the Mission founded the Serampore College to train indigenous ministers for the growing church, and to provide education in Arts and Sciences to anyone. The King of Denmark granted a Royal Charter in 1827 that made the College a degree-granting institution, i.e., the first in the Asian context. As Serampore was a Danish colony, King Frederick VI, the King of Denmark, issued the Serampore College its Royal Charter of Incorporation on February 23, 1827, in Copenhagen, Denmark. The Charter gave Serampore College the privilege of awarding degrees in Arts and Theology. William Carey, Joshua Marshman and John Clark Marshman (Joshua's son) were designated as members of the first council. At its opening, the Serampore Trio/Quartet released a prospectus which proposed *A College for the Instruction of Asiatic Christian and Other Youth in Eastern Literature and European Science*. The college was open to all people regardless of caste or creed, and the founders ensured that no denominational test would apply to the faculty members. The Charter has also been confirmed by the Bengal Government Act IV of 1918. The status accorded by the Danish Charter has since been reaffirmed for the study of theology, and now forms the basis for degrees of all levels conferred by over 58 theological colleges throughout India and is administered by the Senate.

After 22nd February 1845, when Denmark sold all of its Indian assets to Britain, the management and operation of the College continued without interruption under the direction of a Master and a Council. In 1856, the Baptist Missionary Society in England took over the management of the college and, in 1857, the College became affiliated with the newly established University of Calcutta and became a constituent college of that university. In 1883, the College closed as an Arts College and began functioning as a Christian Training Institution and a theological institute for the Baptist churches in Bengal. Re-affiliating with the University of Calcutta in 1911, the Serampore College, in 1913, was authorised to award the Bachelor of Arts degree. The faculty of the college was interdenominational.

Between 1916 and 1927, sixty-nine more students earned their Bachelor of Divinity degree through the Serampore College. During the centenary year of the college, the Bengal Legislative Council passed the Serampore College Act (1918 Act I; 1918 Act II; 1918 Act III; 1918 Act IV) for the purpose of enlarging the college council and forming a new inter-denominational senate that would confer theological degrees for all Christian denominations in India.

Carey's life, call, ministry, and mission are remarkable documentations for the history of world missions. He took upon himself the translation of the Bible, printing as well as writing of books so that all will receive knowledge. For him, education was liberation and Bible in vernacular language was a key to true realization. William Carey's life and ministry have left indelible marks in the history of Christian mission and the history of modern education. Therefore, it is pertinent for us to study his contributions to education in the light of the development of science and technology, literature and culture, social transformation and empowerment of men and women of low castes, and economic statuses. It also addressed the issues of discrimination against women and children by the religious order and also political exploitation of the colonial powers.

The Serampore missionaries found it difficult to start the missionary works in India. The policy of East India Company was to keep the Gospel out of the domain of the natives for their own selfish political and commercial gains. From the beginning, the East India Company realized that Indians are sensitive about their own religions and the company thought that Gospel works might damage the efforts of business and the survival of the company. The conflict between two strong views, one in favour of missionary works and another against, divided not only the Indian public but also the British citizens, both within the British Parliament and in the Church of England. Scholars who were sympathetic to the missionary efforts asserted that the Gospel is transformative and enlightening and that brings education, awareness, and new life in Christ. They were even critical of colonial rulers who wanted to plunder the wealth of other nations. The Serampore Mission had received more support through the means of Raja Ram Mohan Roy who felt that Carey's mission was doing the right thing, though he did not want Hindus to be converted to Christianity.

As a pioneer missionary, Carey educated himself to get into the social and secular discourses within the Indian intellectual tradition and wanted to develop his approach more holistic, contextual, and pluralistic. Therefore, the task continues, and the book titled **Serampore Mission: Perspectives in Contexts** will certainly continue searching newer approaches to mission in the prevailing geo-political and religious contexts. I congratulate Dr. Johnson Thomaskutty and the Union Biblical Seminary for this genuine task. Indian examples and approaches are still relevant, and they must be rightly critiqued to make mission more responsible in approaching the Gospel.

Overture

The Serampore Mission

Roger E. Hedlund

It gives me immense pleasure to be asked to write an overture to this significant volume on the occasion of the Bicentenary of the founding of the Serampore College. My thanks and appreciations are due to Professor Johnson Thomaskutty and the academic committee of the Union Biblical Seminary for their initiatives. Popular as well as scholarly books, articles, essays, and dissertations devoted to William Carey and the Serampore Trio/Quartet are legion, but not so much has been said about the Serampore Mission as such.

Carey and family, arriving as "missionary outlaws" in Bengal, for six years had struggled against great difficulties. In 1799, new recruits of the Baptist Missionary Society (the Particular Baptist Society for Propagating the Gospel among the Heathen) landed in Serampore. The Governor, Colonel Olav Bie, extended protection to the Baptist missionaries in the Danish colony of Serampore. Here Carey became part of a productive team including William Ward, Joshua and Hannah Marshmann, and the other BMS missionaries. Colonel Bie provided a link to the earliest Protestant Mission in India, established by King Frederick IV in 1705 at the Danish colony of Tranquebar in South India where Bie had served previously. Carey in his famous *Enquiry* had made reference to the Tranquebar mission of Ziegenbalg and Plütschau. The Serampore Mission was founded on January 10, 1800. The roots of the Protestant missionary movement are in the Pietism of Germany via the Danish-Halle Mission and the Moravian Brethren.

Carey's egalitarian ideals were put into practice in the Serampore Mission which followed the Moravian precedent of pooling resources. A common purse was distributed according to needs. All property was vested in the Society, not to be sold or to become the private property of any. Carey believed that a missionary must identify with the people among whom he is sent to serve and therefore should be indigenous and self-supporting. This became possible when Carey was employed as Professor of Bengali and Sanskrit at the Fort William College. Carey's generous salary supported the work of the Serampore Mission. A new generation of BMS missionaries, combined with a new BMS committee in London—the original members having died—created misunderstanding leading to the separation of Serampore from the BMS.

Carey's enormous productivity became possible at Serampore as part of a team effort including not only the Serampore Trio/Quartet and other BMS missionaries but also the immense contribution of innumerable—often unnamed yet indispensable—local *pundits*. For thirty years Carey served as Professor of Bengali and Sanskrit at Fort William College, which he reached by boat from his home in Serampore. For a time, Serampore became a centre for Bengali studies and translations. The Serampore Mission also deployed missionaries to Burma, Bhutan, Agra, Chittagong, Ceylon, Malacca, Dhaka, Delhi, and Assam. The Mission published grammars in Bengali, Punjabi, Telugu, Marathi, Kannada, Bhutanese and Sanskrit and dictionaries in Bengali, Marathi and Sanskrit as well as epics such as the Ramayana and the Mahabharata. The Mission organized a number of successful and profitable schools including the earliest schools for girls in and around Serampore. In 1818 Serampore College was established for secular and theological education. The Serampore Mission came to an end in 1937 with the handing over of its assets to the Baptist Missionary Society. Serampore College continues its mission of providing well-recognized secular as well as theological education, the latter including doctoral degrees of the Senate of Serampore College.

It should be noted that Carey never thought of himself as "father" of modern missions. To the contrary, in the *Enquiry* he traces an unbroken continuity of missionary activity from the Apostolic era of the New Testament and beyond including that of the Catholics as well as of Anglicans and Protestants such as John Elliott and David Brainerd in New England, Ziegenbalg in India, the Moravians, John Wesley and much more. Some have protested that Ziegenbalg, not Carey, should be considered the "father" of the Protestant missionary movement because it was Ziegenbalg who brought

Protestantism to Tranquebar in 1706, 87 years prior to the arrival of Carey in Bengal in 1793. Alas, the well-intended "father" designation is at best an exaggeration, a distortion which ignores the prior contributions of others, perpetuated in part by a 1994 revision of the 1934 *William Carey* biography by S. Pearce Carey, now entitled *William Carey, the Father of Modern Missions* edited by Peter Masters and published by the Wakeman Trust in London. In the formation of the BMS in 1792, Carey became a "father" of modern missions for the Particular Baptists of England. More important, the recovery of the missing structure, the voluntary mission society—a counterpart to the missionary orders of the Roman Catholic Church—made mission possible. Earlier missions existed, benefactors of governmental or ecclesial patronage, whereas BMS provided a new model. Soon others followed: the London Missionary Society (1795), Church Missionary Society (1799), Religious Tract Society (1799), British and Foreign Bible Society (1804), American Board of Commissioners for Foreign Missions (1810), Basel Mission (1815), Danish Missionary Society (1821), and many others. This continues today in the contemporary Indian missionary movement. The essays in this splendid collection contribute further to the significance of the Serampore Mission for the emergence and development of world Christianity.

Bibliography

Daniel, J. T. K. and Hedlund, R. E., eds. *Carey's Obligation and India's Renaissance.* Serampore: Council of Serampore College, 1993.

Jeyaraj, Daniel. "Mission Reports from South India and Their Impact on the Western Mind: The Tranquebar Mission of the Eighteenth Century." *Converting Colonialism: Visions and Realities in Mission History, 1706-1914.* Ed. Dana L. Robert. Grand Rapids and Cambridge: Eerdmans Publishing, 2008: 21-42.

Noursangzeli, Marina. "Serampore Mission." *The Oxford Encyclopaedia of South Asian Christianity.* Vol. 2. Eds. R. E. Hedlund, J. Athyal, J. Kalapati, J. Richard. New Delhi: Oxford University Press, 2012: 622-3.

Smith, A. Christopher. *The Serampore Mission Enterprise.* Bangalore: Centre for Contemporary Christianity, 2006.

Walker, F. Deauville. *William Carey.* American Edition. Chicago: Moody Press, 1980: 202-218, 240-256.

Introduction

Serampore Mission: Perspectives in Contexts

Johnson Thomaskutty

As Serampore College—one of the historical institutions in India, founded by the initiatives of William Carey, Joshua Marshman, and William Ward in 1818—celebrated its bicentenary year in 2018, The Union Biblical Seminary in Pune joined the celebrations and organized a series of theological deliberations in honor of the Serampore missionaries and their unique contributions. The Serampore College as a well established educational institution reached its current status by crossing several historical milestones and achieving national and international acclamations such as the Royal Charter of Incorporation (1827) and the confirmation of the Charter by the Bengal Government Act IV (1918). As part of the celebrations in UBS, the academic committee of the seminary selected the theme "Serampore Mission: Perspectives in Contexts" for the Center for Mission Studies (CMS) Consultation that was held in November 1-3, 2018. The theme of the consultation motivated the participants and the resource persons to explore how the Serampore Mission introduced paradigm shifts in the contextual-and-missional hermeneutics and praxes in the Indian Sub-continent. Subsequently, the papers went through several revisions and editorial ventures to appear into the present form.

In the current book, the biblical, historical, hermeneutical, theological, missional, ministerial, and contextual disciplines of the movement are integrally analyzed from multiple perspectives. The contemporary outlook and significance of the movement are investigated in closer relationship with faith, scripture, and theology. As the nation of India advances as a global community, the book attempts to revisit and re-interpret the basic principles and strategies of the Serampore Mission from multiple vantage points. Through the consultation, we ultimately attempted to revisit the Serampore Mission from a holistic perspective and to develop ideas for contemporary application. The Biblical and hermeneutical, linguistic and translational, theological and ethical, historical and ecumenical, dialogical and religious, ecological and contextual, and missional and ministerial aspects of the movement were examined with a key focus on their significance in today's life-situation. It was also an attempt to fill the gap between the contexts of the Serampore Mission in its own *Sitz-im-Leben* and the contemporary realities of the twenty-first century CE with the help of hypothetical brainstorming and critical investigations.

The missionary movement in Serampore and in the extended Indian sub-continent under the leadership of the "Trio" (i.e., William Carey, Joshua Marshman, and William Ward) and the establishment of the Serampore College were key initiatives in the history of Christianity in India. The unique contributions of Hannah Marshman as a woman, who endeavored hard in the movement, enable us to think beyond the traditional boundaries of the "Trio" to the wider level of the "Quartet." The mission's contributions to the academic world, ecclesiastical contexts, and the society as a whole need to be acknowledged with high esteem and at the same time re-evaluated in order to derive new meanings for the twenty-first century missionary, ministerial, and academic exercises. With this outlook in mind, the resource persons evaluated the movement from various critical and ideological standpoints. The consultation ultimately focused on three aspects: first, it investigated the influence of the Serampore Mission and the paradigm shifts that brought into the missional and the ministerial developments in the Indian scenario; second, it attempted to understand the significance of the Serampore Mission and its educational and theological contributions in the contemporary India; and third, it evaluated the role of the mission and its engaged and holistic tasks in the pluralistic Indian scenario.

This book is an attempt to answer some of the significant questions such as: First, how do we understand the Christian identity in the contemporary socio-political and multi-religious context of India? Second, how can the missional and ministerial tasks of the church be integrated with the combined efforts of missiologists, biblical scholars, educators, historians, religious scholars and theologians? Third, what are the challenges we confront in India today to consider the missional, ministerial, and hermeneutical aspects with greater priority? Fourth, how significant is the Serampore Mission in the contemporary Indian context? How does it continue to influence the academic world, the church, and the general public? And fifth, how do the contributions of the Serampore missionaries continue to influence Christian communities in their witness, mission, and evangelism? As we flip through the pages of the book, the above stated questions shall enable us to fathom the realities with a contemporary outlook.

The title *Serampore Mission: Perspectives in Contexts* requires some explanation. The usage "Serampore Mission" is an overarching expression to understand the contributions of the missionaries as biblical expositors, theologians of their own times, vernacular linguists and translators, educators with deep impression, ministerial and missional experts, botanists, liberators, social transformers, founders and administrators, editors and publishers, and the like. The virtue of versatility and multifaceted missional and ministerial strategies of the missionaries are explored here with vigor for further reflection and action. The usage of the term "Perspectives" enables the readers to fathom deep into how scholars from multiple vantage points deliberated their views concerning the contributions of the Serampore missionaries. Moreover, the authors of the essays are experts in different fields of studies, and they reflect their views about the Serampore Mission with profundity and brilliance.

As the Serampore missionaries perceived the reality of God, human struggles, and the cosmic order from a transformative and liberative point of view, it is our task to conceptualize and systematize their contributions with a holistic outlook and a paradigmatic perception. In that way, we can transform our present struggles and future hopes based on the past axioms of the missionaries. The term "Contexts" is used with a broader spectrum of understanding in order to reconstruct the views from multi-religious, multi-cultural, multi-denominational, and multi-lingual contexts of the nation. The authors here represent diverse contexts and with multiple perspectives to invigorate the mission and ministry of the Serampore missionaries. With this view in mind, the authors write the following essays and delineate their views.

In the first essay, entitled *A Theo-epistemological Reflection on William Carey and the Serampore Mission*, **Songram Basumatary** spearheads his discussion from a *theo*-epistemological and *missio*-epistemological standpoint. He places *Theos* [or *God*] and *mission* at the center of his discussion and argues from a broader *theo*-hermeneutical, epistemological, and philosophical framework. He observes William Carey as a visionary-missionary and attempts to understand his *theo*-conscience, faith conviction, and spiritual commitment to the task of Jesus with broader implications in mind. In that process, he compares and contrasts Carey's epistemology and praxis within the extended framework of the western *theo*-hermeneutical patterns and procedures. The essay invigorates how the Reformation and the Calvinistic, Postmillennial, Puritan, and enlightenment roots of Carey's mission-theology develop as a unique theo-mission epistemology with an emphasis on contextually oriented praxis-theology.

Subhro Shekhar Sircar, in his essay *Important Documents of the Serampore College and Their Significance to Higher Education in India*, first of all, provides a historical summary of the Serampore College, and then, analyzes the role and significance of the First Prospectus of the college (1818), the Royal Charter of Incorporation (1827), and the revival of the Royal Charter and the Serampore College Act (1918). He outlines the implications of these documents or events to higher education in India and the future challenges. He takes us closer to the historical realities as well as the kernels of the Serampore Mission perspectives. The essay guides us through the challenges and prospects of theological education in India through the initiatives of the Serampore Quartet. The author also attempts to lead the readers toward the contextual initiatives of the Serampore missionaries. After a highly sophisticated epistemological framework of the first essay by Basumatary, here Sircar attempts to lead us through the historical underpinnings behind the mission and the challenging efforts of the Serampore missionaries.

Through his essay *The Impact of the Bible on Nations through the Protestant Reformation and the Protestant Missionary Movement*, **Prakash Abraham Mathew** takes our attention toward a constructive analysis of the Reformation Movement and the First Protestant Missionary Movement. He foregrounds the challenges and the prospects on the way and the dedication of the stalwarts like Martin Luther and William Carey. As both the movements were born out of the influence of the Scripture, the author pays attention on how the two figures anchored their missions in the Scripture in the German and the Indian contexts respectively. The author invites the attention toward the tasks of translating, distributing, and interpreting the Scripture. The essay further outlines how the Scripture was instrumental for a renaissance in the fields of language and literature, national formation, education, human right aspects, eco-vision, and socio-religious concerns.

Stanly Jones, in his essay *William Carey's Bible Translation Principles: Prospects and Challenges*, demonstrates how the mission of translating the Scripture into various languages was executed contextually. In a context in which theoretical aspects related to linguistics and translation were not developed, Carey's contextual and dynamic translation principles are significant to reckon with. Some of the noteworthy expressions such as "Bible Translation as Mission" and "Bible Translation as Contextualization" invite the attention of the readers. The theological importance of the ministry of Bible translation is expounded through analyzing the biblical events from Gen. 11 (i.e., the Event at Babel) and Acts 2 (i.e., the Event on the Day of Pentecost) with precision. After providing a biblical foundation for the aspect of translatability, the author takes us through William Carey's principles and perspectives of Bible translation with profundity. Further, he challenges the readers to understand the aspect of translation as a key mission enterprise of the Church.

In the essay entitled *Re-reading the Gospel of John in the Light of William Carey's Linguistic Methods*, I (**Johnson Thomaskutty**) attempt to see how Carey developed the Bengali grammar and language through the following means: first, a descriptive and scientific approach; second, advancing the vernacular linguistic styles; third, composition of colloquial linguistic styles through a dialogic genre; fourth, code switching and diglossia; fifth, advancement of a colloquial style called *Sadhu Bhasha*; sixth, a peculiar linguistic style called *Christian Bengali*; and seventh, paying attention on both the popular and the lesser tongues. Thus, the contextual and sociolinguistic approach of Carey is taken up to ponder into the 'H' level linguistics of John's Gospel and its 'L' level linguistic probabilities and possibilities. Carey's linguistic method is employed as a hermeneutical tool to develop a socially inclined linguistic methodology to interpret the Scripture in today's context. The author invites the readers toward the closer realities of the first century Palestinian and the nineteenth century Bengali (and extended Indian) oral cultures and the written Johannine deliberations for a theoretical and hermeneutical analysis.

Annie George, through her essay *Educational Principles of the Serampore Mission and Its Implications for Contemporary Education*, invites our acumen toward the educational principles of the Serampore missionaries. She is particular in stating about the role of Hannah Marshman with emphasis. For her, the Serampore Quartet's educational development, vernacular instruction, and publication are some of the important highlights of their mission initiatives. The essay takes our attention to some of the implications of their educational principles then and now. Through her deliberation, it is affirmed that the Serampore Quartet had a great vision for the educational development of India. She also brings practical implications for our own situation in context. As she deliberates her views, it is argued that the Serampore Quartet emphasized a "contextual educational methodology." The essay inspires us to take up insights from the Serampore missionaries to implement contextually oriented and relevant educational principles and methods.

In his essay *The Contribution of the Serampore Mission toward the Ecumenical Movement: A Historical Perspective*, **Woba James** foregrounds the ecumenical journey of the Serampore Mission right from its inception. He says: "The study of the history of the Serampore Mission can best be understood as one of the histories of ecumenism. Beginning with its inception and onto the present form, it represents a great ecumenical body that is noteworthy." In the essay, the author perceives the ecumenical style of the Serampore Mission as a "National Theological Structure of Ecumenism." While emphasizing the inter-denominational and inter-religious connections of the mission, the author extends his thinking pattern toward a gender balanced ecumenism in the theological and educational arena of the Serampore system. The essay even goes to the extent of suggesting a dialogue between the Senate of Serampore and the Asia Theological Association (ATA) in India. It seems an important suggestion that extends our thinking to new horizons and dialogical initiatives in the area of theological advancement in India.

Shiju Mathew, in his *"Through You all the Families of the Earth Shall be Blessed" (Genesis 12:3c): Reading the Life of Abraham and William Carey from a Missiological Perspective*, invites our attention toward the Genesis narrative and the Abrahamic account in order to see resonances in Carey's life and also in the Indian scenario. Both Abraham and Carey are addressed as "Fathers": one, "Father of the Nations," and the other, "Father of Modern Missions." The author finds some striking similarities between the way Abraham and Carey reacted to the divine call within the framework of their own time and space. The 'centripetal' and 'centrifugal' mission aspects are at focus in his missional hermeneutical reading of the Genesis passage with a reverberation to the Serampore Mission. Finally, the author encourages the readers with the following statement, "The Church is expected to continue the mission of God initiated by Abraham, Jesus Christ, William Carey and others to fulfill the promise of God: 'Through *you* all the families of the earth shall be blessed.'" Thus, the author places the lives of Abraham and Carey as paradigms for the contemporary situation.

Through his essay *the centrality of Christ and the Hermeneutical Perspectives of the Serampore Mission*, **George Philip** emphasizes the centrality of Christ in the endeavors of the Serampore Mission. With this focus in mind, he takes our attention toward the liberative vision and mission of Jesus narrativized in the New Testament and also of Carey and his colleagues in the Indian context. As Jesus was a context-oriented missionary par-excellence, Carey, his slave, became a context-oriented missionary. The author explains how the missionaries used proof-text and literal methods and the 'church-individual' togetherness aspect in the process of interpreting the Scripture. The narrative, Dalit, Tribal, Feminist, and Postcolonial reading practices of the Senate of Serampore are also outlined for our understanding. In that way, the author attunes his readers toward the hermeneutical and interpretative side of the Senate of Serampore College.

Jangkholam Haokip, in his essay *Serampore Mission from a Botanical and Ecological Perspective*, expounds to see how Carey played the role of an ecologist and botanist par-excellence being deeply rooted in his evangelical conviction. The essay demonstrates that Carey was not merely concerned of anthropocentric missional aspects, but rather a missionary with a holistic perspective. Carey was a contextually inclined missionary who raised his level according to the needs and demands of the time and space. His essay discusses the contribution of Carey toward creation care, reflects on his theological foundation, and raises some questions for further reflection and action. Some of his questions for our reflection include: "how do we view nature today?," "how far does Carey's theology of creation care help our understanding of and response to global ecological crises today?," and "do we care for nature because we love it, or are we to care for it because it is part of that God is going to save through the death and resurrection of Christ?" In essence, the author attunes our attention toward some of the pertinent theological aspects like the nature as God's creation, Christ as the agent of God's creative activity, and the responsibility of the human beings in taking part in creation care.

In his essay *Serampore Mission and Dalit Theology*, **Viju Wilson** demonstrates how Serampore Mission sowed the seeds of liberation and liberative perspectives right from its inception. As the Senate of Serampore was further established, the liberative aspects were perspectivized, idealized, and contextualized with new vigor and passion. As Dalits are the downtrodden community of our nation, it is important to understand the way William Carey, Joshua and Hannah Marshman, William Ward, the Serampore College, and the Senate of Serampore College brainstormed and conceptualized their struggles and contextual underpinnings around the marginalized sections of the community. The author of the essay argues that Dalit Theology was spearheaded from the Serampore Mission initiatives. The essay begins with discussing the contextual theological framework of the Senate of Serampore and then convinces the readers that theological education is a life-affirming mission. In the essay, we journey through information on the liberative and contextual framework of the Serampore Mission, the current emphasis on Dalit Theology, and the need for a solidarity approach rather than an advocacy approach in the contemporary Indian scenario. It is also an attempt to show how the Senate of Serampore is particular in incorporating studies related to the Dalit issues and liberation aspects within its curriculum.

Mayang Longkumer, in his essay *Revisiting Serampore Missions and Tribal Worldviews: A Postcolonial Reading*, endeavors to revisit the Serampore Mission and other foreign missionary movements in India from a Tribal perspective. The tribal realities of the North-Eastern India are illuminated in the essay and also it takes the readers along to the theological and missiological evaluations. He does it in his own way by making use of the currently available tool called "Postcolonial Reading." His discussion takes us backward to the historical realities of Carey and his colleagues in the Serampore context. Moreover, he makes an appraisal of the western missionary movements functioned in foreign lands as they orchestrated under the colonial shadow and with a hegemonic mindset. He concludes the essay stating that, "Christian missions should be approached in a holistic sense in order to experience life without domination that degrades and devalues humanity and natural world around us." Thus, the essay makes an evaluation of the Serampore Mission and the North-Eastern tribal mission in order to suggest some corrective measures in our approach to missions.

In his essay *The Modern Missionary Movement of the Serampore Trio: A Missiological Perspective*, **James Patole** attempts to bring an overarching coverage of almost all the areas of Carey's involvements from a missiological perspective: first, at the outset, he narrates the story of the Serampore missionaries and the Serampore Mission; second, he observes the role of the Serampore missionaries and their mission strategies with an emphasis on the centrality of the Scripture, Jesus and the Great Commission, mission praxes, multilingual educational methods, the sodality and modality paradigms, contextualization aspects, statistical analysis, bi-vocational mission paradigm, and the inclusive missiology; and third, he brings implications of his study for the contemporary missions. He concludes his essay stating that, "The movement that began to grow so rapidly with the Serampore Trio continues to inspire and rekindle a passion for the worldwide Great Commission initiatives, networking, and strategic mission movements." The author's attempt here enables us to understand the missional dynamics of the Serampore missionaries with a broader outlook.

Kaholi Zhimomi, through her essay *Beyond the Serampore Mission Historiography: Re-defining Ecumenism from the Context*, throws light on the Serampore Mission with a forward-looking perspective. By placing the Serampore Mission at the analeptical level, she foregrounds the initiatives, needs, and demands of a wider ecumenism. In that way, she redefines ecumenism from the contemporary contextual realities. Thus, the proleptic and analeptic connection between the Serampore Mission and the modern ecumenical initiatives is expounded through her careful deliberation. At the outset of the essay, the author poses a significant question: "Can we look beyond the Serampore Mission historiography and re-define ecumenism from the contemporary context challenging the various qualified ecumenical studies?" This question enables her to make a journey through the Serampore mission history with a contemporary appraisal. After discussing the ecumenical pragmatism of the Serampore missionaries, she goes further to discuss about a "Transformative Receptive Ecumenism" in a contextually experiential way.

In the last essay, entitled *William Carey's Approach to the People of Other Faiths, Religious Practices, Caste System, and Conversion*, **Giri K.** emphasizes the tenets of the Serampore Mission in relation to the people of other faiths. As we understand, Carey was not a narrow-minder and parochial missionary; but rather an inclusivist with an open-ended perspective. In the essay, the author outlines the following aspects with precision: first, Serampore Mission's approach towards people of other faiths; second, their early encounters with people of India and their religions; third, their views on conversion and conversion activities; fourth, their attitude to caste system; fifth, their attitude towards other scriptures; and sixth, their humanitarian concerns. The author concludes that the Serampore missionaries approached people of other faiths with tolerance and benevolence. Their positive approach toward other religions in India paved a new way forward for Christian mission activities.

The above understanding makes it firm that the Serampore Mission was a multifaceted and holistic movement that impacted various areas of human life and social living. The transformative function of the mission touched human lives at various levels and in multiple forms through its theological articulations, secular education, missional and ministerial advancements, biblical interpretation, ethical and moral lessons, ecological concerns, Dalit and Tribal emancipation, feminist concerns, social and religious renaissance, linguistic and translational achievements, and various other global aspects. As we celebrate the bicentenary of the Serampore College, it is significant to restate that William Carey was a visionary-missionary par-excellence and those who accompanied him contributed immensely to the transformation of the individuals, the church, and the society at large. The charismatic, evangelical, and ecumenical natures of the missionaries and their approaches need to be applauded and their balanced approach to missions needs to be revived in the contemporary contexts.

I take this occasion to thank the Board and the Administration of the Union Biblical Seminary for their financial, moral, and intellectual support rendered throughout the process, especially toward the organization of the consultation and the publication of the book. I am deeply indebted to my faculty colleagues and students of UBS for their constant motivation and needed support in multifarious ways. It is my pleasure to thank ISPCK, Delhi, for accepting the manuscript for publication. Above all, all glory and honor go to the Almighty God.

1

A *Theo*-epistemological Reflection on William Carey and the Serampore Mission

Songram Basumatary

Introduction

At the very outset, let me set a clear hypothesis that neither the Serampore Mission started in a theological vacuum nor was it an accidental mission. Also, let not the present inheritors of this mission think that they are the pioneers and the custodians of a life altering vision, life transforming mission, and life affirming theological education that Senate of Serampore College (University) is offering, as it is expressed in its vision and mission statement that reads:

> We believe that the Triune God has offered the possibility of *renewal of life* and *hope for the entire creation* in and through Jesus Christ, and that as *an instrument of God*, the Church is called to be involved in *God's mission of liberation, reconciliation* and *community building* among all peoples through varied forms of ministry. Set in the midst of people of *other faiths and ideologies* as well as situations of *life-negating forces*, we are called upon to equip the whole people of God to respond to the contextual challenges critically and creatively by being *faithful to the Gospel of Jesus Christ.* In light of this faith and self-understanding, we seek to equip ministers, leaders, scholars and the whole people of God to be committed to creative discernment of and active participation in *God's liberative mission* in the world at large and in South Asia in particular by providing programmes of theological study and ministerial formation at various levels through affiliated colleges and institutions.

This is indeed a comprehensive mission statement with sky high *theo*-vision and ground-touching *theo*-praxis. Where did such an encompassing and life altering vision, life transforming mission, and life affirming theological education emerge from? Where is the epistemic stem of such a vision and mission probably be? In a way to answer these questions, this paper attempts to trace the *theo*-epistemological and *missio*-epistemological frameworks of the very Serampore Mission and in particular of William Carey, the visionary-missionary who was very much captivated by *theo*-conscience, faith conviction, and spiritual commitment to the mission and commission of God manifested in and through the life and work of Jesus, the Christ.

Problematizing the Case: Nothing Theology about it?

While talking about the theological and missiological epistemology of the Serampore Mission in general, and William Carey in specific, a natural thought and question pops up in my mind. "Are we theologizing Serampore Mission?" Or "Is it the fruit of Serampore Mission's theology itself?" Further, "Can we consider William Carey as a mere missionary" or at best, "a mere social activist" or "the pioneer of the praxis theology?" In this sense, more than recognizing him as the "Father of Modern Mission," can we consider him as "Father of Contextual Theology," and if not, at least as the "Forerunner of Indian Liberation Theology"? With these preliminary thoughts of where to re-locate Carey, I venture towards a less trodden avenue—re-reading and re-locating Serampore Mission, especially William Carey into the domain of theology proper. As Thomas Schirrmacher captured correctly, perhaps there is a missing link between Carey's Theology and his mission.[1] As it is already mentioned, he is famously known as the "Father of Modern Missions"[2] or "Father of Protestant Missions"[3] in the mission history. As it appears in his writings, he is considered as "begetter of modern mission"[4] and his mission as "Conversion of the Heathens (*sic*)."[5] Even the great mission maxim of Carey, "Expect great things (from God); attempt great things (for God)" is interpreted purely in terms of achievements from the perspective of soul-win-oriented '*mission to*,' rather than seeing it as *missio*-praxis paradigm of *mission at* and *mission within* the people. There seems little or nothing *theo-missio*-epistemological and *theo-missio*-praxiological in the reading of the Serampore Mission as a whole and William Carey in specific.

Evidently, much has been written about the success stories of Serampore Mission and Carey, but surely very little attention has been given, especially the theological framework behind Carey's vision and mission. The biographies[6] available on him do not mention anything direct on the *theo*-epistemological and *missio*-epistemological frameworks behind his commitment for mission which he perhaps adamantly defended even though he was ridiculed and insulted as worthless for mission![7] The best description of Carey's personal optimism of world mission which he derived from postmillennial theology can be found in his biography of his first wife.[8] However, Carey's eschatology is also almost completely ignored in many of the writings on him. Perhaps it is strange that though the Protestant mission societies continually refer to his mission as the origin of their mission, they only describe his life up to the publication of the *Enquiry* and has little to say about his theology.[9]

There are two excellent dissertations by Hermen Oussoren[10] and Daniel Potts[11] that critically discuss the achievements of Carey and his mission. The former presents an exhaustive historical discussion of his life,[12] and the latter contains the most thorough work on Carey and the work of his colleagues. However, these works too largely ignore his theology. Even his eschatological views, which played a major role in his decision to be a missionary is not dealt with. Even Bruce J. Nichols'[13] article that bears the direct title, "The Theology of William Carey," discusses quite little on Carey's theology proper except few passing statements in highlighting five areas of theological concerns.[14] One of the very rare attentions given to his theology in fact is by Iain Murray who in his study on the *Puritan Hope* gives a space to Carey's theological foundation,[15] especially on eschatology which permeated the great missionary societies of the Eighteenth and Nineteenth Centuries.

Reasons for such failure to give attention to Carrey's theology, probably may be due to the fact that his theology differs from that of predominant, post-classical mission societies, which happily claim him as their father, even though he was a Calvinist and a postmillennialist.[16] It may be a strong contention, but from such a portrayal of Carey, especially in German literatures, it is assumed that they did not want to consider Carey as a pioneer missionary and left behind no materials with which to ascertain his theological convictions. This can be ascertained from the expression such as "He was much more of a mission motivator and Bible translator than a pioneer in the heart of India—or a mission strategist."[17]

To my browsing and readings, the two recent works: *Be keen to get going: William Carey's Theology* by Thomas Schirrmacher[18] and "Serampore: *Telos* of the Reformation" by Samuel Everett Masters[19] give an ample space to his theological backgrounds, which come to us as respite to explore the theological framework of Carey and the Serampore Mission as a whole. These works clearly ascertain that as it is observed by Schillbach, "the significance of Carey's work lies not in the 420 converts, 24 in Serampore"[20] but in his theological foundations.[21]

Theological Framework of the Serampore Mission

Serampore Mission has various streams of theological lineage. *First*, from the dogmatic theological point of view, William Carey had priori-knowledge and influence of Reformation theological convictions, particularly the *solas*. *Second*, from a mission theological point of view, he was influenced by a large number of theologians of evangelical awakenings. *Third*, from the aesthetic theological point of view, he had strong influences of Puritan theology and spirituality. *Finally*, and generally, from the epistemological point of view, he had a wider range of knowledge on realities within the church, society and the world at large.

Reformation Theological Root

As it is stated above, the Serampore Mission was not born in a theological vacuum. It is neither a historical accident, but it is a product of Reformation principles or theology. There is evidently Reformation theological root in William Carey's commitment for mission.[22] Surely the evangelistic zeal and the spirit of activism in the Eighteenth Century was a result of Reformation principles. As modern missionary movement has its root in the various branches of Reformation theology, particularly on the genuine concern for the conversion of souls, the expansion of the church, and the establishment of the kingdom of God,[23] the history of the Serampore mission has ample evidences of theological principles evolving from the Reformation that served as the driving forces in all its mission endeavors.

The development of the powerful theological ideas unleashed by the Sixteenth Century reformers can be seen through the English Puritans and English *Particular Baptists* like Jonathan Edwards and Andrew Fuller. As Timothy George notes, "Carey stood most clearly in the Reformation tradition in his confidence in the Scriptures and lifelong labor to see their translation into 40 distinct languages. His plan to evangelize India was simply: 'Preach the Gospel, translate the Bible, and establish schools, proclamation, translation, education.'"[24] His visionary and practical missiology was worked out from the Reformation theological themes. For example, in the second section of his seminal work, *Enquiry*, under the heading, "Containing a Short Review of Former Undertakings for the Conversion of the Heathen(*sic*)," he mentions "the New England Puritans, John Eliot and David Brainerd; Ziegenbalg . . .; the Moravian Brethren . . .; and Wesley . . ."[25] all of whom had Reformation heritage behind their theologies. Therefore, Samuel Everett Masters in his thesis claims that Serampore Mission is the *telos* of Reformation.[26] In fact, it can be said that as Martin Luther ushered the Reformation, likewise, Carey, the modern missionary movement. In other words, as Kane asserts, "What Luther was to the Protestant Reformation, Carey was to the Christian Missionary Movement."[27] This shows that the mission innovation carried out by Carey was a result of protestant theological emphasis and later development of reformed theology.

One of the most significant Reformation theological influences on Carey was the *solas* of Martin Luther, particularly the *Sola Scriptura, Sola Gracia,* and *Solus Christus*. Luther's theological conviction and the declaration of the sufficiency of Scripture in matters of salvation had a great impact on Carey which led him to have a strong faith in the authority of the Holy Scripture, the Word of God. He seems convinced of Luther's hermeneutical principle that the Word of God has creative and transformative power and this could be the reason why Carey translated the Scriptures into as many native languages as he can.[28] Incontestably, perhaps the reformer's insistence on *solas* led the Eighteenth Century Christianity to emphasize on *biblicism, conversionism, crucicentrism* and *activism*. To put it differently, the emphasis on personal conversion and the centrality of the cross of Christ in evangelicalism and mission activism have their roots in *solas* of Reformation.

As with Reformation, beyond the deep concerns about corruption in church and society was all about theological and biblical epistemological quest, both conceptually and functionally. The Reformation helped in shaping the modern world through biblical and theological principles. Along with the *solas*, many other theological insights like priesthood of all believers, the church as an assembly of believers, and the sanctity of all vocations are visible in Carey's theology and mission activism. Here it is apparent that though modern missionary movement emerged after many years, the influence of Reformation theology towards evangelism and mission in Carey's time and in his mission is undeniable. Even his understanding of the Grace of God and personal faith allegiance resembles Luther's, which can be seen from the final words from his lips on his death bed. While Luther said, "We are beggars. This is true," Carey uttered a verse from Isaac Watts' hymn: "A wretched, poor, and helpless worm, on thy kind arms I fall."

Calvinistic Theological Root

Behind Carey's dream about the possibility and bearing the responsibility of mission, there was a strong Calvinistic theological backdrop as well. One of the greatest stimuli of Calvin's theology on Carey, as a positive principle, is the doctrine of *God's sovereignty*. In fact, the Serampore Trio/Quartet were all considered as *evangelical Calvinists* as they, first and foremost, dwelt especially on the belief in the sovereignty of God and on the plan to establish indigenous churches under their own leadership.[29] Carey was indeed driven by the *doctrine of providence*,[30] which in Calvinist theology is described as the very sovereignty of God itself. As evidence to this fact, we could see a number of texts Carey himself had written describing Calvin's thought and his theology.[31]

As a *Calvinist Baptist*, Carey believed in providence unreservedly and continually based on his belief in the necessity of missions on this understanding. He was very much convinced that the heathens (*sic*) were lost unless God brought them the Gospel without human assistance. His simple conclusion was that since God is sovereign, whatever God commands must be obeyed and such obedience will bear fruit. In other words, God acts alone based on God's sovereign will and power apart from all human cooperation. So is his challenge in stating that, "Expect great things (from God)! Attempt great things (for God)!" In his *Enquiry* Carey convincingly wrote:

> It has been said that we ought not to force our way, but to wait for the openings, and leadings of providence . . . neither ought we to neglect embracing those openings in providence which daily present themselves to us . . . . Where a command exists nothing can be necessary to render it binding but a removal of those obstacles which render obedience impossible, and these are removed already. Natural impossibility can never be pleaded so long as facts exist to prove the contrary.[32]

It is observed that Carey never changed this view even in later stages. He never drifted far from his Calvinistic roots when reflecting on his God of providence, order and control.[33] However, it is also interesting to note that Carey in his *Enquiry* distinguished clearly between God's sovereign will, the providence, and the moral will, his sense of duty and responsibility. In this sense, he was also an ardent follower of *Calvinist ethics* which he demonstrated in the churches he served prior to his mission journey to India. He exercised a strict church discipline typical of Calvinism and followed *Puritan ethics* in each and every minor decision, including journeys on Sundays.[34] He was very firm in his faith that the true missionary work is rooted in the gracious, eternal purpose of the triune God. His vision and mission born of repentance, prayer, and self-denial was strictly guided by his belief in the sovereignty of God. Carey seems to have followed Luther and Calvin who stressed the sovereignty of God in salvation and the providence of God that had given a biblical view of human depravity, whereby human's only hope was to be found in God's sovereign grace alone.

Nevertheless, Carey in his *theology of obligation and means* also argues that God's sovereignty does not relieve us of responsibility or the need to exercise "due prudence." In other words, God's sovereignty for him should not be used as an excuse to disobey God's call and command. Though Carey was strongly inspired by the Calvinistic theology that emphasized salvation as the work of the sovereign God as well as the *Great Commission* which was only meant for the apostles, one of the strong theological points he makes in his *theology of means* is that God uses human beings as 'means.'[35] God appoints human beings as agents of bringing the gospel to unevangelized nations. Since such understanding of means had strong implications for preaching and missions, Carey must have, therefore, understood the entire Reformation as 'mission of preaching the gospel,' i.e., 'the Word of God.' He was convinced that belief in God's sovereignty does not lead us to futile speculation, but rather to willing obedience of his commands to preach the gospel. So, as Calvin preached and defended the gospel against all stereotypes, Carey also called believers to active evangelism based on compassion for fellow human beings. Such a zeal of Carey for evangelism and missions can be seen rooted in Calvin's commitment that "where an opportunity presents itself of edifying, let us consider that by the hand of God a door is opened to us for introducing Christ there, and let us not withhold compliance with so kind an indication from God."[36]

Carey also developed his *theology of conversion* based on *Calvinist soteriology*. His take on the question of conversion is to be understood from the soteriological principles basically based on *sola fides*, *sola gratia* and *solus Christus* of the reformers. While many believed that the *doctrine of predestination* quenches down missionary effort rather than intensifying it, Carey like other Protestant missionaries and missionary leaders of his day, agreed with the view that Calvin's *doctrine of predestination* never denied human responsibility towards divine commandments, including the Great Commandment.[37] What was required was not just faith in Christ, but faith in one's faith in Christ. He was firm on the gospel proclamation that "Whoever wills, let him/her take the water of life freely."[38] For he was convinced of the fact that there was no doctrine in the gospel and even no threatening in the law of God that refuses sinners coming to Christ for salvation.[39] Carey too believed that human beings are saved by God's active and sovereign grace, through faith apart from works as other reformers. Luther and Calvin had themselves experienced a radical personal conversion. Salvation was no longer mediated by the church but by Christ himself. This could be the reason why Carey was not much bothered of resulting in his mission only a few converts!

Nonetheless, *the Great Commission* for Carey is still incumbent upon the church. According to Schirrmacher,[40] Carey had two questions to answer about *the Great Commission*: *First*, "Was the *Great Commission* directed only to the apostles or is it valid for all Christians of all eras?" *Second*, "Can the *Great Commission* be fulfilled?" While answering the first question, Carey specifically attacks the view that the *Great Commission* expired with the passing of the apostles"[41] and direct in answers that the *Great Commission* is binding "even to the end of the age."[42] His argument is that the Great Commission was not only directed to the apostles, but to the church as a whole and its validity continues till the end of time.

The answer to the second question is given from the postmillennial expectation that there will be a final success of the mission. His knowledge above and affinity with Reformation Theological themes carried through reformed theologies. The enlightenment rationalities that provided new intellectual tools, perhaps made him to see the *Great Commission* as personally binding for mission activism. He contended that "Means were now held to be obligatory and the *Great Commission* is still binding on believers."[43] Unlike some other theologians' view that the desire for the increase of God's glory as the primary motivation for missions,[44] Carey sees duty as the primary motivation for missions. The missionary endeavor is the proper response to the Lord's command that his disciples "pray that his kingdom may come, and his will be done on earth as it is in heaven . . . ."[45] And yet, it is evident that Carey's point of departure for mission was not the ecclesiology, but the theology proper. He built a theological framework for the use of means on the foundation of the *doctrine of Providence.* Carey devised a *theo-missiological* approach that begins with scripture and works outward to take into account the actual condition of the world. So, he used the *doctrine of providence* effectively to link the gap between his view of duty and his call for the use of means. As it was in the case of Puritans, Carey believed in God working out His purpose in history in his own times and saw God's guiding hand in his mission impossible. Carey also found the Calvinist idea of *compassion* as a motivating factor for mission. In *Enquiry* he appeals for "feelings of humanity"[46] and maintains that motivation should be derived from consideration of the destitute and uncivilized state of most of humankind.[47] Human "ignorance, or cruelty, should call forth our pity, and excite us to concur with providence in seeking their eternal good."[48] It is *compassion* that finally leads to the *call of duty.* He was very much convinced of the fact that expressions of concern for the lost are empty unless accompanied by active obedience to the *Great Commission.*

The above discussions show that certainly *Calvinism* provided a critical theological framework to Carey to safeguard against many of the extremes of evangelicalism and missions that developed later in the history of Evangelical movement. Over against the overly rationalistic approach to theology by earlier generation of *Particular Baptists* who followed *Hyper-Calvinism,*[49] Carey recovered a Biblical view of evangelicalism. His logical conclusion against the theological development of *Hyper-Calvinism*[50] is that "if the gospel was to be freely offered to Englishmen, it should be offered to the world."[51] Carey could not correspond to the views of the hyper-Calvinists with the duty of calling people to Christ. At this point, perhaps it is also appropriate to note that Carey was not inclined to the Methodism of his day as one might expect, but by *Evangelical Calvinism.*[52] This indicates that as a Calvinist, his significance lies in his reconciliation between the theology of the Reformation, particularly Reformed theology, and the church's responsibility for the missions.[53]

Postmillennial Theological Root

As the history of mission reveals, the *Postmillennialism*[54] played yet another significant role in the modern mission movements. The Eighteenth Century was the great age of *Postmillennialism* which played a major role in the development of missionary thought and development of the Anglo-American missions.[55] It is perhaps important to note in our discussion on the root factor of mission that out of three most common eschatologies, *Postmillennialism* has more often been the champion of increasing missionary fervor.[56] The American reformed theologian Jonathan Edwards as well as English and Scottish theologians related postmillennial eschatology with revival and with the missionary idea—a combination which gave rise to the growth of organized missionary activity at the end of the century. The impetus behind the mission awakening was the view that there was an undeniable connection between missions and the Christian hope for the future. Evidently, we see both the modern 'evangelical' missions and modern 'ecumenical' missions having their root in the notion and understanding of Eschatology.[57] In fact, the strong *cosmo-theandric* vision that world is going to come to an end and the God is going to judge the living and the dead played a major role in taking the *Great Commission* in urgency. Carey was strongly influenced by such a postmillennial view of a universal Kingdom of God.[58] The mission of activism and political engagement such as the fight against the caste system, opposition to the burning of widows, and protection of indigenous people are all because of Carey's determinism about *Postmillennialism*.[59]

Puritan Root

The *Puritan hope* is yet another influence on Carey. Since Puritans were motivated by the simple commands of Christ, their view of the Christian ministry included the imperative of preaching the Gospel to the unconverted. They also believed that the Trinitarian God is active in history and the divine purpose cannot be thwarted. Since God is the Lord of history, all God's purposes would be worked out. While the contours of mission's methodology were still taking shape, Puritans had already made the logical jump from a responsibility to preach to one's parish to the responsibility to preach to the world. In his *Enquiry*, Carey extracted the *Puritan hope* for his mission in three ways: *first*, we go because God demands it; *second*, compassion for the lost is an appropriate motivation for missions. It is not inconsistent with a high view of God's glory, for God himself is compassionate; and *third*, obedience requires the grasping of those tools placed providentially within reach.

Enlightenment Intellectual Root

It is important to note that the year Thomas Payne released his work, that is, *The Age of Reason* (1791) and its offshoot *The Rights of Man* (1792),

William Carey's *Enquiry* was published in Leicester. From this it is evident that Carey was not aloof from the rationalistic and scientific temper of the enlightenment. He might have rejected much of *Enlightenment philosophy*, but he had an enthusiastic interest in scientific and social progress. Since the parallel products of the Reformation, the *Evangelicalism* and the *Enlightenment* shared a common social space, certainly the cross-fertilization was obvious. Radical politics and evangelical missions are not exactly binary opposites, but they do represent two differing visions of how to improve the world.[60] Many of the leaders of the modern missionary movement were attracted to radical political movements. Carey himself was reputed to have had republican sentiments,[61] and he was also a lifelong pacifist. While pastoring at Leicester, he was made the secretary of the Nonconformist committee and found himself engaged in the struggle to repeal the Test and Corporation Acts which placed social limits on Catholics and Nonconformists.[62] It is said that at Leicester, Carey came into contact with others who were advocates of scientific progress[63] that probably influenced him to have a lifelong interest in science and eventually make thoughtful contributions in the field of botany.

William Carey's Mission Theology

Methodology of his Mission Theology

Carey's *missio-theological* methodology can be seen as an outworking of Reformation principles, as discussed above. The elements of *biblicism*, *conversionism*, *crucicentrism*, and *activism* were his key approaches from the first day of his step in Serampore. His first method was to engage with religious beliefs of the people and speak from the true *Shastras*, the Bible. Certainly, it is not without dispute in our times today in terms of inter-faith relations. We can see some of Carey's most notable responses to Hindu beliefs in Samuel Pearce Carey's collections.[64] For instances, it is narrated:

> You think you'll be saved by the incessant naming of your god or *debtah*? A parrot's holiness and yours is one. Seeing some idol, he would ask, 'what is that?' 'Our god,' they would reply. He would then retort: 'Did that make men, or did men make that?' Similarly, to a wandering Hindu monk who claimed an ability to change water to milk he said, on inviting him to dinner, that if he had scruples about eating with them, he need not fear, even should the food be forbidden. A person who can change water into milk can surely change forbidden food into lawful.

Such a way of dealing with Indian religion for Carey was in fact fight against the *Brahminic* religious rituals and social practices. Perforce, he dealt very aggressively with the Brahmins. Their biblical anthropology and ecclesiology placed them in explicit opposition to the Indian caste system. They saw that Hinduism and the caste system were the biggest obstacles to the conversion of Indians and to their progress. S. P. Carey summarizes Carey's views on caste and the effect of the Hindu worldview in the following words:

> Never was a people more willing to hear, yet more slow to understand. They heard of the new way but followed the old. Custom was king. The past forbade the least change. 'Caste,' he said, has cut off all motives to *Enquiry* and exertion, and made stupid contentment the habit of their lives. Their minds resembled their mud homesteads, destitute of pictures, ornaments, and books. 'Harmless, indifferent, vacant,' he writes, 'they plod on in the path of their forefathers; and even truth in geography, astronomy, or any other science, if out of their beaten track, make no more impression on them than the sublime truths of religion.[65]

This suggests that Hinduism and the caste system were consistently considered as "binding chains" by the Serampore Trio/Quartet. They saw it as something to be barred from the life of the church. They countered the evil at three critical points. *First*, new believers were not allowed to maintain Hindu rules of commensality on the theological ground the Hindu idea of ritual contamination from sharing a meal with a person of a lower case was obviously contrary to the spirit and letter of the New Testament. As a sign, when Krishna Pal the first convert was baptized, he was immediately invited to dine with the others at Serampore that led Krishna break the caste barrier. Such theological activism was truly in line with what is said, "In Christ there is neither Jew nor Greek, Barbarian, Scythian, bond nor free, all are one in him."[66]

Secondly, the *theo-activism* that overturned the caste system was *marriage*. In April of 1803, the Serampore community celebrated the first marriage between converts. As symbolic resistance, Krisnu Prasad, a Brahmin wedded the daughter of Krisha Pal who was a Sudra with a simple ceremony on mats under a tree. The *third* counteractive challenge against the caste system was *handling of death*. For instance, during his early years in India, Carey had felt the impact of Hindu customs when his child died, and no one could be found to bury. In the same year as the first wedding, the first baptized Hindu died after short illness. John Clarke Marshman reported that his peacefulness at death produced a positive effect on the other new believers. The Serampore missionaries had purchased a plot of land to serve as a cemetery. When the time came for the burial, the coffin bearers were chosen to make a strong Christian statement: "There, in the presence of a silent and astonished multitude, Mr. Marshman and Mr. Felix Carey, Bhyrub, a baptized Brahmin, and Peeroo, a baptized Mahomedan, placed the coffin on their shoulders and singing the Bengalee hymn, 'Salvation through the death of Christ,' carried it through the streets."[67]

The examples cited to justify the theological methodology of Carey may appear romanticizing or oversimplifying Serampore Mission and it may be problematic to the present day inter-faith tensions and relations. However, in accordance with the core of the gospel of God in Jesus, the Christ, we can conclude in the words of Leslie Newbigin that "it is impossible to become true Christians without crossing racial, linguistic, or class barriers."[68]

Theology of the Cross

Carey's obedience to the call of God and commitment for the mission of God in and through his life and experiences are profound examples of the theology of the cross over against the theology of glory that Luther talked about centuries ago. From the inclusion of the Puritans like John Eliot and John Sergeant in his list of missionary predecessors in his *Enquiry*,[69] it is probable that Carey had strong Puritan theology especially drawn to David Brainerd and Jonathan Edwards. Jonathan Edwards' Puritan theology was innovative in many ways behind the Great Evangelical Awakening and it was instrumental in the revival of Baptist life. This definitely had a great influence on Carey.

Carey's theology of the cross can be seen from his life of self-denial and self-sacrifice owing to his obedience to God's obligatory command amidst extreme poverty, the death and psychological challenges faced in the family.[70] While Carey and his friends, in order to discredit false beliefs those were critical about the Indian religions, positively presented the message of the cross. Probably, Carey used it as an apologetic style in order to make the cross as a chief concern in his preaching. We see him making distinction between general "truths" and the specific message of the cross:

> In preaching to the heathen(*sic*), we must keep to the example of St. Paul, and make the greatest subject of our preaching, *Christ Crucified*. It would be

> very easy for a missionary to preach nothing but truths, and that for many years together, without any well-grounded hope of becoming useful to one soul. The doctrine of Christ's expiatory death and all-sufficient merits had been, and must ever remain, the great means of conversion.[71]

How the cross played a guiding role in his life and mission can also be seen from his words of advice to his son Jabez which reads: "I rejoice that you have begun to preach in Malay. Consider this as your greatest work and labor to build up the people in Faith and Holiness but above all *labor to lay Christ Crucified as the foundation on which you build for all that is not built on that foundation will fail*."[72] For Carey, salvation was anticipated to be obtained through *sin confessing, sin forsaking, Christ's righteousness embracing*.[73] Not only in preaching, but there was a theology of suffering or perhaps Luther's theology of the cross in practice in Carey's life. He was certainly influenced by Puritans' *crucicentric* emphasis along with their *Biblicist* and *conversionist* character.[74] It is evident that the Puritan preaching that revolved around 'Christ, and him crucified' was the anchor of Carey's persevering life and pathos-filled untiring mission.

Theology of Social Change

Carey's *ethico-socio-political* concerns[75] and involvement in the battle against social injustices springs up from his liberative theological convictions. Carey was just as outspoken in his opinions on slavery[76] and the caste system, which he in no case wanted to allow within the church, even at the cost of advantages for his missionary efforts.[77] He was so truthful to his *theo-sociological* commitment that even while he was in England, he did not take sugar as it was produced by using slaves as laborers. Not only did he protest in this way, but throughout his entire life he prayed for the emancipation of the slaves.[78] His firm Biblical ethics and theological stand on compassionate justice could bring social transformation by challenging the religio-cultural practices such as *sati*, burning of widows, and infanticide.

Theology of Culture

Respect for all people and all cultures was the hallmark of Carey's theology. The Serampore Trio/Quartet as a whole was convinced that all nations were "of one blood."[79] Their theology told them that all human beings are depraved and so all need Christ. Carey had a high view of India and Indians. In one of his letters, he wrote:

> I suppose that no people can have more completely surrendered their reason than the Hindus. In all matters of business and everything relating to this world, they are not deficient in knowledge, but in all things relating to religion, they are apparently void of all understanding.[80]

Carey, like T. S. Eliot, who saw "the culture of a people as an incarnation of its religion"[81] recognized that their religion had a formative effect on their moral life. Of course, the objective of his approach to Indian culture seems to "guide the native life in such a way that it really makes the missionaries superfluous and that all the treasures of the native culture are Christianized."[82] Therefore, whatever was felt unbiblical must be abandoned. In Oussoren's view, perhaps Carey attempted to "lead their culture to the cross."[83] Oussoren also describes that while Catholicism sacrificed its Christian principles to preserve the local culture, Carey had warned against this approach in the *Enquiry*:

> The Jesuits indeed once made many converts to popery among the Chinese; but their highest aim seemed to be to obtain their good opinion; for though the converts professed themselves Christians, yet they were allowed to honor the image of CONFUCIUS their great law-giver; and at length their ambitious intrigues brought upon them the displeasure of government, which terminated in the suppression of the mission, and almost, if not entirely, of the Christian name.[84]

Carey and his friends found a biblical balance between the syncretism of Catholic missions and the cultural leveling of Zinzendorf. Their position better reflects the unity and diversity which is a characteristic of the New Testament church. Though preaching the gospel was their first priority, they saw no contradiction in engaging in social action to eradicate some of the worst practices of Hindu society. They evaluated all elements of the culture through the filter of Scripture as best they could.[85]

One of the examples of their respect for culture is that the new converts were not required to change their Hindu names. They felt the New Testament provided sufficient examples of Greek Christians who retained their original names. Even Brahmin converts were not required to quit wearing the *poita*, the sacred thread that identified the upper castes as 'twice-born.' They were baptized and preached to their fellow-countrymen with the *poita* across the shoulder. The Serampore Trio/Quartet believed that missionaries, in their anxiety should not interfere unnecessarily with the national habits and customs of the converts, nor make any rule on the subject. Thus, they did a job which was forbidden for even members of the lowest castes.[86] Carey strongly emphasized and himself experienced the communal living[87] as reformers emphasized it strongly.

Though Carey was very cautious about Indian culture and adopted only those forms of cultural elements which they considered compatible with the gospel, it is doubtless that he used culture as means for preaching the Gospel. This is why Carey, for example, took profound delight in the beauties of the Indian languages and dialects. Perhaps, unlike other missionaries who condemned the local cultures and forced to shun them, he and his friends were not cultural chauvinists. As they were well informed by the biblical principles, they also did not fall into the tendency of making English-Indian cultural divide. While they strongly opposed the Indian custom of widow burning and the caste system, they were also equally opposing the class prejudice of the English in India. In fact, they underwent struggles in the process as movement from theology to application because of cultural resistance. Yet, it seems obvious that they were courageous enough to go against the flow of dominant evangelical theology as theology itself is a by-product of culture.

Since culture is never static and theology is the artifact of culture, the word of God which is the core of theology is interacted and articulated according to the cultural milieus of people in different contexts. Carey in particular was aware of the cross-cultural environment he was in. So, he was convinced of the fact that the Word of God which is a transforming power by its very nature according to reformers' theology is meant to be spoken into people's life and language.

Beside these major theological approaches, we could see *holistic vision and mission* in Carey. He refused to divorce conversion from discipleship. Indeed, Carey balanced the propositional and incarnational dimensions of the mission of God in Jesus Christ. He was a practitioner of a holistic mission and incarnational evangelism. He knew that Jesus gave food to the hungry and at the same time presented himself as bread of life. He not only translated the Bible, but planted schools, established newspaper, organized agricultural society, and worked tirelessly to eradicate the social evils which were non-negotiable with the gospel. Undoubtedly, he would have been in hearty agreement with the great Methodist missionary E. Stanley Jones: "A soul without a body is a ghost; a body without a soul is a corpse. The gospel is addressed to living persons, soul and body, in all of their broken humanity and need for wholeness."[88]

Another theological inference we can draw from Carey is his *ecumenical approach*. It can be presumed that the quest for *Christian unity* in our times was born on the mission field of Carey's India and abroad. He paved the way for the ecumenical co-operations by working closely with believers of many denominations in India and by calling for an international conference of missionaries to develop a common strategy for evangelism and witness. However, he was definitely not for an uncritical ecumenism which would sacrifice the distinctiveness of the Gospel just for the sake of bland togetherness. Possibly, we can place him in the position of Richard Baxter's great maxim: "In essentials, unity; in non-essentials, liberty; in all things, charity."

Conclusion

The secret behind Carey's breakthrough in missiological thinking and achievements was his theological convictions. He had a sound theological foundation in his vision of mission itself as he was well aware of the theological and missiological trends of his time. He had a rationally defensible and explanatorily powerful vision and descriptively accurate estimation of his mission. In other words, he set off his mission journey with a sound *theo-epistemological* and *missio-epistemological* framework. Therefore, though others had seen the straight stick submerged in water, bent; and the railway tracks converging in the distance, for Carey, the stick still looked straight and the tracks kept going parallel. He saw a vision of a trajectory of mission progressing and moving far and wide.

Facing the challenges of practicality, Carey's mission theology flowed from his view of God as an active shaper of history and built his mission on the *theology proper*, i.e., the doctrine of divine providence as a biblical principle. He also believed that in God's providence the human cultures are shaped as tools for the spread of the gospel of God in Jesus. He prayerfully depended on God and perseveringly made practical efforts. His strong faith in the 'providence' of God, a clear perception of the mission of God, the rational view of the reality of the world, and correct sense of the necessity and urgency of taking the gospel of God to the world had driven him to oblige to the mission and commission of God.

The beauty of Carey's theological standpoint and activism is that he assiduously balanced the spiritual and social dimensions of mission. Perhaps his self-denying life-style based on the protestant ethos of simplicity, frugality and abstention from worldly things made him a genuine Christian theologian. His ability to contextualize the gospel without compromising the non-negotiable essentials of biblical faith provides a balanced model for a truly witnessing missiology in our times of socio-religious and political upheavals. Indeed, it is apt to conclude that more than living in India a lifetime as a pastor, a teacher, a linguist, an agriculturalist, a journalist, a botanist, a social activist, and a statesman of the world Christian movement, Carey was a *praxis-oriented theologian.* Carey and his colleagues Marshman and Ward were not theologians, but they were the very models of theologically-driven practitioners, the *theo-praxists.*

Endnotes

[1] Thomas Schirrmacher, *Be keen to get going: William Carey's Theology*, tran. Cambron Teupe (Hamburg: RVB International, 2001, corrected edition 2008).

[2] Basil Miller, *William Carey: The Father of Modern Missions* (Minneapolis: Bethany House, n.d.).

[3] Ralph D. Winter, and Steven C. Hawthorne, eds., *Perspectives on the World Christian Movement* (Pasadena: William Carey Library, 1981), 227-228. E. Daniels Potts, *British Baptist Missionaries in India 1793-1837: The History of Serampore and its Missions* (Cambridge: At the University Press, 1967).

[4] Charles L. Chaney, *The Birth of Missions in America* (South Pasadena: William Carey Library, 1976), xi.

[5] William Carey, *An Enquiry into the Obligations of Christians to Use Means for the Conversion of the Heathens* (London: The Carey Kingsgate Press, 1961). [Hereafter: Carey, *Enquiry*].

[6] For instance, Mary Drewery, *William Carey* (Grand Rapids: Zondervan, 1979); James R. Beck, *Dorothy Cary: A Biography* (Grand Rapids: Zondervan, 1979); Frank Deauville Walker, *William Carey* (Chicago: Moody Press, 1980 [1925]); Kellsye Finnie, *William Carey* (Carlisle: OM Publishers; Didcot: Baptist Missionary Society, 1992); Basil Miller, *William Carey: Cobbler to Missionary* (Grand Rapids: Zondervan, 1952), and *William Carey: The Father of Modern Missions* (Minneapolis: Bethany House, n.d.); S. Pearce Carey, *William Carey* (London: The Wakeman Trust, 1993 [1923]); A. Christopher Smith, "William Carey," *Mission Legacies: Biographical Studies of Leaders of the Modern Missionary Movement*, ed. Gerald H. Anderson (Maryknoll: Orbis, 1994). The list of older biographies can be found in Ernest A. Payne, "Carey and his Biographers," *The Baptist Quarterly* 19 (1961): 4-12.

[7] For example, when he proposed for missionary society, he was responded, "There never was a theology of the voluntary society. The voluntary society is one of God's theological jokes, whereby he makes tender mockery of his people when they take themselves too seriously." Andrew F. Walls, *The Cross-Cultural Process in Christian History* (Edinburgh: Orbis, 1970), 246.

[8] Beck, *Dorothy Cary*, 130.

[9] Schirrmacher, *Be keen to get going*, 11.

[10] Aalbertinus Hermen Oussoren, *William Carey, Especially his Missionary Principles* (Leiden: A. W. Sijthoff, 1945), 219-269.

[11] E. Daniels Potts, *British Baptist Missionaries in India 1793-1837: The History of Serampore and its Missions* (Cambridge: At the University Press, 1967).

[12] Oussoren, *William Carey*, 19-121.

[13] Bruce J. Nichols, "The Theology of William Carey," *Carey's Obligation and Indian Renaissance*, eds. J. T. K. Daniel and Roder E. Hedlund (Serampore, West Bengal: Council of Serampore College, 1993), 114-126. The same article can also be found in Thomas Schirrmacher, ed., *William Carey: Theologian – Linguist – Social Reformer* (Bonn: Verlag für Kultur und Wissenschaft, 2013), 86-109.

[14] These are: Biblical Foundations, Christology for Mission, The Gathered Church, Faith and Culture and Integral Mission.

[15] Iain Murray, *The Puritan Hope: Revival and the Interpretation of Prophecy* (Edinburgh: Banner of Truth Trust, 1971), 138-147.

[16] J. A. de Jong, *As the Waters Cover the Sea: Millennial Expectations in the Rise of Anglo-American Missions 1640-1810* (Kampen: J. H. Kok, 1970), 176-181.

[17] Smith, "William Carey," 249.

[18] Schirrmacher, *Be keen to get going*, 35.

[19] Samuel Everett Masters, "Serampore: *Telos* of the Reformation," A Thesis Submitted to the Faculty in partial fulfillment of the requirements for the degree of Master of Arts in Religion at Reformed Theological Seminary, Charlotte, North Carolina, December 2010. [Hereafter Masters, *Telos of Reformation*].

[20] A. Schillbach, "William Carey als Bahnbrecher der evangelischen Mission," *Evangelisches Missions Magazin* (1892), 129-141.

[21] Most of the literatures used and arguments made in this article is mainly taken from these two sources.

[22] For an exhaustive study on this, see Masters, "*Telos* of Reformation."

[23] Sidney H. Rooy, *The Theology of Missions in the Puritan Tradition: A Study of Representative Puritans: Richard Sibbes, Richard Baxter, John Eliot, Cotton Mather & Jonathan Edwards* (Laurel: Audubon Press, 2006), 11.

[24] Timothy George, *Faithful Witness: The Life & Mission of William Carey* (Birmingham: New Hope Publishers, 1991)

[25] Carey, *Enquiry*, 62-63.

[26] Masters, *Telos of Reformation.*

[27] J. Herbert Kane, *A Global view of Christian Missions from Pentecost to the Present* (Baker Book House, 1971), 83.

[28] Oussoren, *William Carey*, 118. For a table of the translations in the various languages with dates of appearance, see note 1; Beck also in his *Dorothy Carey*, 168-170, mentions six Bibles, 23 New Testaments and 10 parts as Carey's own achievements; Similarly, Mary Drewery in her *William Carey*, 155-158, 192 lists six complete Bibles and 29 parts as Carey's works. In cooperation with his team, he also completed 19 Bibles and 17 parts. See also Walker, *William Carey*, 219-232; S. Pearce Carey, *William Carey*, 385-394.

[29] See, Brian Stanley, *The History of the Baptist Missionary Society 1792-1992* (Edinburgh: T & T. Clark, 1992), 36-57; William Travis, "William Carey: The Modern Missions Movement and the Sovereignty of God," *The Grace of God, the Bondage of the Will*, Vols. 1 and 2, eds. Thomas R. Schreiner and Bruce A. Ware (Grand Rapids: Baker Books, 1995), 323-336.

[30] He mentions this term six times in his *Enquiry* [11, 67, 68, 80] and in other writings, Beck, *Dorothy Carey*, 44, 45, 54, 184.

[31] John Clark Marshman, *The Life and Times of Carey, Marshman and Ward, Embracing the History of the Serampore Mission*, Vols. 1 and 2 (London: Longman, 1859). Also see John Clark Marshman, ed., *William Carey, Letters, Official and Private* (London: 1828). For how Calvinism influenced Carey and his mission, see Terry G. Cater, "The Calvinism of William Carey," 13-35.

[32] Carey, *Enquiry*, 10-11.

[33] Beck, *Dorothy Carey*, 184.

[34] Beck, *Dorothy Carey*, 87.

[35] For Carey, "means" was the key word signifying the whole apparatus of human agency." D. W. Bebbington, *Evangelicalism in Modern Britain* (Great Britain: Unwin Hyman, 1989), 41.

[36] Quotes by Paul Helm in this section are all from his chapter on "Calvin, A. M. Toplady and the Bebbington Thesis," *The Advent of Evangelicalism*, eds. Michael A. G. Haykin and Kenneth J. Stewart (Nashville: B & H Academic, 2008), 205. This quote is from Calvin's Commentary on 2 Cor. 2:12.

[37] Andrew C. Ross, "Missionary Expansion," *Encyclopedia of the Reformed Faith*, ed. Donald K. McKim (Louisville: Westminster John Knox Press; Edinburgh: Saint Andrew Press, 1992), 242-244.

[38] Robert Hall, *Help to Zion's Travellers: Being an Attempt to Remove Various Stumbling Blocks Out of the Way, Relating to Doctrinal, Experimental and Practical Religion* (Philadelphia: American Baptist Publication Society, 1851), 125.

[39] Hall, *Help to Zion's Travelers*, 124.

[40] Schirrmacher, *Be keen to get going*, 35.

[41] Carey, *Enquiry*, 36.

[42] Carey, *Enquiry*, 9.

[43] Bebbington, *Evangelicalism in Modern Britain*, 41.

[44] John Piper, *Let the Nations Be Glad! The Supremacy of God in Missions* (Grand Rapids: Baker Books, 1993).

[45] Carey, *Enquiry*, 31.

[46] Carey, *Enquiry*, 31.

[47] Carey, *Enquiry*, 95.

[48] Carey, *Enquiry*, 94.

[49] Hyper-Calvinism is the opinion that the Calvinist doctrine of Predestination refutes missions, because God would save those He wished without human aid, so that the Great Commission is already fulfilled. Although not typical of Calvinism, this viewpoint was popular, particularly among the Particular Baptists Carey knew. See Iain H. Murray, *Spurgeon and Hyper-Calvinism: The Battle for Gospel Preaching* (Edinburgh: Banner of Truth Trust, 1995); Kenneth G. Talbot and W. Gary Crampton, *Calvinism, Hyper-Calvinism and Arminianism* (Canada: Still Waters Revival Books; Lakeland: Whitefield Publishers, 1990).

[50] For a detail on hyper-Calvinism in England during 1700s, see Terry G. Cater, "The Calvinism of William Carey and its Effect on His Mission Work," Thomas Schirrmacher, ed., *William Carey: Theologian - Linguist - Social Reformer*, World of Theology Series 4 (Bonn: Verlag für Kultur und Wissenschaft, 2013), 14-23.

[51] Masters, "*Telos* of Reformation," 17.

[52] Walker, *William Carey*, 35-36. Carey mentions Wesley only briefly in his *Enquiry* on page 37. Reason for this could be for the opposite doctrine of Arminianism held by the Methodists seemed to him to strike at the roots of belief in the grace of God. See Walker, *William Carey*, 37.

[53] Beck, *Dorothy Carey*, 136.

[54] Postmillennialists believe that the Kingdom of God will be realized in the present age by the preaching of the Gospel and by the saving influence of the Holy Spirit in the hearts of individuals, and that at an unknown time in the future, the whole world will be Christianized. They also believe that Christ will return at the end of the so-called Millennium, an epoch of unknown length, marked by justice and peace . . . . The Millennium, according to the Postmillennialist view, is a Golden Age at the end of the present dispensation, the Age of the Church. See Loraine Boettner, *The Millennium* (Phillipsburg: Presbyterian and Reformed, 1984[1957]), 4-14. Loraine Boettner, "The View of Postmillennialism," *The Meaning of the Millennium*, ed. Robert Clouse (Downers Grove: Inter-Varsity Press, 1977).

[55] Allen Carden, *Puritan Christianity in America* (Grand Rapids: Baker Book House, 1990), 94-95, 108-110; Andrew C. Rolls, "Missionary Expansion," *Encyclopedia of the*

Reformed Faith, ed. Donald K. McKim (Louisville: Westminster John Knox Press; Edinburg: Saint Andrew Press, 1992), 242-244.

[56] In contrast to premillennialists, postmillennialists emphasize the present aspects of God's kingdom which will reach fruition in the future. They believe that the millennium will come through Christian preaching and teaching. Such activity will result in a more godly, peaceful, and prosperous world. The new age will not be essentially different from the present, and it will come about as more people are converted to Christ. See R. G. Clouse, "Millennium, Views of the," *Evangelical Dictionary of Theology*, ed. Walter A. Elwell (Grand Rapids: Baker Book House, 1984), 715.

[57] Schirrmacher, *Be keen to get Going*, 13.

[58] Richard J. Bauckham, "Millennium," *New Dictionary of Theology*, eds. Sinclair B. Ferguson, David F. Wright and James I. Packer (Leicester and Downers Grove: Inter-Varsity Press, 1989), 429 (retranslated from the German).

[59] For more detail on Influence of *Postmillennialism* on Carey, see Schirrmacher, *Be keen to get Going*, 13-35; Thomas Schirrmacher, "William Carey, Postmillennialism and the Theology of World Missions," *Contra Mundum*, available at: http://contra-mundum.org/schirrmacher/careypostmil.html.

[60] Masters, *Telos of Reformation*, 85.

[61] Carey, *William Carey*, 60.

[62] Carey, *William Carey*, 59.

[63] Masters, *Telos of Reformation*, 86.

[64] Carey, *William Carey*, 190.

[65] Carey, *William Carey*, 162.

[66] Andrew Fuller, *Memoirs of the Late Rev. Samuel Pearce, A.M.* (London: J. W. Morris, 1800), 48.

[67] John Clark Marshman, *The Life and Times of Carey, Marshman and Ward: Embracing the History of the Serampore Mission* (London: Longman, Brown, Green, Longmans and Roberts, 1859), 1:185.

[68] Lesslie Newbigin, *The Open Secret: An Introduction to the Theology of Mission* (Grand Rapids: William B. Eerdmans Publishing, 1995), 145.

[69] Carey, *Enquiry*, 36.

[70] Such experience can be seen in his words: "I am in a strange land, alone, with no Christian friend, a large family, with nothing to supply their wants." John Clark Marshman, *The Life and Times of Carey, Marshman, and Ward* (London: Longman, Brown, Green, Longmans and Roberts, 1859), 64.

[71] Oussoren, *William Carey*, 276.

[72] Sunil Kumar Chatterjee, *Family Letters of Dr. William Carey* (Serampore: Non-Liner, 2007), 121. [Italics mine].

[73] Carey, *William Carey*, 195.

[74] Sidney H. Rooy, *The Theology of Missions in the Puritan Tradition: A Study of Representative Puritans: Richard Sibbes, Richard Baxter, John Eliot, Cotton Mather and Jonathan Edwards* (Laurel: Audubon Press, 2006).

[75] Vishal Mangalwadi, "India: Perils and Promise Then And Now," ed. Thomas Schirrmacher, *William Carey: Theologian—Linguist—Social Reformer*, World of Theology Series 4 (Bonn: Verlag für Kultur und Wissenschaft, 2013), 86-96.

[76] Oussoren, *William Carey*, 191-193.

[77] E. Daniel Potts, *British Baptist Missionaries in India 1793-1837*, 158- 159; Oussoren, *William Carey*, 195; Kellsye Finnie, *William Carey*, 109; Beck, *Dorothy Carey*, 135-136; Drewery, *William Carey*, 104-105; A. Christopher Smith, "Myth and Missiology: A Methodological Approach to Pre-Victorian Mission of the Serampore Trio," *International Review of Mission* 83 (1994): 451-475, 461-463.

[78] Bruce J. Nichols, "The Theology of William Carey," 121-122, proved that this was founded in Carey's theology as was the case with all his engagement in social affairs.

[79] Ira Mason Allen, from the Church Register, *The Triennial Baptist Register* 2 (1836). As cited in Masters, 164.

[80] Williams, *Serampore Letters*, 61-62.

[81] T. S. Eliot, *Christianity and Culture* (New York: Harcourt, 1948), 105.

[82] Oussoren, *William Carey*, 264.

[83] Oussoren, *William Carey*, 265.

[84] Carey, *Enquiry*, 90.

[85] Masters, *Telos of Reformation*, 168-69.

[86] Carey, *William Carey*, 223.

[87] S. D. L. Alagodi, "Carey's Experiment in Communal Living at Serampore," *Carey's Obligation and India's Renaissanc*, eds. J. T. K. Daniel and R. E. Hedlund (Serampore: Serampore College, 1993), 18.

[88] E. Stanley Jones, *Unshakable Kingdom and the Unchanging Person* (Nashville: Abingdon, 1972), 40.

Bibliography

Alagodi, S. D. L. "Carey's Experiment in Communal Living at Serampore." *Carey's Obligation and India's Renaissance*. Eds. J. T. K. Daniel and R. E. Hedlund. Serampore: Serampore College, 1993.

Bauckham, R. J. "Millennium." *New Dictionary of Theology*. Ed. Sinclair B. Ferguson. Leicester, Illinois: IVP, 1988.

Bebbington, D. W. *Evangelicalism in Modern Britain*. Great Britain: Unwin Hyman, 1989.

Beck, J. R. *Dorothy Cary: A Biography*. Grand Rapids: Zondervan, 1979.

Boettner, L. *The Millennium*. Phillipsburg: Presbyterian Reformed, 1984 [1957].

Boettner, L. "The View of Postmillennialism." *The Meaning of the Millennium*. Ed. Robert Clouse. Downers Grove: IVP, 1977.

Carden, A. *Puritan Christianity in America*. Grand Rapids: Baker Book House, 1990.

Carey, S. P. *William Carey*. London: The Wakeman Trust, 1993 [1923].

Carey, W. *An Enquiry into the Obligations of Christians to Use Means for the Conversion of the Heathens*. London: The Carey Kingsgate Press, 1961.

Cater, T. G. "The Calvinism of William Carey and its Effect on His Mission Work." *William Carey: Theologian—Linguist—Social Reformer*. Ed. Thomas Schirrmacher. World of Theology Series 4. Bonn: Verlag für Kultur und Wissenschaft, 2013.

Chaney, C. L. *The Birth of Missions in America*. South Pasadena: William Carey Library, 1976.

Chatterjee, S. K. *Family Letters of Dr. William Carey*. Serampore: Non-Liner, 2007.

Clouse, R. G. "Millennium, Views of the." *Evangelical Dictionary of Theology*. Ed. Walter A. Elwell. Grand Rapids: Baker Book House, 1984.

De Jong, J. A. *As the Waters Cover the Sea: Millennial Expectations in the Rise of Anglo-American Missions 1640-1810*. Kampen: J. H. Kok, 1970.

Drewery, M. *William Carey*. Grand Rapids: Zondervan, 1979.

Eliot, T. S. *Christianity and Culture*. New York: Harcourt, 1948.

Finnie, K. *William Carey*. Carlisle: OM Pub; Didcot: Baptist Missionary Society, 1992.

Fuller, A. *Memoirs of the Late Rev. Samuel Pearce*. London: J. W. Morris, 1800.

George, T. *Faithful Witness: The Life & Mission of William Carey*. Birmingham: New Hope Publishers, 1991.

Hall, R. *Help to Zion's Travellers: Being an Attempt to Remove Various Stumbling Blocks Out of the Way, Relating to Doctrinal, Experimental and Practical Religion*. Philadelphia: American Baptist Publication Society, 1851.

Helm, P. "Calvin, A. M. Toplady and the Bebbington Thesis." *The Advent of Evangelicalism*. Eds. Michael A. G. Haykin and Kenneth J. Stewart. Nashville: B & H Academic, 2008.

Jones, E. S. *Unshakable Kingdom and the Unchanging Person*. Nashville: Abingdon, 1972.

Kane, J. H. *A Global view of Christian Missions from Pentecost to the Present*. Baker Book House, 1971.

Mangalwadi, V. "India: Perils and Promise Then and Now." *William Carey: Theologian—Linguist—Social Reformer*. Ed. Thomas Schirrmacher. World of Theology Series 4. Bonn: Verlag für Kultur und Wissenschaft, 2013.

Marshman, J. C., ed. *William Carey, Letters, Official and Private*. London: 1828.

Marshman, J. C. *The Life and Times of Carey, Marshman and Ward: Embracing the History of the Serampore Mission*. London: Longman, Brown, Green, Longmans and Roberts, 1859.

Masters, S. E. "Serampore: *Telos* of the Reformation." A Thesis Submitted to the Faculty in partial fulfillment of the requirements for the degree of Master of Arts in Religion at Reformed Theological Seminary. Charlotte, North Carolina: December, 2010.

Miller, B. *William Carey: Cobbler to Missionary*. Grand Rapids: Zondervan, 1952.

Miller, B. *William Carey: The Father of Modern Missions*. Minneapolis: Bethany House, n.d.

Murray, I. H. *Spurgeon and Hyper-Calvinism: The Battle for Gospel Preaching*. Edinburgh: Banner of Truth Trust, 1995.

Murray, I. H. *The Puritan Hope: Revival and the Interpretation of Prophecy*. Edinburgh: Banner of Truth Trust, 1971.

Newbigin, L. *The Open Secret: An Introduction to the Theology of Mission*. Grand Rapids: William B. Eerdmans Publishing, 1995.

Nichols, B. J. "The Theology of William Carey." *Carey's Obligation and Indian Renaissance*. Eds. J. T. K. Daniel and Roder E. Hedlund. Serampore, West Bengal: Council of Serampore College, 1993.

Oussoren, A. H. *William Carey, Especially his Missionary Principles*. Leiden: A. W. Sijthoff, 1945.

Payne, E. A. "Carey and his Biographers." *The Baptist Quarterly* 19 (1961): 4-12.

Piper, J. *Let the Nations Be Glad! The Supremacy of God in Missions*. Grand Rapids: Baker Books, 1993.

Potts, E. D. *British Baptist Missionaries in India 1793-1837: The History of Serampore and its Missions*. Cambridge: At the University Press, 1967.

Rolls, A. C. "Missionary Expansion." *Encyclopedia of the Reformed Faith*. Ed. Donald K. McKim. Louisville: Westminster John Knox Press; Edinburgh: Saint Andrew Press, 1992.

Rooy, S. H. *The Theology of Missions in the Puritan Tradition: A Study of Representative Puritans: Richard Sibbes, Richard Baxter, John Eliot, Cotton Mather & Jonathan Edwards*. Laurel: Audubon Press, 2006.

Ross, A. C. "Missionary Expansion." *Encyclopedia of the Reformed Faith*. Ed. Donald K. McKim. Louisville: Westminster John Knox Press; Edinburgh: Saint Andrew Press, 1992.

Schillbach, A. "William Carey alsBahnbrecher der evangelischen Mission." *Evangelisches Missions Magazin*, 1892.

Schirrmacher, T., ed. *William Carey: Theologian—Linguist—Social Reformer*. Bonn: Verlag für Kultur und Wissenschaft, 2013.

Smith, A. C. "Myth and Missiology: A Methodological Approach to Pre-Victorian Mission of the Serampore Trio." *International Review of Mission* 83 (1994): 451-475.

Smith, A. C. "William Carey." *Mission Legacies: Biographical Studies of Leaders of the Modern Missionary Movement.* Ed. Gerald H. Anderson. Maryknoll: Orbis, 1994.

Stanley, B. *The History of the Baptist Missionary Society 1792-1992.* Edinburgh: T & T. Clark, 1992.

Talbot, K. G. and W. Gary Crampton. *Calvinism, Hyper-Calvinism and Arminianism.* Canada: Still Waters Revival Books; Lakeland: Whitefield Publishers, 1990.

Travis, W. "William Carey: The Modern Missions Movement and the Sovereignty of God." *The Grace of God, the Bondage of the Will* 1-2. Eds. Thomas R. Schreiner and Bruce A. Ware. Grand Rapids: Baker Books, 1995.

Walker, F. D. *William Carey.* Chicago: Moody Press, 1980 [1925].

Walls, A. F. *The Cross-Cultural Process in Christian History.* Edinburgh: Orbis, 1970.

Winter, R. D. and Steven C. Hawthorne., eds. *Perspectives on the World Christian Movement.* Pasadena: William Carey Library, 1981.

2

Important Documents of the Serampore College and their Significance to Higher Education in India

Subhro Sekhar Sircar

Introduction

The Serampore College and the Senate of the College have passed through 200 years and 100 years respectively. Serampore College began its journey on July 15, 1818, under the founding initiative of William Carey, Joshua Marshman, Hannah Marshman, and William Ward, "the Serampore Quartet"[1] representing the British Baptist Missionary Society. On this day, they issued the first prospectus of the College, titled "*A College for the Instruction of Asiatic,*[2] *Christians and other Youth in Eastern Literature and European Science*." The Senate of the College was constituted through the Serampore College Act 1918 (which is also called Bengal Act IV, 1918) by the Council of Serampore College and under the provision of the Royal Charter 1827. Hence, the First Prospectus of the College (1818), the Royal Charter (1827), and the Serampore College Act (1918) are some of the very important documents through which the Serampore College provides higher education in general in the College campus and higher theological education for churches of all denominations throughout India and beyond. Their contributions to higher education in India are of great importance. So this paper is an attempt to look at the significance of these documents and their contributions to higher education in India.

A Historical Summary of the Serampore College[3]

In 1818, William Carey, Joshua Marshman, Hannah Marshman, and William Ward established a college in the Danish settlement of Serampore for the instruction of Indian youth in Christianity and the Sciences. Prior to 1818, the Serampore Quartet had worked together with other Baptist missionaries in providing education for their own children and the children of the native Indians, including females. The college was also open to all irrespective of any caste or creed, and the founders ensured that no denominational test would apply to its faculty members. Since Serampore was a Danish colony, Frederick the VI, King of Denmark, granted the college its Royal Charter of Incorporation in 1827 with University powers under the control of an independent Council. Its main objective was the promotion of piety and learning, particularly among the native Christian population of India.

In 1845, the ownership of the Settlement of Serampore was transferred from Denmark to Great Britain and its chartered rights and immunities were also transferred by the Treaty of Purchase. In 1856, the Baptist Missionary Society in England becomes a part of its educational operations, both Arts and Theological. In 1857, affiliated to the newly formed Calcutta University, the College became the body in India to exercise, though not the first to receive, University Powers.

In 1883, the College closed as an Arts College and began functioning as purely a native Christian Training Institution, a secondary, normal and theological institute for the Baptist churches of Bengal. From 1900, and the following ten years, there was an important discussion in various denominational and inter-denominational conferences concerning the reorganization of the College as a high grade teaching institution. It was proposed to begin to utilize the Charter for the granting of Theological degrees to qualified students of all churches, irrespective of denominational affiliation. In 1910, the Council reorganized the College under the leadership of Principal Dr. George Howells on the lines laid down by the original founders. The appointment of a qualified Theological Staff and the opening of Higher Theological Classes on an inter-denominational basis was organized under the direct control of the college council. Dr. Howells restarted the Intermediate Arts classes in 1911 and re-affiliated with the University of Calcutta after three decades. In 1913, he raised Serampore College up to the standard of the Bachelor of Arts degree.

On December 4, 1915, the Royal Charter was utilized for the first time for the conferring of a degree in Bachelor of Divinity to three students. From 1916 through 1927, up to the Centenary year of granting the Charter, sixty-nine additional students earned B.D. degree through the Serampore College. In 1918, the Centenary year of the College, the Bengal Legislative Council passed the Serampore College Act for the purpose of enlarging the College Council and constituting a new inter-denominational Senate that would administer higher theological education for all Christian denominations in India. By 1960, twenty other Indian colleges and seminaries affiliated themselves with Serampore. However, by 2005, there were 50 colleges and seminaries that received affiliation from Serampore including one each from Sri Lanka and Bangladesh. As of 2018, it is recorded that 59 colleges and seminaries and five Counselling and Training Institutes (offering Diplomas and Masters Courses) are affiliated with Serampore. These are the main landmarks in the history of the Serampore College.

Origin of the Idea of a College by the Serampore Missionaries

The Serampore Quartet, influenced by German Pietism, felt that education (meaning, reading, writing, and arithmetic) should go hand in hand with missionary activity. George Howells affirms this truth when he says that "Education, as a missionary agency, has been carried on from the commencement of the missionary movement."[4] In 1794, Carey, while working as superintendent of an indigo plantation at Madnabati, established his first school there with a few local boys whom he taught reading, writing, arithmetic, the local accounting system, and Christianity.[5] The boys were expected to learn by heart simple catechisms, portions of scripture and hymns, as part of exercises in reading and writing. Carey, however, was not content with this very limited educational program. Writing to Ryland, in January 1795, Carey outlined an ambitious plan:

> for erecting two colleges . . . in each of which we intend to educate twelve lads, six Musselmen, and six Hindoos: A Pundit is to have the charge of them, and they to be taught the Shanscrit, Bengalee and Persian languages. The Bible is to be introduced there, and perhaps a little philosophy and geography. The time of their education is to be seven years. . . .[6]

Although Carey could not implement this plan immediately, it indicates his ambition for higher education even before setting up the Serampore Mission in 1800.

In the face of opposition of the East India Company, the newly arrived English Baptist missionaries, Joshua and Hannah Marshman, William Ward, and others in October 1799 found shelter under Governor Colonel Ole Bie in the Danish settlement of Serampore. This providential event convinced William Carey to relocate in Serampore town from Madnabati, and so after his arrival there on 10th January 1800, the Serampore Mission was born. From the outset of their work, the Serampore missionaries recognized the importance of education. At the initial stages, the schools started in Serampore were boarding schools for European and Anglo-Indian children, both boys and girls. The schools opened in 1800 rapidly grew in popularity and the revenue brought from this source became a means of self-supporting for the Serampore Mission. The first school for Bengali boys was opened on 1st June 1800, which soon became popular. As a consequence, more vernacular schools were planned, and the Serampore Mission opened a series of such schools in surrounding districts. "Carey and his colleagues," writes George Smith, "had founded and supervised, by the year 1818, no fewer than 126 native schools, containing some 10,000 boys, of whom more than 7,000 were in and around Serampore."[7] From 1818, efforts were made to provide schools for Bengali girls. In 1818, Hannah Marshman formed a society in Calcutta 'for the education of native females,' and in 1820, one school was opened with eight students. The growth of these schools was slower than that of the boys' schools. By 1824, there were six schools catering for one hundred and sixty girls.[8] Hannah Marshman is much remembered in the Serampore Mission for her pioneering role in girls' education. Hundreds of girls were enrolled in their schools. Girls' education became a social reform movement and it helped to overcome local conservatism. The emancipation of women through education was accompanied by other reform efforts such as the campaign against *Sati*.[9]

Some of the remarkable features of the Serampore native schools were: they were started with open admission; they were free schools; their main objective was to remove illiteracy and ignorance of the poor and the marginalized of the native society; they taught modern science, history, and geography with tables and charts; there was a synthesis of oriental and western ideas; medium of instruction was the mother tongue; and they were conducted with the help and backing of the villagers themselves.[10] The emphasis on education through the vernacular languages in these schools laid the foundation for the Indian Renaissance.

Encouraged by the success in school education, the Serampore missionaries sought to serve in the education and broadening the general attitude of all classes of the community, which they hoped to achieve by setting up a college. Carey further understood that there is a great need of trained native agents for all the varied missionary activities in which they were engaged, evangelistic, pastoral, educational and literary. Hence, in one of his letters to Dr. Ryland in 1817, he wrote,

> I conceive that the work of duly preparing as large a body as possible of Christian natives of India for the duties of pastors and itinerants is of immense importance. The pecuniary resources and the requisite number of missionaries for the Christian instruction of Hindostan's millions can be supplied from England, and India will never be turned from her idolatry to serve the true and living God, unless the grace of God rests abundantly on converted Indians to qualify them for mission work, and unless, by those who care for India, these be trained for and sent into the work. In my judgment, it is on native evangelists that the weight of the great work must ultimately rest.[11]

The above writing expresses Carey's missionary zeal and vision for the cultural, social and religious transformation of India through education and gospel preaching. But they realized English missionaries will never be able to instruct the whole of India. As the number of converts grew and brightened their whole outlook, Serampore drew up a plan, as J. C. Marshman tells us, "for educating the children of native converts, and youths who might renounce their caste. It was intended to give them instruction in divinity, history, geography, and astronomy, and in the English and Bengali languages."[12] To meet this need, the Serampore College was conceived. Therefore, the crown of their missionary endeavor in this direction is seen in the opening of the College on 15th July 1818.

The First Prospectus of the College, 1818

Determined to concentrate their attention on the foundation of a college, which would meet the urgency of the situation, the missionaries drew up the necessary plans. They issued their first prospectus on the 15th July 1818, according to which the institution was to be *A College for the Instruction of Asiatic, Christian and other youth in Eastern Literature and European Sciences.* The first prospectus runs through 24 pages including the Letter to the Governor of Serampore with his answer. On the 15th August 1818, Joshua Marshman submitted this first College Prospectus "To his Excellency, The Honorable Jacob Krefting, the Governor of Serampore" for his approval with the following forwarding letter:

> Your Excellency will perceive, on examining the plan, that while this College secures to Christian youth instruction and support, it extends to Native Youth of all religions, not only the advantages of its lectures on the various branches of science, but all the advantages of instruction which it affords if they defray the expense of their own support during the period of their stay . . . . We therefore humbly request your Excellency's permission to constitute and organize this College without further delay; and with this view, we beg to leave respectfully to offer the use of the Premises we now occupy, for the various purposes of the College . . . . Should your Excellency be pleased to accede to our wishes, we shall esteem the College formed and established from this day, with which view we beg to leave to recommend the following persons as fit Officers for the Institution. The Rev. W. Carey, D. D. as President. The Three Senior Members of the Serampore Missionary Society as Treasurers to the Institution; the Rev. J. Marshman, D. D., as Corresponding Secretary; and Mr. J. C. Marshman, as Recording Secretary and Examiner.[13]

On the 18th August 1818, Colonel Jacob Krefting approved the prayer of the missionaries, with the following letter:

> To, The Reverend J. Marshman, Serampore: I have had the honor to receive your letter of the 15th instant, conveying to me a printed plan of an intended "College for Asiatic Christian and Other Youth," and which plan you submit to my approbation. It is with the greatest attention that I have perused this plan and am happy to find that it extends to native youths of all Religions, and holds out advantages to the community at large, founded on the most liberal principles, and highly honorable to the respectable Society of the Missionaries at Serampore. It is therefore that I, with the greatest satisfaction, not only consent to the constitution and organization of this College in this Settlement, but farther beg to leave in this public manner to acknowledge your generous endeavors to promote the welfare of so numerous a class of people as are included in your plan . . . .[14]

The forwarding letter with the prospectus to the Governor of Fredericksnagar (Serampore) includes a request to be the first Governor of the College which he gladly accepted. The document also contained proposals and plans as to the financial stability of the College, construction of the required building, and the curricula of teaching. The Governor General of British India, the Marquis of Hastings, to whom the plans were submitted, was pleased with the proposals and agreed to become the first Patron of the College.

The Structure

The entire prospectus runs through 24 pages. The text and layout of the prospectus was originally printed at Serampore in 1818. The following structure will give a pointer to the significance of the first Prospectus about governing the College, that "sketched a more perfect and complete system than any since attempted,"[15] as Smith has commented.

Introduction

The prospectus begins with an introduction that lays out the preamble and the purposes of the College.

Outlines of the Institution

This section has 10 clauses which clearly mention what the College has to offer. Next section provides nine articles each having many sub-clauses concerning the effective governance of the College: specific objects of the college for Asiatic, Christian, and Other Youth; of the college library; of the Government of the college; of the admission of the students on the foundation; of the officers and teachers of the college; of the exercises of the college; of the direction of the students' studies; of students not on the foundation of the College; and concluding remark about governing the change of the above rules.

Salient Features of the Prospectus about the College

The above 'Outlines of the Institution' provide some glimpses of objectives and goals and activities of the College. Space constraints do not allow to give more details of the prospectus. The title of the prospectus, *A College for the Instruction of Asiatic, Christian and other youth in Eastern Literature and European Sciences* demonstrates a summary statement of purpose of the College. Following are the highlights of the main points of the prospectus: first, the College was meant to be a handmaid of evangelization; second, that the instruction would be given in Sanskrit, Arabic, English, including

Chinese and European Sciences; third, the medium was to be the vernacular, and English would be offered as a required subject; fourth, the College was to include a normal section for the training of teachers; fifth, the College was to be considered as 'pre-eminently a divinity school, where Christian youth of personal piety and aptitude for the work of an evangelist should go through a complete course of instruction in Christian theology'; sixth, it was also made imperative that the College should be open to all without distinction of caste and creed; seventh, that this College was to be opened to all denominations, so that Asiatic Christian youth of every name may alike obtain advantages of this institution. Hence, the ecumenical character of the College was promoted from its very existence; and eighth, the College was to have a library consisting of manuscripts of value in any Indian languages, as well as in other languages, and of books in theology, humanities, and philosophies.

In fact, the first prospectus promotes the holistic mission of the College. It emphasized a broader spectrum of courses for the students to focus.

> It embraced the classical or learned languages of Hindoos and Mohammedans, Sanskrit and Arabic; the English language and literature, to enable the senior students 'to dive into the deepest recesses of European Science, and enrich their own language with choicest treasures'; the preparation of manuals of science, philosophy, and history in the learned and vernacular languages of the East; a normal department to train native teachers and professors; as the crown of, a theological institute to equip the Eurasians and native Christian students, by a quite unsectarian course of study, in apologetics, exegetics, and the Bible languages, to be missionaries to the Brahmanical classes.[16]

From its inception, the College had no bar in the admission as it has been enshrined in the Prospectus. The first report of the College states,

> The number of Students already admitted into the College is *Thirty-seven*. These consist of youths who have themselves embraced Christianity—of those who are in the habit of attending Christian worship, being the sons, nephews, and other relatives of those who have been baptized—of native youths sent from various parts of India by gentlemen who are benefactors to the Institution—and of such other youths as have attached themselves to the College for the sake of improving their minds. Of these thirty-seven, *nineteen* are Christians or of Christian families—fourteen are Hindoos of the cast, and four have neither cast nor religion. Of the fourteen Hindoos of the cast, *Eleven are Brahmins*, and three of the Writer cast.[17]

Among these youths, the greater number were from Bengal, and there are already some few from other parts. They speak different languages, practice different religions, and cultures. S. P. Carey, in his "Reminiscences," states,

> They had planned for India the most advanced and progressive of Oriental Colleges devoted to three aims: first, the mastery of India's own learning and literature—just because it was India's very own contribution to man's thinking; second, the fullest possible study of established modern science; Nature's ever-increasing known *facts* against man's wild *fancies*, India's literary fancies especially ungoverned; and third, because of all the faiths that had guided man's steps through the ages, the light of *one* Faith had grown increasingly clear and sure, the frankest investigation into the Hebrew literature and its crowning in Christ Jesus.[18]

Hence, summarizing the above three points, it could be concluded that the curriculum was to be 'Sanskritic, Scientific and Scriptural.'

Every student should be free to follow the course of his own judgment and conscience. No Indian who would wish to be a student of the College should be excluded. The book was not just for preachers, but for aspiring leaders of the destined new Indian journalists, scientists, teachers, writers, jurists, and the like. There was nothing at that time to match it. Even the English Universities were closed corporations. The gates of Serampore were to be wide open; and Hindus and Buddhists, Moslems and Christians were to dwell and study together side by side. Hence, the ideals and ethos laid down by the founders in the first prospectus of the College have its immense significance and impact in the successive documents.

The Royal Charter of Incorporation, 1827

The year 1827 is a landmark in the history of the Serampore College. On the occasion of the Centenary celebration of the Royal Charter, G. H. C. Angus writes, "Carey was a cobbler, Marshman was a weaver, and Ward a printer and journalist; not one had enjoyed a liberal education. Yet, as Christian missionaries, they felt that nothing short of a full University education was adequate to meet the needs of Bengal and India . . . . When it first entered in their minds to obtain official recognition of the academic status of their college work we cannot tell; but in the year 1826 Dr. Marshman traveled to Europe and visited Copenhagen."[19] As a result, Serampore College was presented a Royal Charter of Incorporation on February 23, 1827, in Copenhagen, Denmark, by the Danish King Frederick VI, empowering

Serampore College the privilege to confer degrees on graduates in the same lines as applicable to the other Danish Universities of Copenhagen and Kiel. Hence, Serampore College, not only became the first University in Asia but also the third University of Denmark. According to the provision of the Charter, the Council was constituted, to become the governing body of the College and William Carey, Joshua Marshman, and John Clark Marshman (William Ward being already deceased in 1823) were appointed members of the first Council with William Carey as its first Master of Serampore College (President of the Council).[20] It was to them and to their successors that forever was granted the "power of conferring upon the students of the said College, native Christians as well as others, degrees of rank and honor according to their proficiency . . . ."[21]

These degrees granted at the college gave the possessor a certain rank in the State. It was thought possible that a Danish student might seek a degree at Serampore College, simply for the position, it would bestow on him in his native land. This account enacts in Clause 7 of the Charter that "the said Serampore College shall only have the power of conferring such degrees on the students that testify their proficiency in Science, and no rank or another special right shall be connected there within our dominions."[22] The Charter was issued on the 23rd February 1827, nine years after the founding of the College, and was duly signed by His Majesty, King Frederick VI of Denmark, and a translation, of which the original is at Serampore, was read in the Royal Council of Fredericksnagar (Serampore) on the 18th of June 1829. The granting of the Royal Charter, to confer the degrees along the lines of other universities, became the most significant event in the history of Serampore. Hence, Serampore College became the first College in the East to receive the power to confer degrees.

According to the provision of the Charter, on the 12th June 1833, almost a year before the demise of Carey, the important Statutes and Regulations for the government of the College were incorporated and submitted to His Majesty and received Royal assent. These Statutes and Regulations also underscore the ecumenical and Catholic character of the institution. For from the very beginning, they made provision here for the inclusion of the non-Baptists on the College Council. They made no ecclesiastical barrier to membership on the Council or to a Professorship beyond the acceptance of the belief in Christ's Divinity and Atonement. Clause 13 of the Statutes reads:

> Students are admissible at the discretion of the Council from anybody of Christians, whether Protestant, Roman Catholic, the Greek, or the Armenian Church; and for the purpose of the study, from the Musalman and Hindu youth, whose habits forbid their living in the College. No caste, color or country shall bar any man from admission into Serampore College.[23]

In 1845, six years after the death of King Frederick VI, the then Danish Crown sold all the Danish Settlements on India in payment of a sum of money to the British East India Company. King Christian VIII, however, in accordance with the wishes of his predecessor, King Frederick VI, made it an indispensable condition that the Charter granted to the College should be fully acknowledged. The following Clause (Article VI, Section Two) was therefore inserted in the treaty of the Session: "The rights and immunities granted to the Serampore College by Royal Charter of Dated 23 February 1827, shall not be interfered with, but continue in force in the same manner as if they have been obtained by a Charter from the British Government subject to the general law of British India."[24] The treaty in accordance with its own stipulations was duly ratified on 16th October 1845, and from that date, Serampore became a British possession.

The Statutes and Regulations and Academic Achievements of the College

The years that followed, after the Charter was granted, were the years of commercial depression. Due to bank failures in Calcutta, the College suffered a loss of all endowments and finance meant for it. However, the work of the College went on, but it did not reach the high academic standard that was necessary to justify the use of the Charter for conferring degrees. Nevertheless, it is evident that Carey and his colleagues regarded such use of the Charter as postponed, rather than abandoned. Hence, in June 1833, a year before his death, Carey drew up a series of regulations to serve the purpose of permanent statutes of the Serampore College and subsequently signed by Joshua Marshman, John Clark Marshman and other members of the Council. This document, with its breadth of outlook, is a notable legacy of the Serampore founding missionaries standing as it did for freedom from rigid denominational distinctions, rigid theological tests, and differences of race, color, and creed.[25]

The thirty years that followed, until the founding of Calcutta University in 1857, were years of real academic achievements. But economic pressure and insufficient staff from a University standpoint made the use of the Charter impossible. Once the State Universities came into the field, beginning with Calcutta to which Serampore became affiliated, the importance of the Charter was inevitably diminished. Its very existence was almost forgotten. Side by side with the Calcutta University syllabus, which aimed at training for the service of the Government, Serampore had its own syllabus intended to train Christian youth for the service of the mission and the church. In the Baptist Missionary Society home circles, it was observed that the College had deviated far from the original object with which it was founded, i.e., the training of Christian ministers. As a result of this, in 1883, it was decided to close down the Arts department and the High School and return the College into a purely Theological Institution.

The Revival of the Royal Charter and the Serampore College Act 1918

Rev. Dr. George Howells is gratefully remembered as 'the second founder' of the College. He visited Serampore and was filled with depression: "I felt glad that the authorities in London decided to send me to backward Orissa rather than to Serampore with its dead hopes. A young man sees more hope in an uncultivated wilderness than in a graveyard filled with monuments of the mighty dead."[26] Shortly after his visit at Serampore, George Howells received a copy of a book entitled *The Principles and Methods of Missionary Labor* written by Dr. E. B. Underhill, Honorary Secretary of the BMS. One of the papers of this book that dealt with Serampore College mentioned a proposal to sell the College building. But Dr. Underhill, backed by the then Principal, Mr. Summers, saved the College from its extermination in 1892. In 1896 in the above-mentioned book, Dr. Underhill writes, "The Charter which gives the College the right to confer degrees in Arts and Theology was granted by the Danish Government and confirmed by the British Government . . . . I still cherish the hope that better days may be in store . . . and that the College may yet become the University it was intended to be by its Founders . . . ."[27] In fact, the reading of Dr. Underhill's book planted the seed of revival of the Charter in Dr. Howells mind.

Howells presented a paper to a gathering of Baptist Missionaries from all over the country. In this paper, he proposed the revival of the Charter for the purpose of helping the cause of higher theological education in India. In the following months, Dr. Howells wrote a series of papers and pamphlets making aware of the revival of the Charter. This resulted in overwhelming support from the major missionaries utilizing of the Serampore Charter on University lines. As a part of this revival effort, in 1910, the higher Theological Department was opened. Serampore conferred the degree of Bachelor of Divinity on the first three theological graduates of the College as a full exercise of the rights under the Charter of 1827 for the first time on 4th December 1915. Dr. Howell became the member of Bengal Legislative Council in 1918 and the story of the Charter was revived under the Bengal Act of 1918 and the Serampore College Bill was passed on 28th March 1918. It subsequently received the assent of the Governor General and was gazetted on 1st May 1918. The privileges under Charter and Statutes remained under the Act and were untouched except that if there was a decision to grant degrees in any other branch of knowledge or Science than Theology, it must satisfy the Government to be equipped for the purpose.[28]

The Significance of the Serampore College Act and Higher Theological Education

There was an opposition to the special privilege under Article 13 of the Act, which protects the rights of the College to confer degrees in other branches of knowledge other than theology, on the grounds that there were more than 41 colleges under Calcutta University which can also claim such a privilege. This privilege was already surrendered by the Serampore College in 1858 when it was affiliated to the Calcutta University. It was argued, "if the Treaty was not broken in 1858, it cannot be broken now by leaving matters where they stand."[29] The Regulation was drawn up by the Serampore missionaries in the year 1833 also has the legal validity as that of the Charter, and Section 6 of the Statutes and Regulations of the Serampore College states:

> The first Council and their successors forever being authorized by the Charter "to confer such degrees of rank and honor as shall encourage learning" in the same manner as other Colleges and Universities, they shall from time to time confer degrees in such branches of Knowledge and Science as may be studied there, in the same manner as the Universities in Denmark, Germany and Great Britain. In doing this the Master and Council shall *ad libitum* call in the aid of any or all the Professors of Serampore College. All such degrees shall be perfectly free of expense to the person on whom they may be conferred, whether he be in India, Europe or America.[30]

Under the Serampore College Act, the Council of Serampore College constituted two bodies, one is known as the Faculty of the College (Local Governing Body of the College), concerning this Section 5 of the Act reads: "The Council shall, within one year from the date of the commencement of this Act, constitute and appoint in the manner prescribed in section 6 a body to be known as the College Faculty." The other body is known as the Senate of the College (to administer the Academic Administration of the Theological education) and Section 8 of the Act reads: "The Council shall, within one year from the date of the commencement of this Act, constitute and appoint in the manner prescribed in section 9, a body to be known as the Senate of the College." And the duties of the Senate also specified in Section 11 of the Act as follows:

> The Senate shall frame courses of study and make rules for the conduct of examinations, and shall, subject to the control of the Council, determine the qualifications for degrees and diplomas, and do and perform all other matters and things necessary or proper for or relating to the determination of the eligibility of candidates for degrees, diplomas and certificates to be conferred by the Council.[31]

The most significant part of these documents is that the College has a unique status as a university by virtue of the Royal Charter of Incorporation and the Serampore College Act 1918. Though it is not clearly stated its jurisdiction in the Serampore College Act, it enjoyed an open jurisdiction of affiliation of colleges and seminaries since the Act was introduced in 1918. Unlike other universities in the country, Serampore College (University) does not have any bar or restrictions on the domain of its affiliation or conferring degrees to students because the College was designed to cater the needs of all native Christians in India, irrespective of their denominations.

In its first Prospectus, it is clearly stated that this College will be open to all denominations, so that Asiatic Christian youth of every name may alike obtain advantages of this institution. It implies that the founders of the College envisioned providing education for all Christian denominations in India as well as other Asian countries. It is affirmed also in the Charter of Incorporation (Section 7) reads, ". . . the members of the first Council and their successors for ever shall have the power of conferring upon the students of the said College, native Christians as well as others, degrees of rank and honor according to their proficiency . . . ." This is further reiterated in the Serampore College Act 1918. The fifth paragraph of the Preamble reads,

> And whereas it is considered that in order to give effect, under the conditions now existing, to the intentions of his late Danish Majesty and of the founders of the said College, that is to say, *to promote piety and learning, particularly among the native Christian population of India* [italics are mine], the amendment of the constitution of the College, *by the enlargement of the Council on an inter-denominational basis* [italics are mine], with power to delegate some of its functions, in manner hereinafter appearing, is required.[32]

Further, concerning the constitution of the Senate Clause 9 (a) of the said Act reads, "at least one and not more than three representatives of each of the following Christian denominations, viz., Anglican, Baptist, Congregational, Lutheran, Methodist, Presbyterian, and Syrian, shall, as far as practicable, be members of the Senate." Hence, above clauses sufficiently empower the College to affiliate colleges and seminaries from all Christian denominations in India and beyond. Even during the presentation of the Serampore College Bill at the Proceedings of the Bengal Legislative Council, 1918, the ecumenical and national nature of the College was repeatedly highlighted.[33] Although in recent times, this was challenged by some people who are ignorant of these documents and the status of the College, their attempt failed. Therefore, in line with the vision and mission of the founders, the College continued its journey until today.

The Present Status and the Contribution to the Higher Theological Education

The College began its journey in Higher Theological education when "the Higher Theological Department was opened on 27th October 1910, and under the new regime the names of 121 students are recorded in the Register of the H. T. D., 235 have been registered as Internal students of Serampore, belonging either to the H. T. D. or to one of the five institutions that have been affiliated during the last ten years, and 116 students representing nearly all denominations and very many (*sic*) races in India have been registered for pursuing the External course of studies."[34]

However, in the development of the Serampore College after 1910, the teaching activities of the College were organized in two Departments: The Theology Department and the Arts-Science-Commerce Department (the Arts Department, 1911; Science, 1924, 1928, reintroduced in 1948; and Commerce, 1950). The Arts-Science-Commerce Department of the College as a teaching institution was affiliated to the University of Calcutta. The

Calcutta University was the first among the universities to accept Serampore degrees from its inception and recognize the BD degree as an equivalent to its BA degree. Other universities soon followed its example. The College in its teaching aspect is referred to as the Serampore College (Teaching). As of 2018, the ASC Department offers Master of Science in Botany, Master of Science in Physiology, and Master of Science in Zoology. The Theology Department functions on its own right as a teaching institution in Theology at the College. The Theology Department of the College is not an affiliated college of the Senate of Serampore College (University) but is an integral part of the Serampore structure.[35] This is because the Theology Department came into existence before the Senate was created. Serampore College is a centre of Theological Education that the College is most widely known. In fact, it is for Theology that the College is known in the world at large.

As of 2018, Serampore College (University) confers through its residential program the Diplomas in Clinical Pastoral Counseling (Dip. C.P.C.), Bachelor of Theology (B.Th.), Bachelor of Missiology (B.Miss.), Bachelor of Divinity (B.D.), Master of Theology (M.Th.), Master of Counseling and Psychotherapy (M.C.P.), and Doctor of Theology (D.Th.). It confers through the external program the Diploma in Christian Studies (Dip. C.S.), the Diploma in Worship and Music (D.W.M.), Diploma in Bible Translation (Dip. B.T.), the Degree of Bachelor of Bible Translation Studies (B.B.T.S.), the Degree of Bachelor of Christian Studies (B.C.S.), the Degree of Master of Christian Studies (M.C.S.) and the degree of Doctor of Ministry (D.Min.). Serampore College also confers the degree of Doctor of Divinity (D.D.) *Honoris Causa.* The Diploma in Christian Studies (Dip.C.S.) is offered to everybody without any distinction of faith or no faith, and to those who are interested in studying Christianity as a religion. The Degrees and Diplomas granted by the Serampore College (University) are recognized by Universities in India and abroad for the purpose of higher education.

In recent years, further development has been advanced from 'aims and objectives of Theological Education' in today's context. It is stated, "Theological Education has the broad goal of equipping the people of God and the congregations in their respective contexts."[36] Consequently, numerous courses on Contextual Theologies have been introduced with a strong commitment to liberation, such as Dalit Theology, Adivasi and Tribal Theology, and Feminist Theology, as well as issues like disability, AIDS/HIV, and Ecology. Under the Serampore College theological education system, academic, professional, vocational, personal, and communitarian life formation of students are given high importance. Indian religious issues are also given due importance in the light of present contexts.

Conclusion

As Serampore College is celebrating 200 years and the Senate 100 years, we are reminded from the first prospectus of the College the purpose for which the founders established this College: *A College for the Instruction of Asiatic, Christian and other youth in Eastern Literature and European Sciences*. For the last 200 years, the College has upheld both theological and secular disciplines side by side with lively cooperation and creative tension. Many Baptist leaders in England would have liked Serampore College to be exclusively a divinity school raising leadership for the emerging Asian churches. The Quartet was opposed to narrow-minded theologies that were not concerned with secular disciplines. In other words, they emphasized ecumenical and holistic education upholding sound learning, genuine piety and sterling character in their institution established in the pluralistic context of Asian society which was otherwise divided on the basis of many religions, castes, and denominations. They were against every form of communalism and sectarianism.

Can we call ourselves a university like other Universities in our country? During the Proceedings of the Bengal Legislative Council 1918, the speakers were repeatedly referring Serampore College as Serampore University. Serampore College is a University by the issuing of the Royal Charter 1827 in line with Copenhagen and other European Universities. It never ceased to be a University at any point in time. What is next? Can Serampore College achieve the recognition as a fully-fledged University, perhaps, a Christian University from the perspective of the Christian community as a whole? The Serampore dream and experience, from its very beginning, was ecumenical and broad-based. Serampore College, with its First Prospectus of the College (1818), Royal Charter (1827), Statutes and Regulations (1833), and Serampore College Act (1918), should come forward, on its own, to fill up the gap and help the Christian communities and denominations to be an authentic witness for Christian services in all spheres of life of the church in India and beyond. S. Pearce Carey in his book, *William Carey*, writes, "The Marquis Wellesley had been the first to supply a higher Indian education for the British Civil Service, but Serampore was the first to provide a higher education for Indian themselves: at least, for India's rank and file . . . The Serampore Mission first brought a higher education within the grasp of India's poor."[37] It will be a great tribute fitting to the founders, and all who labored following the founders, "if the College is declared a National Institute for Higher Learning in secular and theological faculties and its privilege in the Charter as enacted in the Act is fully realized and restored."[38] The College Council had the similar future expectation about the College as George Smith affirms, "The Council, however, is not without hope that in due time Carey's noble vision of a great Christian University at Serampore conferring its own degrees, not only in theology but in all branches of useful learning, may powerfully appeal to some of the merchant princes of the West."[39] This expectation is yet to be realized.

Hence, I conclude with recalling what Principal Howells said in his report on "Serampore College, Foundation Day" on 3rd February 1917 about our ideals:

> As a college, we stand for a union of learning. Our Charter sets forth the promotion of piety and learning as our primary object . . . We stand for a union of Theology with Arts and Science. Our Theological Department is highly important indeed the crowning feature of our work. We believe that theological study is best pursued wholly or in part in an open institution and in conjunction with a liberal course of general culture. What the church in India needs today is not a number of narrow-minded theologians trained as in the cloister and looking at life and its realities from a merely sectarian point of view, but saintly men of wide culture and general sympathies in intimate touch with their fellows . . . . We believe in the union for educational purposes of Christians of one body with those of another. For the Professors of Serampore College, there is no denominational test and the only requirements laid down by the Statutes is a belief in Christ's divinity and atonement as essential to vital Christianity . . . . We stand for the union of Christians and non-Christians in their student life . . . . We stand in our educational work for the union of India, North, and South, East and West. Serampore was not founded as a College exclusively for Bengal . . . .[40]

While Howells was uttering these words, he was being true to the spirit and aims of our great founders. Let us "Expect great things from God and Attempt great things for God."

Endnotes

[1] For a long time in the history of the mission, the three men—the founders of the Serampore Mission and Serampore College, William Carey, Joshua Marshman, and William Ward, have been known as 'the Serampore Trio.' However, Mrs. Hannah Marshman, a woman and the wife of Joshua Marshman, was no less a part in the founding of the Serampore Mission as well as the College from the very beginning. About her Mrs. E. L. Wenger aptly records, ". . . the woman who was to be a true colleague and assistant to the missionaries in every way open to a woman in those days was Mrs. Hannah Marshman, of whom it is written: 'She was a woman of feeling, piety and good sense, of strong mind and great disinterestedness, fitted in every respect to be an associate in the great undertaking to which the life of her husband was devoted, and withal of so amiable a disposition that nothing was ever known to have ruffled her temper.' Truly a jewel of a woman! She lived until 1847, being the last survivor of the original pioneers, and having seconded their labors ably and zealously throughout her long life." [See E. L. Wenger, "The Serampore Mission and Its Founders," *The Story of Serampore and Its College*, Fourth edition (Serampore: The Council of Serampore College, [1918] 2005), 4-5]. She is also considered as the pioneer for women education in India and whose leadership in sustaining the Mission and the College with her daily activities has monumental significance. As the College is celebrating its Bicentenary, it would be a fitting tribute and an honor to her to be called 'The Serampore Quartet' in place of 'The Serampore Trio' as used to be known all these years.

[2] There was no comma in the original title of the Prospectus in between 'Asiatic' and 'Christian' that seemed to have led the British evangelical public to believe that the student body was much more 'Christian' in composition than ever was the case; John Clark Marshman rectified this 30 years later when he cited the prospectus issued on 15th July 1818 and inserted a comma. See A. Christopher Smith, *The Serampore Mission Enterprise* (Bangalore: Center for Contemporary Christianity, 2006), 126.

[3] This 'Historical Summary of the Serampore College' appears in almost all annual reports of the College presented by George Howells with slight modifications and changes. This is revised by the writer based on George Howells and A. C. Underwood, "Serampore College: Historical Summary," *The Story of Serampore and Its College* (Serampore and Calcutta: Baptist Mission Press, 1918), and later editions.

[4] George Howells, *The Soul of India: An Introduction to the Study of Hinduism, in its Historical Setting and Development, and in its Internal and Historical Relations to Christianity* (London: James Clarke and Co. and The Kingsgate Press, 1913), 571.

[5] *Periodical Accounts*, Relative to the Baptist Missionary Society (1795): 124; (1798): 436.

[6] *Periodical Accounts* (1795): 124-125.

[7] George Smith, *The Life of William Carey* (London: J. M. Dent and Sons Ltd.; New York: E. P. Dutton and Co. Inc., Reprint, 1935), 273.

[8] Wenger, "The Serampore Mission and Its Founders," 7.

[9] Roger E. Hedlund, "William Carey's American Connections: Implications for the Serampore Mission, Indigenous Christianity and Indian Renaissance" (Ph.D. Dissertation, University of Madras, 2003), 152.

[10] Malay Dewanji, *William Carey and Indian Renaissance* (New Delhi: ISPCK, 1996), 76.

[11] Cited in S. Pearce Carey, *William Carey* (London: Hodder and Stoughton, 1923; Eighth Edition, Carey Press, 1934; London: The Wakeman Trust, 1993), 322.

[12] Cited in Carey, *William Carey*, 321-322.

[13] *A College for the Instruction of Asiatic Christian and other Youth in Eastern Literature and European Sciences*, 1818, 22-23. The text and layout of the *Prospectus* was originally printed at Serampore in 1818. It was reprinted with amendments for Black, Kingsbury, Parbury and Allen, London, 1819.

[14] *A College for the Instruction of Asiatic Christian and other Youth in Eastern Literature and European Sciences*, 1818, 24.

[15] Smith, *The Life of William Carey*, 276.

[16] Smith, *The Life of William Carey*, 276-77.

[17] *First Report of the College for Asiatic Christian and Other Youth, Instituted at Serampore, August, 1818, Under the Patronage of The Most Noble the Marquis of Hastings, K. G.* (1819): 7.

[18] S. P. Carey, "Reminiscences," MSS, Serampore College, Carey Library and Research Centre, 31.

[19] G. H. C. Angus, "The Story of the Charter, 1827-1927," *The Codex: The Centenary Number* (December, 1927), 6.

[20] Angus, "The Story of the Charter, 1827-1927," 6; *The Serampore College Act, 1918, Bengal Act IV of 1918*, Government of West Bengal Legislative Department, As modified up to the 1st July, 1951, (Alipur, West Bengal: Superintendent Government Printing, West Bengal Government Press, 1951), Clause 7.

[21] Angus, "The Story of the Charter, 1827-1927," 6; *The Serampore College Act, 1918*, Clause 7.

[22] *The Serampore College Act, 1918*, Clause 7.

[23] *The Serampore College Act, 1918*, 12.

[24] Cited in Mrs. W. Stewart, "The Serampore Charter," *The Story of Serampore and Its College* (Serampore: Council of Serampore College, [1918] 2005), 42.

[25] Stewart, "The Serampore Charter," 42.

[26] Stewart, "The Serampore Charter," 43.

[27] Cited in Stewart, "The Serampore Charter," 43-44.

[28] *The Serampore College Act, 1918*, Clause 13. Refer Clause 13 of the Serampore College Act, which reads:

> If at any time, the Council shall intend to grant degrees in any branch or branches of knowledge and science other than theology, such degrees shall be confined to students who shall have received regular instruction at the Serampore College; and before the Council proceeds to grant such degrees, it shall satisfy [the State Government] as to the adequacy: (1) of the establishment and equipment of the College; (2) of the academic standard to be maintained; (3) of the financial provision made therefor: Provided that the said Government, on ceasing to be so satisfied, may withdraw [its; This word was substituted for the word "their" by paragraph 5 (2) of the Government of India (adaptation of Indian Laws) Order, 1937] approval of the granting of such degrees.

The words "provincial Government were originally substituted for the words "the Government as defined in section 2 (b) of the Indian Universities Act, 1904, in relation to the University of Calcutta" by para. 3 and Sched. IV, to the Government of India (Adaptation of Indian Laws) Order, 1937, and thereafter the word "State" was substituted for the word "provincial" by paragraph 4 (l) of the Adaptation of Laws Order, 1950.

[29] Abstract from the Proceedings of the Bengal Legislative Council 1918 Serampore College Bill, 1918 (List of Business—Item No. 11). See Ravi Tiwari, *Senate of Serampore College (University) at Ninety: Issues and Concerns* (Serampore: The Senate of Serampore College, 2008), 22.

[30] *The Serampore College Act, 1918,* Schedule II, Section 6.

[31] *The Serampore College Act, 1918,* Clause 11.

[32] *The Serampore College Act, 1918,* 1.

[33] Tiwari, *Senate of Serampore College (University) at Ninety,* 22-24

[34] Angus, "The Story of the Charter, 1827-1927," 7.

[35] *Senate of Serampore College, Faculty of Theology: Regulations and Syllabus Related to the Degree of Bachelor of Divinity*, Vol. 1, Compulsory Courses (rev. ed. 2014; 1st rep. 2015), 9.

[36] *Senate of Serampore College, Faculty of Theology: Regulations and Syllabus Related to the Degree of Bachelor of Divinity*, Vol. 2, Optional Courses (rev. ed. 2014), 3.

[37] S. Pearce Carey, *William Carey*, 325.

[38] Tiwari, *Senate of Serampore College (University) at Ninety*, 9.

[39] Smith, *The Life of William Carey*, 292.

[40] George Howells, "Serampore College, Foundation Day: Principal's Report," 3rd February 1917; *The Students' Chronicle and Serampore College Magazine* (March, 1917): 1-2.

Bibliography

A College for the Instruction of Asiatic Christian and other Youth in Eastern Literature and European Sciences. Serampore: Serampore College, 1818.

Angus, G. H. C. "The Story of the Charter, 1827-1927." *The Codex: The Centenary Number* (December 1927): 6-7.

Carey, S. P. *William Carey*. London: Hodder and Stoughton, 1923; Eighth Edition, Carey Press, 1934; London: The Wakeman Trust, 1993.

Dewanji, M. *William Carey and the Indian Renaissance*. New Delhi: ISPCK, 1996.

First Report of the College for Asiatic Christian and Other Youth, Instituted at Serampore, August 1818, Under the Patronage of The Most Noble the Marquis of Hastings, K. G., 1819.

Hedlund, R. E. "William Carey's American Connections: Implications for the Serampore Mission, Indigenous Christianity, and Indian Renaissance." *Ph.D. Dissertation*. University of Madras, 2003.

Howells, G. "Serampore College, Foundation Day: Principal's Report." 3rd February 1917. *The Students' Chronicle and Serampore College Magazine* (March 1917): 1-5.

Howells, G. *The Soul of India: An Introduction to the Study of Hinduism, in its Historical Setting and Development, and in its Internal and Historical Relations to Christianity*. London: James Clarke and Co. and The Kingsgate Press, 1913.

Howells, G. and A. C. Underwood. "Serampore College: Historical Summary." *The Story of Serampore and Its College*. Serampore and Calcutta: Baptist Mission Press, 1918.

Periodical Accounts. Relative to the Baptist Missionary Society (1795): 124; (1798): 436.

Senate of Serampore College, Faculty of Theology: Regulations and Syllabus Related to the Degree of Bachelor of Divinity. Vol. 1. Compulsory Courses. Revised Edition 2014; First Reprint 2015.

Senate of Serampore College, Faculty of Theology: Regulations and Syllabus Related to the Degree of Bachelor of Divinity. Vol. 2. Optional Courses. Revised Edition 2014.

Smith, A. C. *The Serampore Mission Enterprise*. Bangalore: Center for Contemporary Christianity, 2006.

Smith, G. *The Life of William Carey*. London: J. M. Dent and Sons Ltd.; New York: E. P. Dutton and Co. Inc.; Reprint 1935.

Stewart, W. "The Serampore Charter." *The Story of Serampore and Its College*. Serampore: Council of Serampore College, [1918] 2005.

The Serampore College Act, 1918, Bengal Act IV of 1918. The government of West Bengal Legislative Department. As modified up to the 1st July 1951. Alipur, West Bengal: Superintendent Government Printing, West Bengal Government Press, 1951.

Tiwari, R. *Senate of Serampore College (University) at Ninety: Issues and Concerns*. Serampore: The Senate of Serampore College, 2008.

Wenger, E. L. "The Serampore Mission and Its Founders." *The Story of Serampore and Its College*. Fourth edition. Serampore: The Council of Serampore College, [1918] 2005.

3

The Impact of the Bible through the Protestant Reformation and the Protestant Missionary Movement

Prakash Abraham Mathew

Introduction

The year 2017 was celebrated as the 500th anniversary of the Reformation and the year 2018 marked as the 200th anniversary of the Serampore College—two significant events in the history of Christianity. Both these events not only contributed to the growth of worldwide Christianity but also paved way for the renaissance of two nations. Two leading names in the above movements are Martin Luther and William Carey. If we carefully analyze the history of their contribution to these movements, it will be clear that they spent most of their time in translating the Bible into the local languages. This has made significant impact in the renaissance of the respective nations. Luther who pioneered the protestant reformation brought transformation in the life of the Church as a whole. On the other hand, Carey who is considered as the father of protestant missionary movement eventually came to India and founded the Serampore Mission. One of the uniqueness of these movements is based on their emphasis on the translation of the Bible. History unfolds the challenges of the colossal task which they involved in their respective life threatening contexts.

History demonstrates, not only in the case of Germany and India, in several other nations how renaissance and transformation were introduced through the propagation of the message of the Bible. In spite of its profound influence in different parts of the world, the Bible was also attacked around the world. In their title *Breaking India*, Rajiv Malhotra and Aravind Neelakandan analyze the work of Christian organizations engaged in the Indian context from different dimensions. In his introductory marks, Malhotra asserts that the translation projects of the Bible are "not favorable to Indian unity and overtly hostile to Indian culture."[1] The authors further argue that the western agencies fostered division among the Indian community through the means of promulgating Dravidian and Dalit identity separatism. They call Carey as the "nastiest evangelist" and Serampore College as "notorious."[2] It was in this context, I am motivated to analyze the Protestant Reformation and the Protestant Missionary Movement that laid primary emphasis on the Bible. Thus, an attempt is being made here to do a historical analysis of the following queries: first, how did the Bible give birth to these movements through the initiatives of Luther and Carey? Second, what were the challenges these stalwarts confronted to accomplish their tasks? And third, what were the impacts of these movements upon the renaissance of Germany and India?

The Impact of the Bible for the Birth of the Movements

The Bible was an important medium for the birth of both the Protestant Reformation and the Protestant Missionary Movement. History shows how God's word brought transformation in the lives of Luther and Carey and enlightened them with transforming visions. At the age of twenty, Luther saw a complete Latin Bible in the university Library and realized that the Bible contains more than what is being read and explained in the churches. Luther mentions the reception of the personal copy of the Bible as "the unforgettable hour."[3] This gave him the interest to read and study the Bible. During his time in the Augustinian Monastery, he spent considerable time in reading and studying the Word of God. This eventually brought transformation in his life and he understood that the same transformation can be brought in the lives of the people if they come in direct contact with God's word.[4] Thus Luther attempted to translate the Bible into the German language which became the most significant means for the Protestant Reformation.

On the other hand, Carey, who was a fruit of the Protestant Reformation, had also been transformed by the power of the Scripture and challenged the world in front of him to know its power. While Luther primarily attempted to make transformation within the church, Carey attempted to transform the people who did not know about Christ. As in the case of Luther, Carey was also engaged in reading and studying the Scripture in his early days. He also received guidance from biblical expositors like Thomas Scott, Andrew Fuller, Robert Hall, and John Sutcliff.[5] Thus, the Bible brought considerable impact in him before he shared it with others.

During the two centuries that followed the Protestant Reformation, the Protestants did not show much interest in foreign missions. It is in this context that William Carey challenged the Protestants through his emphasis on the Great Commission of Jesus Christ to take the Gospel into different parts of the world. Thus, 19th century saw the impact of his effort through great protestant missionary efforts.[6] Carey came to know about different communities in the world through reading books such as *The Last Voyages of Captain Cook* and *The Present State of British Empire and Geographical Grammar.* At the same time, his personal Bible studies challenged him to take the gospel to the non-Christian communities around the world. He published a treatise with the following title: "An Enquiry into the obligation of Christians to use means for a conversion of the Heathens in which the religious state of the different nations of the world, the success of former undertakings, and the practicality of future undertakings are considered."[7] Through this he emphasized that the Great Commission is binding for all Christians of all generations. It clarified the need of missions, refuted the objections to mission work, and listed suggestions for formulating a society. Mulholland considered Carey's treatise as the Magna Carta of the Protestant Missionary Movement. This book is as significant as Luther's ninety-five theses which played a significant role in the Protestant Reformation.[8] The historic sermon on 31st May, 1792, based on Isa. 54:2-3, "Enlarge the place of your tent; stretch out the curtains of your dwellings, spare not; lengthen your cords, and strengthen your pegs" (NASB), challenged people to take the gospel to the unreached areas of the world. It is at the end of this message he stated: "Expect great things from God and attempt great things for God." This eventually led him to the formation of the Baptist Missionary Society. Later London Missionary Society and Church Missionary Society were also formed to spread the gospel to the unreached.[9]

It took 275 years since the Protestant Reformation to start a protestant mission and Carey became instrumental for the movement. In fact, the Bible became the vital tool in that transformative mission. One of the watch words of protestant reformation *Sola Scriptura* continues to prove that God's Word alone can transform the lives of the people and it did transform Carey for pioneering a world mission movement. The Protestant missionary movement gave birth to the Serampore Mission with Carey's arrival in India.

The Challenges in the Task: A Comparison

If we analyze the life of Luther and Carey, one thing significant to notice is the time and effort they spent in translating the Bible. Luther spent more than 25 years both in translation and revisions of the German Bible. Though he finished the German New Testament in 1522 and the complete Bible in 1534, he was constantly involved in revising the work until his death.[10] Luther's attempts to translate the Bible into German gave him several challenges on the way to accomplish it.

Luther was in a context where the common people were not allowed to have the Bible in their possession. Interpretation of the Bible was under the authority of the clergy and the common people were only expected to listen what the clergy interpret. Hence, the authority of the church was against the translation of the Bible. People were threatened to death and many faced excommunication from the church due to their involvements in the translation and circulation of the Bible. The Scripture was chained to the pulpit in order to keep them away from common accessibility. The copies of the manuscripts of the Bible were used to find only in the monasteries.[11] The Latin Bible was accessible only to the elite groups and was read mostly by the educated in the society. The church authorities conveyed that the common people are not able to understand the Scripture and that the German language does not express the correct sense of its message.

When Luther was laboring to translate the Scripture into the common people's language, German language was not in a unified form but was spoken in different dialects. During Luther's period, there were a few German translations existed; but they were based on the Vulgate version with certain levels of textual difficulties and several inconsistencies.[12] Luther attempted for this great task in spite of the unavailability of modern translation tools such as grammar books, dictionaries and concordances. The textual criticism was at its initial levels and the biblical scholarship was not in a developed stage to take up such translation projects.[13] Luther had to challenge an age old ecclesiastical system and had to take risks on the way to fulfill his vision.

Being transformed and challenged by the Scripture, Carey also realized that transformation will happen if God's Word reaches people. While Luther was working in his own cultural context, Carey was involved in a completely new socio-cultural and religious context. He was reforming a society that went through a socio-cultural degradation. Vishal and Ruth Mangalwadi describe the situation in which Carey came to the nation of India. They state that, "Asceticism, untouchability, mysticism, the occult, superstition, idolatry, witchcraft, and other oppressive beliefs and practices became the hallmark of Indian culture."[14] It was in such a context that Carey undertook translating the Bible into different and unfamiliar languages. Scott quotes Crockett saying that, "In translation work, Carey stands along with giants—Jerome, Aelfric, Wycliffe, Erasmus, and Tyndale all who gave their lives to spreading the Book's life-changing, freeing, redemptive message."[15] The Serampore Trio understood the fact that the Bible can transform the lives of the people and thereby the destiny of the nation of India. Thus, one of the purposes of the Serampore mission stated in the Serampore Covenant is that: "labor unceasingly for Bible Translation."[16] Carey and his team had to develop languages from their initial levels to translate the Bible into those languages. Luther had one language before him whereas in a multi-linguistic context of India, Carey had a massive task to perform.

Carey acquainted with biblical languages before he arrived in India and that helped him in his initiatives of translating the Scripture. He studied several languages such as Hebrew, Greek, Latin, Dutch, French and Italian all by himself. When he came to Bengal, he started learning Bengali and was determined to gain command over the language in order to fulfill the mission of God. There was significant gap between the literate and the illiterate Bengali during the time of Carey. Thus, he created a style known as *Sadhu Bhasha* and this style used Sanskrit words. He also listened to people in order to pick up correct idioms and expressions.[17] Similarly, Luther was thorough with the Latin, Hebrew and Greek. Even though he was a German citizen, he took special effort to learn the depths of the German language. He travelled extensively in order to familiarize with different dialects of it. Luther moved through the streets and market places in order to understand their expressions and idioms.[18] Translator's ability to handle both the source and the target languages (receptor's language) is an important factor for effective translation. Luther's aim was to translate the Scripture into the language of the common people. With that aim in mind, he took special attention to learn their language. When Carey was in the process of translation, the literary style that prevailed in Bengal was predominantly poetic. He and his friends took up the challenge and with the help of the local *pundits*, they involved in translating the Bible for the Indian communities.[19]

Carey did not receive much welcome from the Anglicans in Kolkata because of various reasons. The Church of England looked at Carey and his colleagues as dissenting non-conformists. They were also not authorized by the archbishops of Canterbury or York. Their family backgrounds also increased the tension between the Anglicans and the missionaries. The learned and the leaders alike thought that Carey cannot do such a task which requires knowledge and special abilities. The East India Company neither supported him nor encouraged his missionary activities.[20]

Carey's job in the indigo factory helped him to deepen his understanding about the culture and language of Bengal. He also got help from individuals like Ramram Basu for improving his knowledge of the Bengali and he learned the basics of the language from *Bengali Grammar* that was prepared by John Thomas and Nathaniel Brassey. George Udney donated a wooden press to Carey in 1798 which helped him to publish the Bengali Bible. Carey, Marshman and Ward printed the Bengali New Testament in February 7, 1801.[21] Keeping the first copy in the communion Table and dedicating it to God, Carey preached from the text: "Let the word of Christ dwell in you richly in all wisdom" (Col. 3:11).[22] This was a great achievement and that was resulted into the transformation of the society. Carey believed that the Word of God is the fountain of life and it can bring about a radical transformation in the lives of the people. This motivated Carey to translate the Scripture into several vernacular languages.

It is observed that about thirty-six years Carey worked as a translator involving in translating the Bible into various languages. He was continuously working to improve the Bengali New Testament as he aimed to make the message clearer and closer to the original text. Carey used to circulate his translations to people from different background in order to get opinions from them.[23] He also consulted with the scholars at the Fort William College for improvement. Luther also took help from the language experts to make his translation better. His friends Reuchlin, Lyra, Erasmus and Melanchthon helped him in the translation process.[24] Luther experienced a lot of difficulty while translating the Old Testament and it took several years to complete it in comparison to the New Testament. He finished the project in 1534 and because of the challenges that he faced, he commented that Hebrew does not want to become German.[25] While Luther translated the Bible into the German language, the Serampore mission translated the Bible into 42 different languages.

No translation is perfect and therefore both Luther and Carey faced several criticisms. Carey was criticized for using Sanskrit words and colloquial forms of Bengali in his translations. Thus, it was argued that he was not consistent in style and language. Another criticism against him was the use of 'Christian Bengali,' that is, framing Bengali words equivalent to the Hebrew and the Greek words.[26] Similarly Luther also faced certain criticisms because of certain principles he held in the task of translation. Since his attempt was to make the Bible into the common human language, in several places he emphasized on the content rather than the form of the text. Both Carey and Luther revised their translations based on the criticism they received. It is not correct to evaluate their work in the light of the modern linguistic or translation theories. Carey worked in a context where he did not have any of the linguistic tools to aid his translation work.

Luther attempted the task more than 250 years before Carey and thus the task was more challenging for him. He had to fight against an existing system which was powerful and universally accepted. Carey, on the other hand, took up this task in a different socio-cultural context.

The Bible and the Renaissance of the Nations

Both Luther and Carey launched the transformative Word of God to the people of Germany and India. Both the Protestant Reformation and the Protestant Missionary Movement emerged as a result of expounding the Scripture. The formation of the German Bible contributed colossally to the nation building. The Protestant Missionary Movement eventually gave birth to the Serampore mission and played a key role in building the modern India. In the following section, we will analyze how these movements impacted the nations.

The Renaissance of Germany

Luther's German Bible not only brought spiritual renewal but also played a pivotal role in bringing revival in several other aspects of the country. It helped the people to have a direct access to the message of the Bible which eventually brought transformation in the society.

Development of Language, Literature, and National Identity

The German Bible made significant contribution in unifying the German language. During the period of Luther, the German language existed not in a standardized form. The German Bible bridges both the written and spoken languages of that time. Luther considered both the high and low forms of German in his translation in order to impact every strata of the society.[27] As he initiated to unify the language, it created a momentum for a common tongue. Haemig states that it became the basis for both the spoken and written German today.[28] In the process of creating the Bible as a common people's book, Luther incorporated several art works within the text in order to convey different themes from the German culture. There were 117 paintings included within the text and they became a masterpiece in the German literature.[29]

A common language for a nation creates a collective identity for the community. It is precisely what Luther's translation contributed to the nation of Germany. Latourette says that Luther's Bible created a profound influence upon the Germans than the KJV did to the English.[30] The Bible became a matter of prestige to the nation as a whole and it changed the fate of the people in the country.

Translation Movements

Luther's German Bible became an inspiration to translate the Bible into different languages. Several other translators used Luther's German Bible and the principles he used to make the Bible available in other languages. William Tyndale was influenced and used Luther's Bible for the translation of the English Bible. Michael Agricola, the translator of the Finnish Bible, also used it as a guide for his translation.[31] When the Bible reached the hands of the common people, it transformed individuals, communities and the nations. Thus, translation of the Bible into vernacular languages became a major emphasis after the Reformation.

The Bible and the Reformation

When Luther encountered the divine word, it became a pivotal document for the reformation of the church. Later when the German New Testament was printed and then the complete Bible, it gave great impetus for the spread of the movement. When the Bible reached the hands of the common people, they realized that the Scripture is the only authority for faith and practices. It fostered the movement in a greater way and helped to spread the message of Reformation. Wood observes that, "for at heart it is none other than the word, and to distribute the scriptures was to further the reformation. As Luther again and again insisted, it was not what he did which effected the transformation of European Christianity: the word did it all."[32] The amount of circulation of Luther's Bible shows its wider reception and impact on the people.

Renaissance in the Indian Context

Serampore Mission is one of the fruits of the Protestant Missionary Movement. It focused not only on the spiritual aspects of the people but also attempted to bring changes in several other aspects of the life of the community in India. In fact, translation of the Bible was a major concern of the mission and the accomplishment of the task impacted India in several ways.

The Contribution to Language and Literature

Carey's contribution to the language and literature is undeniable. He served as a teacher of Bengali and Sanskrit at Fort William College for several years. He prepared a *Bengali Grammar* book and written a Bengali prose and both of them were used as text books. Carey edited a Bengali dictionary and translated the Mahabharata and the Ramayana in Bengali.[33] In fact the publication of the Bengali New Testament was one of his significant contributions. These developments in Bengali language and literature made Serampore as a centre of Bengali Studies. Several stories, plays, novels, and dramas were emerged immediately after the death of Carey. They not only contributed to the development of literature but also became avenues for critiquing the social issues of the day.[34]

Carey's opportunity to become a Bengali and Sanskrit teacher at the Fort William College helped him to translate the Bible into several of the Asian languages. He prepared a grammar for Marathi and Bengali languages. He also made a grammar for Sanskrit believing that Sanskrit is the source language to understand several other Indian dialects.[35] Though languages have been developed to translate the Bible, we also need to know how they enhanced the life of the people. Carey's associates at the Fort William College developed Urdu, Hindustani and Hindi.[36] Though initially they developed for the translation of the Bible, it brought tremendous development in governance, education, and other areas of the life of the Indian society.

History tells us that a press was bought to print Bible and later it was used to produce other materials. The modern press brought huge development in the history of India. A steam engine was installed in order to produce paper. The introduction of the steam engine brought revolution in the industry.[37] The production of paper fostered literatures in vernacular languages and brought advancement in the field of education.

The production of paper and the installation of the press ushered a new era in journalism. Carey launched a newspaper to fight against the social injustices. Despite the difficulties faced, he published *Samachar Darpan* and *Friend of India*. Carey and his friends unfolded the social evils and attempted to impact the educated in the society. The periodical, *Dig Darshan* published articles on physics, chemistry, geography and biology.[38]

Bible in the Unification and Formation of the Identity of the Nation

Christianity is often criticized for dividing India on the basis of languages and cultures. While translating the Bible into the common people's language, Luther revived Germany and unified the nation. The translation of the Bible into German and English brought great renaissance in Germany and England respectively and Europe as a whole. Though Carey was criticized for dividing the nation linguistically by developing different languages, the fact of the matter is that it fostered the birth of modern India. It fostered good governance, education, development and liberated communities of different cultures.[39] The beauty of a peaceful co-existence amidst of the diversities of cultures became an example before the world. The natural identity of the nation is displayed through the linguistic diversities.

Carey propagated equality of all human beings based on the biblical principle that all human beings are created equally in God's image. He fought against all caste distinctions and this paved way for the emergence of the current Indian leaders from the marginalized communities.[40] The presence of the message of the Bible in the land of India creates a sense of freedom from the oppressive structures. It helps to fight against social injustices and envisions for a peaceful co-existence with diversities. The challenges of caste, oppression of the marginalized, exploitation of women, disparities between rich and poor shatter our nation's unity.[41]

Bible and the Renaissance in Education

The translation of the Bible was essential for the propagation of the Gospel. The Baptist Missionary Society realized this fact and prioritized Bible translation as one of its projects. They understood that translation of God's word to the vernacular languages will help them to make a good rapport with the local people.[42] The Bible portions are not just used for the propagation of the gospel but also used as a material for education. Gine narrates the impact it made on education. The translated Bible portions were used in the initial days for the purpose of studying. Through the use of Bible as a study material, the life of Jesus was introduced as a model for people to develop their character.[43] The missionaries did not confine themselves to the translation work of the Bible alone, but they also translated other literatures as well. Carey and Marshman translated Valmiki's Ramayana into English. They also translated books on science and philosophy, and they became materials for education.[44] The right to education irrespective of caste and gender is a strong impact upon uplifting the lower strata of the society.

When different languages have been developed, it brought about a big movement in the field of education. It gave opportunities for people from various linguistic backgrounds to study in their mother tongue and understand the secular literature in their own languages. It created an educated society and formed people with potentials. Thus, religious and secular materials were made available for the people in vernacular languages.[45] They created a longing for learning in Indian minds and eventually brought social changes. In fact, it gave opportunities for the marginalized communities to equip themselves through education.

Carey realized that, as an outsider, he was not able to understand the deepest sense of the local language and thus not able to express it in a powerful way. Thus, he felt the need to train the local people in the biblical languages so that they will be equipped in translating the Bible into their mother tongues. Carey realized that Hebrew and Greek have similarities with Sanskrit and therefore easy for Indians to learn these languages.[46] Thus the team laid the foundation to raise local translators which resulted in the formation of Serampore College in 1818. It became a place for Christians and people of other faith traditions trained in various disciplines. They also included theology as one of the disciplines. One of the aims was to train people in the oriental languages.

The birth of theological education under Serampore College marks the greatest revolution in the history of theological education in India. Today with its affiliated colleges, it is the largest body of theological training in India. The contextual emphasis in its curricula is strong enough to train the young people to involve in transforming the nation. The Serampore College paved way for the Indians to theologize in touch with the larger Indian society and thereby bring changes in the society. In fact, theological articulation must be done with contextual significance. The colleges affiliated to the Senate of Serampore and the theological education it imparts show the impact of Carey's vision to transform India. Snaitang calls Carey as "the architect of modern theological education—at least in the protestant tradition."[47] The College produced Christian leaders to the churches and other related agencies. One of their significant contributions is the development of indigenous leaders for the Indian churches and organizations. The formation of theology department along with secular studies displays Carey's integrative approach and the development of persons in multidimensional ways. It gave opportunities for people to interact with people of other faith traditions and develop new social relationships.[48]

Translation of the Bible in the Indian Languages

Though Carey first translated the Bible into Bengali, he translated and supervised translation of the Bible into several other languages. He realized the importance of Sanskrit in the Indian context and translated a Sanskrit New Testament in 1808 and the complete Bible in 1818.[49] Later, Bibles were made available in several Indian languages and a movement for translation had been started. The scholars from the Fort William College assisted Carey and a department of Bible translation itself was formed. Later the East India Company closed the Department.[50] Thereafter, the British and Foreign Bible society came to lend their support. The Kolkata auxiliary of this society was later founded, and it was the first of its kind to foster the translation projects. The Sanskrit New Testament in Devanagri script was published in 1863 and several other Indian languages were also considered. All these attempts helped to the development of different vernacular languages in the Indian context. These developments helped in the formation of the auxiliaries of British and foreign Bible society in different parts of the sub-continent and eventually led to the formation of a Bible society at the national level.[51] Several of the later translations used Carey's principles and impacted the movement of translation in India. Carey created a zeal for translation while the Bible societies involved in translation and distribution of the Bible.

Bible as a Solution to Human Rights Concerns

The situation in which Carey came to India, specifically Bengal, was a period when human rights violations were rampant. It was in this context that Carey voiced against the age-old evil practices that existed in the society. God of the Bible does not endorse any human rights violations but envisions a peaceful co-existence of his creations. Carey believed that if the actual message of the Bible reaches people in their own language, it will bring a transformative effect in them. The Bible in their mother tongue helped the people in the lower strata of the community to understand God's liberative activity in a more meaningful and personal way. It also helped the people to evaluate their worldviews, traditions and practices in the light of the redemptive message of the Bible. Following are a few human right concerns which Carey addressed during his time and how they transformed the socio-cultural milieu of India.

Carey strongly protested against human rights violations. In his early days in England he witnessed slave trade which was common in Portugal and Spain under British colonialism. Slaves were shipped to the British colonies during that period. Many lives were lost in the voyage due to brutality, starvation and diseases. Carey criticized slave trade and reacted to it by avoiding the use of sugar from British colonies so that his hands will be cleansed from the blood of the innocent.[52] In Bengal also Carey witnessed the sale of children for slavery and agitated against this practice. By the middle of the 19th century, the government took legal action against such practices.[53] He was moved by the emphasis of humanism in the French Revolution and convinced that the best way to transform people is to bring them to Christ. T. V. Philip quotes the words of Pearce Carey who says that "when France rose for the rights of men, Carey was meditating on the rights of God. The surest way of securing man's right is to find them included in

God's."[54] Carey understood that by making the message of the Bible available to the people, it would transform them and therefore he focused a major part of his work dedicated to translating the Bible.

Carey himself underwent a strange experience at the death of his son and was treated as an outcaste by the society. But he was filled with the compassion of Christ and attempted to spread the values of "equality, human dignity, service and social justice."[55] The evil of caste system was dominant in the Indian society and it was a threat to the basic fabric of the country. Though certain other missions in India did not oppose caste system, Serampore Mission rejected it strongly and set aside any of such distinctions which divide the people. Carey believed that God's kingdom will not be real if the caste system dominates in the society particularly within the church.[56] The upliftment of the marginalized communities and the emergence of political leaders from such communities have owed to Carey and the Christian missions. In his discussion with Mangalwadi, R. M. Pandit says that the reason why political parties now witnessed the emergence of dalit leaders is because Carey had sown the seed of equality from the Bible years ago. He further says that the reason political parties are forced to appoint the "untouchables" as chief ministers is because of Carey.[57]

Carey was a person who raised his voice for the rights of the women. God's word was the basis for Carey to fight against the social evils that destroy the lives of women in Indian society. The laws of Manu make the life of the women miserable in the society.[58] Carey believed that the righteousness and justice of the God of the Bible alone which envisions equality to both men and women could only save the lives of Indian women.

In fact, Carey was the man who steered the fight against *sati* (widow burning). After witnessing an incident, he decided to fight against this evil practice. In 1804, the government asked Carey to submit a report of the custom of widow burning. He submitted the report, but the officials did not act upon the report initially. Carey's effort was later supported by the Indian leader, Raja Ram Mohan Roy and in 1829 sati was legally banned.[59] Carey and his team also raised voice for remarriage of widows.

Infanticide was another evil practice that existed in the society at time of Carey's arrival in India. A sick child was considered to be under the control of evil spirit. Parents wanted to destroy these children or give them for sacrifices. Children were thrown to the rivers to be drowned or devoured by crocodiles in order to fulfill the vows made by parents. Since women had low status in the society, killing of female infants was also a common practice in the society. Carey's fight against such practices resulted in proclaiming infanticide as illegal in 1804.[60]

The practice of burning lepers existed in the society during the time of Carey's ministry in India. He fought against this inhuman act after witnessing an incident. Lepers faced alienation from the society and were sent out from homes without food or clothes. This prompted the missionaries to establish the oldest leprosy hospital.[61] Similarly, we find that later in history Mother Teresa also stood for the care and rehabilitation of the lepers.

Education of women is one of the major contributions of the Serampore Mission. It was started in a situation where women were considered as inferior to men. The move to give education to women created awareness of the value of women. This gave women social uplifting and opportunities to play leadership roles and also opportunities to work as teachers, professors, principals, and government officers.[62] Though our nation has still reservations to allow women to come in the forefront, or accept them as equal with men, we have witnessed women becoming, president, prime minister, cabinet ministers, governors, chief ministers and holding other portfolios as well. Thus, Carey attempted to fight against the social evils and stood for the cause of the marginalized in the society. The theological conviction behind these is the idea that human life is precious, and the humanity bears the image of God. He also believed that all human beings are equal in the sight of God.

Eco-vision of the Serampore Mission

One of the uniqueness of Carey's holistic approach to mission was his concern for environment. While we now think of protecting the nature, Carey thought about it years before and took effort to care the environment for a sustainable human life. The guiding force for him to take such effort must be the mandate God has given to humanity in the Genesis creation narratives. The creation narratives state that the creation is entrusted to humanity in order to take care of it. Carey felt that the mother earth needs care and healing, he planned environmental care programs at the beginning of the nineteenth century. Carey's held the view that since nature displays God's handiwork, it must be treated properly. It is part of humanity's existence and therefore would have equal treatment with that of human being.[63] Even though India was not his home country, his concern to instruct people in the area of caring the environment is a commendable point. These efforts of Carey are best examples for people who criticize that his motive was only converting people to Christianity.

With the care of creation in mind, Carey established an Agri-horticultural society in India in 1820. The objective was to develop fruits, vegetables and food crops. He also started a botanical garden for planting and developing varieties of trees. He also took time to study about various plants, trees and flowers and published his ideas in books. This helped people to have concern about tending plants and vegetations which eventually created awareness among the people about the proper care of nature. It is also noted that Carey established a library and a museum for research and analysis.[64] Carey understood the relationship between human being and nature and thus realized that exploitation will have adverse effect on people. It is noteworthy to see that the Senate of Serampore continues to emphasize creation care through incorporating courses related to ecology. The liberative aspect of the message of the Bible for the environment and its emphasis in the contemporary theological education is one of the significant contributions by the Serampore mission.

Conclusion

We will limit the significance if we say Protestant Reformation and Protestant Missionary Movement are just movements within the history of Christianity. They are movements in the world history—movements that impacted the destiny of the nations. The irrefutable fact is that the basis of these movements is rooted in the Bible. Luther and Carey who experienced the transformative power of God's word used the same to transform the nations. Their vision to bring reformation in the church and in the society was based on the message of the Bible. Translation of the Bible was the heart and soul of their work. It is God's Word that gave birth of these movements and at the same time played significant role in birth of modern India and Germany. Therefore, if we give credit to Luther and Carey—the credit ultimately goes to the Bible. It is the Bible that transformed people and thereby the nations.

As we celebrate the bicentenary of the Serampore College, the theological fraternity must revisit the vision of its founder—to transform the people through the message of the Bible. The Bible must be given focus in our theological endeavors and that will transform individuals and eventually make them pillars for rebuilding the nations. The revolution that Serampore Mission brought in India is an example of how gospel can penetrate the hearts of the people and change their lives. Bible does not dichotomize between evangelism and social actions. Therefore, whoever attempts to transform people must bring transformation holistically. This is what history witnessed through the work of Luther—the Protestant Reformation—and Carey—the pioneer of Protestant Missionary Movement. Amidst of the life threatening challenges, they worked hard to accomplish the task and inspired several others in the world to know the importance of the Scripture. In the past, several people labored and sacrificed their lives for giving the Scriptures to the world. The Word continues to inspire people to cross the cultural boundaries and enable them to give life-transforming Word to the people.

Endnotes

[1] Rajiv Malhotra and Aravindan Neelakandan, *Breaking India* (Princeton: Infinity Foundation, 2011), 4.

[2] Book Review: "Breaking India," *Ethne* 10/3-4 (2011), 4; Also see Malhotra and Neelakandan, *Breaking India.*

[3] Hans Kasdorf, "Luther's Bible: A Dynamic Equivalence Translation and Germanizing Force," *Missiology: An International Review* 6/2 (1978): 214.

[4] Carl S. Mayer, "Luther," *The New International Dictionary of the Christian Church*, ed. J. D. Douglas (Grand Rapids: Zondervan, 1978): 609-10.

[5] Christopher A. Smith, *The Serampore Mission Enterprise* (Bangalore: Centre for Contemporary Christianity, 2006), 5.

[6] T. V. Philip, *Reflections on Christian Missions in India: William Carey Lectures and Other Essays* (Delhi: ISPCK/CSS, 2000), 28.

[7] Kenneth B Mulholland, "From Luther to Carey: Pietism and Modern Missionary Movement," *Bibliotheca Sacra* 156/621 (1999): 88.

[8] Mulholland, "From Luther to Carey: Pietism and Modern Missionary Movement," 88.

[9] Barkat Masih Khokar, "Remembering William Carey (1793-1993)," *National Council of Churches Review* CXIII/11 (1993): 681.

[10] Mary Jane Haemig, "Luther on Translating the Bible," *Word and World* 31/3 (2011): 255-56.

[11] A. Skevington Wood, *Captive to the Word* (Toronto: The Paternoster Press, 1969), 96-97.

[12] Kasdorf, "Luther's Bible: A Dynamic Equivalence Translation and Germanizing Force," 219.

[13] Philip Schaff, *History of the Christian Church*, revised edition (Peabody: Hendrickson, 2006), 7: 202.

[14] Vishal Mangalwadi and Ruth Mangalwadi, *The Legacy of William Carey: A Model for the Transformation of Culture* (Wheaton: Crossway Books, 1993), 24.

[15] Bennie Crockett, "H. I. Hester Lecture: William Carey's Integrated Christian Vision," in Hummel Scott, "The Legacy of William Carey at the Bicentennial of the Founding of Serampore College," *William Carey: The Multifaceted Genius* (Serampore: Council of Serampore College, 2018), 19.

[16] Philip, *Reflections on Christian Missions in India: William Carey Lectures and Other Essays*, 38.

[17] C. Arangaden, "Carey's Legacy of Bible Translation," *Indian Church History Review* 27/1 (1993): 19-20.

[18] Kasdorf, "Luther's Bible: A Dynamic Equivalence Translation and Germanizing Force," 271-218.

[19] Pratap Chandra Gine, "Educationist William Carey: Translation in Education," *Mission and the Local Congregations: Essays in Honor of William Carey's 250th Birth Anniversary*, ed. Solomon Rongpi (Delhi: ISPCK, 2011), 6.

[20] Daniel Jeyaraj, "Embodying Memories: Early Bible Translations in Tranquebar and Serampore," *International Bulletin of Mission Research* 40/1 (2016): 50.

[21] Jeyaraj, "Embodying Memories: Early Bible Translations in Tranquebar and Serampore," 50-51.

[22] Arangaden, "Carey's Legacy of Bible Translation," 21.

[23] Gine, "Educationist William Carey: Translation in Education," 7-8.

[24] Kasdorf, "Luther's Bible: A Dynamic Equivalence Translation and Germanizing Force," 220.

[25] Joseph Keller, "Luther's Bible Translation and the Wartburg Project" (October 2015): 2.

[26] Gine, "Educationist William Carey: Translation in Education," 9-10.

[27] Ruth Little Dewhurst, *The Legacy of Luther: National Identity and State-Building in Early Nineteenth Century Germany* (M. A. Diss., Georgia State University, 2013), 21-22.

[28] Haemig, "Luther on Translating the Bible," 260-61.

[29] Kasdorf, "Luther's Bible: A Dynamic Equivalence Translation and Germanizing Force," 233.

[30] K. C. Latourette, *A History of Christianity* (New York: Harper and Row, 1953), 1: 719.

[31] Haemig, "Luther on Translating the Bible," 261.

[32] Wood, *Captive to the Word*, 95.

[33] Roger E. Hedlund, "Carey, A Missiologist Before Time," *Indian Church History Review* 27/1 (1993): 44.

[34] Hedlund, "Carey, A Missiologist before Time," 44.

[35] Jeyaraj, "Embodying Memories: Early Bible Translations in Tranquebar and Serampore," 51-52.

[36] Arangaden, "Carey's Legacy of Bible Translation," 26-27.

[37] Vishal Mangalwadi, "William Carey: The Father of Modern India," *Ethne* 10/3-4 (2011): 7.

[38] Ashish K. Massey and June Hedlund, "William Carey and the Making of Modern India," *Indian Church History Review* 27/1 (1993): 13.

[39] Mangalwadi, "William Carey: The Father of Modern India," 7.

[40] Mangalwadi, "William Carey: The Father of Modern India," 5.

[41] O. L. Snaitang, "William Carey's Vision and Its Relevance Today," *Indian Church History Review* 27/1 (1993): 63.

[42] Gine, "Educationist William Carey: Translation in Education," 4-5.

[43] Gine, "Educationist William Carey: Translation in Education," 11.

[44] Jeyaraj, "Embodying Memories: Early Bible Translations in Tranquebar and Serampore," 52.

[45] Mangalwadi, "William Carey: The Father of Modern India," 7.

[46] Jeyaraj, "Embodying Memories: Early Bible Translations in Tranquebar and Serampore," 52.

[47] Snaitang, "William Carey's Vision and Its Relevance Today," 57.

[48] Snaitang, "William Carey's Vision and Its Relevance Today," 57.

[49] Arangaden, "Carey's Legacy of Bible Translation," 22-23.

[50] Arangaden, "Carey's Legacy of Bible Translation," 25.

[51] Arangaden, "Carey's Legacy of Bible Translation," 26.

[52] Philip, *Reflections on Christian Missions in India: William Carey Lectures and Other Essays*, 33-34.

[53] Snaitang, "William Carey's Vision and Its Relevance Today," 60.

[54] Philip, *Reflections on Christian Missions in India: William Carey Lectures and Other Essays*, 35.

[55] Massey and Hedlund, "William Carey and the Making of Modern India," 12.

[56] Snaitang, "William Carey's Vision and Its Relevance Today," 59.

[57] Mangalwadi, "William Carey: The Father of Modern India," 5.

[58] Massey and Hedlund, "William Carey and the Making of Modern India," 12.

[59] Massey and Hedlund, "William Carey and the Making of Modern India," 12.

[60] Swati Dutta, "The Significance of William Carey's Contribution towards the Status of Women in India Today," *William Carey: The Multifaceted Genius* (Serampore: Council of Serampore College, 2018), 84.

[61] Massey and Hedlund, "William Carey and the Making of Modern India," 13.

[62] Snaitang, "William Carey's Vision and Its Relevance Today," 56.

[63] Snaitang, "William Carey's Vision and Its Relevance Today," 60.

[64] Snaitang, "William Carey's Vision and Its Relevance Today," 61.

Bibliography

Arangaden, C. "Carey's Legacy of Bible Translation." *Indian Church History Review* 27/1 (1993): 19-28.

Dewhurst, R. L. "The Legacy of Luther: National Identity and State-Building in Early Nineteenth Century Germany." *M.A. Dissertation*. Georgia State University, 2013.

Dutta, S. "The Significance of William Carey's Contribution towards the Status of Women in India Today." *William Carey: The Multifaceted Genius*. Serampore: Council of Serampore College, 2018: 83-88.

Gine, P. C. "Educationist William Carey: Translation in Education." *Mission and the Local Congregations: Essays in Honour of William Carey's 250th Birth Anniversary*. Ed. Solomon Rongpi. Delhi: ISPCK, 2011: 3-12.

Haemig, M. J. "Luther on Translating the Bible." *Word and World* 31/3 (2011): 255-62.

Hedlund, R. E. "Carey: A Missiologist Before Time." *Indian Church History Review* 27/1 (1993): 29-49.

Jeyaraj, D. "Embodying Memories: Early Bible Translations in Tranquebar and Serampore." *International Bulletin Mission Research* 40/1 (2016): 42-59.

Kasdorf, H. "Luther's Bible: A Dynamic Equivalence Translation and Germanizing Force." *Missiology: An International Review* 6/2 (1978): 213-34.

Keller, J. "Luther's Bible Translation and the Wartburg Project" (October 2015).

Khokar, B. M. "Remembering William Carey (1793-1993)." *National Council of Churches Review* CXIII/11 (1993): 679-88.

Latourette, K. C. *A History of Christianity*. Vol. 1. New York: Harper and Row, 1953.

Malhotra, R. and Aravindan Neelakandan. *Breaking India*. Princeton: Infinity Foundation, 2011.

Mangalwadi, V. "William Carey: The Father of Modern India." *Ethne* 10/3-4 (2011): 5-8.

Mangalwadi, V. and Ruth Mangalwadi. *The Legacy of William Carey: A Model for the Transformation of Culture*. Wheaton: Crossway Books, 1993.

Massey, A. K. and June Hedlund. "William Carey and the Making of Modern India." *Indian Church History Review* 27/1 (1993): 7-18.

Mayer, C. S. "Luther." *The New International Dictionary of the Christian Church*. Ed. J. D. Douglas. Grand Rapids: Zondervan, 1978: 609-611.

Mulholland, K. B. "From Luther to Carey: Pietism and Modern Missionary Movement." *Bibliotheca Sacra* 156/621 (1999): 85-95.

Philip, T. V. *Reflections on Christian Missions in India: William Carey Lectures and Other Essays*. Delhi: ISPCK/CSS, 2000.

Schaff, P. *History of the Christian Church*. Revised Edition. Vol. 7. Peabody: Hendrickson, 2006.

Scott, H. "The Legacy of William Carey at the Bicentennial of the Founding of Serampore College." *William Carey: The Multifaceted Genius*. Serampore: Council of Serampore College, 2018: 15-30.

Smith, A. C. *The Serampore Mission Enterprise*. Bangalore: Centre for Contemporary Christianity, 2006.

Snaitang, O. L. "William Carey's Vision and Its Relevance Today." *Indian Church History Review* 27/1 (1993): 50-63.

Wood, A. S. *Captive to the Word*. Toronto: The Paternoster Press, 1969.

4

William Carey's Bible Translation Principles: Prospects and Challenges

J. Stanly Jones

Introduction

William Carey is an iconic figure of the modern missionary movement. Though known for a wide range of works that he and his colleagues undertook in Serampore, Carey's fame is most closely associated with his efforts to translate the Bible into many of the Indian and South Asian languages. Carey though was not the first Bible translator in India, he appeared on the scene at the very beginning of the modern missionary movement and along with his associates produced an explosion of translated materials. Despite having no official linguistic training, Carey by his own efforts learned more than forty languages and translated the Bible in most of them. Indeed, this translation ministry became the central focus of Carey's life and work. Carey was convinced that the Scripture in vernacular language itself is sufficient enough to bring transformation and salvific work in a person. This paper briefly deals with the theological importance of Bible translation and examines Carey's Bible translation principles, attempting to trace the challenges and prospects of his translation work.

Theological Importance of the Bible Translation

The positive effect of Bible translation in the vernaculars is attributed to how the gospel is so readily translatable. This is because the message of the Bible demonstrates a "refusal of a 'sacred' language" and instead "developed a 'vernacular' faith."[1] Lamin Sanneh observes that "without translation there would be no Christianity or Christians. Translation is the church's birthmark as well as its missionary benchmark: the church would be unrecognizable or unsustainable without it."[2] Similarly, Bediako states,

> In matters of religion, no language speaks to the heart, mind and inner-most feelings as does our mother-tongue. The achievement of Christianity with regard to this all-important place of language in religion is truly unique. For Christianity is, among all religions, the most culturally translatable, hence the most truly universal, being able to be at home in every cultural context without injury to its essential character.[3]

The significance of this fact is theological, that the Bible in the vernacular remains in every aspect of the Word of God, and the basis for this translation ministry can be traced to the events of incarnation and Pentecost.

Babel and Pentecost

The two great stories about language in the Bible, the Babel and the Pentecost event, stand at two critical junctures in the biblical narrative about community and the importance of vernacular languages. The narrative of the confusion of languages at Babel (Gen. 11) is placed just before the events that led to the "establishment of the ethnically particular" covenant nation (Gen. 12).[4] Babel highlights the origin of "linguistic pandemonium and cultural fragmentation," and explains how this diversity of language interferes with wider communication.[5] Allan Smalley describes Babel as the "biblical story of vernaculars."[6] Thus, it has been God's plan from the beginning to create diverse peoples, nations, tribes and languages. Particularly, from the time of humanity's migration since the Babel incident to the uttermost parts of the earth "has resulted in more people speaking more languages within more unique cultural and national settings."[7]

The New Testament counterpart to the Babel narrative is the story of Pentecost (Acts 2) that illustrates the reversal of the Babel effect. The story of Pentecost is told just before the events leading to the establishment of the "ethnically universal people of the new covenant," the church.[8] In the account of the day of Pentecost, the Jews who had gathered in Jerusalem from all over the world (15 regions and countries) heard the disciples miraculously empowered by the Holy Spirit speak the languages of all who were assembled. It was so dramatic that the people gathered were amazed and perplexed and acknowledged saying, "in our own languages we hear them speaking about God's deeds of power" (Acts 2:11). Tennent states that the speech of the disciples in other tongues is "a theological statement whereby God takes the initiative to overturn the chaos of Babel . . . and in its place empowers the church for a global mission of redemption to the ends of the earth."[9] Thus, "Pentecost is the biblical story of breaking the limits on vernaculars to enable universal communication of the word of God" and of people who speak different languages turning to God as they hear God's deeds and power in their native language.[10]

It also demonstrates God's acceptance of everyone's language, and the authorization to translate the gospel in every language and culture. In the words of Tennent, at Pentecost "a small group of Jewish followers of Jesus are baptized into the reality of the infinite translatability of the gospel for every language and culture."[11] Thus, the "Pentecost event establishes the translatability of the gospel and the importance God places on the vernacular language as a primary means of communicating the truths of God."[12] Instead of favoring a 'monotonous standardization of cultures and languages' through some global monolingual scheme, the Pentecost event illustrates how Godself is revealed in the mother tongue of every tribe and nation.[13] Although the linguistic miracle was unique in the sense that it was not repeated since then, "the missiological miracle of communicating 'the glorious works of God in our own native language' has been repeated innumerable times through translation."[14]

Another way to consider the Bible translation as an act of God is to examine the activity of the Holy Spirit in the charismatic translation of tongues (*hermeneia*, 1 Cor. 12-14). It is important to note that these hermeneutics of tongues is to build up the church as the body of Christ (cf. 1 Cor. 14:5). Thus, it helps to understand the role of translation in the divine economy in the New Covenant. In a broader sense, the gift of translation may be understood to be applicable also to Bible translation, as it both provides the basis for and represents the primary form of the church proclamation.[15]

The Incarnation and the Translatability of the Bible

Incarnation provides the most theological foundation for effective cross-cultural Gospel communication, and it serves as the model for contextualizing or translating "the universal gospel message into a potentially infinite number of particular settings."[16] In the words of Andrew Walls, "when God in Christ became *human*, Divinity was translated into humanity, as though humanity were a receptor language."[17] Christian faith rests on this divine act of translation: "the Word became flesh, and dwelt among us" (John 1:14).[18] This 'translation' act enabled Christ to be born as a person in first century Jewish Palestine, and this act provides an important theological and missiological justification to a constant succession of new translations.[19]

However, the fact of incarnation has few important consequences. Matjaz Crnivec in his article "Theology of Translation" mentions three consequences that the incarnation model provides for the translation ministry. First, as the incarnate Christ has two natures, so does the translation of the Bible: it is both an act of God and of human, potentially fully divine and necessarily fully human. Hence, Bible translation "should be more than just a human act and a product of accurate linguistics, hermeneutics, cultural studies and other purely human endeavors."[20] Similarly, the human dimension confirms that the process should make full use of all the scientific and scholarly expertise available.[21]

The second consequence relates to the manner in which this 'primordial mediation' occurred, i.e., "Christ's incarnate culture" was effected under the very culture-specific conditions.[22] Christ became a person in a particular locality and in a particular ethnic group, at a particular place and time. On the one hand, he fully took part of the contemporary Jewish culture: he spoke the language, observed the rites and customs, and expressly affirmed many of its values. Graham Ogden observes, "Incarnation cannot mean anything less than a full immersion into a particular culture."[23] But on the other hand, we notice that Jesus did challenge some of the cultural core values of his time, such as the purity laws, the use of violence, and the like. This challenge on the foundations of the society and its authority structures was an act necessary for the constitution of a radically different "culture" of the kingdom of God. Thus, we are presented here with a significant paradox that "Jesus is fully part of the culture and at the same time he presents a total, radical challenge to its core tenets, with a view to a possibility of establishing something essentially different." Thus, in Bible translation, this fundamental creative tension should rule and fuel the process.[24]

The third consequence is from the viewpoint of understandability. Jesus' teaching was deeply grounded in the language of his people. Instead of the sacred language 'Hebrew,' he chose to speak in Aramaic, the language of the people. He also used the "common rhetorical devices and metaphorical expressions" that were familiar to his audience. But at the same time there were some sayings that were enigmatic, and difficult to interpret (cf. Mark 4:12-14 and parallels). This tension between general understandability and occasional intended obscurity has significant implications for the translation process.[25] Hence as a form of incarnation, translation should take seriously the concepts such as enculturation, indigenization, and contextualization. Bible translation is more than a simple transfer of meanings, concepts and terms from one language and culture to another. Thus, one cannot separate translation of Scripture from incarnation, and this translatability, is an in-built nature of the Christian faith that is capable of subverting the cultural possessiveness of the faith in the process of its transmission.[26]

Bible Translation and Contextualization

Translatability rescued Christian faith from a western possessiveness and led to the emergence of a genuine indigenous Christianity in terms of *Missio Dei*, in the local setting.[27] If first century Christians had only passed the gospel "by means of the cultural grids that were unique to them, the Christian faith would have been robbed of the insights of various Christians since then."[28] As Tennent states, "If the gospel had stayed contained within the single ethnicity of Judaism, we would not have benefited from the insights of the Hellenistic Christians. In the same way, as the gospel has been translated into *other* cultures . . . we have gained more and more insights into the beauty and reality of Jesus Christ."[29] This is largely because the church "followed the 'mission by translation' option—with all of the pitfalls and dangers of mistranslations in mind."[30]

Language does not exist apart from culture, and so in order to be able to translate, the translator must have knowledge, not only of the language, but also of the culture in which the language is embedded.[31] Citing Kosuke Koyama, Gilles Gravelle says, Bible translation is not about replacing the cultural and faith elements of receptive language with western forms of Christianity, but instead, "Bible translation is to recover, reconnect and transform what already exists by way of the richness of the language and religious culture, and not the religion per se. This then allows for the contextualization of theology for practical needs."[32] However, Koyama maintains that the process should include two critical movements: first, "to articulate Jesus Christ in culturally appropriate, communicatively apt words," and second, "to criticize, reform, dethrone, or oppose culture if it is found to be against what the name of Jesus Christ stands for."[33] This process of translation reveals a significant difference between what a western cross-cultural translator would attempt in comparison to what a mother-tongue translator would like to attempt. The indigenous stage of translation requires "this dangerous and unavoidable task" for the appropriation of the gospel in local language and culture.[34]

Gravelle gives an illustration for this effect. He says, nineteenth and twentieth-century western cross-cultural translators treated native religious terminologies as suspect and errant. They considered indigenous languages as not having the linguistic facility to express key theological concepts. This led the translators to replace important theological terms with those that mirrored the equivalent western concept or borrowed terms from other national or contact languages. They did this to avoid blending the message of the gospel with local religious beliefs. This puts the users of the translation at disadvantages, because, the recipients of the translation were forced to learn the meaning of a new foreign term or phrase, before applying the meaning of the term in their cultural context. Instead a contextual translation should allow the people to grasp the depth of the meaning of the text fully without having to learn a foreign term or phrase.[35]

Therefore, the Bible translator's role extends beyond evangelism. According to Gerald West, translation "is much more than a technical discipline, it is a metaphor for forms of inculturation."[36] Bible Translation is an activity of identity building as well as a means of liberation, for communities. "Such liberation comes about by the theological praxis of the Scriptures being translated not only into indigenous languages but also into its opposite: from the indigenous cultures."[37] Hence, the term 'contextualization' encompasses both the roles of identity and liberation. Bible translation should be understood as a prime example of contextual theology, which has been central to Christianity from its beginning. The concept accentuates the relationship of faith to its context, whether it is the context's socio-economic structures or its cultural traits of language, traditions, and cosmological assumptions.[38]

Throughout the history of the church, translation of the Bible into the languages of the world was considered to be an indispensable foundation for the sustainable mission of God. Since the beginning of the church, when the Jewish disciples on the day of Pentecost began telling the wonders of God's works in multiple languages, the practice of the gospel being introduced by linguistic and cultural outsiders (missionaries) in new linguistic and cultural contexts continued.[39] Though this has been the pattern for over 2,000 years, it was mostly so during the last 200 years, the Modern Missionary era. However, this stage of cross-cultural translation was only 'partial enculturation' in the sense that the translators, mostly the foreign missionaries sought after a one-to-one meaning correspondence with words wherever possible. In places where a one-to-one correspondence did not appear to exist, foreign terms were commonly brought in to rectify assuming that meaning is generally predictable based on the source language alone. As a result, it placed significant constraints on a receiving language's lexicon in that meaning units were assumed to be based on specific word classes.[40]

It was in this context, Carey established the practice of cross-cultural transmission by translating the scriptures into the local languages. This was followed by the establishment of the Bible Societies, beginning with the British and Foreign Bible Society in 1804, whose mission was to provide the Bible for people living in foreign nations, at first in the colonial language and then eventually in the local languages. Regardless of the limitations, it is important to accept that this cross-cultural transmission of God's Word over the past 200 years has resulted in the injection of biblical information into many of the world's languages and cultures.[41]

William Carey and Bible Translation

Carey was passionate to learn as many as languages possible and attempted to translate the Bible into almost all the languages he knew. His first translation was the Bengali Bible. To learn Bengali, Carey used manuscripts of a translation of parts of the Bengali New Testament translated by a colleague (John Thomas) who had earlier worked in India. However, once Carey became aware that the translation, he was studying was not adequate, he began his own translation of the Bible into Bengali using Greek and Hebrew texts. In 1796, only three years after his arrival in India, he completed a draft of the New Testament and parts of the Old Testament in Bengali. Further, he revised the New Testament several times before it was published, "writing each draft out by hand in Bengali script."[42] According to the details provided by Smalley:

> The Bengali New Testament progressed through eight editions, each of them incorporating at least a revision, sometimes a complete retranslation. The

> Old Testament was published in sections, parts of it revised and republished two times, other parts three. The final page of the final revision came off the press the year before Carey died in 1833.[43]

Carey realizing the importance of Sanskrit as 'India's hallmark of culture,' the language in which scholarly debates were carried out, started studying Sanskrit along with Bengali, and translated the Bible into Sanskrit. Assuming that most of Indian languages had their roots in Sanskrit, he believed that a Sanskrit translation could be a source text from which Indians who did not know Greek and Hebrew could translate. The last part of the Sanskrit Bible was published in 1822. Carey did not revise and re-translate the Sanskrit Bible, however, as he repeatedly did the Bengali.[44]

Carey also learnt Marathi. Though he lived outside the Marathi-speaking area, he learned the language from an educated speaker and translated the whole Bible into Marathi, publishing it in 1819. Carey revised the Marathi New Testament in 1824. He also wrote a Marathi grammar and dictionary. Carey turned to Hindi as well and translated the Bible in 1818. He also revised the Hindi New Testament in 1818, after which he undertook some further revisions and new translations of the gospels, including one in a different script.[45] These four languages—Bengali, Sanskrit, Marathi and Hindi—were the ones in which Carey was the primary translator. Later, a different pattern of work was used for Oriya, Carey's fifth language, in which Carey entrusted the drafting to an Oriya who translated from the Bengali translation. Meanwhile Carey learned the language by studying the draft, wrote a grammar of it, and checked and revised the draft against the Greek and Hebrew original texts. The revision was carried out in consultation with the Oriya translator, and the Oriya Bible was completed in 1815.[46]

The success of the Oriya translation led to a new pattern where Carey supervised numerous translations done by Indian assistants. The assistants would translate the Bible into their own languages, and Carey's role was limited to examining, revising, editing and proofreading the drafts. Following this procedure Carey produced a full Bible in one additional language, the New Testament with part of the Old Testament in five more languages, the full New Testament in eighteen languages, and parts of the New Testament in several more, for a total of thirty-four languages.[47] Quoting the church historian John Foster, S. K. Chatterjee says, that during the first eighteen centuries of the history of the church, the Bible was translated into about thirty languages. But in the first third of the nineteenth century, the number was doubled by Carey and his associates.[48] Thus, in the first three decades of the modern missionary movement, forty-nine percent of first translations into new languages anywhere in the world were published at Serampore, most of them translated by Carey or under his supervision, and virtually all of them edited and proofread by him. By 1832, the Serampore press had produced religious materials in forty-four languages and dialects, apart from the translation of the Indian epic poem, the Ramayana.[49]

Carey is often praised for his tireless labors at translating the Bible into Indian languages. But critics have questioned the quality of the translations that Carey produced. Smalley remarks that Carey's work was "seriously flawed" and that if competent translation consultants had existed at that time none of the translations that Carey did or supervised would have been approved for publication.[50] However, these judgments on Carey's translations should not surpass the fact that his work in India was a powerful inducement for the start of translations in many languages throughout the world in the 19th and 20th centuries.

Translation Principles of Carey

Carey believed that the Word of God to be of eternal significance. Mangalwadi remarks, "Carey spent enormous energy in translating and promoting the Bible, because as a modern man he believed that God's revelation alone could remove superstitions and inculcate a confidence in human rationality."[51] Carey believed that the circulation of translated scriptures would lay the foundation of the church in any region and lead the people to liberation from immorality, superstition and oppression.

Carey's translation work was centered on the chief derivations of Sanskrit works. He insisted that Sanskrit was a philosophical key that unlocked the meaning to many other languages and etymological issues. It was because of this reason, believing that a Sanskrit translation could be a source text for translators into vernaculars, Carey studied and translated the Bible into Sanskrit as early as 1822. However, Carey was very cautious in using Sanskrit terminologies in his translations due to the aversion he had towards the idolatrous system of Hinduism. For instance, in spite of the difficulty in finding a suitable Indian term to communicate the Christian concept of 'God' or *theos*, Carey rejected the idea of using the Sanskrit term *deva*.[52] According to Christopher Smith, "Carey in particular was reluctant to employ its religiously-nuanced philosophical vocabulary in the communication of Christian dogma. As a result, an awkward, textual "Church Sanskrit" was created which others had to refine before Bible translations could be rescued "from the cloud of ridicule" that enveloped them in Brahmin circles."[53]

Though Carey and his colleagues had a high regard for Sanskrit and were intellectually interested in Hinduism, they did that fundamentally for apologetic purposes. Smith states,

> Such an approach was probably counter-productive because it resulted in the short-circuiting of their hermeneutical endeavor. Western concepts and styles obtruded in their translation of their message and made their communication much less effective than it might have been. Thus, Serampore's hybrid version of Sanskrit failed to take firm root in India's soil and withered away after a few decades.[54]

In this sense, Carey's and Marshman's translation projects demonstrated that their work derived its inspiration from the European Enlightenment dualism of their time. Such was the atmosphere in which Carey and his colleagues operated as they struggled to provide the Bible into a remarkable number of Oriental languages.[55] The challenges Carey and his colleagues faced in terms of Bible translation may be characterized by the following missiological axiom, "Linguistic translation was not enough; conceptual translation was necessary"[56] if they were to convey the significance of Christ to Bengal's people and their neighbors.[57]

Though, they did their best to communicate the gospel, by preaching and by translating the scriptures, Smith critiques that "as their mission institutionalized, the time that they gave to public evangelistic activities diminished significantly. *Inter alia*, they assumed that once they had made significant parts of the Bible available in some of India's most significant vernacular languages, then their task would be largely accomplished."[58] However, unfortunately, their effort turned out to be a "finished product from the West," instead of communicating the gospel in culturally appropriate ways in terms of using the cultural and linguistic richness of the receptive language.[59]

Carey's Translations in Perspective

Carey's massive translation program was not as successful as expected, and during Carey's lifetime itself better translations appeared, or were under process, which replaced the ones produced at Serampore. All Serampore versions were superseded by better translation in the near future. The reasons for this are many. So, it is important that we need to be carefully fair to Carey and his context, while seeking to understand the reasons for his poor results and their application to translation issues in India today. Carey presumably would have welcomed a constructive critique of his work for the purpose of better communication of the Gospel.[60] Because, Carey's own remarks suggest that he was aware of the flaws in his translations, and that the translations he made and supervised were not perfect. However, he hoped that his successors and others would build on them. His search for quality in translation is evident in the fact that he revised the Bengali translation several times, the language he knew best. However, most of the translations which Carey supervised lasted longer than those in which he was the primary translator.[61]

One of the reasons for the short lives of some of the Carey translations was due to Carey's understanding that the North Indian languages were similar to Sanskrit. This is true in languages such as Hindi and Marathi which were not spoken where Carey lived. For instance, among other problems, "the dialect of his Marathi New Testament was not widely known, and the script was inappropriate."[62] Probably, Carey failed to understand that even though certain languages are very similar in grammar and vocabulary, each significantly differed from others in more ways than obvious. Similarly, Carey's Bengali translation on which he had worked for 32 years, lacked idiomaticity and naturalness. Carey followed the English way of writing which was quite different from the way of Bengali writing making it difficult for the people to understand them. Because of these faults, the people of Bengal contemptuously dubbed the language translated and written by the missionaries as 'Serampore Bengali.'[63] Some of the other reasons for the short life of Carey's major works are as follows:

Political Reasons

Translational faults were not the only reasons. In fact, the translations which replaced Carey's were also not always much better than his. Ecclesiastical politics was also the reason for this.[64] The Serampore Trio/Quartet were Baptists, who were part of a minority in Britain, while the Protestant Church in Calcutta was dominated by the Anglican state-church majority. There were conflicts between the Anglican dominated British and Foreign Bible Society and the Baptist dominated Serampore Mission which is evident in their unwillingness to work together in committees and projects.[65]

This led the Calcutta Auxiliary of the British and Foreign Bible Society which was formed in 1811, to promote rival translations to the ones being done at Serampore. Smalley gives one example of such: In 1827 some Anglicans and others who practiced infant baptism by sprinkling began to object to Greek *baptidzo* being translated with a word meaning 'immerse' in the Serampore translations and requested the British and Foreign Bible Society to withdraw the support which it had been giving them. The Calcutta auxiliary, without accepting the explanation of Carey, sided with those who had protested the translation and recommended that the British and Foreign Bible Society withdraw support. The Bible Society went along with the request and required that the Greek word be transliterated, carried over into each language without being translated. The Serampore men refused to capitulate. As a result of this conflict, rival translations were developed.[66]

Lack of Institutional Framework

Unfortunately, the Serampore translation ministry did not last after Carey and Marshman died. Possibly because, they left no institutional framework in which their literary heritage could be directly carried on by either juniors or native workers. Though one of the purposes of founding the Serampore College was to train Indians who could improve the translations, it was only recently that Serampore College developed a new curriculum for training mother-tongue translators. Further, Carey and his colleagues could not tolerate junior missionaries and assistants who were not as single minded as they were, and who did not follow the exhausting work schedule of the Serampore Mission.[67]

Limited Linguistic Knowledge

Carey was in a pioneering situation with only the most basic understanding of linguistics. Smalley notes, "Part of the reason for the poor Bengali in translated material was certainly Carey's inadequate understanding of the nature of translation, of language and of communication."[68] Hooper and Culshaw recognize these shortcomings in commenting on "the state of philological knowledge" at that time.[69] For instance, one specific linguistic misunderstanding that dominated Carey's translations was a bias for Sanskrit.

Carey made Sanskrit too central to his vernacular translation processes, based on the understanding that Sanskrit influenced the vernacular languages. The following statement from Anand Amaladass and Richard Young explain the problem:

> Carey was convinced, erroneously as we now know, that Sanskrit was the "parent" of the modern Indian languages that he called "secondary cognate languages." Estimating that at least three-fourths and in some cases as much as seven-eighths of the words in these languages were "understood through the Sanskrit," Carey believed that "there is little variation throughout the whole of the Indian family" in construction, idiom, and figures of speech.[70]

This was one reason why Carey tried to translate the Bible into languages he did not know and which were spoken over a thousand miles away from where he lived.[71] Das states the result of introducing Sanskrit words into the Bengali Bible: "mixed vocabulary of this sort was bound to be displeasing to a native reader."[72] According to Smalley, Carey failed to sense that "reliance on translation from Sanskrit made his vernacular translations heavy, wooden and bookish."[73]

Too Much Attempted

Another reason that Carey produced poor translations is that he tried to do too much. Here some difficult questions need to be raised as to whether Serampore translation program was motivated by competition with other translators who were already at work in various languages.[74] For example, Carey's Gujarati translation was released (in 1820) just ahead of another local production in Gujarati. The same was in the case of the Chinese version too. Similarly, Carey's Telugu New Testament was published in the same year (1818) as a locally produced version which was considered to be more superior.[75] We should however note that the data regarding who was translating what may not have been available to them.[76]

Questions were raised within Serampore mission about Carey's and Marshman's translation strategies. For instance, in 1806, within few years of the founding of the Serampore mission, William Ward openly expressed his concerns about the scale of the translation projects and literally warned Carey and Marshman against attempting too far more than was prudent. Ward writes,

> As to making Bibles for other missionaries, into languages which we ourselves do not really understand, I Recommend them [Carey and Marshman] to be

> cautious, lest they should be wasting time and life . . . . I remind them that life is short, that this life may evaporate in schemes of translations for China, Bootan, Mahratta and . . . By spending so much of our time on translations which we can never distribute, we may leave undone translations nearer home, and leave the Mission at our deaths in such an unestablished state, that all may come to nothing.[77]

Thus, even as early as 1806, Ward challenged his colleagues on both the degree of emphasis they gave to Bible translation and the quality of the resulting output. Of course, attempts were made by Carey and Marshman to overcome such misgivings. It could be argued that little else could Carey do when their mission was affected by threats from the East India Company to their very survival. Thus, the Serampore Trio/Quartet was aware that their efforts in translation were only preparatory or only the first phase of mission enterprise, and that their translations were rudimentary and that they would be 'perfected' when their junior partners and native workers would take over the mission.[78]

Misplaced Focus on Words and Word Order

Another reason for the weaknesses of Carey's translations, also mentioned by H. L. Richard in his 2018 article "Some Observations on William Carey's Bible Translations," is with regard to the theory of translation. Richard states, Carey placed an undue emphasis on words in his translation work. Modern linguistics has demonstrated that words and sentences vary in meaning according to contexts, and so the central units in communication are sentences and paragraphs. But Carey assumed that words were central and that words in one language have counterparts in other languages, which convey the same meaning.[79] J. C. Marshman reported that Carey, in his first Bengali translation, "presented a simple translation of the English words arranged in the English order of collocation."[80] Smalley provides the following summary of this point:

> Carey believed that "accuracy" was enhanced by as literal a translation as possible, with the wording and the grammatical structure of the translation geared to the wording and grammatical structure of the Greek or Hebrew original. Ironically, as with many other translators his overwhelming drive to make the Scriptures accessible in the languages of India and beyond was thwarted partly by the distortion he introduced through fear of distorting the Bible by making it truly accessible.[81]

With regard to the Bengali translation, Sisir Kumar Das mentions five features that Carey employed in his translation: first, the English order of subject-verb-object was followed rather than the Bengali order of subject-object-verb; second, the English pattern of a relative clause following its antecedent ("the missionaries who translate the Bible") was used instead of the Bengali pattern of the clause preceding ("the who-translate-the-Bible missionaries"); third, the regular use of the conjunction "and" is a mark of English and particularly of the English Bible, but Bengali does not contain such a proliferation of conjunctions; fourth, Bengali generally does not use verb copulas ("the translations [were] disappointing") at all; and finally, adverbial clauses, like relative clauses, precede the main clause in Bengali rather than following the main clause.[82] This problem intensified when local terminologies were linked to and dependent on their Sanskrit roots. Amaladass and Young point out this issue in their analysis of Carey's Sanskrit Bible. They state, "What rankles most is that Carey so strictly adhered to the syntax of the King James Bible, as if to deviate from it would have detracted from the gospel itself."[83]

New Approaches to Translation

The above observations of Carey's translations are not merely a concern for historians but have relevance to the Christian community in India. In a context, where the church is "linguistically isolated from the mainstream of society because it has learned a strange dialect from the Bible itself" (such as Carey's Christian Bengali), the implications of this are many. The 'Christian dialect' is not an issue as long as the focus is on the Christian community, but in communicating the message beyond the Christian community, this becomes a major challenge. In such contexts, Bible translations are needed that "resonate with people outside the church."[84] Until this is achieved, the task of the Bible translation into India's languages that Carey began is far from accomplished.

Second, what stands out from Carey's translation approaches, is the fact that translation needs to be teamwork of experts well versed in the local language and the source languages. This is different from Carey's times when translation almost invariably was the work of a single person, even though he was helped by the local pundits. It is observed that, among Carey's translation projects, the most successful ones were those that involved both a local pundit as the primary translator who was well versed in the local language and Carey as the editor and supervisor who was well versed in the source languages. Hence, translation needs to be community oriented with multiple translators, instead of a small independent team with usually one translator.

Third, throughout much of the modern history of Bible translation, literacy has been taken as the mode of transmission. However, not all societies are comfortable with reading and writing because of their oral traditions. It is important so that literacy alone not be the presupposed medium for biblical translation. It is therefore important that oral strategies to introduce the themes and stories of the Bible are documented and implemented for such societies.[85] Whiteman comments, "Literacy is nearly always seen as the panacea for any development ills, when in fact the record is a mixed one. In some cases, it has been helpful, in other situations it has not been."[86] While literacy is an important and ongoing need in any translation project, a translation team also needs to look for alternative methods and media in communicating the Scripture, such as crafting oral Bible stories, audio-visuals, putting Scripture into songs or poetry, and so on.[87] In this context, it is also important to note that historically, the first-century world consisted of a predominantly oral setting in which the New Testament was composed, and the same biblical texts were at one point in history oral compositions, performed in public, in interaction with the audience.[88]

Fourth, although translatability aims at the accommodation of languages, cultures and context, the use of gender sensitive language has often been neglected. Since a basic purpose of translation is to express a text in terms of modern language, gender-inclusivity and gender-sensitivity should be part of the process.

Fifth, translators should utilize more local material including cultural, religious terms and concepts, rather than try to fit in western or national material in places where the concepts appear to be missing or the local terms are deemed unacceptable.[89] As Hwa Yung states, "contextualization is not simply a fad or a catch-word but a theological necessity demanded by the incarnational nature of the Word."[90]

Sixth, translations should be impact or action oriented rather than product or outcome oriented. The traditional model followed during Carey's time sought to provide rational knowledge of Scripture through the completion of translation, assuming that people reading these vernacular versions of the Scripture would immediately respond to the gospel. On the other hand, translations should also focus on bridging traditional religious and cultural understanding of the gospel and seek to transform cultural and religious worldviews instead of replacing them.[91]

Seventh, translation as a theological act, should seek the liberation of those oppressed, including linguistic oppression. Most often it is the national and official languages that determine to a great extent how theology is done. Today with about ninety-five percent of the world's population having access to at least some portion of the Scripture in the language they understand, the remaining five-percent minority are significantly neglected.[92] According to Maxey's statistics, this five percent includes over three hundred million people and more than two-thirds of the world's languages. From a linguistic perspective, these minority-language speakers are oppressed religiously "by the confines of theological reflection that is in languages not their own."[93] In such contexts, Bible translation in these minority languages will serve as a means of liberation for these people.

Finally, it has been observed that there is no theologically or ideologically neutral translation. No translation occurs in theological vacuum, and every Bible translation has a theological purpose or even an agenda. In such contexts, it is important that the translator approaches the text with openness, instead of approaching the text with a fixed set of theological presuppositions which can cause a certain degree of distortions to the product. This shift from a static model to a dynamic model is essential.[94]

Conclusion

It seems to indicate that the 200-year period of largely western and cross-cultural Bible translation work begun by William Carey and his colleagues has already come to an end and today the translation periphery has become the translation heartland. It is important at this stage that we reflect on the translation principles of Carey and the challenges he faced in this process. However, we need to realize that these challenges should not overshadow the magnanimous amount of work he and his colleagues along with the local pundits accomplished through their translation ministry but help us to move in the right direction in terms of translating, interpreting and communicating the Word of God in our own cultural context. Scripture should no longer be a third person's communication filtered through other people's language and culture, but instead should help people to have a direct communication with God, through their own culture. The translation of the Bible should empower people and societies to this extent and help them to be better equipped through their vernaculars to deal with the challenges they face in today's context. Examining Carey's Bible translation principles and in the light of it deriving new approaches to translation that resonate with people both inside and outside the church will certainly help to achieve this objective. Until this is achieved, the mission of Bible translation ministry that Carey envisioned is far from accomplished.

Endnotes

[1] Kwame Bediako, *Jesus and the Gospel in Africa: History and Experience* (Maryknoll: Orbis Books, 2004), 32.

[2] Lamin Sanneh, *Whose Religion is Christianity? The Gospel Beyond the West* (Grand Rapids: William B. Eerdmans, 2003), 97.

[3] Bediako, *Jesus and the Gospel in Africa*, 32.

[4] William A. Smalley, *Translation as Mission: Bible Translation in the Modern Missionary Movement* (Mercer: University Press, 1991), 252.

[5] Smalley, *Translation as Mission*, 253; "Beyond Babel: Pentecost and Mission," *International Bulletin of Missionary Research* 30/2 (2006): 57.

[6] Smalley, *Translation as Mission*, 253.

[7] Gilles Gravelle, "Bible Translation in Historical Context: The Changing Role of Cross-Cultural Workers," *International Journal of Frontier Missiology* 27/1 (2010): 12.

[8] Smalley, *Translation as Mission*, 253.

[9] Timothy C. Tennent, *Invitation to World Missions: A Trinitarian Missiology for the Twenty-First Century* (Grand Rapids: Kregel Publications, 2010), 412.

[10] Smalley, *Translation as Mission*, 253.

[11] Tennent, *Invitation to World Missions*, 412.

[12] K. J. Franklin and C. J. P. Niemandt, "Vision 2025 and the Bible Translation Movement," *HTS Teologiese Studies/Theological Studies* 69/1 (2013): 3/8. http://dx.doi.org/10.4102/ hts.v69i1.1332, accessed on 7th October 2018.

[13] "Beyond Babel: Pentecost and Mission," 57.

[14] Smalley, *Translation as Mission*, 253.

[15] Early reformers used these passages and the manifestation of *glossolalia* to support their conviction that Scriptures and liturgies must be translated into the vernacular. Cf. Matjaz Crnivec, "Theology of Translation," http://kud-logos.si/2002/theology-of-translation/, posted on May 5, 2002, accessed on 13thOctober 2018.

[16] Tennent, *Invitation to World Missions*, 353.

[17] Andrew F. Walls, *The Missionary Movement in Christian History: Studies in the Transmission of Faith* (Maryknoll, New York: Orbis Books, 1996), 27.

[18] Walls, *The Missionary Movement in Christian History,* 26.

[19] Walls, *The Missionary Movement in Christian History,* 27; Franklin and Niemandt, "Vision 2025 and the Bible Translation Movement," 4/8.

[20] Crnivec, "Theology of Translation," http://kud-logos.si/2002/theology-of-translation/.

[21] Crnivec, "Theology of Translation," http://kud-logos.si/2002/theology-of-translation/.

[22] Crnivec, "Theology of Translation," http://kud-logos.si/2002/theology-of-translation/. Also, Andrew F. Walls, "The Translation Principle in Christian History," *Bible Translation and the Spread of the Church*, ed. Philip Stine (Leiden: E. J. Brill, 1990), 25.

[23] Graham S. Ogden, "Translation as a Theologizing Task," *Bible Translator* 53/3 (2002): 312, cited by Crnivec, "Theology of Translation," http://kud-logos.si/2002/theology-of-translation/.

[24] Crnivec, "Theology of Translation," http://kud-logos.si/2002/theology-of-translation/.

[25] Crnivec, "Theology of Translation," http://kud-logos.si/2002/theology-of-translation/.

[26] Kwame Bediako, *Christianity in Africa: The Renewal of a Non-Western Religion* (Edinburgh: University Press, 1997), 110.

[27] Bediako, *Christianity in Africa,* 122.

[28] Franklin and Niemandt, "Vision 2025 and the Bible Translation Movement," 3/8.

[29] Tennent, *Invitation to World Missions*, 336.

[30] Franklin and Niemandt, "Vision 2025 and the Bible Translation Movement," 3/8.

[31] Eugene Albert Nida, *Customs and Cultures: Anthropology for Christian Missions* (California: William Carey Library, 1954), 223.

[32] Gravelle, "Bible Translation in Historical Context," 16. Kosuke Koyama gives an example from the Thai Buddhist context, saying, "For the Thai translators of the Bible, there was no language other than the language of the Buddhist-animist culture . . . With great care Thai translators insured richness. It is not a distortion." Cf. K. Koyama, *Water Buffalo Theology* (Orbis, 1999), cited by Gravelle, "Bible Translation in Historical Context," 16.

[33] Gravelle, "Bible Translation in Historical Context," 16, citing K. Koyama, *Water Buffalo Theology* (1999).

[34] Gravelle, "Bible Translation in Historical Context," 16.

[35] Gravelle, "Bible Translation in Historical Context," 16-17.

[36] Gerald West, "Mapping African Biblical Interpretation: A Tentative Sketch," *The Bible in Africa: Transactions, Trajectories and Trends*, eds. Gerald O. West and Musa W. Dube (Leiden: Brill, 2000), 46.

[37] James Maxey, "Bible Translation as Contextualization: The Role of Orality," *Missiology: An International Review* 38 (2010): 177.

[38] Maxey, "Bible Translation as Contextualization," 175.

[39] Gravelle, "Bible Translation in Historical Context," 11.

[40] Gravelle, "Bible Translation in Historical Context," 14.

[41] Gravelle, "Bible Translation in Historical Context," 12. According to 2017 Wycliff Bible Translation Statistics, approximately: 670 languages have completed Bibles; 1,521 languages have completed New Testament; and 3,312 languages have some Bible portions. Therefore, of the world's about 7,000 languages, 5,503 languages have some or the entire Bible. And because many of these translations were done in large language groups, about 95 percent of the world's populations have some portions of the Bible in their language. Cf. http://wycliffenz.org/about/our-work/bible-translation-statistics/, assessed on 28th October 2018.

[42] Smalley, *Translation as Mission*, 42.

[43] Smalley, *Translation as Mission*, 44.

[44] Christopher Arangaden, "Carey's Legacy of Bible Translation," *Carey's Obligation and India's Renaissance* (Serampore: Council of Serampore College, 1993), 178-179; Smalley, *Translation as Mission*, 45-46. Carey wrote a Sanskrit grammar. Compared to his Bengali grammar, which was less than 200 pages, his Sanskrit grammar was much larger running to 1,040 pages. Cf. Smalley, *Translation as Mission*, 45.

[45] Smalley, *Translation as Mission*, 46.

[46] Smalley, *Translation as Mission*, 46.

[47] Smalley, *Translation as Mission*, 46. For a complete list of Carey's translation works, see Arangaden, "Carey's Legacy of Bible Translation," 180-183; and S. K. Chatterjee, "William Carey and the Linguistic Renaissance in India," *Carey's Obligation and India's Renaissance* (Serampore: Council of Serampore College 1993), 165.

[48] Chatterjee, "William Carey and the Linguistic Renaissance in India," 164.

[49] Lamin Sanneh, *Translating the Message: The Missionary Impact on Culture* (Maryknoll, New York: Orbis Books, 2001), 102; Smalley, *Translation as Mission*, 47.

[50] Smalley, *Translation as Mission*, 47. A similar view is expressed by Culshaw in his 1967 article "William Carey—Then and Now." Wesley J. Culshaw, "William Carey—Then and Now," *The Bible Translator* 18 (April 1967): 53-60. Cf. Roger L. Omanson, "Bible Translation: Baptist Contributions to Understanding God's Word," *Baptist History and Heritage* 31 (1996): 14.

[51] Vishal Mangalwadi and Ruth Mangalwadi, *The Legacy of William Carey: A Model for the Transformation of a Culture* (Wheaton, Illinois: Crossway Books, 1993), 81.

[52] Cf. Richard Fox Young, "Church Sanskrit: An Approach of Christian Scholars to Hinduism in the Nineteenth Century," *Wiener Zeischrift fur die Kunde Sudasiens* 23 (1979): 115, cited by A. Christopher Smith, *The Serampore Mission Enterprise* (Bangalore: Centre for Contemporary Christianity, 2005), 321.

[53] Smith, *The Serampore Mission Enterprise*, 321, citing Young, "Church Sanskrit," 205-231.

[54] Smith, *The Serampore Mission Enterprise*, 321-322.

[55] Smith, *The Serampore Mission Enterprise*, 322.

[56] Andrew F. Walls, "Converts or Proselytes? The Crisis over Conversion in the Early Church," *International Bulletin of Missionary Research* 28/1(2004): 4.

[57] Smith, *The Serampore Mission Enterprise*, 322.

[58] Smith, *The Serampore Mission Enterprise*, 323.

[59] Smith, *The Serampore Mission Enterprise*, 323.

[60] Smalley, *Translation as Mission*, 47; H. L. Richard, "Some Observations on William Carey's Bible Translations," *International Bulletin of Mission Research* 42/3 (2018): 242.

[61] Smalley, *Translation as Mission*, 48.

[62] Smalley, *Translation as Mission*, 49; J. S. M. Hooper and W. J. Culshaw, *Bible Translation in India, Pakistan and Ceylon* (Oxford: University Press, 1963), 105.

[63] K. P. Sen Gupta, *The Christian Missionaries in Bengal: 1793-1833* (Calcutta: Firma K. L. Mukhopadhyay, 1971), 96; Smalley, *Translation as Mission*, 49.

[64] Smalley, *Translation as Mission*, 50, citing Sen Gupta, *The Christian Missionaries in Bengal*, 44-49.

[65] Smalley, *Translation as Mission*, 50-51.

[66] Smalley, *Translation as Mission*, 51.

[67] E. Daniel Potts, *British Baptist Missionaries in India: 1793-1837* (Cambridge: University Press, 1967), 22-26; Smalley, *Translation as Mission*, 52.

[68] Smalley, *Translation as Mission*, 49.

[69] Hooper and Culshaw, *Bible Translation*, 20.

[70] Anand Amaladass and Richard Fox Young, *The Indian Christiad: A Concise Anthology of Didactic and Devotional Literature in Early Church Sanskrit* (Anand, India: Gujarat Sahitya Prakash, 1995), 38, cited by Richard, "Some Observations on William Carey's Bible Translations," 243.

[71] Richard, "Some Observations on William Carey's Bible Translations," 243.

[72] Sisir Kumar Das, *Early Bengali Prose: Carey to Vidyâsâgar* (Calcutta: Bookland, 1966), 61, cited by Richard, "Some Observations on William Carey's Bible Translations," 244.

[73] Smalley, *Translation as Mission*, 49.

[74] John Clark Marshman, *The Life and Times of Carey, Marshman, and Ward: Embracing the History of the Serampore Mission*, Vol. 1 (London: Longman, Brown, Green, Longmans and Roberts, 1859), 244-245.

[75] Richard, "Some Observations on William Carey's Bible Translations," 244-245.

[76] However, Smith provides documentation of unhealthy competition in Bible translation between Marshman and Robert Morrison in China. Cf. Smith, *The Serampore Mission Enterprise*, 61.

[77] William Ward's *Missionary Journal*, 27 April 1806, cited by Smith, *The Serampore Mission Enterprise*, 319.

[78] Smith, *The Serampore Mission Enterprise*, 320.

[79] Richard, "Some Observations on William Carey's Bible Translations," 246.

[80] Marshman, *The Life and Times of Carey, Marshman, and Ward*, 180.

[81] Smalley, *Translation as Mission*, 49-50. Also cited by Richard, "Some Observations on William Carey's Bible," 247.

[82] Das, *Early Bengali Prose*, 50-54, cited by Richard, "Some Observations on William Carey's Bible," 246.

[83] Amaladass and Young, *The Indian Christiad*, 36, cited by Richard, "Some Observations on William Carey's Bible Translations," 246

[84] Richard, "Some Observations on William Carey's Bible Translations," 247.

[85] Maxey, "Bible Translation as Contextualization," 179.

[86] Darell L. Whiteman, "Bible Translation and Social Development," *Bible Translation and the Spread of the Church. The Last 200 Years. Studies in Missions*, Vol. 2, ed. Philip C. Stine (Leiden/Boston: E. J. Brill, 1990), 135.

[87] Gravelle, "Bible Translation in Historical Context," 18.

[88] Maxey, "Bible Translation as Contextualization," 179-180.

[89] Gravelle, "Bible Translation in Historical Context," 14.

[90] Hwa Yung, *Mangoes or Bananas? The Quest for an Authentic Asian Christian Theology* (Delhi: Oxford, 1997), 13.

[91] Gravelle, "Bible Translation in Historical Context," 16.

[92] Maxey, "Bible Translation as Contextualization: The Role of Orality," 177.

[93] Maxey, "Bible Translation as Contextualization: The Role of Orality," 177.

[94] Crnivec, "Theology of Translation," http://kud-logos.si/2002/theology-of-translation/.

Bibliography

Arangaden, C. "Carey's Legacy of Bible Translation." *Carey's Obligation and India's Renaissance*. Serampore: Council of Serampore College, 1993.

Bediako, K. *Christianity in Africa: The Renewal of a Non-Western Religion*. Edinburgh: University Press, 1997.

Bediako, K. *Jesus and the Gospel in Africa: History and Experience*. Maryknoll: Orbis Books, 2004.

"Beyond Babel: Pentecost and Mission." *International Bulletin of Missionary Research* 30/2 (April 2006): 57-58.

Chatterjee, S. K. "William Carey and the Linguistic Renaissance in India." *Carey's Obligation and India's Renaissance*. Serampore: Council of Serampore College, 1993.

Crnivec, M. "Theology of Translation." http://kud-logos.si/2002/theology-of-translation/. Posted on 5th May 2002. Accessed on 13th October 2018.

Franklin, K. J., and Niemandt, C. J. P. "Vision 2025 and the Bible translation movement." *HTS Teologiese Studies/Theological Studies* 69/1 (2013), 8 pages. http://dx.doi.org/10.4102/ hts. v69i1.1332. Accessed on 7th October 2018.

Gravelle, G. "Bible Translation in Historical Context: The Changing Role of Cross-Cultural Workers." *International Journal of Frontier Missiology* 27/1 (2010): 11-20.

Gupta, K. P. S. *The Christian Missionaries in Bengal: 1793-1833*. Calcutta: Firma K. L. Mukhopadhyay, 1971.

Hooper, J. S. M. and W. J. Culshaw. *Bible Translation in India, Pakistan and Ceylon*. Oxford: University Press, 1963.

Mangalwadi, V. R. *The Legacy of William Carey: A Model for the Transformation of a Culture*. Wheaton, Illinois: Crossway Books, 1993.

Marshman, J. C. *The Life and Times of Carey, Marshman, and Ward: Embracing the History of the Serampore Mission*. Vol. 1. London: Longman, Brown, Green, Longmans and Roberts, 1859.

Maxey, J. "Bible Translation as Contextualization: The Role of Orality." *Missiology: An International Review* 38 (2010): 173-183.

Nida, E. A. *Customs and Cultures: Anthropology for Christian Missions*. California: William Carey Library, 1954.

Omanson, R. L. "Bible Translation: Baptist Contributions to Understanding God's Word." *Baptist History and Heritage* 31 (1996): 12-22.

Potts, E. D. *British Baptist Missionaries in India: 1793-1837*. Cambridge: University Press, 1967.

Richard, H. L. "Some Observations on William Carey's Bible Translations." *International Bulletin of Mission Research* 42/3 (2018): 241-250.

Sanneh, L. *Translating the Message: The Missionary Impact on Culture*. Maryknoll, New York: Orbis Books, 2001.

Sanneh, L. *Whose Religion is Christianity? The Gospel beyond the West*. Grand Rapids: William B. Eerdmans, 2003.

Smalley, W. A. *Translation as Mission: Bible Translation in the Modern Missionary Movement*. Mercer: University Press, 1991.

Smith, A. C. *The Serampore Mission Enterprise*. Bangalore: Centre for Contemporary Christianity, 2005.

Tennent, T. C. *Invitation to World Missions: A Trinitarian Missiology for the Twenty-First Century*. Grand Rapids: Kregel Publications, 2010.

Walls, A. F. "Converts or Proselytes? The Crisis over Conversion in the Early Church." *International Bulletin of Missionary Research* 28/1 (2004): 2-7.

Walls, A. F. *The Missionary Movement in Christian History: Studies in the Transmission of Faith*. Maryknoll, New York: Orbis Books, 1996.

Walls, A. F. "The Translation Principle in Christian History." *Bible Translation and the Spread of the Church*. Ed. Philip Stine. Leiden: E. J. Brill, 1990.

West, G. "Mapping African Biblical Interpretation: A Tentative Sketch." *The Bible in Africa: Transactions, Trajectories and Trends*. Eds. Gerald O. West and Musa W. Dube. Leiden: Brill, 2000.

Whiteman, D. L. "Bible Translation and Social Development." *Bible Translation and the Spread of the Church. The Last 200 Years. Studies in Missions*. Vol. 2. Ed. Philip C. Stine. Leiden/Boston: E. J. Brill, 1990.

Yung, H. *Mangoes or Bananas? The Quest for an Authentic Asian Christian Theology*. New Delhi: Oxford, 1997.

5

Re-reading the Gospel of John in the light of William Carey's Linguistic Methods

Johnson Thomaskutty

Introduction

Here I attempt to understand William Carey's linguistic methods in the Bengali context in particular and in the Indian context in general. Though Carey, with the help of several Indian *pundits*, initiated to bring transformative attempts in the Indian context, his contributions did not receive due attention from the academic communities in the Indian context and elsewhere. As Carey endeavored for the linguistic renaissance in the Bengali/Indian context, his achievements and contributions should be acknowledged and be given due respect. In this article, I attempt to understand the linguistic contributions of Carey and also explore how his linguistic methods can be expounded for interpreting the biblical documents in their own sociolinguistic contexts. With that aim in mind, I will implement some of the linguistic methods of Carey into the narrative framework of John's Gospel and will explore the sociolinguistic matrix of the Fourth Gospel for interpretative avenues.

Answering the following questions might be significant in our investigation: How did Carey develop his linguistic methods in the Bengali/Indian context? Was Carey able to implement his linguistic methods effectively in the Bengali context? Can we use Carey's linguistic methods for interpreting the scriptures? How do Carey's linguistic methods help us to understand the sociolinguistic matrix of the Fourth Gospel? How is such a hermeneutical method useful for understanding the scriptures in the contemporary context? My attempt here is to answer these and many other questions. The task of this study is threefold: understand the linguistic contributions and methods of William Carey in the Indian context; implement the methods in interpreting the sociolinguistic and communitarian dynamics of the Fourth Gospel; and develop a new hermeneutic for understanding the scriptures in the contemporary context.

William Carey's Linguistic Methods

In the following section, we attempt to analyze Carey's linguistic methods in the Bengali context in particular and the Indian context in general. That will bring a broader outlook of Carey's linguistic methods in order to see their interpretative avenues in the NT interpretation.

Grammar and Linguistics: A General Understanding

Linguistics is understood as a science devoted to the study of language in all its aspects such as structure, interrelationship with the rest of human activity, history and mutual relations.[1] Walter R. Bodine comments that, it is "the study of language as language, in contrast to the study of any specific language."[2] Linguistics as a discipline evaluates human language capability and other cognitive abilities.[3] Kutscher and Werning state that, "The current state of knowledge suggests that on the basis of common biological sensory systems, the human perception of space is driven by universally-applicable principles of signal processing and interpretation. This leads one to hypothesize that universal special concepts are to be found in human language."[4] In that sense, human language perceives the universals in particularistic contexts. It is mostly understood through the process of grammar and its syntactic connections.

It is believed that the Greeks were indeed greatly interested in the grammar of their language and that Plato is one of the first to speculate on it.[5] But what is most admirable in the Greek conception of the business of grammar is that it includes rhetoric, prosody, and literary criticism.[6] The section on diction in Aristotle's *Poetics* is an early extant treatment of grammar in Greek and it is significant that the parts of speech are here examined as a part of critical activity.[7] In Latin too grammar includes everything that relates to the making and understanding of literature.[8] Quintilian of the first century CE divides grammar into two parts, the science of correct speech and the interpretation of poets.[9] In the Middle Ages, grammar was the most important branch of learning and the first of the seven arts.[10] Leonard Bloomfield considers Pānini's grammar that "it is one of the greatest monuments of human intelligence."[11] And those who know about the great Tamil grammar in *Tolkappiyam*, a work belonging to the Third Sangham, that is, the early centuries of the Christian era, would know how grammar in Dravidian letters was as comprehensible a literary discipline as it was in ancient Greece.[12] Thus grammar as a discipline within the study of language was well-explored in the Western and in the South Indian contexts.

William Carey's Linguistic Initiatives

It is impossible to imagine life without the influence of language. The nation of India is popularly known for its plurality of languages and dialects. The term 'Indian' is perceived as a blend of all kinds of pluralities based on languages, socio-cultural ethos, religions, customs, beliefs, ethnicity, color, caste and creed. During the Enlightenment in the eighteenth century, there was a renewed interest in grammar emerged in Europe.[13] This was the period in which the educated middle classes had assumed leadership in society and the vernaculars had become an effective instrument of communication for social change and intellectual progress.[14] When William Carey landed in Calcutta on 11th November 1793, the European Enlightenment was at its height and its manifestation in the study of language is to be found in great achievements in lexicography and grammar.[15] As a product of Enlightenment, Carey transformed many of the Indian vernaculars from their debased condition.[16]

Carey's Bengali Grammar published in 1801 reflects the new urge for a scientific study of living languages.[17] Carey's Bengali grammar appeared at a time when the Brahmin scholars of Bengal thought that the language was not respectable enough to deserve the attention of qualified grammarians.[18] As Gupta comments, "A society that values grammar values propriety in expression and when that society has no sense of propriety about anything it must not be expected to care for propriety in the use of language. Rule of law in language is guaranteed only by rule of law in public life."[19] As a youth, Carey learned Greek, Latin, and Hebrew. Moreover, he acquired substantial knowledge in Sanskrit, Oriya, Marathi, Punjabi, and Bengali languages. Bengali was his first-love apart from his deep love and attachment for Sanskrit.[20] The learned people of Bengal were not willing to dissociate themselves from the orthodox conventional style, largely derived from and shaped by classical Sanskrit language and literature.[21] William Carey and his Serampore associates started to advocate strongly for development and improvement of all the popular Indian languages.[22]

Carey's Linguistic Blend

Many held the view that William Carey's uncommon genius was best manifested in his linguistic works.[23] If he could concentrate his labor in this field only he undoubtedly would have been regarded as one of the greatest linguistic scholars of the world.[24] Though he emphasized on the Vernacular school of thought, he also attempted to link the *Vernacularist* school with the *Orientalist*[25] and *Anglicist* schools of thought.[26] He was able to achieve greater heights in the fields of translation works, vernacular grammar, creating dictionaries and polyglots, and building vocabularies.[27] He developed his love toward Sanskrit language alongside of his special interest in Bengali.[28] Carey believed that the development of vernaculars would lead to a country's quick modernization.[29] With that aim in mind, he worked for the development of Bengali language and literature.

In a context in which Bengali was mostly used as a spoken language and rarely used as a written language, Carey attempted to develop the language through various means.[30] Ray comments that, "Carey was the first among the scholars and authors to have felt the need of recording the colloquial language with its own diction and distinctive style."[31] Though he was considered as a missionary, his attempts helped to promote the Indian languages in the educational, commercial, administrative and cultural activities. Carey's attachment to Serampore College and Fort William College enabled him to foster the vernaculars with focus. He worked, on the one hand, as a professor of Bengali and Sanskrit in Fort William College and, on the other hand, as a Baptist missionary in Serampore.[32] In 1921 Rabindranath Tagore observed that, "Carey was a pioneer of revived interest in the vernaculars."[33] Carey realized the complexity of India's socio-cultural problems due to its multilingual character. He strongly felt that the people should be made aware of their mother tongues and should be conversant in some languages other than their mother tongues.[34] The missionaries must know several Indian languages to work in this country. In order to facilitate this purpose, he envisaged to develop a language study center in Serampore.[35] One of the objects of this center would be to help the European missionaries, coming to work in India, to learn quickly some Indian languages so that they could come closer to the common people.[36] Through all these attempts, Carey was able to give the Bengalis several linguistic and grammatical tools to work with.[37]

Carey and His Colloquialism

Carey wrote two books in lucid and colloquial Bengali prose style: *Kathopākathan* and *Ithihāsamālā*.[38] He used some natives to complete *Kathopākathan* or *Dialogues*.[39] As an important contribution demonstrating human life as it is, this work was intended to facilitate Bengali language.[40] The text relates encounters experienced in recruitment of domestic hands, conversation between Sahib and his Moonshi, between money-lender and the debtor, gentry and gentry, between women and women, clergy and the parishioner, zemindar and the riot, besides market scene and the style of speech current among laborers, quarrelling people, and gesticulating women.[41] Ray says that, "The dialogues were meant to serve as a lingual bridge between the Englishmen and the so-called lower ranks of the Bengali people."[42] The text was mainly intended to flourish the colloquial words and to communicate human life in day-to-day affairs.[43] Chatterjee comments that, "*Kathopākathan* using the dialect of the common people also established that Bengali, unaided by Sanskrit, could be developed as a powerful expressive language."[44] The text uses common phrases and idioms to express ideas in colloquial terms. This book has thrown much light on the manners, customs, social ideas, daily dialogues and the like.[45] Some even argue that the simple language of the book clearly established that it had not come all on a sudden, but it existed in unwritten or manuscript form before the final compilation of it.[46]

Colloquial expressions of different districts of Bengal are presented in it because the compilers came from different parts of Bengal.[47] De wrote in 1919: "It [*Kathopākathan*] had still not lost all the force and precision of realism and was a rich source for the literary historians of the idioms and slangs spoken in Bengali. Reflecting the results of Carey's minute and sympathetic observation and familiarity with the people, it proved that he had a thorough acquaintance with the resources of the language in all odds and different colloquial forms."[48] Through all these means, Bengali literature progressed astonishingly between 1800 and 1830. If Carey with the help of Serampore Mission and Fort William College had not come forward to enrich Bengali literature giving it due recognition, the elite society of Calcutta including Ram Mohan Roy would not have started writing in Bengali but rather preferred Persian or Sanskrit.[49] Similarly, *Ithihāsamālā* is a collection of various types of fictitious stories of earlier period. The language of the book is more lucid and simpler than that of the earlier publications of Serampore Mission.[50] These writings under the initiative of Carey demonstrate how Bengali as a language developed from its oral and colloquial form to its elegant and flourishing literary style.

Other Linguistic Methods

Through the establishment of a Language Study Center in Serampore, Carey initiated to build a cultural bridge between the East and the West.[51] That introduced a new style of a linguistic mix in the society. Carey's approach to language can be best explained through the following points. *First*, he developed a socio-linguistic approach to understand the language system of Bengal.[52] The *code switching* and *diglossia* of language systems in which a classical form of language ('H' form) exists alongside of another form or forms of the same language ('L' form).[53] When we consider the Indian languages in general, all other languages including Bengali are rooted in Sanskrit and that can be counted as the 'H' form. It was again true in the case of Bengali, that is, the elegant Bengali (the classical 'H' form) which was distinct but at the same time related to the colloquial ('L') forms of the same language.[54] Carey's understanding of the language system of Bengal enabled him to foster the language from multiple angles. In Carey's assessment, Sanskrit was at the center of Indian languages. Therefore, he approached other languages ('L' forms) through the means of Sanskrit.[55]

Second, Carey pioneered a style of Bengali language called *sadhu bhasha*. This style made use of loan words from Sanskrit, a natural course to follow where the sanskritic overlay of religious terms was manifest even in some languages belonging to other linguistic families such as the Dravidian.[56] Third, Carey was known for his style of language called *Christian Bengali*, a form that developed through the interaction of colloquial Bengali under the western influence.[57] As a result, the biblical text and its contents continued to remain under the domain of western thinking and the language of the Bengali Bible continued to exist as *Christian Bengali*.[58] Thus, there was a prevailing 'European-Indian mixed culture' in the colonial India, especially in the context of Bengal.[59] Fourth, Carey spent a considerable time in translating the New Testament into a multitude of minor Indian tongues. The names of these languages were at that time scarcely known to the linguists of Europe.[60] Carey did not remain content with his intimate acquaintance with numerous languages; he also tirelessly utilized his knowledge in undertaking publications.[61] These and other linguistic methods of Carey made profound influence in the Indian context.

The above discussion enables us to understand some of the linguistic methods developed by Carey and the Serampore mission. Those linguistic methods were instrumental for the advancement of colloquial languages in the Indian context. Some of them are important to be restated here: first, development of a descriptive and scientific approach to the languages that emphasized vocabulary, grammar, and structure to translate them from their oral traditions to the written form; second, advancement of a Vernacular linguistic style in closer relationship with the Oriental and Anglicist styles; third, composition of a colloquial dialogic style that facilitates a linguistic bridge between the natives and the foreigners; fourth, perceiving the colloquial languages through the means of *code switching* and *diglossia*, that means, understanding 'L' forms of language in relation to their 'H' forms;[62] fifth, facilitating a style of *sadhu bhasha* to accommodate the lower strata of the society; sixth, formation of a new style of language called *Christian Bengali*; and seventh, paying attention on both the popular and lesser tongues of the society. These linguistic methods of Carey are significant in today's interpretative contexts. In his study of languages, Carey attempted to understand the following aspects: the forms of speech and patterns of communication; community differences in the 'ways of speaking' they have adopted; typical patterns in multilingual people's use of languages; and involvement of language in social transformation.[63] In the following section, we will examine how the above stated linguistic methods are significant to understand the narrative framework of John's Gospel.

Re-Reading John's Gospel in the Light of Carey's Linguistic Methods

William Carey's implementation of his linguistic methods introduced some of the transformative measures in the sociolinguistic context of India.[64] Some of his linguistic methods can be used as hypothetical tools to throw more light on the understanding of the New Testament. In the current study, we attempt to apply some of his linguistic methods in the socio-linguistic context of the Johannine community. Carey's linguistic methods can be used as hermeneutical tools for understanding the core realities of John's community.[65] The seven methods recapitulated in the previous section can be used to demonstrate their reverberations in the Johannine community situation. In that process, the Johannine implied author is considered as a linguist who communicates his message to the implied reader with rhetorical punch and narrative efficacy. The principles of language adopted by Carey in the Indian context and their interpretative significance can be introduced as innovative methods for developing contextual hermeneutics pertinent to the Johannine community.

Carey developed a descriptive and scientific approach to the languages that emphasized vocabulary, grammar, and narrative structure to translate the oral traditions to their written form. At the semiotic level of the Fourth Gospel, the semantic domains, the narrative syntactic, and the pragmatic interplay reveal the author's idiosyncrasies.[66] A simple impressiveness of presentation and repetition of words and phrases enable the Gospel elegant in appearance.[67] Abbott understands that the authors of the New Testament, especially the Evangelist John, "knew Greek more from hearing others speak it than from reading authors."[68] Barrett says that, "It [the Greek of John] is neither bad Greek nor (according to classical standards) good Greek."[69] The narrator builds an "insider" linguistic dynamics through the repetitive use of love, truth, life, light, witness, and abide over against the "outsider" linguistic pattern.[70] Through all these means, the Johannine community developed its own sociolinguistics and semantic domains. Though the range of vocabulary in John is comparatively less, the range of meaning appears profound.[71] For John words are signs of communication that build the semantic domains.[72] He uses words both as denotative and connotative vehicles to convey the message in his own idiom.[73]

John's style of *relexicalization*[74] and *overlexicalization*[75] of words is demonstrated as follows: the expressions such as *following*, *abiding*, *loving*, *keeping the word*, *receiving*, *having*, and *seeing* are used to describe "believing in Jesus," and *spirit*, *above*, *life*, *light*, *not of the/this world*, *freedom*, *truth*, and *love* are used to describe "the realm of God."[76] Similarly, he uses two sets of words that are variants to describe contrasting spheres of existence, opposing modes of living and being; there is a contrast between *spirit*, *above*, *life*, *light*, *not of the/this world*, *freedom*, *truth*, and *love*, and their opposites, *flesh, below, death, darkness, the/this world, slavery, lie*, and *hate*.[77] Moreover, his repetitive uses of the *hour, lifting up*, and *glorification* of the Son of Man direct the attention of the reader toward the death of Jesus.[78] Abbott makes much of the fact that in the Fourth Gospel, often within the limits of one verse, words of different root are used to express the idea of *seeing*.[79] Some of John's vocabularies like *agapē/agapaō* (44 times), *alētheia* and its cognates (46 times), *ginōskein* (56/57 times), and *kosmos* (78 times) make a noticeable distinction in comparison to other gospels.[80] When we observe Carey's method of emphasizing vocabulary, grammar, and narrative structure in the Bengali context, we can also see how the Johannine narrator picks up words and other linguistic elements with focus and community consciousness. Analyzing Johannine words, phrases, clauses, sentences and micro-sections, and their interplay within the macro-structure of the Gospel provides us new insights for Johannine hermeneutics.[81] The language of John and its community dynamics enable the reader to develop Johannine contextual hermeneutics.

Not only relexicalization and overlexicalization of words, but also John constructs grammar in his own way. The author conveys his message with the help of a widespread use of *kai* as a parataxis to join words, phrases, clauses, and sentences together to build his semantic domains (1:19-21; 2:9).[82] Alongside of that, John prefers his peculiar style of using the conjunctions *oun* (2:16-18; 3:23-25; 4:8-9; 6:3-5; 9:4-6; 11:12-14; 11:57-12:1; 18:1-3, 5-6) and *de* (2:8; 6:71; 11:45-46, 54-55), and asyndeton (1:17, 39; 2:6-7, 17; 4:22; 6:59; 9:9; 12:12, 22).[83] Grammarians point out that colloquial Greek as a source for asyndeton in John.[84] Within the literary Aramaic and the Mishnaic Hebrew, asyndeton becomes a frequent feature.[85] Buth comments that, "It appears that a colloquial substratum in Hebrew, and probably Aramaic and Greek, could all have influenced John in the direction of a 'normal' narrative function for asyndeton."[86] John orchestrates a distinctive grammatical structure in John through the means of a cluster of words and their semantic integration. Carey was concerned of developing vocabulary, grammar, and structure in the Bengali context to develop the language from the oral tradition to the literary form. Carey's sociolinguistic approach was demonstrable when he considered the Bengali socio-cultural and linguistic dynamics together into account.[87] Once when we apply this method into the Johannine narrative framework for interpretative purposes, we can perceive that the Johannine vocabulary and language lie much closer to the core realities of the community life.[88] In that sense, it appears as if it was closer to the oral level of the community language. A serious question to be posed from the hermeneutical point of view is: "How did John build his own lexicon and his own grammar based on the community demands or the *Sitz im Leben Kirche*?" An interpreter of John's Gospel has to respond to this question before s/he addresses any other questions derived out of the text.

As Carey emphasized a Vernacular linguistic style in relationship with the Oriental and Anglicist styles, an analysis of John's sociolinguistic interplay shall enable us to throw light on its semantic underpinnings.[89] Christianity began in a Jewish cultural environment, with a Hebrew or Aramaic vocabulary and a background of Semitic hopes and longings.[90] At the time of Jesus, Hebrew was the language which had been in use among the Jews of Palestine for the longest time.[91] Moreover, there had come to be a standard Literary Aramaic and its various spoken dialects.[92] At the time of Jesus most educated Palestinian Jews of the upper classes knew at least some Greek.[93] In that sense, John's Gospel integrates literary styles from the Hebrew, Aramaic, Greek, and Latin linguistic thought-worlds.[94] As John demonstrates the Johannine community's idiomatic style, he accommodates the linguistic and literary features of the Greco-Roman and Jewish worlds. Brown comments that, "The community or part of it may have moved from Palestine to the Diaspora to teach the Greeks (7:35), perhaps to the Ephesus area—a move that would cast more light on the Hellenistic atmosphere of the Gospel and on the need to explain Aramaic names and titles (e.g., rabbi, Messiah)."[95] As the Johannine community was formed as a sect within the Synagogue set-up and later on excommunicated (9:22, 34; 12:42; 16:2), the Johannine Christians would have developed a different rhetoric.[96]

The colloquial styles of Hebrew, Aramaic, Greek, and Latin and their integration would have given birth to a new style in the community of John.[97] As scholars had identified, John also had influences from the Old Testament,[98] Qumran, Platonic,[99] Hermetic, Mystery religious, Philonic, Gnostic, Mandaean,[100] and Samaritan backgrounds.[101] Furthermore, John also would have developed his own linguistic and ideological style to make his community identity distinct from the Synoptic and Pauline communities.[102] In that way, John's method of *evaluation* and *acceptance* of ideas enabled him to build a distinctive identity in semiotic terms.[103] As Carey emphasized the Vernacular linguistic style in relationship with the Orientalist and Anglicist styles, John's mixed phenomenon provides an amalgam of linguistic and literary interaction.[104] In the hermeneutical procedures, a reader who neglects this important aspect of the Fourth Gospel may miss its linguistic, stylistic, and ideological flavor.

Carey's composition of a colloquial dialogic style through *Kathopākathan* facilitated a linguistic bridge between the Bengali nationals and the missionaries who came to India. The Johannine dialogues show how the narrator makes use of this literary category to dramatize the *Sitz-im-Leben Jesu* in the *Sitz-im-Leben Kirche* context.[105] A genre analysis of the Johannine dialogues, which takes into consideration the content, form, and function, helps us to understand the semantic, syntactic, and pragmatic aspects of the Fourth Gospel.[106] We are informed that dialogue is a recognizable and established literary category which is spread throughout John.[107] In John's narrative, a reader can recognize several common conventions of dialogue that form the text into a specific literary category.[108] John's narrative develops with a focus on the characters and their verbal exchanges.[109] Some narrative similarities between the Platonic and the Johannine dialogues are conspicuous to the reader.[110] Plato's literary style transformed the real-life conversations of Socrates with his friends and students into creative 'inventions' which incorporated various dramatic elements for the purpose of progressing toward a philosophical truth.[111]

Similarly, in John, the narrator attempts to imitate the real life conversations of Jesus with his interlocutors.[112] The synagogue and church dialogue in the Johannine community context is well connected to other layers of dialogues. While the community was in constant conflict with the world and their existence was under threat, 'eternal life' was the key concept introduced to them.[113] The evangelist reinterprets the 'divine'/'transcendental' story (at the rear of stage) and the story of the earthly Jesus to the community (at the front of stage) in his own idiom.[114] Thus, a reader of the dialogue can notice the way linguistic, literary, historical, and theological aspects blend together within the text.[115] As *Kathopākathan* demonstrates the day-to-day affairs of the common people in colloquial language, John's dialogues reveal how God in flesh reveals himself to humanity. In that way, the socio-religious, socio-cultural, and sociolinguistic conventions of the community are at view. Carey and his colleagues foster a linguistic category through *Kathopākathan* to redeem the language from its oral condition to a literary form. Considering the dialogues in John as a literary category and recognizing their proximity to the oral pre-condition, a reader of the text can reconstruct new hermeneutics that take into consideration the sociolinguistic and literary roots of the Fourth Gospel.[116]

Carey perceived the colloquial languages through the means of *code switching* and *diglossia*, that means, identifying the 'L' forms of the dialects and their geographical concentration distinct from their 'H' forms. As Jesus's character in John demonstrates his knowledge in the Pentateuch (Exo. 16:4 in 6:31; Num. 21:9 in 3:14; 35:30 in 8:17), the Prophetical writings (Isa. 6:10 in 12:40; 40:3 in 1:23; 53:1 in 12:38; 54:13 in 6:45; Zech. 13:7 in 16:32; 12:10 in 19:37) and in the Wisdom literature (Psa. 22:18 in 19:24; 35:19 in 15:25; 41:9 in 13:18; 69:9 in 2:17; 69:21 in 19:28; 82:6 in 10:34; 118:26 in 12:13), a reader gets the impression that Jesus was knowledgeable in the 'H' form of the Hebrew language.[117] At the oral level of communication, Jesus, his disciples, and the Johannine community exercised their scriptural knowledge in the oral (or 'L') forms of the languages. This is the nature of the linguistic attitudes at the heart of code switching.[118] Wise says that, "in ancient Palestine, Jesus's Aramaic sayings, if they were such, might well come down in writing in an 'H' form of the language rather than the actual 'L' form in which they were spoken."[119] The Johannine community, emerged in Jerusalem and flourished in the Ephesian context, was exposed to various linguistic, cultural, and ideological phenomena.[120] In that sense, the Aramaisms, Hebraisms, and Semitisms (i.e., constructions abnormal in Greek, but normal in Aramaic, in Hebrew, or both in these Semitic languages) paved way to the distinctive Greek structure of the Gospel.[121]

The poetic format of John reveals his literary style and that led Burney and Torrey to suggest a theory of an Aramaic origin of John.[122] Based on all these available information, we come to a point that Jesus might have been a multilingual or at least a bilingual. Recent discoveries of ossuary inscriptions in Judea have revealed that the inhabitants of first century Palestine were trilingual, speaking Hebrew, Aramaic, and Greek.[123] Jesus the Galilean and the apostles, who were predominantly if not exclusively Galilean, might have used Greek in addition to the Semitic tongues.[124] Carey distinguished the 'L' level of the Bengali language from its 'H' level and from other elegant 'H' (i.e., Sanskrit) forms and made all efforts to translate the colloquial language to the literary level. When Fourth Gospel is placed in its own sociolinguistic context, we might notice that the 'L' forms of languages might have converted into 'H' forms in his writing.[125] In that sense, Jesus's 'L' forms of communication might have received an *inferior* 'H' form in the Johannine community context and later on into a *superior* 'H' form in the literary composition of John.

Carey facilitated a style popularly known as *sadhu bhasha* to accommodate society's lower strata of people. Let us see how John has to be perceived from this perspective. Jesus spoke both in Aramaic and in Hebrew; similarly, the Johannine community shared their concerns in Aramaic and in Hebrew.[126] Jesus's use of Greek or a varied dialect of Aramaic or even an 'L' form of Latin can be perceived at least in the following occasions: first, Matthew 8:5-13 par. John 4:46-54: Jesus's conversation with the centurion or commander (probably in Greek); second, John 4:4-26: Jesus's conversation with the Samaritan woman (either in Greek or in Samaritan Hebrew/Aramaic); and third, Mark 15:2-5 par. Matthew 27:11-14; Luke 23:2-4; John 18:29-38: Jesus's trial before Pilate (dialect of either Greek or Latin).[127] Jesus and, later on, the Johannine community developed their rhetoric based on the linguistic codes available to them from Aramaic, Hebrew, Greek, and Latin thought-worlds.[128] That further means, the *ipsissima verba Jesu*[129] or at least his *ipsissima vox*[130] developed from an amalgam of Aramaic, Hebrew, Greek, and Latin dialects.[131] John's message with *extra-linguistic*,[132] *para-linguistic*,[133] and *linguistic*[134] reveals this unique and multifaceted semiotics.[135] The above details enable us to systematize a multi-lingual rhetoric that absorbs multifaceted social reactions.[136] Just as Carey developed his own peculiar style that bridges the gap between the literate and illiterate and adopting loan words from Sanskrit,[137] Jesus and the Johannine community at the 'L' level and the literary Gospel at the 'H' level reflect a flexible dialect that incorporates loan words from other dialects.[138] This peculiar style of John is persuasive to attract people from varied backgrounds.[139]

Carey approached the Bengali language in a different way and that resulted into the formation of a new style called *Christian Bengali*. This hybrid style of language in the Bengali context can be used as a model to ponder deep into the realities of the Johannine community.[140] The 'L' style of language(s) at the *Sitz im Leben Jesu*, the *Sitz im Leben Kirche*, and the *Sitz im Leben* of the evangelist himself reflect the multilingual and multicultural hybridity of the oral reflections around Jesus.[141] When the language received its 'H' status through the written composition(s), many of those hybrid aspects also might have survived.[142] In that sense, through the oral ('L') level and written ('H') level communications, the community of John developed its own peculiar linguistic style. John's in-group dynamism of language over against the out-group dimensions is expressed through its peculiar dualistic framework: light (vs. darkness, 1:5), born of water/spirit (vs. born of blood/flesh/humans, 1:13), above (vs. below, 8:23), spirit (vs. flesh, 3:6), life (vs. death, 3:36), truth (vs. lie, 8:44-45), sky (vs. land [earth], 3:31), God (vs. Satan, 13:27), Israel (vs. Judeans (1:19, 47), and not of this world (vs. this world = Israelite society, 17:1). This phenomenon reveals the community's style of antilanguage (1:19-28).[143]

John's characterization develops based on its dualistic framework and linguistic phenomena that results into a series of conflicts between the protagonist and the antagonists.[144] Within the literary and narrative framework of the Fourth Gospel, John develops a peculiar Greek style that is Greco-Roman in dialect, Hebraic/Semitic in rhythm, Syrian and Antiochene in influences, and Aramaic in proximity.[145] Semitic literary parallelisms are obvious in John's passages like 3:11, 18, 20-21, 31-32, and others.[146] This style of John can be considered as a hybrid form called *Christian Greek* in particular and *Semitic Greek* in general.[147] When John develops his language, he adopts several linguistic and ideological aspects from the Greco-Roman and Jewish thought-worlds and that helped him to develop a purely Johannine sociolinguistics and narrative rhetoric.[148] Carey paid attention on both the popular and lesser tongues of the society.[149] As Carey developed a peculiar style emerged out of his sociolinguistic context, in John a reader can notice a rhetoric that reflects the in-group dynamism of his community. That means, the social and religious matrix of the Jesus movement was emerged out of a multilinguistic context.[150]

Conclusion

In recapitulation, William Carey's linguistic methods were instrumental for the linguistic and literary renaissance in the Indian context and that further contributed to several areas of human life in Bengal. He spearheaded a new movement in India with intellectual insights from the European Enlightenment. In his nativistic and vernacular emphasis on linguistics, Carey brought into focus a dynamic interwovenness between vocabulary and social ethos, a cultural interlocking of grammar, and a colloquial dialogic style. His interest in a scientific approach to language that emphasizes development of vocabulary, grammar, and literary structure, and the advancement of vernacular linguistic style in relation to the Orientalist and Anglicist methods was well-placed in sociolinguistic terms. Carey's involvement in the composition of colloquial dialogic genres, usage of linguistic methods such as *code switching* and *diglossia*, facilitation of the literary and linguistic phenomenon called *sadhu bhasha*, formation of the sub-dialect called *Christian Bengali*, and attention to both the popular and lesser tongues reveals his sociolinguistic approach in the advancement of languages. As his linguistic methods were taking into consideration the socio-cultural realities of the Bengali community, they can be explored as hermeneutical tools to understand the matrix behind the biblical documents.

In our analysis of the Gospel of John, we found that John's relexicalization and overlexicalization, simple grammatical and literary structures, Semitic linguistic styles (Aramaism and Hebraism), Greco-Roman influences, dialogic and monologic language, continuous asyndeton and parataxis, *code switching* and *diglossia* from oral communications to written language, the usage of antilanguage through the means of dualistic narrative framework and other phenomena together demonstrate the linguistic nexus of the literary masterpiece. John's linguistic matrix takes our attention to the life situations of Jesus and the Johannine community and also invites our acumen to the final written composition of the Gospel. Thus, we understand how a linguistic configuration developed from the 'L' level in Jesus's and the community's life situations to the 'H' level in the written framework of the Gospel. A reader of the Fourth Gospel can go closer to the linguistic framework that is derived out of a multilinguistic and pluralistic socio-cultural reality of the Johannine community.

As John's literary composition, historical underpinnings, and theological insights are integrally connected to the sociolinguistic and communitarian dynamics, it is important to understand the linkage between the community existence and the usage of language in the process of textual interpretation. Porter comments that, "Interpretation of the Bible should rightly involve a significant linguistic component, since biblical studies, regardless of whatever else it may be, is a textually based discipline."[151] As Porter says, the role of sociolinguistic analysis of the scripture should be emphasized in the exegetical and hermeneutical explanations of the Fourth Gospel.

With that standpoint in mind, the current study challenges the readers of the scripture to consider the following aspects in the process of interpreting the scripture in the contemporary context: first, integrating the dynamics of sociolinguistics both within the biblical traditions and within the contemporary socio-political and religio-cultural realities of the reader; second, applying the sociolinguistic methods enables us to fathom deep into the matrix of the text and to explore the social dynamics closer to the message; third, understanding the language dynamics of the scriptures and the contextual dynamics of the interpreter in relation to the semiotic aspects (i.e., semantics, syntactic, and pragmatics) and assimilating them for a dialogue between the narrator of the text and the contemporary reader; fourth, evaluating the way *code switching* and *diglossia* occurs as the language(s) alter(s) from its/their 'L' levels to the 'H' levels to enable a linguistic transition from the communitarian (i.e., oral) traditions to the literary (i.e., written) traditions; and fifth, demonstrating how language can be used as an unavoidable means to derive community dynamics and contextual underpinnings from the textual framework. In short, language is used as a powerful means that connects oral reality, social dynamics, linguistic matrix, epistemological details, historical insights, and literary rhetoric to develop a contextual and ideological artistry.

Endnotes

[1] See "Linguistics," *Encyclopaedia Britannica*, 162.

[2] See Bodine, "Linguistics and Biblical Studies," 327.

[3] See Kutscher and Werning, *On Ancient Grammars of Space*, VII.

[4] See Kutscher and Werning, *On Ancient Grammars of Space*, VII.

[5] Law comments, "In a series of dialogues Plato depicts Socrates deep in debate, showing how, through a careful process of questioning, it is possible to elicit knowledge that a person has never been taught." See Law, *The History of Linguistics in Europe*, 18.

[6] See Gupta, "William Carey and Bengali Grammar," 189-190.

[7] See Modrak, *Aristotle's Theory of Language and Meaning*, 1-9.

[8] See Oniga, *Latin a Linguistic Introduction*, 1-8.

[9] See Chakkuvarackal, "Serampore Mission and the Linguistic Renaissance in India," 124-125; also see Law, *History of Linguistics in Europe*, 62.

[10] See Gupta, "William Carey and Bengali Grammar," 189-190.

[11] See Bloomfield, *Language*, 11; also see Gupta, "William Carey and Bengali Grammar," 191. Kapoor's text describes: "It [Panini's *Ashtadhyayi*] is a complete, explicit and comprehensive grammar of both spoken and textual (compositional) Sanskrit." See Kapoor, *Dimensions of Pānini Grammar*.

[12] See Athithan, *Linguistic Structures in Tamil*, 1-30.

[13] The period of Enlightenment in the 18th century was marked by the intellectual and philosophical conviction that truth could only be obtained through the powers of human reason, observation, and experiment. See McKim, *Westminster Dictionary of Theological Terms*, 90.

[14] Delon comments that, "European Enlightenment thinkers were interested in diverse aspects of language and languages: their structure, their historical relationships, their 'moral' and philosophical qualities, the methods used to teach languages, their function in society, and their role in science and literature." See Delon, *Encyclopedia of the Enlightenment*, 617.

[15] See Gupta, "William Carey and Bengali Grammar," 188.

[16] Mangalwadis say, "Carey transformed Bengali, previously considered 'fit only for demons and women' into the foremost literary language of India." See Mangalwadi, *The Legacy of William Carey*, 20.

[17] See Gupta, "William Carey and Bengali Grammar," 188.

[18] See Gupta, "William Carey and Bengali Grammar," 188. Bengali was called by those who speak it, *Banla* or *Bangla-bhasha*, the language of *Benga* or *Vanga* (in Sanskrit, the word 'Vanga' meant Eastern and central Bengal). See Chakkuvarackal, "The Serampore Mission and the Linguistic Renaissance in India," 126.

[19] See Gupta, "William Carey and Bengali Grammar," 188.

[20] See Mangalwadi, *The Legacy of William Carey*, 20.

[21] See Ray, "William Carey—Linguist with a Difference," 157.

[22] See Chatterjee, "William Carey and the Linguistic Renaissance in India," 159.

[23] Recognizing Carey's courageous missionary works and remarkable success in Bible translation into Oriental languages, Carey was awarded the Diploma of Doctor of Divinity by the Brown University of America on 8th March 1807. See Ray, "William Carey—Linguist with a Difference," 155-158; also see Mukhopadhyaya, "William Carey's Contribution for the Promotion of Sanskritic Studies," 194.

[24] See Chakkuvarackal, "The Serampore Mission and the Linguistic Renaissance in India," 123-140.

[25] Thomas says that, "Orientalism, a Western scholarly discipline of the 18th and 19th centuries that encompassed the study of the languages, literatures, religions, philosophies, histories, art, and laws of Asian societies, especially ancient ones." See Thomas, "Orientalism," 1.

[26] See Chakkuvarackal, "The Serampore Mission and the Linguistic Renaissance in India," 124.

[27] The following are some of Carey's works on language: (1) *Grammar*: Bengali, Marathi, Sanskrit, Punjabi, Telugu, Bhotani, and Kurnataka; (2) *Dictionaries*: Bengali, Marathi, Bhotani, and Sanskrit; and (3) *Polyglot*: 13 Indian languages and 4 hilly languages. See Chakkuvarackal, "The Serampore Mission and the Linguistic Renaissance in India," 129.

[28] See Mukhopadhayay, "William Carey's Contributions for the Promotion of Sanskritic Studies," 193-202; also see Chakkuvarackal, "The Serampore Mission and the Linguistic Renaissance in India," 128.

[29] See Chakkuvarackal, "The Serampore Mission and the Linguistic Renaissance in India," 127.

[30] Carey considered Bengali as one of the most expressive and elegant languages of the East. Bengali of Iswarachandra, Bankim, Rabindranath, and others is now honored as a world language. Carey's endeavors behind such a development cannot be ignored. See Tapan Banerjee, "Growth and Development of Bengali Literature from Serampore"; also see Murshid, *Kalantare Bangla Gadya*, 184; Sen, "Bengali Language, Literature and William Carey," 4.

[31] See Ray, "William Carey—Linguist with a Difference," 157.

[32] See Gupta, "William Carey and Bengali Grammar," 187; also see Chakkuvarackal, "The Serampore Mission and the Linguistic Renaissance in India," 128.

[33] See Carey, *Life of William Carey*, 209.

[34] See Bhattacharya, *Ravindranath Tagore: Adventure of Ideas and Innovative Practices in Education*, 16-17.

[35] See Ray, "William Carey—Linguist with a Difference," 155-158.

[36] See details about Carey's translations: Christopher Arangadan, "Carey's Legacy of Bible Translation," 177-186. Carey's Bible translations include: (1) *The whole Bible*: Bengali, Oriya, Hindi, Marathi, Sanskrit, and Assamese (6 languages); (2) *New Testament and Old Testament up to Ezekiel 26*: Punjabi (1 language); (3) *New Testament and Old Testament up to 2 Kings*: Pashtoo and Kashmiri (2 languages); (4) *New Testament and Pentateuch*: Telugu and Konkani (2 languages); (5) *New Testament*: Lahnda, Gujarati, Rajastani, Bikaneri, Pahari, Nepali, Hindi, Bangheli, Hindi Kanouji, Rajastani Marwari, Rajastani Harauti, Kanarese, Bhatneri, Hindi Braj Bhasha, Pahari Dogri, Bihari Maghadi, Rajastani Malvi, Pahari Garhwali, Manipuri, Pahari Palpa, Khasi, and Pahari Kumaoni up to Colossians (19 languages); and (6) *One or more Gospels*: Balochi (Matthew, Mark, and Luke), Rajastani Jaipuri (Matthew), Rajastani Mewari (Matthew), Hindi Awadhi (Matthew and Mark), and Sindhi (Matthew; 5 languages). Also he translated Sanskrit works to English, such as *Mahabharata* (1795), *Ramayana* (1806) and philosophical treatises like *Samkhya*. For more details, see Chakkuvarackal, "The Serampore Mission and the Linguistic Renaissance in India," 129-130, 135-136; also see Mangalwadi, *The Legacy of William Carey*, 20; Chatterjee, "William Carey and the Linguistic Renaissance in India," 161.

[37] H. H. Wilson of Oxford University would say of Carey's 80,000-words Bengali dictionary that "it was unique in those days for its erudite and minute philological exactness." See Arangadan, "Carey's Legacy of Bible Translation," 148-150. Similarly, from 1794 to 1810 Carey collected more than 40,000 Sanskrit words with synonyms in twelve different languages. See Urmi Gangopadhyay, "Carey's Contributions to Linguistics."

[38] See George, *Modern Indian Literature and Anthology*, 74.

[39] See Mukherjee, *A Dictionary of Indian Literature*, 174.

[40] See Ray, "William Carey—Linguist with a Difference," 157.

[41] See Ray, "William Carey—Linguist with a Difference," 158.

[42] See Ray, "William Carey—Linguist with a Difference," 158.

[43] See Ray, "William Carey—Linguist with a Difference," 158.

[44] See Chatterjee, "William Carey and the Linguistic Renaissance in India," 169.

[45] See Das Sajanikanto, *Sahilya Sadak Charitmala* 15, 54.

[46] See Chatterjee, "William Carey and the Linguistic Renaissance in India," 170.

[47] See Chatterjee, "William Carey and the Linguistic Renaissance in India," 170.

[48] See De, *History of Bengali Literature*, 136-137.

[49] See Chatterjee, "William Carey and the Linguistic Renaissance in India," 168.

[50] See Chatterjee, "William Carey and the Linguistic Renaissance in India," 170.

[51] See Chatterjee, "William Carey and the Linguistic Renaissance in India," 159; also see Chakkuvarackal, "The Serampore Mission and the Linguistic Renaissance in India," 130-131.

[52] For more details about socio-linguistics, see Jaffe, *Stance: Sociolinguistic Perspectives.*

[53] See Gangopadhyay, "Carey's Contribution to Linguistics"; also see Gardner-Chloros, *Code-Switching*, 1-19.

[54] See Chakkuvarackal, "The Serampore Mission and the Linguistic Renaissance in India," 131-132.

[55] See Chakkuvarackal, "The Serampore Mission and the Linguistic Renaissance in India," 131-132.

[56] See Arangadan, "Carey's Legacy of Bible Translation," 176-177. Mangalwadis say, "The Bengali songs of Tagore's Gitanjali display both on the influence on the language of Carey as well as the worldview of the Bible, which Carey translated." See Mangalwadi, *The Legacy of William Carey*, 93-94; Carey, *William Carey*, 209.

[57] See Chakkuvarackal, "The Serampore Mission and the Linguistic Renaissance in India," 132-133.

[58] See Gine, *'Nomos' in Context*, 184-185.

[59] See Chakkuvarackal, "The Serampore Mission and the Linguistic Renaissance in India," 133.

[60] See Chakkuvarackal, "The Serampore Mission and the Linguistic Renaissance in India," 133.

[61] Several of these languages were vernaculars of only a few hundreds of thousands. Yet they had been distinct languages from time immemorial, and some had substantial literary traditions (i.e., Awadhi, Braj Bhasha, Kanouji, Malvi and others). See Chakkuvarackal, "The Serampore Mission and the Linguistic Renaissance in India," 133.

[62] Carey's approach to the study of languages was in a sense sociolinguistic, because he studied and analyzed languages in their social contexts and the study of social life through linguistics. See Chakkuvarackal, "The Serampore Mission and the Linguistic Renaissance in India," 136.

[63] See Chakkuvarackal, "The Serampore Mission and the Linguistic Renaissance in India," 136.

[64] See Chakkuvarackal, "The Serampore Mission and the Linguistic Renaissance in India," 131.

[65] For more details about Carey's linguistic principles, refer the previous section.

[66] See Blomberg, *A Handbook of NT Exegesis*, 117-142.

[67] See Guthrie, *NT Introduction*, 335. In the words of Petersen, "One of the most distinctive features of the Gospel of John is its blatantly self-conscious use of language. Everyone in the narrative, including the narrator, speaks everyday language, but the narrator and Jesus also speak what we will call a special language, one that employs the grammar and vocabulary of the everyday but uses the vocabulary in a different way, leading to misunderstanding on the part of those who only speak the everyday language." See Petersen, *The Gospel of John and the Sociology of Light*, 1; cf. Grelot, *The Language of Symbolism*, 7-24.

[68] See Abbott, *Johannine Vocabulary*. Stanton states that, "John's Gospel is like a stream in which children can wade and elephants swim. For many readers the gospel's main themes are simple and clear, and the evangelist's dramatic presentation of the story of Jesus compelling." See Stanton, *The Gospels and Jesus*, 97.

[69] See Barrett, *Gospel according to St. John*, 5-6. W. F. Howard considered that the author "was a man who, while cultured to the last degree, wrote Greek after the fashion of men of quite elementary attainment." See Moulton and Howard, *A Grammar of New Testament Greek*, 33.

[70] Guthrie says, "in the reverse direction, many of the expressions used frequently in the synoptics are little used, or do not occur at all, in John (e.g., kingdom, people [*laos*], call, pray or prayer)." See Guthrie, *NT Introduction*, 336.

[71] For more details about repetition as a style in John, see Van der Watt, "Repetition and Functionality in the Gospel according to John," 87-108.

[72] See Van der Watt, "Ethics through the Power of Language," 139-167.

[73] *Denotation* is the meaning that words have for most everyone who hears them in most contexts. *Connotation* is the special meaning that a word has for a particular person or group of people, perhaps only in certain contexts. See Cotterell and Turner, *Linguistics and Biblical Interpretation*, 45-47; Blomberg, *A Handbook of NT Exegesis*, 121.

[74] Malina and Rohrbaugh define, "Relexicalization refers to the practice of using new words for some reality that is not ordinarily referred to with those words." See Malina and Rohrbaugh, *Social-Science Commentary on the Gospel of John*, 4.

[75] Malina and Rohrbaugh define, "To overlexicalize is to have many words for the central area of concern." See Malina and Rohrbaugh, *Social-Science Commentary on the Gospel of John*, 5.

[76] See Malina and Rohrbaugh, *Social-Science Commentary on the Gospel of John*, 4.

[77] See Malina and Rohrbaugh, *Social-Science Commentary on the Gospel of John*, 5.

[78] See Van der Watt, "Repetition and Functionality in the Gospel according to John," 87-108.

[79] See Nicklin, *Aboott's Johannine Vocabulary*, 172-175.

[80] See Martin, *NT Foundations*, 271-272.

[81] See Martin, *NT Foundations*, 271-272.

[82] Guthrie comments that, "Perhaps the most characteristic feature of John's style is the widespread use of *kai*, instead of subordinating clauses, in joining sentences (*parataxis*). It is this feature more than any other which creates such an impression of simplicity in Greek. The author is clearly more intent on imparting a message than on stylistic niceties." See Guthrie, *NT Introduction*, 336.

[83] See Buth, "Oun, De, Kai, and asyndeton in John's Gospel," 144-161.

[84] For more details about Johannine grammar, refer Abbott, *Johannine Grammar*; also see Fitzmyer, *The Semitic Background of the New Testament*, 3-186.

[85] See Turner, *A Grammar of New Testament Greek*, 1963: 340-341

[86] See Buth, "Oun, De, Kai, and asyndeton in John's Gospel," 159.

[87] See Chakkuvarackal, "The Serampore Mission and the Linguistic Renaissance in India," 131-132.

[88] Cf. Blomberg, *A Handbook of NT Exegesis*, 117-142.

[89] See Barr, *The Semantics of Biblical Language*, 1-30.

[90] The author's knowledge of Jewish customs, Jewish history, and Palestinian geography reveal the Palestinian background of the Gospel. See Guthrie, *NT Introduction*, 261-263; also see Chakkuvarackal, "Important Issues in the Translation of the Bible in the Indian Context," 165; Thompson, "John, Gospel of," 371-372.

[91] See Wise, "Languages of Palestine," 435.

[92] See Wise, "Languages of Palestine," 437.

[93] See Wise, "Languages of Palestine," 439; also see Guthrie, *NT Introduction*, 266-267.

[94] See Wise, "Languages of Palestine," 434-444. Robertson considers John's Gospel as a "Jewish Gospel." See Robertson, *John: The Jewish Gospel*, 1-4. The crime of Jesus, written as a superscription over His head, was inscribed in three languages: Hebrew, Latin, and Greek (John 19:20). See Gromacki, *NT Survey*, 23. Gromacki states that, "Since there was such a language mix, public documents had to be written in several languages in order to reach all of the people. This is why the crime of Jesus, written as a superscription over His head, was inscribed in three languages (John 19:20)." Latin was spoken only by native Romans and key political subjects. The language

most spoken and read throughout the Mediterranean area was Greek. In Palestine and throughout the Near East, Aramaic was very popular. Hebrew was no longer spoken and read by the average Jew; the orthodox, including the rabbis of the Pharisaic order, still embraced its usage.

[95] See Brown, *An Introduction to the New Testament*, 375.

[96] See Lamb, *Text, Context, and the Johannine Community*, 1-35.

[97] See Brown, *The Community of the Beloved Disciple*; Martyn, *History and Theology of the Fourth Gospel.*

[98] For more details about OT influence in John, see Guthrie, *NT Introduction*, 248-249; Thomaskutty, *Dialogue in the Book of Signs*, 34-36.

[99] See Thomaskutty, *Dialogue in the Book of Signs*, 443-444.

[100] See Dodd, *The Interpretation of the Fourth Gospel*, 9; also see Brown, *The Gospel according to John*, 1:lii-lxiv.

[101] Brown states that, "much of the Qumran-like vocabulary appears in the speeches of Jesus in John (to a much greater extent than in the Synoptics) need not lead us to conclude hastily that the raw materials in those speeches were the artificial compositions of the evangelist. If Qumran exemplifies a wider range of thought, Jesus could well have been familiar with its vocabulary and ideas; for the Word-made-flesh spoke the language of his time." See Brown, *An Introduction to the New Testament*, 373; also see Dodd, *The Interpretation of the Fourth Gospel*, 9; Guthrie, *NT Introduction*, 291; Thomaskutty, *Dialogue in the Book of Signs*, 3-4.

[102] See Thompson, "John, Gospel of," 375; Thomaskutty, *Dialogue in the Book of Signs*, 36-39; Beasley-Murray, "Synoptics and John," 792-795.

[103] John's ideas would have developed from various other sources. But, the evangelist would have used them with a scrutiny. Thus, he clustered his ideas with that of the ideas from the surroundings.

[104] See Fitzmyer, *The Semitic Background of the New Testament*, 3-186.

[105] Martyn considers the John as a *two-level drama*. See Martyn, *History and Theology of the Fourth Gospel.*

[106] Van Aarde comments that, "The tern *genre* refers to the *generic* characteristics of a specific literary form, which differ from the characteristics of other forms, and which enable us to identify a specific *literary type*." See Van Aarde, "Narrative Criticism," 381; cf. Thomaskutty, *Dialogue in the Book of Signs*, 433-474.

[107] See Stibbe, *John's Gospel*, 54.

[108] See Greimas and Courtés, *Semiotics and Language*, 78.

[109] See Thomaskutty, *Dialogue in the Book of Signs*, 476-477.

[110] See Van Kooten, *The Creation of Heaven and Earth*, 168; Thomaskutty, *Dialogue in the Book of Signs*, 444.

[111] See Denning-Bolle, *Wisdom in Akkadian Literature*, 72 and 76.

[112] See Brant, *Dialogue and Drama*, 13; Thomaskutty, *Dialogue in the Book of Signs*, 444-445.

[113] See Thomaskutty, *Dialogue in the Book of Signs*, 480.

[114] See Thomaskutty, *Dialogue in the Book of Signs*, 480.

[115] See how John's dialogues are framed as follows: 1:19-2:12; 2:13-22; 3:1-21; 3:22-36; 4:1-42; 4:43-54; 5:1-47; 6:1-71; 7:1-52/8:12-59; 9:1-10:21; 10:22-42; 11:1-53; 11:54-12:50; and the like. See Thomaskutty, *Dialogue in the Book of Signs*, 480.

[116] See Martin, *NT Foundations*, 272.

[117] See Fitzmyer, *The Semitic Background of the New Testament*, 3-186.

[118] Cf. Wise, "Languages of Palestine," 444.

[119] See Wise, "Languages of Palestine," 444.

[120] See Gromacki, *NT Survey*, 23.

[121] Brown says that, "Still another factor is that the Christian message in the Greek world was first preached in the diaspora synagogues and consequently was phrased in the religious vocabulary of Greek-speaking Judaism—a Greek which was influenced by the Semitized style of the LXX, the Greek OT." Brown continues saying that, "Personally, we tend to agree with the majority of scholars who do not find adequate evidence that a complete edition of the Gospel according to John ever existed in Aramaic. It is possible, however, that bits of the historical tradition underlying John were written in Aramaic, especially if the source of this tradition was John son of Zebedee." See Brown, *The Gospel according to John*, CXXIX.

[122] See Burney, *The Poetry of the Lord*; cf. Burney, *The Aramaic Origin of the Four Gospels*; Torrey, *The Four Gospels*; Torrey, "The Aramaic Origin of the Gospel of St. John," 305-344.

[123] See Hiebert, *An Introduction to the NT*, 29; Ong, *The Multilingual Jesus*, 32-37.

[124] See Gundry, "The Language Milieu of First-Century Palestine," 407.

[125] See Porter, *Linguistic Analysis of the Greek New Testament*, 113-132.

[126] Porter says, "Jesus was born to a Palestinian Jewish family and was apparently well versed in the institutions of the Jewish people, including the use of Aramaic, the language of the Jews since their return under the Persians from exile in Babylon." See Porter, "Greek of the New Testament," 433.

[127] See Porter, "Greek of the New Testament," 433-434.

[128] Malina and Rohrbaugh comment that, "John indeed highlights the interpersonal and textual functions of language. The linguistic dimensions of how Jesus speaks (textual component) and with whom he speaks (interpersonal component) come through in a way not found in the Synoptic narratives." See Malina and Rohrbaugh, *Social-Science Commentary on the Gospel of John*, 6; also see Halliday, *Language as Social Semiotic*, 8-36.

[129] Jesus's own very exact words.

[130] Jesus's own very exact voice.

[131] While the Synoptics and Paul emphasize new structures to replace old ones (i.e., Kingdom of God/Heaven, Church, Body of Christ, those "in Christ," and the like), John and his group seek the implementation of new values, not new structures, in place of old ones.

[132] Such as time and place, typography, format, medium of presentation, and background and history of a text. See Louw, "Reading a Text as Discourse," 18.

[133] Such as punctuation, intonation, pause, speech acts, genre (e.g., epic, lyric, drama, conversation, parable). See Louw, "Reading a Text as Discourse," 18.

[134] Such as word order, embedding, nominalization, levels of language, style, and, in particular, the discrepancy between syntax and semantics. Louw, "Reading a Text as Discourse," 18.

[135] Malina and Rohrbaugh state that, "In the Gospel of John . . . who is involved and how things are said are everything." See Malina and Rohrbaugh, *Social-Science Commentary on the Gospel of John*, 6; also see Louw, "Reading a Text as Discourse," 18.

[136] John's language and literary artistry are informative, cognitive, performative, expressive, and cohesive in nature. See Caird, *The Language and Imagery of the Bible*, 7-36; also see Malina and Rohrbaugh, *Social-Science Commentary on the Gospel of John*, 7; also see Halliday, *Language as Social Semiotic*, 8-36; Barrett, *The Gospel according to St. John*, 70-72.

[137] See Chakkuvarackal, "The Serampore Mission and the Linguistic Renaissance in India," 132.

[138] See Stambaugh and Balch, *The NT in Its Social Environment*, 87-88.

[139] See Fitzmyer, *The Semitic Background of the New Testament*, 3-186.

[140] See Torrey, *The Four Gospels*.

[141] Aune discusses about the nature of the Gospels as a "Nonliterary" Genre. See Aune, *The NT in Its LiteraryEnvironment*, 23-25.

[142] See Guthrie, *NT Introduction*, 337. In the classical period different dialects, such as Attic, Ionic, and Doric, existed side by side. Of these, the Attic became the foremost literary dialect, and it was adopted as the official language of the Macedonian Empire after the conquests of Alexander the Great. Wenham comments that, "Alexander himself ardently desired to propagate Hellenistic culture throughout his domains, and in time Greek became the *lingua franca* of the civilized world." "This 'common' language" Wenham says, "the so-called Koine or Hellenistic Greek, developed somewhat simpler (and sometimes less precise) forms than the present Attic Greek and it incorporated some forms from other dialects." See Wenham, *The Elements of NT Greek*, 17.

[143] Malina and Rohrbaugh comment that, "'Antilanguage' is the language of an 'antisociety,' that is 'a society that is set up within another society as a conscious alternative to it. It is a mode of resistance, resistance which may take the form either of passive symbiosis or of active hostility and even destruction." See Malina and

Rohrbaugh, *Social-Science Commentary on the Gospel of John*, 7; Halliday, *Language as Social Semiotics*, 164-182.

[144] See Petersen, *The Gospel of John and the Sociology of Light*, 23-79.

[145] Porter says, "The New Testament, apart from a few Aramaic and/or Hebrew words and phrases, is written in a form of ancient Greek. This Greek, however, is not the Greek of the classical writers, such as Plato, Thucydides or the tragedians, but is that of the Greek of the Greco-Roman world of the first century." See Porter, "Greek of the New Testament," 426-427. Eusebius quoted Papias as saying that Matthew composed his logia in the Hebrew (Aramaic). See Hiebert, *An Introduction to the NT*, 31; Martin, *NT Foundations*, 281-282.

[146] See Martin, *NT Foundations*, 272.

[147] See White, "Ancient Greek Letters," 85-105; Fitzmyer, *The Semitic Background of the New Testament*, 3-186.

[148] More details about language during NT times: Stambaugh and Balch, *The NT in Its Social Environment*, 87-88.

[149] See Gromacki, *NT Survey*, 23.

[150] Hezser says that, "Jews who lived in Roman Palestine were Roman subjects who reacted to the experience of Roman imperialism in different ways, depending on their socio-economic status, geographical location and religious persuasion." See Hezser, "The Torah Versus Homer," 5.

[151] See Porter, *Linguistic Analysis of the Greek New Testament*, 83.

Bibliography

Abbott, E. A. *Johannine Vocabulary: A Comparison of the Words of the Fourth Gospel with Those of the Three*. London: Adam and Charles Black, 1905.

Abbott, E. A. *Johannine Grammar*. London: Adam and Charles Black, 1906.

Arangadan, C. "Carey's Legacy of Bible Translation." *Carey's Obligation and India's Renaissance*. Eds. J. T. K. Daniel, and R. E. Hedlund. Serampore: Council of Serampore College, 1993: 177-186.

Athithan, A. *Linguistic Structures in Tamil, A Historical Study: The Grammar of Tolkappiyam and the Language of Patinenkilkkanakku, A Comparative Study*. Madurai: Madurai Kamaraj University, 1989.

Aune, D. E. *The New Testament in Its Literary Environment*. Philadelphia: The Westminster Press, 1987.

Banerjee, T. "Growth and Development of Bengali Literature from Serampore." *Carey Day Souvenir*. Serampore: Serampore College, 2001.

Barr, J. *The Semantics of Biblical Language*. Eugene, Oregon: Wipf & Stock, 2004.

Barrett, C. K. *The Gospel according to St. John*. London: SPCK, 1978.

Beasley-Murray, G. R. "Synoptics and John." *Dictionary of Jesus and the Gospels*. Eds. J. B. Green. and S. McKnight. Downers Grove: Inter-Varsity Press, 1992: 792-795.

Bhattacharya, K. *Ravindranath Tagore: Adventure of Ideas and Innovative Practices in Education*. Springer Briefs in Education. Heidelberg/New York: Springer, 2014.

Blomberg, C. L. *A Handbook of New Testament Exegesis*. Grand Rapids: Baker Academic Press, 2010.

Bloomfield, L. *Language*. Delhi: Motilal Banarsidass, 1935/2005.

Blount, B. K. *Cultural Interpretation: Reorienting New Testament Criticism*. Minneapolis: Fortress Press, 1995.

Bodine, W. R. "Linguistics and Biblical Studies." *Anchor Bible Dictionary*. Vol. 4. New York: Doubleday, 1992.

Brant, J. A. *Dialogue and Drama: Elements of Greek Tragedy in the Fourth Gospel*. Peabody: Hendrickson, 2004.

Brown, R. E. *An Introduction to the New Testament*. Bangalore: Theological Publications in India, 2009.

Brown, R. E. *The Community of the Beloved Disciple: The Life, Loves, and Hates of an Individual Church in New Testament Times*. New York: Paulist Press, 1979.

Brown, R. E. *The Gospel according to John*. Vol. 1. Garden City, New York: Doubleday, 1966.

Burney, C. F. *The Poetry of Our Lord*. Eugene, Oregon: Wipf & Stock, 1925.

Buth, R. "*Oun, De, Kai*, and Asyndeton in John's Gospel." *Linguistics and New Testament Interpretation: Essays on Discourse Analysis*. Ed. Black, D. A. Nashville: Broadman Press, 1992: 144-161.

Caird, G. B. *The Language and Imagery of the Bible*. Philadelphia: The Westminster Press, 1980.

Carey, S. P. *William Carey: The Father of Modern Missions*. London: Wakeman Trust, 1923.

Chakkuvarackal, T. J. "The Serampore Mission and the Linguistic Renaissance in India." *Bangalore Theological Forum*. Vol. XXXV. No. 2 (2003): 123-140.

Chakkuvarackal, T. J. "Important Issues in the Translation of the Bible in the Indian Context." *Bangalore Theological Forum*. Vol. XXXIV. No. 1 (2002): 163-175.

Chatterjee, S. K. "William Carey and the Linguistic Renaissance in India." *Carey's Obligation and India's Renaissance*. Eds. J. T. K. Daniel. and R. E. Hedlund. Serampore: Council of Serampore College, 1993: 159-176.

Cotterell, P. and Turner, M. *Linguistics and Biblical Interpretation*. Leicester and Downers Grove: Inter-Varsity Press, 1989.

De, S. K. *History of Bengali Literature in the Nineteenth Century, 1800-1825*. Chizine Publications, 2018.

Delon, M., ed. "Grammar." *Encyclopedia of the Enlightenment*. Vol. 1. London/New York: Routledge, 2001.

Dodd, C. H. *The Interpretation of the Fourth Gospel*. Cambridge: University Press, 1953.

Denning-Bolle, S. *Wisdom in Akkadian Literature: Expression, Instruction, Dialogue.* Leiden: Ex Oriente Lux, 1992.

Fitzmyer, J. A. *The Semitic Background of the New Testament.* Grand Rapids: Eerdmans, 1997.

Gardner-Chloros, P. *Code-Switching.* Cambridge: Cambridge University Press, 2009.

George, K. M. *Modern Indian Literature and Anthology.* Vol. 1. New Delhi: Sahitya Akademi, 1992.

Gibson, A. *Biblical Semantic Logic: A Preliminary Analysis.* The Biblical Seminar 75. London/New York: Sheffield Academic Press, 2001.

Gine, P. C. *'Nomos' in Context: Philo, Galatians and the Bengali Bible.* Delhi: ISPCK, 2001.

Greimas, A. J. and Courtés, J. *Semiotics and Language: An Analytical Dictionary.* Bloomington: Indiana University Press, 1979/1982.

Grelot, P. *The Language of Symbolism: Biblical Theology, Semantics, and Exegesis.* Peabody: Hendrickson Publishers, 2006.

Gromacki, R. G. *New Testament Survey.* Grand Rapids: Baker Book House, 1974.

Gundry, R. H. "The Language Milieu of First-Century Palestine." *Journal of Biblical Literature* 83 (1964): 405-407.

Gupta, R. K. D. "William Carey and Bengali Grammar." *Carey's Obligation and India's Renaissance.* Eds. Daniel, J. T. K., and Hedlund, R. E. Serampore: Council of Serampore College, 1993: 187-192.

Guthrie, D. *New Testament Introduction.* Fourth Revised Edition. Downers Grove: Inter-Varsity Press, 1990.

Halliday, M. A. K. *Language as Social Semiotic: The Social Interpretation of Language and Meaning.* Baltimore: University Park, 1978.

Hezser, C. "The Torah Versus Homer: Jewish and Greco-Roman Education in Late Roman Palestine." *Ancient Education and Early Christianity.* Library of New Testament Studies 533. Eds. Hauge, M. R., and Pitts. London/New York: Bloomsbury T & T Clark, 2016: 5-24.

Hiebert, D. E. *An Introduction to the New Testament.* Three Volume Collection. Waynesboro: Gabriel Publishing, 2003.

Jaffe, A., ed. *Stance: Sociolinguistic Perspective.* Oxford: Oxford University Press, 2009.

Kapoor, K. *Dimensions of Pānini Grammar: The Indian Grammatical System.* D. K. Printworld, 2005.

Kutscher, S. and Werning, D. A., eds. *On Ancient Grammars of Space: Linguistic Research on the Expression of Spatial Relations and Motion in Ancient Languages.* Berlin/ Boston: Walter de Gruyter, 2014.

Lamb, D. A. *Text, Context, and the Johannine Community: A Sociolinguistic Analysis of the Johannine Writings.* New York/London: Bloomsbury T & T Clark, 2014.

Law, V. *The History of Linguistics in Europe: From Plato to 1600*. Cambridge: Cambridge University Press, 2003.

"Linguistics." *Encyclopaedia Britannica*. Vol. 14. Chicago: William Benton, 1963.

Louw, J. P. "Reading a Text as Discourse." *Linguistics and New Testament Interpretation: Essays on Discourse Analysis*. Ed. Black, D. A. Nashville: Broadman Press, 1992: 17-30.

Malina, B. J. and Rohrbaugh, R. L. *Social-Science Commentary on the Gospel of John*. Minneapolis: Fortress Press, 1998.

Mangalwadi, V and R. *The Legacy of William Carey: A Model for the Transformation of a Culture*. Wheaton: Crossway Books, 1993/1999.

Martin, R. P. *New Testament Foundations: A Guide for Christian Studies*. Vol 1: The Four Gospels. Exeter: The Paternoster Press, 1975.

Martyn, J. L. *History and Theology of the Fourth Gospel*. Nashville: Abingdon, 1968.

McKim, D. K. *Westminster Dictionary of Theological Terms*. Louisville/London: Westminster John Knox Press, 1996.

Modrak, D. K. W. *Aristotle's Theory of Language and Meaning*. Cambridge: Cambridge University Press, 2001.

Mukherjee, S. *A Dictionary of Indian Literature*. Vol. 1. Hyderabad: Orient Longman, 1998/1999.

Mukhopadhayay, I. "William Carey's Contributions for the Promotion of Sanskritic Studies." *Carey's Obligation and India's Renaissance*. Eds. Daniel, J. T. K., and Hedlund, R. E. Serampore: Council of Serampore College, 1993: 193-202.

Murshid, G. *Kalantare Bangla Gadya*. Calcutta: Ananda Publishers, 1992.

Nicklin, T. *Book Review: Abbott's Johannine Vocabulary*. The Classical Review. Vol. 20/3 (1906): 172-175.

Ong, H. T. *The Multilingual Jesus and the Sociolinguistic World of the New Testament*. Leiden/Boston: Brill, 2016.

Petersen, N. R. *The Gospel of John and the Sociology of Light: Language and Characterization in the Fourth Gospel*. Eugene, Oregon: Wipf & Stock, 1993.

Porter, S. E. *Linguistic Analysis of the Greek New Testament: Studies in Tools, Methods, and Practice*. Grand Rapids: Baker Academic Press, 2015.

Porter, S. E. "Greek of the New Testament." *Dictionary of New Testament Background*. Eds. Evans, C. A., and Porter, S. E. Downers Grove: Inter-Varsity Press, 2000: 426-435.

Ray, N. R. "William Carey—A Linguist with a Difference." *Carey's Obligation and India's Renaissance*. Eds. Daniel, J. T. K., and Hedlund, R. E. Serampore: Council of Serampore College, 1993: 155-158.

Robertson, R. *John: The Jewish Gospel*. Blommington: Thomas Nelson & Zondervan, 2017.

Sen, A. K. "Bengali Language, Literature and William Carey." *Carey Day Souvenir*. Serampore: Serampore College, 2002.

Stambaugh, J. E. and Balch, D. L. *The New Testament in Its Social Environment*. Philadelphia: The Westminster Press, 1986.

Stanton, G. *The Gospels and Jesus*. Oxford Bible Series. Second Edition. Oxford: Oxford University Press, 2002.

Stibbe, M. W. G. *John's Gospel*. New Testament Readings. London/New York: Routledge, 1994.

Thiselton, A. C. *New Horizons in Hermeneutics: The Theory and Practice of Transforming Biblical Reading*. Grand Rapids: Zondervan Publishing House, 1992.

Thomas, M. C. "Orientalism," published in https://www.britannica.com/science/Orientalism-cultural-field-of-study. Accessed on 14th October 2018.

Thomaskutty, J. *Dialogue in the Book of Signs: A Polyvalent Analysis of John 1:19-12:50*. Biblical Interpretation Series 136. Leiden/Boston: E. J. Brill, 2015.

Thompson, M. M. "John, Gospel of." *Dictionary of Jesus and the Gospels*. Eds. Green, J. B., and McKnight, S. Downers Grove: Inter-Varsity Press, 1992: 368-383.

Torrey, C. C. *The Four Gospels: A New Translation*. New York: Harper, 1933.

Turner, N. *A Grammar of New Testament Greek*. Vol. 3: Syntax; Vol. 4: Style. Edinburgh: T & T Clark, 1963-1976.

Van Aarde, A. G. "Narrative Criticism." *Focusing on the Message: New Testament Hermeneutics, Exegesis, and Methods*. Pretoria: Protea, 2009: 381-418.

Van der Watt, J. G. "Ethics through the Power of Language: Some Explorations in the Gospel according to John." *Moral Language in the New Testament*. Eds. Zimmermann, R., and Van der Watt, J. G. Vol. 2. Tübingen: Mohr Siebeck, 2010: 139-167.

Van der Watt, J. G. "Repetition and Functionality in the Gospel according to John." *Repetitions and Variations in the Fourth Gospel: Style, Text, Interpretation*. Eds. Van Belle, G., Labahn, M., and Maritz, P. Leuven: Uitgeverij Peeters, 2009: 87-108.

Van Kooten, G. H. *The Creation of Heaven and Earth: Re-Interpretations of Genesis 1 in the Context of Judaism, Ancient Philosophy, Christianity, and Modern Physics*. Leiden/Boston: Brill, 2005.

Verghese, B. K. *Let There be India! Impact of the Bible on Nation Building*. Chennai: WOC Publishing/Mumbai: Media Concerns, 2014.

Wenham, J. W. *The Elements of New Testament Greek*. Cambridge: University Press, 1965.

White, J. L. "Ancient Greek Letters." *Greco-Roman Literature and the New Testament*. Ed. Aune, D. E. Atlanta: Scholars Press, 1988: 85-105.

Wise, M. O. "Languages of Palestine." *Dictionary of Jesus and the Gospels*. Eds. Green, J. B., and McKnight, S. Downers Grove: Inter-Varsity Press, 1992: 434-444.

6

Educational Principles of the Serampore Mission and its Implications for Contemporary Education

Annie George

Introduction

Hailing from humble backgrounds, the Serampore Trio, William Carey (1761-1834), Joshua Marshman (1768-1837), and William Ward (1769-1823) made exceptional contributions to Indian missions in the 19th century. Observing the long years of partnership of Hannah Marshman (1767-1847), the mother of the Serampore Mission,[1] it is unfair not to mention her in this introduction. They realized the advantages of synergy among themselves and with natives in their mission endeavors which might be one of the reasons for their monumental impact to the missions in India. Together they labored for the emancipation of the people and inspired many social reforms based on Christian values and ideals. Their holistic approach to mission prompted them to untiringly address the spiritual and social needs which opened the eyes of the colonial rulers, the Bengali intelligentsia, and common people to various reforms. The Trio/Quartet, before they came to India, as British Missionary Society (BMS) missionaries, had experience in teaching.[2] Education became a missionary tool for the Trio/Quartet. Their sacrificial service to educate the common people in Bengali naturally led to the development of the Bengali language and publications of materials in the vernaculars.[3] This paper attempts to derive the educational principles of these missionary educators and formulate various implications for today.

Educational Principles of the Serampore Trio/Quartet

The efforts of the Serampore Mission to open the doors of education to everyone without discrimination reveal their three educational principles: institutional development, vernacular instruction, and publications. Establishment of educational institutions and promotion of vernacular languages through various publications opened the world of literature to the common people. Schools became the places where people learned to read and write in their own languages, and publications became textbooks to use in the schools. The following pages will discuss these aspects in detail.

Institutional Development

This section deals with the contributions of Carey and the Marshmans in establishing educational institutions. Their contributions include schools for children and higher education: a college with liberal arts and theology faculties and teacher training institution known as Normal Schools.

William Carey

Even before the formation of the Mission, Carey, the father of the Serampore Mission,[4] had a strong educational ambition. Soon after founding the Baptist Missionary Society in Britain in 1792, he along with John Thomas reached India in 1793. Carey focused on preaching, teaching and translating the Scripture. But education and establishment of educational institutions had a prominent place in his missionary endeavor.[5] This is evident in the establishment of a boarding school soon after his arrival in India. His instruction to his sons, William Carey Jr. and Jabez further reveals his commitment to the establishment of schools. In 1811, he wrote to Carey Jr.: "One of the first things to be done there (Catwa) will be to open a charity school."[6] His instruction to Jabez in 1814 echoed similar concern about the need of establishing schools in Ambovana.[7]

There were first phases of elementary education in Bengal began with Carey's first school for poor native boys in Madnabati in 1794.[8] In the school, children learned scripture, to read and write, and to keep accounts. Even during those times, he had plans to work with Thomas to establish two colleges and each college was to admit twelve lads—six Mussulmans and six Hindoos. The plan was to teach Sanskrit, Bengali, and Persian, the Bible, philosophy and geography under the leadership of a pundit.[9] Even though Carey's first school was unsuccessful, he continued to derive plans to expand educational activities. "Plan for the Education of the Children of Converted Natives" written in 1802 explained his vision.[10] Carey's goal was to promote curiosity and inquisitiveness among Bengalis even though he exhibited a strong missionary consideration. So, he hoped to include subjects like vernacular language, history, geography, moral fables, natural history which were not part of Pathsalas.[11]

Joshua and Hannah Marshman

The second phase of elementary education in Bengal began when Carey, Joshua and Hannah Marshman, and Ward[12] together moved to Serampore in January 1800 and founded the Serampore Mission. The contributions of Joshua and Hannah Marshman, as accomplished and enthusiastic teachers, gave momentum to native education. Soon after their arrival in Serampore, Joshua and Hannah Marshman began fee-based boarding schools for European and Anglo-Indian girls. Following the plan depicted in his memorable pamphlet "Hints Relative to Native Schools, together with an Outline of an Institution for their Extension and Management," 45 schools were established in a 20 mile circumference of Serampore within two years of its publication. Beginning with the first school in Cutwa in 1800, they established 111 schools in and around Serampore by the year 1811. Besides, as founding members of Calcutta School Society, the Trio/Quartet hoped to upgrade education in the Pathsalas.

Joshua and Hannah Marshman were the architects of modern and organized female education even though there were many others who had established schools for girls beginning with Mrs. Hedges in 1760.[13] The Mission began schools for girls not only in and around Serampore but also in several districts of Bengal. Girls from poor families and low castes attended the schools. Upper caste families had many reasons for not sending their girls to these missionary schools: superstitious beliefs (such as "educated women become widows soon after their marriage"), Christian instruction in schools, and attitudes towards the missionaries. Even though the Marshmans were not the first to establish schools for girls, they were the pioneers in bringing awareness about the need for girls' education. Although many of these schools discontinued later, they contributed greatly to the cause of educating women. Later historians reported that Marshman found joy to witness the diligence and improvement in a child[14] which shows the passion of the teacher among the Trio/Quartet.

Serampore College and Other Normal Schools

Establishing Serampore College in 1818 was another milestone of the Serampore Mission. It was not the first college in India, but it was unique as it had a theological faculty and a separate faculty for arts. The Trio/Quartet hoped to equip Christian students as potential missionaries and provided arts and science education to non-Christians who have excelled in elementary education. Carey's vision to educate Christians and non-Christians, men and women, in the college is clear in his statement in the Statutes and Regulations of the College: "no caste, color, country shall bar any man (woman) from admission into Serampore College."[15] The theological faculty in Serampore College contributed to train nationals in various missionary activities. The Trio/Quartet saw the great need to train natives to equip them in evangelistic, pastoral, educational and literary activities. They knew that for Christianity to be deep rooted in India, natives must lead the churches.[16] Thus they attempted to train and raise up strong and active Indians yet at the same time did not want Indians to adopt Western names, clothes, and manners.

Serampore College had a holistic curriculum with linguistics, science, religion and ethics as subjects. It brought together western science and eastern literature. While preparing the curriculum of Serampore schools and College, the Trio/Quartet gave equal importance to the secular curriculum of the East India Company, moral educational system of the Christian missionaries, and the indigenous educational system. Amrita Mondal identifies the uniqueness of the educational approach of the Serampore Mission: unlike the other Christian Missions, the Serampore Mission incorporated indigenous knowledge both rational as well as scientific knowledge into their schools and college curricula, especially while promoting science education. However, they did not give up their missionary zeal while making such negotiation with the native people.[17]

The missionaries constantly requested their missionary society to send trained teachers to India. This led to establish their own means to train teachers. The Trio/Quartet in their attempts to enhance the quality of teaching began Normal Schools in 1818. This was to provide trained teachers for village primary schools.[18] Normal school was a French concept. In Serampore the objectives of these schools were as follows: to teach the norms of pedagogy and curriculum, to train teachers for missionary and native schools. Later Normal Schools were established in different parts of Bengal and in other parts of British India..

Transformative Education

The Mission's educational endeavor did not lead to many conversions but there emerged citizens who questioned traditional customs and rejected dehumanizing patterns in the society. They educated common people with passion when the indigenous schools were inadequate, and the government did not show any concern for education. Their endeavor equipped common people not only to read but also to be inquisitive learners and some of them became teachers in schools. These pioneers inspired public opinion in favor of education. The fruits of education "were in innumerable cases a fresh love for truth, justice and compassion, which has effectively changed Indian society for the better; less than the full and conscious acceptance of Jesus Christ, but it could not simply be dismissed as a humanitarian 'cul-de-sac.'"[19] Thus the educational efforts of the Mission were surely holistic and transformative in nature. It was definitely counter-cultural but with the vernacular medium of instruction and with incorporation of indigenous knowledge the education was contextual.

The educational reforms of the Mission brought hostile reactions from Baptist Missionary Society (BMS). When BMS limited missionary activities only to proselytization through effective preaching,[20] the farsighted Trio invested their resources in the field of education in the Indian soil even at the cost of BMS severing all financial assistance with the Mission upon their claim that the latter has deviated from their original missionary purpose.

Vernacular Instruction

The insistence on vernacular education was the key characteristic of the Serampore Mission.[21] Vernacular instruction enabled the missionaries to provide an opportunity for the common people to expand their mind and language which was traditionally considered as the privilege of the elites. It is to be remembered that establishment of elementary educational institutions in vernacular languages was an important step towards education of women.[22]

The two patterns in vernacular education of the mission were as follows:[23] native schools focusing on the converts, and Christian community centered (Moravian),[24] and missionary endeavor education (Lancasterian).[25] In the first pattern, only missionaries and converts were teachers, but in the second pattern non-Christians became teachers and they sent their children to learn in these schools. The second pattern did not have the predominance of Christian teaching but had a humanitarian concern. The medium of instruction in Serampore College was Bengali and Hindi. Students also learned Sanskrit, Persian and Arabic. The curriculum included eastern literature and western science. Science text books were translated into Bengali. In 1820 there was a demand for English Education and in 1829 an English tutor was appointed in the college.[26]

Marshman saw that efficient instruction of people in any nation can be rendered only in their own language, if not it is "completely fallacious."[27] Carey's reasons for vernacular instruction were as follows:[28] first, vernacular teaching can enable teachers to communicate with ease and efficiency; and second, he compared the knowledge of Sanskrit in Bengal to that of Greek in Europe at the time of Reformation. Knowledge of Greek can uplift their mind of those in England who have leisure and fortune. But it is not reasonable to impart Greek in Sunday schools or charity schools in the Kingdom. Thus, Carey and Marshman argued that it will be impracticable to provide education in English or Sanskrit in Bengal. Besides, they saw that English education would not only have occasional success but also be expensive.

Translation activities and publications of the Trio/Quartet in vernacular languages have undoubtedly led to the development of the languages. Beginning with Carey's voyage to India, he became diligent in learning vernacular languages and translation to vernacular languages. Carey undertook the massive task to develop Bengali which had no printed material and few written literature.[29] Carey began his Bengali translation of the Bible in 1795. He translated the Bible or portions of it into 35 different languages. No one has translated the Bible into as many different languages as Carey even though many continue to labor to translate the Bible into various languages. Because of the zeal he displayed in the translation and his achievements in this area, Timothy George, the European Protestant Reformation historian, compared Carey with Jerome, Wycliffe, Luther, Tyndale and Erasmus.[30]

Carey's commitment to vernacular languages gave him many accolades. Soon after Carey's arrival in Serampore in January 1800, he became a teacher of the Bengali language in the College of Fort William. Later he was appointed to teach Sanskrit and Marathi languages. His efficiency in Bengali language led him to become the Government translator in the language in 1823.[31] However, Marshman devoted his time to study the Chinese language and to translate the Bible and other literature into the Chinese language.

Publications

For the Mission, publication of the Scripture was a top priority. When he was in Madnabati, Carey purchased a press which shows his interest in publications even before the formation of the Serampore Mission. Carey, Marshman and Ward were involved in publications even though Ward was in-charge of the Serampore Press. Felix Carey assisted Ward, the expert printer in printing Bible, tracts and other literature. It is noted that the Serampore Mission Press "stabilized scattered exercises in printing and publishing"[32] in India. The Serampore press brought forth 47 translations of the Bible in various languages between 1800 and 1834. John Ellerton's Bengali treatise, *Gooro Shisya* and Carey's Bengali Bible published from the Serampore Mission Press were widely used in the schools run by the missionaries.[33] The Mission first published translations of the Bible in different languages. Later on, they published dictionaries and English translations of many Sanskrit and Persian languages masterpieces. Textbooks and journals published in the press enable students to be inquisitive and curious learners.[34]

Carey excelled in various dimensions as a reformer: social, economic, ecological, agricultural and linguistic. Besides focusing on translation of the Bible, he also translated classic Hindu texts from Sanskrit.[35] He wrote text books to educate people in agriculture and history. He published dictionaries and grammar books for Bengali and other Indian languages.[36] Besides he edited Grammar and a Dictionary in the "Bootan" (Bhutan) language. Later Carey edited and published W. Roxburgh's *Flora Indica* in 1820 and republished it in 1832.

Marshman's fourteen years of vigorous work led to the publication of the first Chinese Bible, a copy of which was presented to the British and Foreign Bible Society at their annual meeting in May 1823.[37] Later he published the English translation of the Works of Confucius and a Key to the Chinese Language. His pamphlet "Hints relative to native schools, together with an Outline of an Institution for their Extension and Management" gave an impetus to begin vernacular schools in and around Serampore. He also worked behind the publications of the first prospectus of the Serampore College, *A College for the Instruction of Asiatic Christian and other Youths in Eastern Literature and European Sciences.*

Several publications from Serampore press inspired public discussion. More publications were in English than in Bengali. Credit for many of these publications chiefly goes to Dr. Marshman: *Digdarshan* or *Magazine for Indian Youth* in 1818, *Samachar Darpan* or *Mirror of News* in 1818, *Friends of India* in 1821, and *Quarterly Friend of India* in 1822. The purpose of *Digdarshan* was "to stimulate a spirit of enquiry and diffuse information."[38] It had many scientific and historical essays and accounts on various subjects in the vernacular language. It was translated to Hindi and Dev-Nagree to use in schools outside of Bengal.[39] The Calcutta School Book Society requested to publish *Digdarshan* in English. Subsequently the society used it as a text book for schools. *Samachar Darpan* discussed geographical and historical topics, political and administrative news, educational news, and contemporary public issues. During the times prior to the abolition of *Sati*, it published articles defending the abolition of it. The Trio/Quartet published the second religious monthly in Bengali, in May 1822. It was called *Increase of the Kingdom of Christ*.[40] The newspapers of the Serampore Press not only drew the attention of the government to the contemporary social problems but also played a remarkable role in the advancement of Bengali prose literature.[41]

Ward set the typefaces for the Bengali Bible by his own hand and printed the first sheet of the Bengali Bible in 1800. He also made typefaces for different scripts. He was not only a printer but also, he penned books. In 1810, he published the first edition of his work on the "History, Literature, and Mythology of the Hindoos, including a minute description of their manners and customs, and Translation from their principal works."[42] It was a remarkable piece of literature with accurate and complete information about the topic. After his visit to England he resumed his duties in the press in 1821. But he focused more on equipping youths in the college for missionary activities. He published another book *Reflections on the Word of God for Every Day in the Year, to be used in Family Devotions*. When he died in 1823, he had begun the work, *A History of Hindu Philosophy and A Treatise on the Character of a Christian Missionary*.[43] Meanwhile, Serampore College delivered many scientific lectures which lead to public discussions. The Trio/Quartet published several scientific books in the vernacular language. In the publication of scientific books, Felix Carey took an important role. He also wrote many valuable scientific works in Bengali and translated many science books. He translated the first anatomy book in Bengali, *Vidya-Harabali*, a two volumes publication.[44]

John Clark Marshman's work was also significant. He joined the Serampore Mission in 1815. He became the staff of Serampore College in

1821 and later took the charge of the Serampore college along with John Mack from 1837-1855.[45] He was involved in education and publications. He assisted his father to launch *Digdarshan* and *Samachar Darpan* and *Friend of India*. After the death of Ward in 1823, he took the responsibility of the Serampore Press. He became a "versatile and voluminous writer for the educated lay people"[46] who supported the Serampore College with his literary earnings till 1855. He is remembered as a leading scholar in Indian history and philology. His writings became textbooks for Bengali schools. Marshman's Guide to the Civil Law of the Presidency of Fort William (1848) is one of his reputed works.

Implications for Education

India has drastically changed since the 19th century. The last decades of the 20th century witnessed rapid social changes due to technology and digital media. On one hand, globalization of education and employment led to prefer English education in an international standard to vernacular education. On the other hand, many social evils continue to rob Indians from educational opportunities. Looking at the educational principles of the Serampore Mission, what are the implications for education in the contemporary Indian context?

Work to Promote Literacy

The educational efforts of the Trio/Quartet to promote literacy in Bengal are highly appreciated. Government and various NGOs continue to labor towards literacy in India. But illiteracy is still a reality in the country. The census of 2011 demonstrates that there is a great improvement in the literacy rate in India compared to 2001: literacy rate has increased by 8.15%. According to the census of 2011, overall literacy rate is 72.99%; male literacy is 80.99%; and female literacy is 64.64%.[47] Bihar and Telangana are the least literate states with 63.82% and 66.50% respectively. Lowest female literacy is in Rajasthan (52.66%) and lowest male literacy is in Bihar (73.39%).[48] In this context, the churches in India are expected to strive hard for promoting literacy by establishing formal educational institutions and non-formal educational systems.

Hannah Marhsman's effort to promote education to women in Bengal is highly valued. However, the literacy rate of women is still a matter of concern. They are still behind men in literacy rate. Educational institutions can provide various creative ways to continue promote education among women.

Use of Digital Media in Education

This paper has discussed the role of the Trio/Quartet to bring publications to the hands of the common people. Not only the Bible in various languages but also tracts, pamphlets, educational and scientific resources reached the common people. This attempt led to generate inquisitiveness and discussions on various social issues in Bengal.

Today India has embraced digital revolution. During the last 20 years, communication technologies have brought about significant changes in the development of the Indian society through information dissemination.[49] Indians have access to instant information for their personal and professional lives. Simultaneously mobiles and hand-held devices are available at an affordable cost. Smartphone holders in India will be 250 million in the next five years and 200 million will have access to Internet.[50] In different states of our subcontinent, use of audio/visual tools and Smart Classes in schools are not a novelty anymore. In recent years, social media has emerged as a tool to enhance e-learning. It brings to learners not only engaging, relevant, and culturally diverse learning experiences but also current concerns and issues. Audio-visual files on social media can be viewed at one's own convenience on small or large screen devices. Technology enhanced learning experiences enable learners to engage in learning more than in typical classroom setups. It can bring information to the hands of common people even in remote areas.

In such a context, the use of digital technology in education is no more a choice rather a requirement. Educational institutions can incorporate digital media in education to bring information to an audience who otherwise have no access to receive learning. Information can be disseminated through audio/visual with text can be useful for both illiterates and literates. A word of caution is to use it with responsibility and discernment and instruct others to do so.

Accumulation of Resources

The Trio/Quartet through their translations, writings, and publications created a pool of resources in various languages which hardly had any written or print resources. Their legacy continues to influence our nation as we see a proliferation of print and digital resources in recent years. Various organizations continue to labor for the cause of translation of the Bible. Besides, in the digital era, the internet brings to us digital Bibles. For example, *You Version* now includes a number of Indian languages in their application. Dramatized audio and video Bible stories are available on YouTube. This can be a tool to be used for children and illiterates.

Developing a repository of resources, print and digital materials in vernacular languages will be an asset for our community. Educational institutions can gather resources not only for their students but also for their communities. Many have undertaken translations of devotional books to many Indian languages. But still there is a scarcity of theological books in vernacular languages. So, publications of books in the vernacular languages need to be a serious concern of theological institutions and educators.

Mass Communication

The newspapers and magazines published by the Mission were their attempt for mass communication. Many organizations continue this legacy to bring print media to the masses through newspapers and magazines. Recently eBooks, digital newspapers, and magazines have furthered the scope of mass communication. Churches and theological institutions can collaborate with other agencies to explore how pertinent resources in the hands of the common people both literates and illiterates through print and digital media.

Equip the Laity

The Trio/Quartet realized the role of Indians in mission work. They willingly educated Indians for this purpose by providing not only elementary education but also higher education, teacher's training, and theological education. They appointed educated local people as teachers in many of the educational institutions. Equipping lay people towards involvement in mission and humanitarian tasks has been a cardinal principle of the Protestant churches. Indian churches have literate and illiterate lay people, and their participation in ministry is vital considering the vastness of our land. For the literate laity, distribution of relevant vernacular materials in print at a low cost or free of cost is a viable option. Churches can employ oral teaching, repetition, discussion, pictures, and music to teach the vast illiterate population. Audio and/or video lessons based on Bible stories, missionary stories, history of Christianity, and practical issues in the vernacular are the need of the hour to equip laity. Creative use of digital media will further help to equip the literate and illiterate laity in the Indian churches.

Theological Education

The Senate of Serampore College continues the legacy of theological education of the Mission. Colleges and seminaries from various Christian denominations and states in India and beyond seek affiliation with the Senate of Serampore College for theological education. Just like the Trio/Quartet, the Senate continues in the commitment to include vernacular instruction in selected seminaries. Distance learning programmes promote theological education to non-residential students across India. However, with the availability of digital media, colleges and seminaries need to exploit the online classes, video lessons, and smart classrooms in theological education.

Women have opportunities for theological education in all seminaries under the Senate but opportunity for their participation in ministry is still a matter of concern. Churches and institutions still uphold a patriarchal mode of operation and interpretation of the Bible. Many women have come to believe that their role is to be passive listeners in churches. These mindsets along with churches following the traditional understanding of the role of women hinder even many theologically trained women from participating in various church related activities. This can hinder women from seeking theological education and ministry as their vocation. Theological institutions and educators have a role to unveil this issue for public discussion.

Holistic Mission

The Serampore Mission's activities gave importance to evangelism and development of people and society. Along with impacting our nation with social involvement, we need to explore the opportunity for evangelism. The needs of our country are great and never ending, but the great commission cannot be ignored. My church tradition, Pentecostalism has leaned toward the spiritual dimension and has ignored the social concern. Other church traditions have emphasized the social concern with less focus on the spiritual dimension. The understanding that the church is a people of God among the peoples of the world wakens the church to her social responsibility.[51] By involving in the holistic ministry we can overcome artificial divisions between social action and evangelism, between ministering to individuals and seeking social justice. Providing educational opportunities, promotion of vernacular languages through education and publications were actions through which the mission addressed social concern. This legacy of holistic mission of the Trio/Quartet remains a challenge to the Indian churches.

Conclusion

The Serampore Trio/Quartet and their associates were pioneers in establishing educational institutions, vernacular education and publications. Establishment of educational institutions in the vernacular languages opened doors of education to many people. Publications in vernacular languages stimulated a spirit of enquiry among common people and they became aware of the need for social reforms. Many of the publications became textbooks in schools. So before asking the question of which was Carey's primary missionary methods, we need to look at how preaching, teaching and translation of scared and scientific books had a cumulative effect not only transmitting the knowledge but also for the transformation of Bengal. Their extensive works laid foundations for many others to carry on these activities. As we look forward to the future, the realities in India with 22 major languages, written in 13 different scripts, with over 720 dialects continue to challenge educators in their efforts to provide meaningful learning experiences to everyone in vernacular languages. It is not only our privilege to discuss the implications of the Mission's missionary activities but also our responsibility to derive action plans for holistic mission in our local contexts and to work together with others with a vision for the wider Indian context.

Endnotes

[1] A. Christopher Smith, "The Protege of Erasmus and Luther in Heroic Serampore, 1812-1855," *Indian Journal of Theology* 37/1 (1995): 31.

[2] G. E. Smith, "Patterns of Missionary Education: The Baptist India Mission 1794-1824," *The Baptist Quarterly* 22/6 (1968): 294, https://biblicalstudies.org.uk/pdf/bq/20-7_293.pdf, accessed on 1st August 2018, 294.

[3] "History of Serampore Mission," 47, http://shodhganga.inflibnet.ac.in/jspui/bitstream/10603/156444/12/12_chapter%208.pdf, accessed September 30, 2018.

[4] Smith, "The Protege of Erasmus and Luther in Heroic Serampore," 24.

[5] "History of Serampore Mission," 46.

[6] Smith, "Patterns of Missionary Education," 294.

[7] "History of Serampore Mission," 46.

[8] Smith, "Patterns of Missionary Education, 294. This was not the first of this kind. The European Indigo planters, George Uday and others had already began elementary

schools for natives. Also there were Indigenous institutions such as Pathsalas, Tols and Madrassas in medieval times in Bengal.

[9] George Smith, *The Life of William Carey, Shoemaker and Missionary*, Ebook, 2009, https://www.gutenberg.org/files/2056/2056-h/2056-h.htm, accessed on 30th November 2018.

[10] Priyanka Sen, "'New Learning' and Missionary Fashioning of Pedagogy at Serampore in the Early Nineteenth Century," *The Criterion: International Journal of English*, http://www.the-criterion.com/new-learning-and-missionary-fashioning-of-pedagogy-at-serampore-in-the-early-nineteenth-century/, accessed on 10th September 2018.

[11] "History of Serampore Mission," 48.

[12] Carey along with his family moved from Madnabati to Serampore when the Marshmans and Ward came to India as BMS missionaries in 1800.

[13] Firoj High Sarwar, "Christian Missionaries and Female Education in Bengal during East India Company's Rule: A Discourse between Christianized Colonial Domination versus Women Emancipation," *IOSR Journal Of Humanities And Social Science* 4/1 (Nov. - Dec. 2012): 39, http://iosrjournals.org/iosr-jhss/papers/Vol4-issue1/E0413747.pdf, accessed on 20th October 2018.

[14] "The Serampore Mission as Educationists 1894-1829," https://biblicalstudies.org.uk/pdf/bq/22-6_320.pdf, 325.

[15] "Serampore Mission's Attempt to Introduce Vernacular Higher Education," http://shodhganga.inflibnet.ac.in/jspui/bitstream/10603/156444/20/20_chapter%2016.pdf, 150.

[16] Joe L Coker, "Developing a Theory of Mission in Serampore: The Increased Emphasis upon Education as a 'Means for the Conversion of the Heathens,'" *Mission Studies* 17/1 (2001): 46.

[17] Amrita Mondal, "Educational Intervention and Negotiation: A Case Study of Serampore Mission and New Education," http://www.academia.edu/8025055/Educational_Intervention_and_Negotiation_A_Case_Study_of_Serampore_Mission_and_New_Education, 86.

[18] Arindam Bhattacharyya, "William Carey: The Initiator of Teacher: Education in India," In Subhro Sekhar Sircar, and Sanjoy Mukherjee, eds., *William Carey: The Multifaceted Genius*. Serampore College Bicentenary Special 1818-2018 (Serampore: The Council of Serampore College, 2018), 115-116.

[19] Cul-de-sac means something of a limiting factor. The idea here is that education was not just limited to a humanitarian task. "The Serampore Mission as Educationists 1894-1829," 325.

[20] Sen, "New Learning' and Missionary Fashioning of Pedagogy at Serampore in the Early Nineteenth Century."

[21] According to G. E. Smith vernacular instruction of the Mission was because of the Moravian influence on Carey. Smith, "Patterns of Missionary Education," 306

[22] Firoj High Sarwar, "Christian Missionaries, 39.

[23] Smith, "Patterns of Missionary Education," 308. Lancasterian follows the thoughts of Zinzendorf and later Pestalozzi. They reasoned that all true learning derives from the God of truth and in Him all true knowledge finds unity. Then in one sense all education is religious. But the difficulty is that schools may not be able to express the unity through teaching.

[24] Smith presents many evidences to show that the Serampore mission is indebted to Moravians in the use of the Bible hymns in schools and the pattern of community living in Serampore, living "in one family, in one house" eating at a common table, with no private property. Everything was considered as their common stock, their weekly meetings to settle disagreements, and their love feasts. Smith, "Patterns of Missionary Education, 298.

[25] In the later years, schools followed the Lancasterian pattern in its organization and curriculum, Smith, "Patterns of Missionary Education," 299-306.

[26] "Serampore Mission's Attempt to Introduce Vernacular Higher Education," 147.

[27] Smith, "Patterns of Missionary Education," 301-302

[28] Smith, "Patterns of Missionary Education," 307.

[29] Smith, "Patterns of Missionary Education," 306.

[30] A. Christopher Smith, "The Protege of Erasmus and Luther In Heroic Serampore, 1812-1855," *Indian Journal of Theology* 37/1 (1995): 20.

[31] "History of Serampore Mission," 52

[32] Rita Kothari, *Translating India: The Cultural Policies of English* (London: Routledge, 2014), 59. Jesuit missionaries were the first to publish. They printed the Gospels in 1550s.

[33] "History of Serampore Mission," 47.

[34] "Serampore Mission's Attempt to Introduce Vernacular Higher Education," 149.

[35] Timothy George, "Let it Go: Lessons from the Life of William Carey," *Expect Great Things, Attempt Great Things: William Carey, Adoniram Judson Missionary Pioneer*, eds. Alle Yeh and Chris Chun, (Eugene: Wipf and Stock, 2013), 4.

[36] "History of Serampore Mission," 51.

[37] "History of Serampore Mission," 54.

[38] "Magazines and Journals from Serampore Mission and Their other Important Activities," http://shodhganga.inflibnet.ac.in/jspui/bitstream/10603/156444/20/20_chapter%2016.pdf, 165.

[39] Mondal, "Educational Intervention and Negotiation," 81.

[40] "Magazines and Journals from Serampore Mission and Their other Important Activities," 166.

[41] "Condition of Education in Pre-Colonial and Colonial: Bengal-An Overview," https://www.google.co.in/url?sa=t&source=web&rct=j&url=http://shodhganga.inflibnet.ac.in/jspui/bitstream/10603/137158/6/06_chapter_01.f &ved=2ahUKEwiz87bzgZzeAhVIqI8KHSGLA7IQFjAAegQIAxAB&usg= AOvVaw1t5eERW2nvfpEVfO5reYzl, accessed on 10th September 2018, 3.

[42] A Christopher Smith, "The Edinburgh Connection: Between the Serampore Mission and Western Missiology," *Missiology: An International Review* 18/2 (April 1990), 187.

[43] A Christopher Smith, "The Edinburgh Connection," 187.

[44] Mondal, "Educational intervention and Negotiation," 84.

[45] "History of Serampore Mission," 59.

[46] Smith, "The Protege of Erasmus and Luther in Heroic Serampore," 31.

[47] Sunanda Gosh and Radha Mohan, *Education in Emerging Indian Society: The Challenges and Issues* (New Delhi: PHI Learning Pvt. Limited, 2016), 136.

[48] Mamta Chandrashekhar, *Political and Social Change and Women in India* (Hamburg: Anchor Academic Publishing, 2016), 24.

[49] Himakshi Goswami, "Opportunities and Challenges of Digital India Programme," *International Educational and Research Journal* 2/11 (2016): 1.

[50] Sumer Sharma, "How India is inching closer to becoming digitally literate," 24th June 2016, https://yourstory.com/2016/06/national-digital-literacy-mission/, accessed on 11th July 2017.

[51] M. M. Thomas "The Ecumenical Movement and Christian Social Thought in India," https://biblicalstudies.org.uk/pdf/ijt/10-2_064.pdf, accessed on 24th December 2018.

Bibliography

Bhattacharyya, A. "William Carey: The Initiator of Teacher: Education in India." *William Carey: The Multifaceted Genius.* Serampore College Bicentenary Special 1818-2018. Eds. Subhro Sekhar Sircar and Sanjoy Mukherjee. Serampore: The Council of Serampore College, 2018: 115-116.

Chandrashekhar, M. *Political and Social Change and Women in India.* Hamburg: Anchor Academic Publishing, 2016.

Coker, J. "Developing a Theory of Mission in Serampore: The Increased Emphasis upon Education as a 'Means for the Conversion of the Heathens.'" *Mission Studies 17/1* (2001): 42-60.

"Condition of Education in Pre-Colonial and Colonial Bengal—An Overview," 9-47, https://www.google.co.in/url?sa=t&source=web&rct=j&url=http://shodhganga.inflibnet.ac.in/jspui/bitstream/10603/137158/6/06_chapter_01.pdf. Accessed on 10th September 2018.

George, T. "Let it Go: Lessons from the Life of William Carey." *Expect Great Things, Attempt Great Things: William Carey, Adoniram Judson Missionary Pioneer*. Eds. Alle Yeh and Chris Chun. Eugene, OR: Wipf and Stock, 2013: 3-14.

Gosh, S., and Mohan, Radha. *Education in Emerging Indian Society: The Challenges and Issues*. New Delhi: PHI Learning Pvt. Limited, 2016.

Goswami, H. "Opportunities and Challenges of Digital India Programme." *International Educational and Research Journal* 2/11 (2016).

"History of Serampore Mission," 46-63, http://shodhganga.inflibnet.ac.in/jspui/bitstream/10603/156444/12/12_chapter%208.pdf. Accessed on 30th September 2018.

Ingleby, J. C. *Missionaries, Education and India: Issues in Protestant Missionary Education in the Long Nineteenth Century*. Delhi: ISPCK, 2000.

Kothari, R. *Translating India: The Cultural Policies of English*. London: Routledge, 2014.

Lalhmangaiha, A. *Holistic Mission and The Serampore Trio*. Delhi: ISPCK, 2010.

Mondal, A. "Educational Intervention and Negotiation: A Case Study of Serampore Mission and New Education," 75-89, http://www.academia.edu/8025055/Educational_Intervention_and_Negotiation_A_Case_Study_of_Serampore_Mission_and_New_Education. Accessed on 30th September 2018.

Sarwar, F. H. "Christian Missionaries and Female Education in Bengal during East India Company's Rule: A Discourse between Christianised Colonial Domination versus Women Emancipation." *IOSR Journal of Humanities and Social Science* 4/1 (Nov. - Dec. 2012): 37-47. http://iosrjournals.org/iosr-jhss/papers/Vol4-issue1/E0413747.pdf. Accessed on 20th October 2018.

Sen, P. "'New Learning' and Missionary Fashioning of Pedagogy at Serampore in the Early Nineteenth Century." *The Criterion: International Journal of English*. http://www.the-criterion.com/new-learning-and-missionary-fashioning-of-pedagogy-at-serampore-in-the-early-nineteenth-century/. Accessed on 10th September 2018.

"Serampore Mission's Attempt to Introduce Vernacular Higher Education," 165-170, http://shodhganga.inflibnet.ac.in/jspui/bitstream/10603/156444/20/20_chapter%2016.pdf. Accessed on 30th September 2018.

Sharma, S. "How India is inching closer to becoming digitally literate." (24th June 2016). https://yourstory.com/2016/06/national-digital-literacy-mission/. Accessed on 11th July 2017.

Smith, C. A. "The Edinburgh Connection: Between the Serampore Mission and Western Missiology." *Missiology: An International Review* 18/2 (April 1990): 185-208.

Smith, C. A. "The Protege of Erasmus and Luther In Heroic Serampore, 1812-1855." *Indian Journal of Theology* 37/1 (1995): 15-44.

Smith, C. A. *The Serampore Mission Enterprise*. Bangalore: Center for Contemporary Christianity, 2006.

Smith, G. E. "Patterns of Missionary Education: The Baptist India Mission 1794-1824." *The Baptist Quarterly* 22/6 (1968): 294-312, https://biblicalstudies.org.uk/pdf/bq/20-7_293.pdf. Accessed on 1st August 2018.

"The Serampore Missionaries as Educationists, 1794–1824." *Baptist Quarterly* 22/6 (1968): 320-325. DOI: 10.1080/0005576X.1968.11751252. Accessed on 12th September 2018.

7

The Contribution of the Serampore Mission towards the Ecumenical Movement: A Historical Perspective

Woba James

Introduction

The modern Ecumenical Movement traces its historic beginning from Edinburgh 1910. While its historic memoirs have several noteworthy pioneering personalities whom we refer to as 'ecumenists,' responsible for the ecumenical movement in general, we are also at the same time reminded of the fact that a century back (counting from 1910) in 1810, it was William Carey, who sowed the seeds of the vision of the modern ecumenical movement. As such, Edinburgh 1910 could also stand as the realization of that long-awaited vision of Carey—the Father of the Modern Missions and one of the pioneers of the Serampore Mission.

The story of the Serampore Mission's contribution to the life and ministry of the Church at large and especially to the Church in India is not one that could easily be told as it covers more than 200 years from where we stand at present. The Church as a whole and the growing number of theological institutions will no doubt continue to be indebted to those pure and selfless souls of the past—the founders namely William Carey, Joshua Marshman, William Ward, and also not forgetting those dynamic leaders like George Howells who had to invest their everything in order to preserve the life of, and develop the mission of Serampore especially through the College.

The study of the history of the Serampore Mission can best be understood as one of the histories of ecumenism. Beginning with its inception and onto the present form, it represents a great ecumenical body that is noteworthy. Therefore, this paper is a humble attempt in presenting the contribution of the Serampore Mission towards the modern ecumenical movement in the context of India. Considering the constraints of time and space, we shall confine our attention to select few areas that vividly reflects the Serampore mission's ecumenical contribution.

Serampore Mission and its Ecumenical Beginnings

The Serampore Mission was established under the missionary leadership of three great missionaries: William Carey, Joshua Marshman and William Ward. Carey, a Baptist missionary under the delegation of the Baptist Missionary Society arrived in Calcutta on 11th of November 1793 and there he at first worked as a planter at an Indigo factory under the British East India Company.[1] Then he was followed by William Ward and Joshua Marshman in the year 1799, who were dropped at Serampore under the Danish territory.[2] It was on 10th of January 1800 that Carey moved to Serampore with his family to join his two friends and together they began the Serampore Mission under the Danish flag of Serampore.[3] Serampore Mission carried out its missionary work mainly through the College that was founded on 15th July 1818. It was to be a college for the instruction of Asiatic Christian and Oriental Youth in Eastern Literature and European Science.[4]

Serampore's Ecumenical character can be seen in its very foundation. The vision and mission of the college that it established reflect its ecumenical nature as portrayed in the formation of two departments—secular scientific education and evangelical theological education.[5] From the very beginning, the founders made it a point to make the college open to all without any caste, race, or creed distinction in its admission of the students.[6] While sure-footing the primary purpose of their mission of evangelization, they also gave equal importance to the necessity of educating the native Indians in the knowledge of the world and its living realities. This was done due to the recognition that the people need not only spiritual training but also need the secular scientific education in order to meet the challenges of life for the development of the total standard of life.

This ecumenical character of the Serampore Mission's foundation is also clearly noted by the then secular society at the early part of its history. Excerpts from the pages of Calcutta Gazzette, Thursday 27th May 1824 reports about the Serampore College as follows:

> . . . that its grand and ultimate object is, to diffuse the light of Divine Revelation as widely as possible in India . . . through means congenial with the nature of the human mind, as well as consistent with the dictates of revelation. It sanctions no means which have the most distant approach to deception . . . that it creates confidence even before Divine Revelation shines fully on the soul, and does all within the reach of human power, towards facilitating its entrance into the mind. The precepts of Manu, the tenets of Mohamed, and the doctrines of Divine Revelation are laid open to the native youth who study in Serampore College, precisely as they are; as well as the state of the various nations in the world, its age, its history both ancient and modern, the size and figure of the earth, the laws of the heavenly bodies, the composition of natural substance all these are laid open to them without the least disguise or misrepresentation. Thus, in the work of enlightening the native mind, there are no after disclosures to dread . . . .[7]

Another beautiful addition to this report is given in the following description that reads:

> Hence, while the native Christian youths in the college, whether their parents were Brahmins or Shudras, eat all from one table, convinced that "nothing which entereth the mouth defileth the man." The Brahmin youth in whom there is not this knowledge, is requested to eat nothing and do nothing which he deems contrary to his ideas of right and wrong respecting caste; and should he retain all these mistaken ideas till his mind be filled with knowledge, after years of studies he departs with no other injury done to his caste, than that of being practically taught by the example of youths around him equal to himself in knowledge and virtue, that it is really nothing, that God hath made of one blood all nations of the earth; and that to every class of men truth and love comprehend all virtue.[8]

Besides this ecumenical vision and praxis in its educational structure, Serampore also represents international co-operation in its establishment and functioning of the College. The story of Serampore is one of the amazing endeavors in co-operation among people of diverse Christian and national backgrounds. Many nationalities contributed to its history—Indian with K. C. Jacob, Thomas Sitther and C.E. Abraham; Denmark with Dr. Larsen, Principal of the United Theological College, Bangalore; Sweden with Bishop

Sandegren; American with Dr. Banninga of Pasumallai, Dr. M. H. Harrison of Bangalore, W.G. Griffiths and M. H. Harper; including also successive principals of Scottish Church College, Calcutta, with Dr. J. F. McFadyen of the staff; English with George Howells, John Drake, G. H. C. Angus, W. W. Winfield and others.[9] Hence, Serampore as we know today was strongly built upon the ecumenical foundations from the very beginning.

Serampore Mission as One National Theological Structure of Ecumenism

Serampore through its negotiations with the BMS and the Danish government, the higher theological education for B.D. degree started in the year 1910, and its first batch were sent out in the year 1915.[10] It was in 1918 that it started its inter-denominational Senate. It was therefore with the constitution of the Senate of Serampore College in that year that it opened up its ecumenical doors to welcome other theological institutions throughout the country under its affiliation.[11] Hence, by 1955, it had 18 institutions under it and by 2006-2007 it had 49 affiliating institutions[12] within its umbrella. It was this overarching structure of the Serampore that served to unite diverse colleges and seminaries in the country.

The earlier Board of Theological Education (BTE), a wing of the National Council of Churches in India (NCCI), together with the Senate took care of the theological education in India especially in relation to its relevant service to the needs of the church and its ministry. Gradually this co-operation between the BTE and the Senate led them to the recognition of the need for the formation of 'One National structure' of theological education. As a result, after a series of consultations, the Board of Theological Education of the Senate of Serampore College (BTESSC) was constituted in the year 1975. By that the BTESSC became the advisory body by the approval of the outgoing BTE, the Senate, and the Council of Serampore College.[13] In 1979 a Review Committee was set up for the revision of the Constitution of the BTESSC along with the definition of the duties of various officers and committees and in 1994 the revised form of the Constitution was adopted and thus officially formed the 'One National Structure' of Theological Education in India.[14] Thus, Serampore's vision for unifying theological education under one common umbrella enabled it to give a sound academic standard throughout the country.[15]

As Serampore is committed to respond to the needs of the church and society, it designed a system of Common Curriculum applicable to all the affiliated institutions. By critically assessing the form of its theological education, which very often seem to be either of western or of outdated traditional form, it recognizes the urgency of being made contextually meaningful to the concrete needs of the contemporary Indian situation. As a result, it worked out a common curriculum that incorporates the issues that are of serious concern for all within its structure of curricula and courses syllabi. While it make provision for core subjects of studies, accepted by all colleges as basic to sound theological training, Serampore also gives the freedom to different individual colleges to have subjects of their choice in order to meet the immediate contextually-situated needs of the church and society.[16] It thus grants autonomous status to the colleges to exercise their freedom in designing new courses and modify existing ones as per the changing needs of their given contexts.

Serampore Mission and Its Inter-denominational Relations

The family of Serampore comprises of vast backgrounds of theological institutions/seminaries, churches' affiliations/denominations and doctrinal differences. It ranges from Orthodoxy to Charismatic, Pentecostal and other Protestant faith persuasions.[17] Since all the institutions affiliated to the Senate of Serampore College come from diversified rich doctrinal and denominational backgrounds, it forms an ecumenical body in the family of Serampore.

During the Senate of Serampore College Act of 1918, the Constitution of the Senate spelled out clearly concerning the ecumenical nature of the Senate of Serampore College. The Article 9 of the Constitution stated that "at least one and not more than three representatives of the following Christian denominations, viz. Anglican, Baptist, Congregational, Lutheran, Methodist, Presbyterian and Syrian . . . be members of the Senate."[18] This was incorporated with a clear view in mind concerning the interest of people coming from diverse denominational backgrounds.

It was in 1960s and 70s that the Senate of Serampore College welcomed the Evangelical seminaries and colleges with the understanding that through ecumenical living together and growing together that people would be led to a rich theological pluralism.[19] It is believed therefore that through such a dynamic encounter of different denominations people could move toward a pluralistic form of ecumenism. This inter-denominational ecumenism of the Senate of Serampore College helped the diverse denominational churches to come under a common structure in training their candidates for mutual commitment to the Gospel and its service in India's pluralistic context.

Serampore Mission and its Concern for Other Living Faiths

The question of other living faiths had been one of the core concerns of the Modern Ecumenical Movement through the 1950s and 1960s. This concern gave birth to the necessity of the concept and praxis of dialogue or interreligious dialogue. Dialogue is aimed at enabling the pluralistic faith society to respect each other's faiths, have an adequate knowledge of their beliefs, enter into a closer relationship with others, and to refrain from accusing each other or to stop themselves from indulging in an unending game of blame.

India's reality is defined by its multicultural and multireligious context. The issue of interfaith relationship thus becomes more pronounced and urgent. With regard to Serampore's ecumenical contributions, it is to be understood that it is not only preoccupied with the inter-denominational aspect of ecumenism but is also very much sensitive to the serious issue of interfaith relations. Serampore thus recognizes the importance of teaching and doing theology in relation to the people of other faiths. Indian Christian theologians like P. D. Devanandan and M. M. Thomas through their pioneering contributions toward studies in religious dialogue in the 1950s[20] continued to encourage the Senate of Serampore College and the churches[21] to play significant roles in organizing several meetings and seminars on the importance of interreligious dialogue in the Indian context.[22]

Senate of Serampore College, recognizing the necessity of interfaith dialogue incorporates in its course syllabi studies on the subject of interreligious relations and the importance of dialogue. Theological institutions under the Senate of Serampore College thus offer subjects that deal with the issue of interfaith reality and its concerns. This is done with the aim of promoting mutual understanding and respect toward each other's faith affirmations, for promoting mutual enrichment as well as for the peaceful co-existence of all within our richly-bestowed pluralistic society/context. Ecumenical theological education under the Senate of Serampore College thus strives to enable and enlighten the students (and teachers as well) to understand the plurality of humanity and of the universe, and to establish a just, liberating, enriching and peaceful relationship between people of different faith traditions.

Prospective Challenges for Expanding the Serampore Mission

Making theological education relevant to the people in their local setting has become the priority today and that too especially in India's context. The earlier classical theological education that has been imparted within the curriculum of Indian theological education was necessitated by the needs of the established educational structures of the churches. Gradually this was found to be insufficient as it was unable to respond meaningfully to the challenges of the church within the given context. Likewise, theological education in India and in particular within the Senate of Serampore College needs to move away from the traditional pattern and method of functioning whenever and wherever necessitated by our local Indian context. It is therefore in this regard that the present writer wishes to briefly demarcate two areas as examples of illustrating our point of argument here with the purpose of provoking our thoughts toward combined deliberations on them:

Ecumenism and Gender Concerns

Theological developments in contemporary Indian context confirm that ecumenical theological education within the Senate of Serampore College needs to make a paradigm shift as far as its male clergy-dominated leadership is concerned in order to create possibilities for empowering the entire congregational fold in the ministry. The present society and church call for a new and inclusive approach that will equip people as a whole for involvement in ushering changes. It is true that the theological education under the Senate of Serampore College is noteworthy for its ecumenical involvement and contribution in many different areas. But unfortunately, it falls somewhat short due to its seemingly 'half-hearted' commitment toward the ecumenism of men-women relationship.[23] Despite its theoretical academic commitment to the issue of gender justice, it has a rather long way to go in order to fulfill its academic vision in this regard.

A Dialogue between the Senate of Serampore and Asian Theological Association Bodies in India

As the heading suggests, the issue at hand is specifically related to the role of the Senate of Serampore in fostering ecumenism beyond the present coverage of its ecumenical relationships. Besides its ecumenical ventures among diverse churches, traditions, denominations, and living faiths; diverse senate-affiliated colleges/institutions and the subsequent extension toward diverse cultures, races and so forth, it needs to also seriously take into account the possibility of creating an ecumenical platform for dialogue between the above cited structures of theological education in India for mutual benefit as well as for the larger mission and ministry of the church.

The rationale behind this argument/suggestion is that in places like the North Eastern region of India (and Nagaland in particular), there exists several experiences and instances of conflicts, tensions, misunderstandings and even some unappealing confrontations in the fields of ministry and also especially in the church. Factors such as suspicion, preference, mutual battle of accusations over which one is 'liberal'/'spiritual'/'worldly'/'academ ic-oriented'/'poor academic standard' and the like.[24] These are some of the apparent tensions that create a huge barrier between the Senate-affiliated theological education and the Asia Theological Association and others that greatly disturb not only the immediate individuals' inter-relationships in the ministry but also the overall theological and ministerial atmosphere in the region.

Conclusion

Serampore Mission thus had its beginning on an ecumenical note and continues to work and contribute toward ecumenism in India. With its ecumenical vision and mission especially in and through the work of theological education, it recognizes the importance of, and thus incorporates ecumenical elements both in its structure and content.

With its one National Structure of Theological Education, Serampore Mission fosters ecumenism by bringing several theological institutions from different regions of the country, thus promoting ecumenical relations between various institutions and colleges under its umbrella. Next, there is also its ecumenical contribution in the form of relations between diverse church traditions in India by bringing them together under one platform for common theological vision and mission. Lastly but not the least, the Serampore Mission extends its ecumenical mission toward people of other living faiths and convictions. This is made possible not only in its innovative participation in organizing seminars on Interreligious Dialogue but also in making interreligious concern one of the pertinent subjects of reflection and action within the core syllabi of its theological education. This not only imparts its candidates in the knowledge of religious pluralism but also in training and preparing them for responsible and sensitively-effective ministry in the concrete context of India's religious pluralism. Thus, Serampore Mission's contribution toward ecumenical movement can be seen in the above select aspects of its theological vision and mission and therefore is noteworthy in today's context of ecumenism. At the end, it is also safe to say on our part that there are still prospective challenges for the Serampore Mission to transcend or go beyond its already-covered areas in its ecumenical vision and mission—to further spread its wings and embrace many more that call out for help and assistance for realizing a truly ecumenical family of God.

Endnotes

[1] Cf. J. C. Marshman, *The Life and Times of Carey, Marshman and Ward: Embracing the History of the Serampore Mission*, Vol. 1 (London: Longmann and Roberts, 1859), 60-63. (Hereafter Marshman, *The Life and Times of Carey, Marshman and Ward*).

[2] Cf. Marshman, *The Life and Times of Carey, Marshman and Ward*, 200. Cf. S. K. Chatterjee, *William Carey and Serampore* (Serampore: Laserplus, 2004), 23-25; Arthur C. Chute, *William Carey: A Sketch of Beginning in Modern Mission* (Chicago: Goodman and Dickerson, 1891), 15.

[3] Cf. E. L. Wenga, "The Serampore Mission and Its Founders," *The Story of Serampore and Its College* (Serampore: The Council of Serampore College, 1961), 12.

[4] Cf. J. C. Marshman, *History of Serampore Mission or Life and Times of Carey, Marshman and Ward*, Vol. 2 (Calcutta: 1859), 168. (Hereafter Marshman, *History or Serampore Mission*). Cf. *Senate of Serampore College Regulations for Internal and External Candidates: Relating to the Bachelor of Divinity (BD) Degree, 1962*, 6-10.

[5] Cf. D. A. Christadoss, "The Story of Serampore College, 1818-1929," *The Story of Serampore and Its College*, ed. Wilma S. Stewart (Serampore: The Council of Serampore College, 1961), 20. Cf. Pratap Chandra Gine, *The System of Elementary Education of the Serampore Mission* (Jorhat: ETC, 2001), 31-38.

[6] Marshman, *History of Serampore Mission*, 170.

[7] Cf. "Serampore College: From the Pages of Calcutta Gazzette," *Carey Day Souvenir 2004, Serampore College*, 41. (Hereafter *From the Pages of Calcutta Gazzette*).

[8] Cf. *From the Pages of Calcutta Gazzette*, 41.

[9] Cf. W. Stewart, "The Ecumenical Character of Serampore College, Part 1," *The Story of Serampore and Its College* (Serampore: The Council of Serampore College, 2006), 101, 102. (Hereafter Stewart, *The Ecumenical Character of Serampore College, Part 1*).

[10] Cf. *Serampore College Theological Department Prospectus*, 1965, 2.

[11] Cf. *Serampore College Handbook for the Year 1954-1955*, 2.

[12] *Annual Report of the President of the Senate of Serampore College, 2006-2007*, 12.

[13] Cf. Ravi Tiwari, "The Ecumenical Character of the Serampore College, Part 2," *The Story of Serampore and Its College* (Serampore: The Council of Serampore College, 2006), 112, 113. (Hereafter Tiwari, *The Ecumenical Character of Serampore College, Part 2*).

[14] Cf. Tiwari, *The Ecumenical Character of Serampore College, Part 2*, 113.

[15] Cf. Stewart, *The Ecumenical Character of Serampore College, Part 1*, 101.

[16] Cf. Stewart, *The Ecumenical Character of Serampore College, Part 1*, 102.

[17] Cf. D. S. Satyarajan, *Senate of Serampore College Registrar's Report, 1990-1991* (1991), 845. (Hereafter Satyarajan, *Senate of Serampore College*).

[18] *Bengal Act No 4 of 1918, The Serampore College Act, 1918, as modified up to the 1st of July, 1981*, 3.

[19] Satyarajan, *Senate of Serampore College*, 845.

[20] Cf. Paul Tillich, *Christianity and the Religions of the World* (New York: Columbia University Press, 1963), 22.

[21] It is to be noted here that in 1975, the National Council of Churches in India started a unit on Unity, Fellowship and Dialogue.

[22] Cf. Mathai Zachariah, *Beyond Ecumenism: A Journey in Light* (Thiruvalla: CSS, 2002), 80.

[23] Cf. Woba James, *Revisiting Ecumenical Theological Education in India: With Special Reference to the Senate of Serampore College* (New Delhi: CWI, 2016), 225.

[24] Cf. James, *Revisiting Ecumenical Theological Education in India*, 234-235.

Bibliography

Annual Report of the President of the Senate of Serampore College, 2006-07.

Bengal Act No 4 of 1918, The Serampore College Act, 1918, as modified up to the 1st of July 1981.

Chatterjee, S. K. *William Carey and Serampore*. Serampore: Laserplus, 2004.

Chute, C. A. *William Carey: A Sketch of Beginning in Modern Mission*. Chicago: Goodman and Dickerson, 1891.

Gine, P. C. *The System of Elementary Education of the Serampore Mission*. Jorhat: ETC, 2001.

James, W. *Revisiting Ecumenical Theological Education in India: With Special Reference to the Senate of Serampore College*. New Delhi: CWI, 2016.

Marshman, J. C. *History of Serampore Mission or Life and Times of Carey, Marshman and Ward.* Vol. 2. Calcutta: 1859.

Marshman, J. C. *The Life and Times of Carey, Marshman and Ward: Embracing the History of the Serampore Mission.* Vol. 1. London: Longmann and Roberts, 1859.

Satyarajan, D. S. *Senate of Serampore College Registrar's Report, 1990-1991* (1991).

Senate of Serampore College Regulations for Internal and External Candidates: Relating to the Bachelor of Divinity (BD) Degree, 1962, 6-10.

"Serampore College: From the Pages of Calcutta Gazzette." *Carey Day Souvenir 2004, Serampore College.*

Serampore College Handbook for the Year 1954-1955.

Serampore College Theological Department Prospectus, 1965.

Stewart, W. "The Ecumenical Character of Serampore College, Part 1." *The Story of Serampore and Its College.* Serampore: The Council of Serampore College, 2006.

Tillich, P. *Christianity and the Religions of the World.* New York: Columbia University Press, 1963.

Tiwari, R. "The Ecumenical Character of the Serampore College, Part 2." *The Story of Serampore and Its College.* Serampore: The Council of Serampore College, 2006: 112, 113

Wilma, S. S., ed. *The Story of Serampore and Its College.* Serampore: The Council of Serampore College, 1961.

Zachariah, M. *Beyond Ecumenism: A Journey in Light.* Thiruvalla: CSS, 2002.

8

"Through *You* all the Families of the Earth Shall be Blessed" (Genesis 12:3c): Reading the Life of Abraham and William Carey from a Missiological Perspective

Shiju Mathew

Introduction

God called Abraham to be a 'blessing' to 'all nations' (i.e., 'all *Jathis*'). In order to be a blessing for all, Abraham was asked to leave his country, his kindred and father's house and move to the land that God would show him. The movement and mission are progressive in outlook. There were many who took the mantle of mission initiated by Abraham and one among them was William Carey. He was called to leave the land of England to the nation of India. Like Abraham, he obeyed the voice of God in the midst of several challenges, oppositions and struggles. The immediate outlook was bleak, but the future result was glorious. Both Abraham and Carey received the title 'Father,' Abraham as 'Father of many nations' and Carey as 'Father of Modern Missions.' They both had not seen the results, but generations received blessings through their faith initiative.

Receiving the title 'Father' is great but paying the price for such an occasion is tasking and quite challenging. Witnessing one's faith has become a major divisive issue in the current religious and political scenario of India. Christian missionaries and churches are now openly attacked by Hindutva forces. In such a context, how to carry the mission? Abraham and Carey are to be considered paradigmatic figures in the contemporary contexts. They both had 'vision' and were willing to do 'mission' with 'passion.' This paper is an attempt to read the life of Abraham and William Carey from a missional perspective drawing its relevance to the present day mission of the church. It will cover Abrahamic call and covenant, Carey and his mission; and the mission of the Church/New Israel towards the people of other faith traditions.

Through 'You': Gospel of Salvation for All *Ethnos/Jathis*

According to Christopher J. H. Wright, "Mission means our committed participation as God's people, at God's invitation and command, in God's own mission within the history of God's world for the redemption of God's creation."[1] The covenant responsibility flows from and participates in that is the heart beat of God. To make it more specific, the covenant community had a salvific role to play, i.e., witnessing Yahweh to other nations. They had an identity and role connected to God's ultimate intention of blessing the nations[2] (see Gen. 12:3; Isa. 42:6; 49:6; cf. Luke 2; Acts 13:46-48). This aspect can be seen in the blessings of Abraham, the Exodus event, the prophetical messages, and the like. Thus, Israel had a major role in the salvation history.

One of the significant questions needed to be discussed is: Does the covenant community execute their responsibility? From the very beginning it has been God's purpose to bring all the *Jathis* (people groups) into the domain of salvation. That was the gospel announced to Abraham and continued throughout the Biblical narratives (Gen. 12:1-3; cf. Gal. 3:6-9). The Abrahamic covenant is the starting point of salvation which connects the preceding Adamic (Gen. 3) and Noahic covenants (Gen. 9) with Mosaic (Exo. 19), Davidic (2 Sam. 7) and the New Covenant (Jer. 31). It is from Abrahamic covenant the task of God towards salvation initiates (i.e., the theme of blessings).[3] Hence, Israel's existence and living among the nations throughout the centuries must be looked in the backdrop of God's call to Abraham and His covenantal agreement. It was with one man and with one family the history of salvation begins.

Abrahamic Call and Covenant

God's call and covenant with Abraham narrated in Genesis 12 and 15 is such a notable event in the history of the redemption that Paul describes as God's evangelizing the gospel 'in advance' to Abraham (Gen. 3:8). Genesis 12 and 15 becomes the cornerstone of God's covenant with the Jewish people as well as the initial self-discloser concerning His mission to the nations.[4]

Yahweh's covenant with Abraham must be seen within the larger context of the previous eleven chapters of the Book of Genesis.[5] Chapters 1-11 present us a picture of humanity disconnected with their creator and in open rebellion with God. The effects of human rebellion are shown to be both personal and systematic, not only separating individuals from God (e.g., Adam and Eve), but also fracturing all relationships (e.g., Cain and Abel) and the society as a whole (e.g., Noah's world).[6] The story reaches its climax in the story of the tower of Babel with people trying to reach God by their own efforts and attempting to make a name for themselves.[7] The Tower of Babel[8] narrative in Gen. 11 represents the wider effects of the fall and serves as an important theological backdrop to God's covenantal agreement with Abraham in Genesis 12.[9] For Allen P. Ross, Gen. 11:1-9 is structured in antithetical parallelism and in chiasm. Chapter 11:5-9 is a reversal of 11:3-4. In verses 3-4, humankind decided to do everything in their own way whereas in verses 5-9 God foils the plan of the humankind. In this account, a great extent of parallelism can be seen with verse 5 as the central fact: 'the Lord came down.'[10] Three facts in the Babel narrative are important in relation to Abrahamic Covenant: first, people through their own efforts wanted to reach the sky; second, they wanted to make a name for themselves;[11] and third, this event has global consequences (i.e., *scattered abroad*). The worldwide effect of this event is underscored by the fact that five times the narrator mentions 'whole earth' (Gen. 11:1, 2, 4, 8, and 9). This is an important background to the Abrahamic covenant, which represents God's initiative to 'make a name for Abraham' and to bless 'the whole earth.' Gen. 12 therefore should be seen as both God's initiative with Abraham and his response to the culminating effects of a worldwide human rebellion.[12]

The Abrahamic call begins with an imperative 'Go' (Gen. 12:1: The Lord said to Abraham '*Go* from your country, and your kindred and your father's house to the land that I will show you'). It is in direct contrast with the people who wanted to 'settle down' and 'not be scattered' (11: 4). The ideas of going, settling and scattering are also be seen in Acts of the Apostles (Acts 1:8; 8:1). God tells Abraham that he will make him a great nation, and make his name great . . . and in him all the families of the earth shall be blessed.[13] In contrast to the people of the Tower of Babel who were proud[14] and openly rebelled against God (cf. Gen. 9:1), Abraham obeyed the voice of God to leave his people, culture and religion in order to become Father of blessings for many nations. Abraham's going out will bring blessings not only to him and his descendants but eventually to the entire world. According to David Bosch, "what Babel has been unable to achieve is promised and guaranteed in Abraham, namely the blessings of all nations."[15] The overall structure of Abrahamic call is chiastic.[16] The passage reveals that what Abraham is called to forsake is the largest frame and gets increasingly narrow. He is asked to leave his *land, his kindred,* and *his father's house.* However, the corresponding blessings are in direct reverse, encompassing an ever winding circle of blessings, i.e., God will personally bless Abraham, he will bless the nation that will come from him, and finally all the families of the earth will be blessed through him.

The phrase 'Through you' is important for our understanding of mission. God promises to bless not only Abraham and the nation of Israel but through Abraham's obedience all the nations of the world (cf. Isa. 42:6; 49:6; Luke 2:32; Acts 13:46-48). The Hebrew word for 'all nations' is *kol mishpechot,* which is equivalent to the Greek word *ethnos,* not denoting geo-political boundary but 'all kinship groups.' Here begins the story of salvation/redemption that reverberates throughout the rest of the Bible. In the final picture, we see God and the nations are reconciled in the new creation (Rev. 21:1-3, 24-26; 22: 2; cf. Zeph. 3:9-11; Acts 2:6-11). According to Chris Wright, Gen. 12 is the story of 'God's mission for world's redemption.'[17] It is launched by the obedience of Abraham and thus God's promises are released in the history of the nations. While the call of Abraham included posterity, covenant blessing, and land for a particular people called Israel, it has a universal goal: 'through you all the nations of the earth will be blessed' (Gen. 12:3; 18:18; 22:18; 26:4-5; 28:14; 35:11).

God's initial choice, address, command, and promise to Abraham were all unconditional in the sense that they did not depend on any prior condition that Abraham had fulfilled. They emerged out of unexpected and unmerited grace of God and out of His determination to bless the human race which has rejected His will. Yet on the other hand there is an implied conditionality in the call and choice of Abraham. God's promise of making Abraham a great nation and making his name great were all depended on Abraham's obedience to His call.[18] Likewise, the second command 'and be a blessing' with its anticipated universal scope was depended on Abraham's obedience to the first command.[19] The implied thrust is 'if you go, then I will do these things . . . and all nations will be blessed.'

God's intention to bless the nations is combined with human commitment to a quality of obedience that enables us to be the agents of that blessing. The glorious gospel of Abrahamic covenant is that God's mission is ultimately to bless all the nations. Between the obedience to the call and covenant, Abraham went through a series of challenges like famine, fear of life, family feud, and sacrifice of his son. Abraham's faith in God and his concern for others ultimately resulted into a covenantal relationship and to the experience of having a different name (see Gen. 15 and 17).

Carey and the Mission

Abraham faithfully followed the mission of God and passed it to his son Isaac (Gen. 24). The mantle was passed then to Jacob, Israel, and then to the Church through Christ. The Church went through various forms of suffering, but her service to the world continued. In the course of time there came a young man who decided to leave his country and culture to embrace a foreign land where all sorts of evil practices such as *Sati* system and *child marriage* were on an increase. The little candle that was born in Paulerspury, England, on August 17, 1761, bloomed in the land of India and extinguished at Serampore, India, on June 9, 1834. When he was 16, he was apprenticed to a shoemaker and later he continued in that area of work, an occupation for which he was never ashamed. Later on, the shoemaker became a missionary-maker. While he was in the business of shoemaking, he drew a map of the world marking the places where the gospel had not been preached. The statement of Andrew Fuller that "If it is the duty of all men to believe whenever the Gospel is presented to them, it must be the duty of all who have received the Gospel to endeavor to make it universally known" convicted him.

Carey's decision to share the gospel to the unreached was not welcomed. One of the occasions, he suggested 'The conversion of the heathens' as a topic for discussion. Quickly a minister stood up and said, 'young man, sit down! When God pleases to convert the heathens, he will do it without your help or mine.' Such rebuffs did not dishearten him. He came to India leaving aside the comfort zone and faced many challenges both from within his family and from outside. The sacrifice paid rich dividend. As we all know the history, though he lost his dear ones and even the printing press and all his labor turned into ashes, he decided not to give up. He could complete translating the New Testament and the Old Testament into many Indian languages like Bengali, Sanskrit, Marathi and Punjabi. Moreover, he completed a dictionary of Bengali and English. Apart from this, he was instrumental in abolishing the age old evil practice called the *Sati* System. The Danish king granted charter for the College at Serampore. The light which ignited through Carey with the help of God in Serampore spread like a wildfire for all these 200 years and it will continue further. The word 'you' in Gen. 12:3 is the Abraham and his 'seed.' The 'seed' includes all those who follow. The pertinent question needs to be addressed is: How to understand 'through you' towards the people of other faith? Whether the Church should limit the Gospel of Salvation within or extend it to others.

Mission of the Church towards People of Other Faiths

Before moving to the mission of the Church, i.e., witnessing Christ with people of other faith traditions, it is important to know that the seed of Abraham was chosen to witness the faith as seen in the Great Commission of Jesus (Matthew 28:18-20; and Acts 1:8). There are two schools of thought regarding witnessing Israel's faith to people of other faiths. On the one side, there are scholars who consider the mission of Israel as centripetal, i.e., inward moving.[20] On the other hand, there are others who think Israel's mission to the nations was centrifugal, i.e., outward moving. Here mission of witnessing is seen as actively sharing one's faith with others.

Scholars such as H. H. Rowley, Walter C. Kaiser, Chris Wright, and others think that the mission of Israel was outward moving. H. H. Rowley calls the Hebrew Bible as a missionary document. For him, Israel had a wider vision that passed beyond the borders of Israel and embraced 'others' in the Kingdom of God. But he thinks that Israel came slowly to the conviction of a universal purpose of God and it appeared clearly and definitely in the exilic and postexilic periods.[21] Kaiser says that Israel's witnessing was 'centrifugal witnessing' not 'centripetal.'[22] For Wright, from the very beginnings of the Bible till the end of it, the centrifugal universalism is obvious. Israel is called to become a light to the nations by actively sharing their faith with others. Barry L. Ross considers God's call to Salvation as universal. His argument is based on Isa. 45:20-25. The call is to 'the refugees of the nations' who when fleeing before Cyrus carried their wooden idols hoping to find help from their gods. To those defeated idolaters the word of God comes as: 'Turn to me and be *saved* all the ends of the earth; for I am God, and there is no other' (cf. Acts 4:12). This Isaianic passage looks forward to a new non-ethnic and non-political concept of the future people of God gathered from *all the ends of the earth.*[23] On the other hand, there are scholars like Robert Martin-Achard and Lucien Legrand who think that Israel's mission was a centripetal one. Martin-Achard says, as the history of the Old Testament reaches its term, what is depicted is centripetal movement, not Israel going to the nations but nations streaming to Israel's sanctuary in Zion. He concludes that the mission of Israel to the nations consisted not in evangelizing but witnessing through her presence.[24] Legrand uses terms like 'universalism centered on Zion' and 'decentralized universalism.' For him, Israel will not go to the nations but nations will see the light of Zion and come to it. The eschatological pilgrimage of the nations to Zion represents universalism centered on it, but some texts go beyond this to imply that God's covenant with Israel will be extended to other nations, who would then stand on the same footing with God as Israel.[25]

There are a few scholars who emphasize the aspect of acculturation. Carroll Stuhlmueller's treatment on this subject is quite far-reaching.[26] For him, Israel borrowed many of its beliefs and practices from their surrounding culture. For example, law codes, kingship, the priesthood, and the sacrificial system were all borrowed from Canaan. For him, also the mission of Israel was centripetal, not centrifugal. David J. Bosch in his memorable work *Transforming Mission* emphasizes the aspect of God's compassion, a compassion that embraces the nations. For him, the purpose of Israel's election was service, and when this is withheld, election loses its meaning. Primarily Israel is to serve the marginals in its midst: the orphans, the widows, the poor, and the strangers. Whenever the people of Israel renew their covenant with Yahweh, they recognize that they are renewing their obligations to the victims of the society.[27] He states that "if there is a missionary in Old Testament, it is God who will as eschatological deed par excellence, bring the nations to Jerusalem to worship there together with covenant people."[28] Thus his approach also appears to be more centripetal than centrifugal.

Thus, the mission of Israel in witnessing their faith to the *Jathis* is seen as either centrifugal or centripetal. But to have a comprehensive understanding of Israel's salvific role to the nations both aspects must encompass. Israel was called to witness God both centrifugally and centripetally. The existence of Israel was to bring blessings to others. Israel was instrumental in making known the true God to the Egyptians at the time of Exodus (Exo. 14-15), to the Ninevites at the time of Jonah (Jonah 1-4), to the Babylonians at the time of Daniel (Dan. 1-4) and to the Persian Empire at the time of Esther. There are scores of individuals who recognized the true God through Israel like Rahab in the book of Joshua and the Philistines in 1 Samuel.

The supreme example of Abrahamic promise 'Through you all the families of the earth shall be blessed' can be seen in the person and work of Jesus (Matthew 1:1, 21; John 4:21; Rom. 3:21-4:25; cf. Isa. 49:1-7). [29] Christopher J. H. Wright states that,

> When Matthew announces Jesus as the Messiah, the son of Abraham, then, it means not only that he belongs to that particular people (a real Jew), but that he belongs to a people whose very reason for existence was to bring blessing to the rest of the humanity. He shared that mission, and indeed, as the Messiah, he had to make it a possibility and a reality at last. A particular man, but with a universal significance.[30]

The life and work of Jesus, like the Hebrew prophets, was missional and revolutionary in nature.[31] The Sermon on the Mount (Matthew 5-7) and Nazareth Manifesto (Luke 4:16-20) are clear examples. Jesus broke all the hierarchical and ethnic boundaries to encompass the 'others,' though there are passages referring salvation to the Jews (Zech. 2:1-5; Matthew 15:22-24; Luke 4:16-20; 7:11-14; John 4 and 12). The mission of Jesus is carried further by His disciples who stepped out of Jerusalem to the other parts of the globe including India. Paul, in his missionary journey, first turned to the Jews,[32] and when the Jews rejected, he turned towards the Gentiles. The special relationship and responsibility enjoyed by the elected Jews was extended to the Church. Just as Israel was called to be a light to the nations (blessings to all), so Christ has entrusted the missional task to the Church (Acts 2, 8, 10, 19). The centrifugal (outward moving) and centripetal (inward moving) aspects are seen both in the life of Abraham and William Carey. Both of them received the call of God and left their land of birth to a foreign land. Their obedience to the divine call in the midst of challenges and oppositions yielded blessings to many (outward moving). In the course of period, people of diverse cultures/*Jathis* witnessed the light and in turn received the blessings (inward moving). Hence, both outward and inward moving aspects are required to carry out the mission. The Church is expected to continue the mission of God initiated by Abraham, Jesus Christ, William Carey and others to fulfill the promise of God: 'Through *you* all the families of the earth shall be blessed.'

Conclusion

Abraham left the land of Mesopotamia (a place of idols) to the land of Canaan (the Promised Land). William Carey left the land of England to the land of India (the place of idols). They both faced uphill tasks and challenges, but the call/vision enabled them to be blessings to others. Their life and missions illuminated 'others.' Like Abraham and Carey, the Church is chosen/elected to be a light to the nations (Acts 13:46-48). The Israelites were elected to be a blessing to the nations, but they failed to execute their responsibility. The Church like Israel is chosen to witness faith to all *Jathis*. The Great Commission (Matthew 28:18-20; Acts 1:8) initiated in Acts 2 and 8:1 continued throughout and still in progress. The Church faced opposition from extremists throughout her history. Despite various levels of persecution, the chosen people of God witness the resurrected Christ and never died out rather increased in number. It is the responsibility of the Church to witness the path of salvation to all *jathis* amidst oppositions and persecutions.

Endnotes

[1] Christopher J. H. Wright, *The Mission of God: Unlocking the Bible's Grand Narrative* (London: Authentic, 2006), 23.

[2] A closer reading shows change of word-expression. In Gen. 12:3c, the word of promise is 'through you all the families of the earth shall be blessed.' The same promise is repeated thereafter with change of words. In Gen. 18:18, 'families' is replaced by 'nations.' In chap. 22:18, the same promise is repeated to Abraham as a reward for not sparing his son Isaac. It says 'through your seeds shall all the nations of the earth bless themselves because you have obeyed my voice.' Here the word 'through you' is replaced by 'through your seeds.' The promise to Abraham is confirmed to Isaac and Jacob (Gen. 26:4; 28:14). See E. W. Hengstenberg, *Christology of the Old Testament* (Secunderabad: OM Books, 2000), 42.

[3] See Hengstenberg, *Christology of the Old Testament*, 42. For Hengstenberg, "The Undeniable meaning of these promises made to the Patriarchs is that through their posterity salvation should be conferred upon all the nations of the earth."

[4] Timothy C. Tennent, *Invitation to World Missions: A Trinitarian Missiology for the Twenty-First Century* (Grand Rapids: Kregel Academic and Professionals, 2010), 106.

[5] See Lucien Legrand, *The Bible on Culture* (Bangalore: TPI, 2001), 64.

[6] See Tennent, *Invitation to World Missions*, 106. In Genesis 3 and 4, the questions of God to Adam and Cain, where are you? And Where is your brother Abel? point out the vertical and horizontal imbalances thereby breaking relationship. In turn it resulted to further breakdown in family and societal relationships (Genesis 6-9).

[7] The Tower of Babel is the climax of the rebellious act of humankind.

[8] Derek Kindner, "Genesis," *Tyndale Old Testament Commentary*, ed. D. J. Wiseman (England: Intervarsity Press, 1967), 110-111. Also refer Gordon J. Wenham, "Genesis," *Word Biblical Commentary*, eds. David A. Hubbard and Glen W. Barter (Texas: Word Books Publisher, 1987), 233-238.

[9] Kindner, "Genesis," 106.

[10] Allen P. Ross, "Genesis," *The Bible Knowledge Commentary: Old Testament*, eds. John F. Walvoord and Roy B. Zuck (Hyderabad: Authentic, 2012), 44.

[11] The Hebrew word *lanu* is used here. The expression 'for ourselves' is used to emphasis the significance of an action for a particular subject. See Gordon J. Wenham, "Genesis," 233-234.

[12] In Genesis chap. 11, the narrator mentions the word 'whole earth' five times pointing out the rebellious act of humankind and in Gen. 12:1-3 the word of God to Yahweh carries the word 'bless/blessing' and that too five times. In Genesis, seeing the act of humankind, God came down whereas in Gen. 12, Abraham hearing the command of God went. It refers to act of disobedience (chap. 11) and act of obedience (chap. 12). See Tennent, *Invitation to World Missions*, 107.

[13] For Wright, the 'blessing' is multinational and Christological. See Wright, *The Mission of God*, 216-18.

[14] Ross, "Genesis," 44-45.

[15] David Bosch, *Transforming Mission: Paradigm Shifts in Theology of Mission* (Bangalore: Center for Contemporary Christianity, 1991), 20.

[16] The structure in Gen. 12:1-3 is a well- structured one with two commands and six promises. The First command is to 'Go' with three promises focusing to Abraham (I will make of you a great nation; I will bless you; and I will make your name great). The second command is based on first set of command and promises 'Be a blessing' with three promises focusing to others through Abraham (I will bless those who bless you; I will curse he who disdains you; and through you all the families of the earth shall be blessed/bless themselves).

[17] Wright, *The Mission of God*, 200.

[18] See Ronald E. Diprose, *Israel and the Church: The Origin and Effects of Replacement Theology* (USA/UK: Authentic Media, 2000), 6-7. For Ronald, the blessings in Abrahamic Covenant did not include eternal salvation rather, Israel as a whole was to be the special object of God's love and through them blessing was to flow to the

whole earth. The unconditional covenant and the blessings promised to Abraham and to his seeds remained operational despite disobedience and blatant transgression of the Mosaic Covenant (cf. Hos. 1-3).

[19] Ross, "Genesis," 46-47.

[20] Israel's role in witnessing and spreading the good news was considered to be passive, i.e., blessing others by being light, merely through our lives and actions.

[21] H. H. Rowley cited by James Chukwuma Okoye, *Israel and the Nations: A Mission Theology of the Old Testament* (New York: Orbis Books, 2006), 5.

[22] Walter C. Kaiser. *Mission in the Old Testament* (Secunderabad: OM Books, 2000), 9.

[23] Barry L. Ross, "An Old Testament Perspective on Conversion," *Conversion in a Pluralistic Context*, eds. Krickwin C. Marak and Plamthodathil S. Jacob (Delhi: CMS/ISPCK, 2000), 8-9.

[24] Robert Martin-Achard cited by James Chukwuma Okoye, *Israel and the Nations: A Mission Theology of the Old Testament* (New York: Orbis Books, 2006), 5.

[25] Lucien Legrand cited by James Chukwuma Okoye, *Israel and the Nations: A Mission Theology of the Old Testament* (New York: Orbis Books, 2006), 5.

[26] Okoye, *Israel and the Nations*, 8.

[27] Bosch, *Transforming Mission*, 20.

[28] Bosch, *Transforming Mission*, 20.

[29] Diprose, *Israel and the Church*, 26-27.

[30] Christopher J. H. Wright, *Knowing Jesus through the Old Testament* (Chennai: UESI Publication Trust, 2001), 4.

[31] For John Desrochers, 'The intention of Jesus behind the founding of new Israel was integrating the Gentiles into it. This is in line with the Jewish expectations, namely the longing for the new Israel. The Jews were deeply convinced that they had been selected as the People of God. The God who had liberated them from the hand of Egypt had made a special covenant with the twelve tribes of Israel. In the course of their tragic history, the Jews had come to expect the appearance of the new and perfect Israel. The promises will be reserved for a remnant of Israel (Isa. 10, 46; Jer. 31). Yahweh will make a new Israel of this remnant and will make a new covenant with it (Jer. 31:31) and a new king (33:17). Then Israel will become the centre of the union of the nations (Isa. 19:24-26). The nations, seeing in Israel the presence of the true God (Isa. 45:15) will turn toward him; their conversion will coincide with the salvation (45:17) and glory of Israel (45:25)' See John Desrochers, *Christ the Liberator* (Bangalore: The Centre for Social Action, 1984), 114-128, for new Israel and the inclusion of the Gentiles in it.

[32] Paul though he turned to the Jews first and then to the gentiles, but he makes his intention clear by affirming that salvation is not merely by being the descendants of Abraham rather through the righteous of faith, i.e., Abraham believed in God and he was reckoned as righteousness (Rom. 9:6-8; cf. Gal. 3:28-29; 6:15-16). In

letter to the Romans, he points out clearly that the promise to Abraham and his descendants, that they should inherit the world, did not come through the law but through the righteous of faith . . . that is why it depends on faith, in order that the promise may rest on grace and be guaranteed to all his descendants—not only to the adherents of the law but also to those who share this faith of Abraham, for he is the father of us all, as it is written, "I have made you the father of many nations (Rom. 4: 16-18). For Hengstenberg, "a difficulty occurs . . . where St. Paul lays a peculiar stress upon the singular 'seed,' which is so often used in a collective sense; and seems desirous of showing from it, that Christ alone could have been intended by the seed of Abraham through whom the heathen shall be blessed." Hengstenberg, *Christology of the Old Testament*, 43.

Bibliography

Bosch, D. *Transforming Mission: Paradigm Shifts in Theology of Mission*. Bangalore: Center for Contemporary Christianity, 1991.

Desrochers, J. *Christ the Liberator*. Bangalore: The Centre for Social Action, 1984.

Diprose, R. E. *Israel and the Church: The Origin and Effects of Replacement Theology*. USA/UK: Authentic Media, 2000.

Hengstenberg, E. W. *Christology of the Old Testament*. Secunderabad: OM Books, 2000.

Kaiser, W. C. *Mission in the Old Testament*. Secunderabad: OM Books, 2000.

Kindner, D. "Genesis." *Tyndale Old Testament Commentary*. Ed. D. J. Wiseman. England: Inter-Varsity Press, 1967.

Legrand, L. *The Bible on Culture*. Bangalore: TPI, 2001.

Okoye, J. C. *Israel and the Nations: A Mission Theology of the Old Testament*. New York: Orbis Books, 2006.

Ross, A. P. "Genesis." *The Bible Knowledge Commentary: Old Testament*. Eds. John F. Walvoord and Roy B. Zuck. Hyderabad: Authentic, 2012.

Ross, B. L. "An Old Testament Perspective on Conversion." *Conversion in a Pluralistic Context*. Eds. Krickwin C. Marak and Plamthodathil S. Jacob. Delhi: CMS/ISPCK, 2000.

Tennent, T. C. *Invitation to World Missions: A Trinitarian Missiology for the Twenty-First Century*. Grand Rapids: Kregel Academic and Professionals, 2010.

Wenham, G. J. "Genesis." *Word Biblical Commentary*. Eds. David A. Hubbard and Glen W. Barter. Texas: Word Books Publishers, 1987.

Wright, C. J. H. *Knowing Jesus through the Old Testament*. Chennai: UESI Publication Trust, 2001.

Wright, C. J. H. *The Mission of God: Unlocking the Bible's Grand Narrative*. London: Authentic, 2006.

9

The Centrality of Christ and the Hermeneutical Perspectives of the Serampore Mission

George Philip

Introduction

Serampore mission has been a life-transforming project initiated by the Serampore Trio (William Carey, Joshua Marshman and William Ward) and continues through the theological training of the Senate of Serampore College for the ministerial candidates. This article has three major parts: the first part is an attempt to answer the question how can we understand the centrality of Christ in the activities of the Serampore Trio?; the second part is an inquiry into the hermeneutical principles of the Serampore mission; and the last part is a probing into the hermeneutical paradigms of the current theological education in the development of contextual scriptural readings. As a whole, one can see the centrality of Christ in the missional activities of the Serampore Trio.

The Centrality of Christ and the Serampore Mission

William Carey and his associates were exceptional personalities in the history of the Indian mission. Carey was influenced by the first Evangelical Awakening of the 18th Century Europe.[1] The Serampore Trio engaged in various activities with an integral spirit of holistic mission. The two mutually linked words in the mission are, 'event' and 'proclamation.' The event we are concerned with is the resurrection. The proclamation is the result of the experience of encounter with the Risen One which does not take us out of the world and history but, in revealing himself in the one who was crucified. This experience of encounter is transformed into a living and liberating witness, producing a new life and anticipating justice and future of the Kingdom.[2] This means that the future of the Kingdom, anticipated by the encounter and experience of the Risen One, reveals himself in the mission of the church in the building up of a transforming hope.

The beginning of 1800 was a difficult period for any English men to survive in the rural Indian context. Ward died of cholera in 1823. His own hymn describes the rewards of the Serampore work, struggles as well as their passion for Christ:

> Yes, we are safe beneath Thy shade,
> And shall be so midst India's heat:
> What should a missionary dread,
> For devils crouch at Jesus' feet.
> There, sweetest Savior! let Thy cross
> Win many Hindoo hearts to thee;
> This shall make up for every loss,
> While Thou art ours eternally.

Serampore Trio centered all their work on the Christ event. Their whole emphasis was to propagate the saving knowledge of Christ. They neither tried to focus the attention on them nor over-emphasized their work. For example, at his deathbed, Carey cautioned a Scottish young man, Mr. Duff, who addressed him Dr. Carey in his interview:

> You have been speaking about Dr. Carey, Dr. Carey; when I am gone, say nothing about Dr. Carey. Speak about Dr. Carey's savior.[3]

Another example of Carey's Christ-centeredness is clear from the lines of a song on his epitaph. Nearing to his death, Carey wanted to place a stone tablet on his tomb. He wanted only a flat stone with his name, date of birth, date of death, and a line from a song by Isaac Watts:

> A guilty weak and helpless worm,
> On your kind arms I fall.[4]

'Word' and 'Deed' were inseparable for the Serampore Trio. Some of the salient features of the Serampore mission are given below.

Integral Mission

Carey and Marshman(s) opened numerous schools for the downtrodden community. Serampore College catered the needs of pastors and teachers. Carey opened a Saving Bank to enable the poor to educate their children and to assist the unemployed.[5] He was instrumental in the founding of the Agro-Horticulture Society in order to raise the level of agricultural production to provide a better diet for the poor. He also engaged in dialogue with political leaders to carry forward the social reforms. Their periodicals, *Samachar Darpan* and *Friend of India*, were eye-openers against socio-political injustices. Once Carey did not attend a Sunday worship service as he had to translate and dispatch a Government order against Sati. Although Marshman reminded Carey about his preaching assignment, Carey said:

> It must be published at once. Someone else must preach for me. If I delay one day, the lives of many poor women will be lost. This is acting the Gospel, and I think a legitimate use of the Sabbath.[6]

The whole things what the Serampore Trio did were centered on the propagation of Gospel message in India. Serampore mission was an encouragement to many. Carey and his colleagues were an inspiration to Indian social reformers like Raja Ram Mohan Roy and in turn, it led to the Bengali Renaissance.

Importance to Native Missionaries

The Serampore Trio identified the need of trained natives from India for mission works. Carey wrote in one of his letters to Ryland, "English missionaries will never be able to instruct the whole India."[7] The Trio was so much satisfied with the progress of native people's evangelistic works. Similarly, the finance required for the sustenance of a European missionary was enormous. Thus, Marshman wrote, "the sum required for the support of a European family would be sufficient to meet the wants of twenty native laborers."[8] They in turn under his guidance might itinerate a large district and fill it with the Scriptural knowledge. In October 1805, the Serampore Trio drew up a "Form of Agreement" in which eleven points were outlined as their mission strategy emphasizing the fact that the church must be indigenous from the beginning. The 8th principle stated, "it is only by means of native preachers that we can hope for the universal spread of the Gospel throughout this immense continent. We think it is our duty as soon as possible, to advise the native brethren who may be formed into separate churches to choose their pastors and deacons from their own countrymen."[9] Carey's own Baptist colleagues were critical of his indigenous policies and separated from him. Thus, the Serampore Trio recognized that the native pastors needed to be trained and become self-supportive and also must be self-governing.

Importance to Local Languages

Dialects of the common people play an important role in the communication of the Gospel. Carey was a missionary with the scientific zeal of a linguist. Till the coming of Carey and his associates, local vernaculars in India did not get any recognition as the official languages.[10] The progress of Indian vernaculars had not been remarkable during the Mohammadean rule. With the patronage of Fort William College of the East India Company, the Serampore missionaries promoted all Indian languages. It is to be acknowledged that Indian local languages and its written text had been confined to a narrow circle of the educated elite. Carey and his associates were the first among the scholars and authors to have felt the need for recording the colloquial languages with its own diction and distinctive style. About the literary developments of the 19th century, Cassell's Encyclopedia noted that, "literary renaissance in this period was due to three causes: first, the new rulers realized that success depended upon the sympathetic knowledge and understanding of the languages and literature of the Indian people; second, the work of the Protestant missionaries of the Danish colony in Serampore; third, substitution of English for Persian as official language in 1853."[11] A good number of Indian learned scholars (*pandits*) closely associated with Carey. It is estimated that Carey himself wholly or partly translated the Bible in 29 Indian dialects. In most cases, Carey retained the language of the common people.

Importance to Native Culture

The Serampore Trio had deep respect toward Indian religions, cultures and languages. Carey's publication of Bengali Dictionary stands even today as a magnum opus. As early as 1802, Carey completed the Bengali Mahabharata in four volumes and the Ramayana in five volumes.[12] Similarly, William Ward had the vision to preserve the history, literature, and mythology of Hindoos (sic). He recommended to BMS:

> . . . that a Society should be formed, either in Calcutta or London, for improving our knowledge of the History, Literature, and Mythology, of the Hindoos; . . . that after collecting sufficient funds, this Society should purchase an estate, and erect a Pantheon which should receive the images of the most eminent of the gods, cut in marble—a Museum to receive all the curiosities of India, and a Library, to perpetuate its literature.

The reason for the preservation is mentioned as:

> . . . that the ancient writings and the monuments of the Hindoos are daily becoming more scarce, and more difficult of acquisition; they will soon irrecoverably perish.[13]

Although the Baptist Mission Society would not have accepted such a proposal, Ward's motivation for such a project was out of his respect for Indian culture and Eurocentric pride in the early nineteenth-century British rule. The Serampore Trio took the Indian culture and belief seriously.

Carey was particular to resist all attempts to replace Indian culture with the Christian culture of the west. As an example, Carey did not ask his first convert, Krishna Pal, to change his name even though his name included a famous Hindu deity. [14] However, the pioneers of the Serampore mission were against social evils of the native culture like caste system, sati, dowry system, exposure of the aged on the banks of rivers, *devadasi* system, and female infanticide.[15] It reflects their commitment toward social transformation through education. Carey and his colleagues were an inspiration to Indian social reformers like Raja Ram Mohan Roy and in turn, it led to the Bengali Renaissance. The centrality of Christ was so visible in their activities. The things that the Serampore Trio did were centered on the propagation of Gospel message in India. Thus, critics would say: "the main object of the Serampore Mission was to communicate to the Christian missionaries a knowledge of Indian Classics so as to enable them to influence the minds of the 'native' people."[16] Based on the above facts, one has to evaluate the hermeneutical perspectives of the Serampore Mission.

Hermeneutical Perspectives of the Serampore Mission

Proof Text and Literal Interpretation

'Proof-text' is the method by which a person appeals to a biblical text to prove or justify a theological position without regard for the context of the passage they are citing. Prior to the development of critical studies, Christian writers generally used this method. The New Testament authors support this idea in their own citations of the Old Testament text. The desire for such method is to base a particular theology on a canonical text.

For Carey, the Bible was the sole means to know the truth of God and the way of salvation. Word of God was the final authority in all aspects of his life. He used Matthew 28:18-20 as a proof text in his booklet, *Enquiry* in order to prove God's dislike of idolatry and the idolatrous practices of the "heathens." Carey quoted extensively from Romans chapter one in order to substantiate the preaching in the unreached areas. Carey quoted a negative example from the lives of Paul and Silas who were forbidden to preach in Bithynia; but still Carey argued that Paul and Silas did not neglect the other parts of the world (Acts 16:6-7).[17] Again Carey depicted that when a God-given command exists, then it was to be implemented no matter how much obstacles seems to be, or if, any natural impossibility of putting it into execution.[18]

It has been said that some learned biblical scholars used to prove from the scripture that the time had not yet come that the heathen should be converted and that first the *witnesses must be slain*, and many other prophecies must be fulfilled such as the down pouring of the Holy Spirit on all people and the like. Then Carey counter-argued that if this is not the time, then how could some missionaries have succeeded in some parts of the world. Carey continued to quote the *Acts of the Apostles* to prove the need for missionary activities in the unknown land. Carey also appealed for the unity of Christians in arranging the means for "pagan" mission. For that he quoted, "*for he that is joined to the Lord is one spirit* (1Cor. 6:17)."[19] Similarly, numerous quotations of prophetical books which describe the glorious picture of God's kingdom are available in his booklet called *Enquiry*.

Another example of his 'proof text' quotation was in relation to his decision to go to India. On 17th January 1793, Carey wrote a letter to his father expressing his willingness to go to India as a missionary. On receiving his letter, his father commented that it was folly for Carey to go to India. Similarly, Carey's wife, Dorothy, also out-rightly rejected Carey's proposal. But Carey proceeded with his plan by quoting Matthew 10:37: "He who loves father or mother more than me is not worthy of me." And "No one who puts a hand to the plough and looks back is fit for the kingdom of God" (Luke 9:62). Throughout his life, Carey made it a point to "live by faith" and "walk by faith."

Fulfilling the Great Commission

Carey considered the Great Commission is as valid to his generation as it was valid for the apostles in the first century. When a Baptist association meeting sought topics for discussion by late 1786, Carey proposed his growing passion: "Whether the command given to the apostles to teach all nations was not binding on all succeeding ministers to the end of the world."[20] In the first year of Carey's life in Bengal, in May 1794, he wrote in his diary, about his interaction with two Brahmins with the help of a *moonshi* (translator), in the presence of about 200 people concerning the things of God:

> . . . I, therefore, discoursed with them upon . . . the folly and wickedness of idolatry, the nature and attributes of God, and the way of salvation by Christ . . . . I cannot tell what effect it may have, as I may never see them again.[21]

Moreover, William Ward, a printer and editor, was a good preacher. Some considered him as the finest preacher of Serampore. Two years after his arrival, he toured the interior with the first convert Krishna Pal preaching and distributing Scriptures. "His knowledge of the character and habits of the natives surpassed that of either of his colleagues," wrote one observer, "and few Europeans have ever been more successful in dealing with [the natives]."[22] Similarly, Marshman joined in translating and preaching. He was a sharp-tongued speaker, and often he came home bloodied from bricks thrown by Indians who were irritated by both his manner and his message. Carey once contrasted his personality and Marshman's with the Reformers, saying, "In point of zeal, he is Luther, I am Erasmus."[23] In one of the letters to his son Jabez, Carey made his intention clear: "Consider that and the spread of Gospel as the great object of your life, and try to promote them by all the wise and prudent methods in your power."[24] For Carey, fulfilling the Great Commission was a mandate to be followed by all Christians.

Translation as a Means of Mission

The major contribution of the Serampore Trio was the translation and printing of the Bible into various languages. Carey was a good linguist. In 1801, Carey published the Bengali New Testament and thereafter it was revised many times. In 1808, his Sanskrit New Testament was published, and over the next 28 years, his pundits and he would translate the entire Bible in six languages such as Bengali, Oriya, Marathi, Hindi, Assamese, and Sanskrit, and parts of it into 29 other languages and dialects. Moreover, Carey translated Indian literatures and his work on grammars proceeded. What all Carey and his associates did was to enhance the mission works. George Smith commented about Carey's work as "every printed Bengali leaf of Scripture or pure literature was a missionary."[25] Carey wanted to attempt great things for God and often the target was too much for a human being to achieve. In 1806, he wrote to Andrew Fuller: "If we are given another fifteen years, we hope to translate and print the Bible in all the chief languages of Hindustani." It would have meant one complete Bible translation every year. But his associates thought of him mad. Ward argued against it, as did Andrew Fuller from England, cautioning if "by aiming at too much we may accomplish the less."[26] But Carey disregarded the warnings and proceeded. Most of Carey's translations were wooden and had to be significantly revised.

'Church-Individual' together as the locus of Interpretation

The Church is the prime locus of interpretation for Roman Catholic and Orthodox churches. Exegesis is the function of the worshipping and witnessing community of faith.[27] Having been functioned as a pastor in both England and in India, Carey never undermined the need of a church and the importance of worshipping community in interpreting the Word of God. Carey was introduced to the personal experience of Christ when he was fourteen by John Warr, one of his fellow apprentice cobblers and a devout Dissenter. Warr shared his "radical" ideas and books which gradually turned Carey a Dissenter.[28] About this Carey says: "he became importunate with me." As a result, Carey took the decision to be a missionary when he was seventeen. Thus, Carey knew the need of personal evangelism and gospel literature.

Carey and his associates were not focusing on the churches alone as they engaged themselves in translating the Bible. Their desire was that each one should get the Word of God in their own local language. Thus, the Serampore Trio focused their attention on Bible translation. This paved the way for the intensified study of the Word of God by lay people. Serampore Trio's vision for imparting the Word of God resulted in the formation of a university for theological and non-theological students.

The Senate of Serampore College and the Hermeneutical Paradigms

According to their first prospectus released on 15th July 1818, the institution was to be "a college for the instruction of Asiatic Christian and other youth in Eastern Literature and European Science." In a lengthy document, Marshman made it clear that the College was to be a handmaid of evangelization.[29] It is meant that the College was to be considered as 'pre-eminently a divinity school, where Christian youth of personal piety and aptitude, for the work of an evangelist, should go through a complete course for the instruction in Christian theology.' Because of the years of commercial depression after the demise of Serampore Trio, Arts and Theology wings lost its pre-eminence. Later by the earnestness of George Howell, Arts and Theology departments were reopened. Serampore conferred its first BD degree on three students in 1915. The Charter of the King of Denmark was revived under the Bengal Act of 1918.

Although the Senate of Serampore College makes use of the western hermeneutical principles, it encourages the use of Indian hermeneutical tools, relevant to the context. From the beginning, Carey was in favor of educating Indian youths in Indian languages within the Indian framework. As Sam P. Mathew mentions, "the complex Indian context demands a plurality of critical biblical readings with the people in pluri-religious community, open to the dynamic activity of the Spirit with a goal to transform our society and promote communal harmony."[30] India has its own unique social problems like poverty, caste system, subjugation of tribals-adivasis, patriarchy, and the like. Therefore, our biblical interpretations should meet the needs of Indian social problems[31] and cultural peculiarities. The focus of contextual theologies is the transformative aspect of the texts. A biblical researcher should present the readers to creatively expand their imagination of the new possibilities and alternatives of the text in the current context.[32] Thus, theological students should develop Indian hermeneutical tools that are relevant to Indian realities.

Narrative Reading

Stories are an important communication tool for human history. People use stories to convey the reality of life and the origin, continuation and the purpose of cosmos and life. And on this premise, Narrative Theology formulates its arguments. Biblical communication about God occurs mostly through stories. Every narrative has a storyteller/implied author, a plot and a few characters. Most often a tradition develops around a story and legitimizes its worldview. Community identity and its existence cannot be understood apart from the way they "story" their lives. Narrative Reading analyzes the stories about God, world, people, religious practices, and the like.[33] One needs to identify and classify various fabrics of these stories so as to empower people against injustices and oppression instead of legitimizing injustices. The narrative reading is more contextual as the readers get an active part and their response is very much important.

Although Carey did not make use of the Narrative Criticism in its modern sense in analyzing the biblical narratives, the narrative style of Carey in convincing his readers should be appreciated. Carey in his *Enquiry* dealt with Matthew 28:18-20 and argued about the continuation of the command of God to all nations. He astutely argued the pros and cons of engaging in mission activity for "heathens." Carey used dramatic language to make his appeal for mission. At the end of his pamphlet *Enquiry*, Carey narrated about the harvest waiting for Paul, Eliot, and Brainerd and other missionaries, who gave themselves fully to the work of the Lord by their mission activities. He concluded the narrative by saying, "surely it is worthwhile to lay ourselves out with all our might in promoting the cause of the kingdom of Christ." By these exhortations, Carey brought awareness and aroused interest to his lethargic Baptists and Calvinists to respond to the command of God.

Dalit Reading

By the inspiration and success of Latin American Liberation theology, Dalit Christians have been theologizing biblical passages to unlock the message of liberation for the last few decades.[34] Since the Bible has the potential of liberation, Dalit liberative reading envisions the Bible as a source of emancipation. The Serampore Trio's work especially the education project should be seen as spreading light over the caste oriented darkness.

Using the hermeneutics of suspicion, retrieval and representation, Dalit hermeneutics undertakes the task of re-reading the biblical texts. Based on the Indian reality of caste system, *dalitness* is taken as an oppressive and unjust condition which functions as a hermeneutical tool to interpret the text. Therefore, both Dalits and non-Dalits can make use of this hermeneutical tool in the process of interpretation. The objective of this reading is to transform the predicament of the Dalit people in India towards a just society. The God in Christ is the real champion of the cause of the sufferers, underprivileged and helpless community. Besides the work of Jesus, individual characters and events in the Bible are taken as models of inspiration to fight against the oppression in the society. A Dalit interpreter approaches biblical texts with hope and aspiration in order to retrieve what is lost.[35] Thus, Dalits are called to fight against any form of unjust and oppressive structures in society (and in the church).

Tribal Reading

Christianity came to the tribal areas of the North-East India in the second half of the nineteenth century. The first contact was with the Khasis occurred in 1812-1813. Krishna Chandra Pal, an evangelist working under William Carey of Serampore, converted two Khasis. The Serampore Baptists established stations, Cherrapunjee in the Khasi Hills and at Guahati in the Assam valley. However, these early contacts did not produce any tangible results and the work was given up after the death of the Serampore Trio. Later Welsh Calvinist Presbyterian Mission and American Baptist Mission took care of most of the evangelistic works in the North Eastern India.[36]

The cultural outlook of Christian Tribals, both the tribal of the plain area and the hill area, seems to be the cultural outlook of the western missionaries who evangelized them. In order to have a native outlook, a proper hermeneutic is essential. The world-view of the tribal people, their concept of God, forms of worship, arts and culture, and their way of life must be taken into serious account in order to have tribal hermeneutics.

Tribal theology addresses the socio-economic problems of the community. Land is the source of life and identity and is sacred. The livelihood of the tribals is generally intertwined with land. However, tribal communities face land alienation, mainly because of the Land Acquisition Act-1894. Similarly, tribal communities often face social isolation and discrimination from the main stream society. The human rights of the tribal are often violated by the government.[37] Therefore, tribal reading of the text addresses such concerns of social justice and social identity.

Feminist Reading

Women's concerns, experiences, and problems are not adequately taken care in traditional Christian theology, which is, therefore, patriarchal in nature. Feminist reading and theology thus seeks to analyze the effects of the exclusion of women and negative anthropology about women in the shaping of the understanding of God, nature, sin, grace, Christology, redemption and ecclesiology. Feminist theology is a quest for alternative traditions which will include both women and men. It also looks for a transformation of male symbols and use of inclusive symbols for God and humans.

As one acknowledges the Serampore Trio, one needs to acknowledge the contributions of Hannah Marshman who has been often silenced. She ran the large mission household and cared for many: mentally ill Dorothy Carey; the widow and children of William Grant (who had died less than three weeks after arriving in India); and the young and pregnant widow of John Fountain. And with Ward, she disciplined the unruly Carey boys.[38] Moreover, Hannah and her husband Marshman operated two boarding schools for English children and one non-fee school for Indian children. The schools' income, in fact, helped make the Serampore mission financially independent. Similarly, she started schools for women. By 1926, there were 14 other such institutions in the country.

Postcolonial Reading

Postcolonial theory, as a tool for Biblical interpretation, deals with the Bible as a "cultural product" in time and space. The Western hermeneutics are considered to be incapable of explaining the harsh realities of inequality, oppression and exploitation that are common experiences of Asian, African, and Latin American countries. Postcolonial biblical criticism is concerned with the sociopolitical context in which the voice of the *other* is being silenced. It deals with the contexts whereby socio-political powers and identities are constructed. The postcolonial theory takes into consideration the situation of the colonizer as well as the colonized in order to reconstruct a negotiating space of equality.[39] Sugirtharajah's edited work on *Voices from the Margin*[40] is recognized as a good contribution to postcolonial theory in biblical criticism. Postcolonial reading brings out the silenced voices of the colonial period. Voices are silenced with respect to gender, race, nativity, culture, and the like because of the colonial viewpoint. The researcher looks for "the expressions of freedom for space."[41]

Serampore Mission is also intertwined with colonial history. News of Captain Cook's explorations in the South Pacific came back to England, expanding peoples' understanding of the world. When Carey read *The Last Voyage* of Captain Cook, it stirred his interest in missions. Although Carey had to face opposition from Britishers in the early part of his stay in Calcutta, gradually, Britishers changed their policy and accommodated him as a professor at Fort William College, which partly supported his expenses of translation projects. As part of his appointment as Professor of Fort William College, British Governor, Lord Wellesley, had been assured that Carey was "well affected to Government" and could be of great use in preparing young Anglos for its operations in Bengal.[42] Marshman openly expressed his love towards British Empire:

> . . . no one in Leaden Hall Street, nor even in Britain, more ardently wishes for the permanence and prosperity of the British empire in India than myself.[43]

Christopher Smith also notes down some derogatory remarks from that period, "the Serampore Baptists believed that the Almighty had committed to 'Britain alone' the task of providing wretched India with 'instruction and relief.'"[44] Moreover, Carey and his associates had the identity of 'British citizens,' 'officer of the college,' and 'missionaries'[45] which in a way helped them from locals' religious attack. This may be the reason, perhaps, Christianity in India is still considered as westerners' religion.

Conclusion

Serampore mission was centered on Christ and His commission to be His witnesses. All of their activities were focusing on the propagation of the Gospel. Experience of Christ event and the propagation of His saving works always transform society. Serampore Trio/Quartet established institutions like schools, colleges, hospitals, printing press, translation projects, and so on to make transformation in the society and to win India for Christ. The pioneers of the Serampore mission were known for their deep respect for Indian languages, literature, religion and culture. Their openness is carried forward in the formation of the Serampore College and later the Senate of Serampore College for the training of ministerial candidates. The hermeneutical principles of the Serampore Trio were proof-text method and literal interpretation of the text. They followed translation as a means of mission. By making the Bible available to everyone in their own language, the Serampore Trio made church-and-individual together as the locus of interpretation.

The continuation of the Serampore mission now focuses on the theological education and development of contextual theologies. The emphasis of Contextual theology in the curriculum of the Senate of Serampore College paves way for furthering the transformation of the Indian societies and the development of native leaders. Thus, the function of the Senate of Serampore College now is in line with the motives of the Serampore Trio/Quartet. The Senate of Serampore graduates are better equipped to address the social and ecclesiastical problems of the day. The theological education produces research scholars and new hermeneutical methods relevant to the context.

Endnotes

[1] Bartholomew Ziegenbalg and Heinrich Plütschau were Pietists from the University of Halle (in Germany) who came to the Danish colony of Tranquebar in India in 1706. Susannah Wesley, mother of John and Charles Wesley, was greatly influenced by reading the memoirs of Ziegenbalg and Plütschau. Her sons deeply felt the spiritual impact of the Moravians. The evangelical awakening in England was led primarily by John and Charles Wesley and George Whitefield. The movement led to renewal in various churches, and Carey was awakened in his faith by the movement. It is significant that Carey wrote his famous "Enquiry," his missions manifesto, only one year after John Wesley died.

[2] Cesar Kuzma, "Mission and Identity of the People of God: An Outgoing Church called to service of the Kingdom," tran. Francis McDonagh, *Concilium* 3/2018: 24-25.

[3] J. J. Ellis, *William Carey: Faithful Translator of God's Word for India*, cf. https://bibletruthpublishers.com/chapter-8-say-nothing-about-dr-carey-or-speak-about-dr-carey/james-joseph-ellis/william-carey/j-j-ellis/la121922, accessed on 10th October 2018.

[4] These words were taken from the last verse of hymn 181 in John Rippon's Arrangement of the Psalms, Hymns and Spiritual Songs, of Rev. Isaac Watts. They were used by Joshua Marshman at William Ward's funeral, eleven years before Carey's death, when they became his epitaph-to be used by biographers.

[5] Bruce J. Nichols, "The Theology of William Carey," *Carey's Obligation and India's Renaissance* (Serampore: Council of Serampore College, 1993), 123-124.

[6] Ellis, *Faithful Translator of God's Word for India,* Chapter 8.

[7] Cf. D. A. Christadoss, "The Story of Serampore College," *The Story of Serampore and Its College* (Serampore: The Council of Serampore College, 2005), 20.

[8] Cf. Christadoss, "Serampore," 20.

[9] Cf. Nichols, "The Theology of William Carey," 118.

[10] S. K. Chatterjee, "William Carey and the Linguistic Renaissance in India," *Carey's Obligation and India's Renaissance* (Serampore: Council of Serampore College, 1993), 157.

[11] *Cassell's Encyclopedia of Literature*, Vol. 1, 295, as cited in Chatterjee, "William Carey," 158.

[12] Kalidas Nag, "Carey's Contributions to Bengali Literature," *The Story of Serampore and Its College* (Serampore: The Council of Serampore College, 2005), 150.

[13] A. Christopher Smith, *The Serampore Mission Enterprise* (Bangalore: CFCC, 2006), 134-35.

[14] Carey and his colleagues encouraged their new converts to retain their traditional dress and even their sacred thread of higher castes. Bruce J. Nichols, "The Theology of William Carey," *Carey's Obligation and India's Renaissance* (Serampore: Council of Serampore College, 1993), 120-121.

[15] O. L. Snaitang, "Challenges from William Carey to the Mission of the Church in India," *Mission in the Past and Present* (Bangalore: BTESSC/SATHRI, 2006), 39.

[16] N. R. Ray, "William Carey—A Linguist with a Difference," *Carey's Obligation and India's Renaissance* (Serampore: Council of Serampore College, 1993), 153.

[17] Carey, *Enquiry,* section 1, (page 10 in the online pdf: https://www.wmcarey.edu/carey/enquiry/anenquiry.pdf).

[18] Carey, *Enquiry,* section 1.

[19] Carey, *Enquiry*, section 5.

[20] Many Christians of Carey's day believed that "when God pleases to convert the heathen, he'll do it without consulting you or me." Carey argued instead that Christ's command to "Go into all the world" was still binding and required action now. Cf. *Enquiry.*

[21] Cf. Mark Galli, "The Man Who Would Not Give Up," *Christian History,* Issue 36 (1992).

[22] Galli, *Christian History*, 14.

[23] Desiderius Erasmus (1469-1536) was a Dutch humanist known for his intense zeal for language. His works paved way for Reformation and Counter-Reformation.

[24] *Letter sent to his Son, Jabez*, 15th August 1820. Also see Sunil Kumar Chatterjee, *Family Letters of Dr William Carey* (Serampore: The Author, 2007), 28.

[25] George Smith, *The Life of William Carey: Shoe Maker and Missionary* (London: John Murray, Albemarle Street, 1885), 157.

[26] See Galli, *Christian History*, 10.

[27] J. Breck, *Scripture in Tradition: The Bible and Its Interpretation in the Orthodox Church* (New York: SVS Crestwood, 2001), 40.

[28] Galli, *Christian History,* Issue 36 (1992), 12.

[29] Cf. Christadoss, "Serampore," 21.

[30] Sam P. Mathew, "Indian Biblical Hermeneutics: Methods and Principles," A paper presented in the consultation on the Indian Bible Commentary Project held at Gurukul Lutheran Theological College and Research Institute, on September 2003.

[31] Cf. P. A. Sampathkumar, "Current Trends in Indian Biblical Studies," *Bible Bashyam: An Indian Biblical Quarterly* 25/1 (March, 1999): 65-74.

[32] The role of the Bible Scholar is to create an appropriate atmosphere for (Dalit) subjectivity to be activated in dialogue with Biblical subjectivity. A. Maria Arul Raja, "Dalit Layers of Consciousness in Dialogue with the Biblical World," *Dalit-Tribal Theological Interface: Current Trends in Subaltern Theologies* (New Delhi/Jorhat: TSC/ WSC/ CDS), 199-200.

[33] Cf. George Stroup, *The Promise of Narrative Theology* (Atlanta: John Knox, 1981), 87-89; D. R. Stiver, *Theology After Ricoeur: New Directions in Hermeneutical Theology* (Louisville: Westminster John Knox Press, 2001), 115.

[34] K. Jesurathnam, *Dalit Liberative Hermeneutics: Indian Christian Dalit Interpretation of Psalm 22* (Delhi: ISPCK, 2010), 6.

[35] Jesurathnam, *Dalit Liberative*, xvii.

[36] Renthy Keitzar, "Tribal Perspective in Biblical Hermeneutics Today," *Indian Journal of Theology* (July-Dec 1982), 319. See https://biblicalstudies.org.uk/pdf/ijt/31-3-4_293.pdf, accessed on 10th October 2018.

[37] Human rights can be understood as abstract norms and values protected in laws, constitutions, and international conventions. At the same time, human rights are cultural concepts that are slowly evolving in response to social change or contestation. Ravi Nair, *Human rights in India: Historical, Social and Political Perspectives* (New Delhi: Oxford University Press, 2006), as quoted by Krishna Halavath, "Human Rights and Realities of Tribals' Lives in India: A Perfect Storm," *IOSR-JHSS* 19/4 (Apr. 2014), 43.

[38] "Hannah and Joshua Marshman (1767–1847; 1768–1837): First woman missionary to India and brilliant educator," *Christian History*, Issue 36 (1992): 15.

[39] Lazare S. Rukundwa, "Postcolonial theory as a hermeneutical tool for Biblical reading," *HTS* 64/1 (2008): 343.

[40] Sugirtharajah, R. S., ed., *Voices from the margin: interpreting the Bible in the Third World* (London: SPCK, 1995).

[41] David Joy, *Overlooking Voices: A Postcolonial Indian Quest* (California: Borderless Press, 2015), 41.

[42] Carey to Fuller, 18 November 1806; Carey to Sutcliffe, 8 April 1801. Cf. Smith, *The Serampore Mission*, 166.

[43] Joshua Marshman, "Advantages of Christianity in Promoting the Establishment and Prosperity of British Government in India: Containing Remarks Occasioned by Reading a Memoir of the Vellore Mutiny" (London: Smith's Printing Office, 1813), 6-7, as cited in Smith, *The Serampore Mission*, 167, footnote 13.

[44] Smith, *The Serampore Mission,* 167.

[45] Only white people were considered as "missionaries" and "ordained" pastors among Protestants till Indian Independence, 1947. It is also to be noted that Colonel Bie and the Governor of Serampore protected Carey, his colleagues and their work. Cf. Daniel Jeyaraj, "Protestant Missionary Work in India, particularly in Calcutta before the arrival of William Carey," *Mission in the Past and Present,* 28.

Bibliography

Breck, J. *Scripture in Tradition: The Bible and Its Interpretation in the Orthodox Church.* New York: SVS Crestwood, 2001.

Carey, W. *An Enquiry into the Obligations of Christians, To Use Means for the Conversion of the Heathens.* Cf. www.wmcarey.edu/carey/enquiry/anenquiry.pdf

Chatterjee, S. K. *Family Letters of Dr. William Carey.* Second Edition. Serampore: The Author, 2007.

Chatterjee, S. K. "William Carey and the Linguistic Renaissance in India." *Carey's Obligation and India's Renaissance.* Serampore: Council of Serampore College, 1993.

Christadoss, D. A. "The Story of Serampore College." *The Story of Serampore and Its College.* Serampore: The Council of Serampore College, 2005.

Ellis, J. J. *Faithful Translator of God's Word for India,* Chapter 8, cf. https://bibletruthpublishers.com/chapter-8-say-nothing-about-dr-carey-or-speak-about-dr-carey/james-joseph-ellis/william-carey/j-j-ellis/121922. Accessed on 10th October 2018.

Galli, M. "The Man Who Would Not Give Up." *Christian History.* Issue 36 (1992). Cf. https://christianhistoryinstitute.org/magazine/article/man-who-would-not-give-up. Accessed on 10th October 2018.

"Hannah and Joshua Marshman (1767–1847; 1768–1837): First woman missionary to India and brilliant educator." *Christian History.* Issue 36 (1992). Cf. https://www.christianhistoryinstitute.org/uploaded/50cf7f6c8edab1.22614948.pdf.

Jesurathnam, K. *Dalit Liberative Hermeneutics: Indian Christian Dalit Interpretation of Psalm 22.* Delhi: ISPCK, 2010.

Joy, D. *Overlooking Voices: A Postcolonial Indian Quest.* California: Borderless Press, 2015.

Keitzar, R. "Tribal Perspective in Biblical Hermeneutics Today." *Indian Journal of Theology* (July-Dec 1982), cf. https://biblicalstudies.org.uk/pdf/ijt/31-3-4_293.pdf. Accessed on 10th October 2018.

Kuzma, C. "Mission and Identity of the People of God: An Outgoing Church called to service of the Kingdom." Tran. Francis McDonagh. *Concilium* 3 (2018).

Marshman, J.C. *The Life and Times of Carey, Marshman and Ward.* Vol. 1 and 2. London: Longman, Brown, Green, Longmans, and Roberts, 1859; Republished by Council of Serampore College, 2005.

Mathew, S. P. "Indian Biblical Hermeneutics: Methods and Principles." A paper presented in the consultation on the Indian Bible Commentary Project held at Gurukul Lutheran Theological College and Research Institute, on September 2003.

Nag, K. "Carey's Contributions to Bengali Literature." *The Story of Serampore and Its College*. Serampore: The Council of Serampore College, 2005.

Nichols, B. J. "The Theology of William Carey." *Carey's Obligation and India's Renaissance*. Serampore: Council of Serampore College, 1993.

Raja, A. M. A. "Dalit Layers of Consciousness in Dialogue with the Biblical World." *Dalit-Tribal Theological Interface: Current Trends in Subaltern Theologies*. New Delhi/Jorhat: TSC/ WSC/ CDS, 2007.

Ray, N. R. "William Carey—A Linguist with a Difference." *Carey's Obligation and India's Renaissance*. Serampore: Council of Serampore College, 1993.

Rukundwa, L. S. "Postcolonial theory as a hermeneutical tool for Biblical reading." *HTS* 64/1 (2008).

Sampathkumar, P. A. "Current Trends in Indian Biblical Studies." *Bible Bashyam: An Indian Biblical Quarterly* 25/1 (March 1999): 65-74.

Smith, A. Christopher. *The Serampore Mission Enterprise*. Bangalore: CFCC, 2006.

Smith, G. *The Life of William Carey: Shoe Maker and Missionary*. London: John Murray, Albemarle Street, 1885.

Snaitang, O. L. "Challenges from William Carey to the Mission of the Church in India." *Mission in the Past and Present*. Bangalore: BTESSC/SATHRI, 2006.

Stiver, D. R. *Theology After Ricoeur: New Directions in Hermeneutical Theology*. Louisville: Westminster John Knox Press, 2001.

Stroup, G. *The Promise of Narrative Theology*. Atlanta: John Knox Press, 1981.

Sugirtharajah, R. S., ed. *Voices from the margin: interpreting the Bible in the Third World*. London: SPCK, 1995.

10

Serampore Mission from a Botanical and Ecological Perspective

Jangkholam Haokip

Introduction

Serampore Mission was a missionary enterprise founded by those in the periphery of the society in the sense of social and economic standings. Along with William Carey, both Joshua Marshman and William Ward did not have the pleasure of receiving social and material wealth when they were young. Basil Miller's description of Carey's life throws some light on this: "Practically untaught, he became learned. Poor himself, he made millions spiritually rich. By birth obscure, he scaled the heights of eminence, seeking only to follow the Lord's leadership, inspired by the forward mark of God's plans."[1] Being poor themselves, their mission was different from that of others. They were able to foresee things that others didn't, expanded the meaning and dimensions of mission into areas that no one was able to do before them, and they had their own theological foundation for all that they were doing in mission. This essay discusses the contribution of William Carey toward creation care, reflects on his theological foundation, and raises some questions for further reflection.

William Carey—The Botanist

The Council of Serampore College in its Bicentenary Special at the commemoration of the 257th Birthday Anniversary of William Carey on August 17, 2018 fittingly entitled their Souvenir 'William Carey: The Multifaceted Genius'[2] and with a similar conviction, the Executive Vice

President and Provost and Professor of Religion in William Carey University, USA, Dr. Scott Hummel comments, "If Protestants had saints, William Carey would be one."[3] The 'saint' and 'genius' William Carey achieved what he called 'great things for God' and one of them was his contribution for the welfare of nature.

Before we look at Carey's contribution for the welfare of nature, a brief mention of his background will help us to understand and appreciate his contributions better. It was not possible that a person like Carey could become what he became. Carey had to persevere and overcome many challenges in his life as a young man. Leaving aside his lack of education, Carey did not enjoy a healthy life during his youth. On the top of that he did not have a gift of speaking and management. In spite of all these challenges, Carey had a strong and uncompromising zeal for mission, grounded in a theology of his time, and that kept him going until his last day. His letter to his father written on January 17, 1793 expressed this clearly:

> The importance of spending our time with God alone is the principal theme of the Gospel . . . . To be devoted like a sacrifice to holy uses is the great business of a Christian. I, therefore, consider myself devoted to the sole service of God, and now I am appointed to go to Bengal in the East Indies, a missionary to the Hindus . . . . I hope, dear father, you may be enabled to surrender me to the Lord for the most arduous, honorable, and important work that ever any of the sons of men were called to pursue. I must part with a beloved family . . . but I have set my hand to the plough.[4]

With such uncompromising conviction, Carey, along with his family finally left England on June 13, 1793 and arrived Kolkata on November 11, 1793 to begin his work. Arguably, Carey is best known for his contribution to other fields including Bible translation and social reform but not in ecology. This does not mean that Carey had less interest in nature. Carey had a keen interest in nature right from his early youth, particularly in the study of botany and in fact, he "piled his rooms with specimens of plants and also insects' life as a result of his quests among the local lanes and forests."[5] Carey was also interested in rocks and minerals. Sanjoy Mukherjee, an Associate professor of Botany in Serampore College, puts it in this way:

> He [Carey] was a captain of labor, a schoolmaster, a printer, the great developer of the vernacular speech, expounder of the classical language, founder of pure literature. Moreover, he was a reformer of society, the watchful philanthropist, a savior of the widows and father of the fatherless, a symbol of hope to the

> despairing and the would-be suicide, a champion of the downtrodden and suppressed, a friend of India and last of all a great Naturalist.[6]

Carey devoted a lot of time to study diverse plants in India. He enriched knowledge not only in the field of Botany but also in Horticulture and Soil Science. Soon after his arrival in India in 1793, Carey came to know that the post of Superintendent in the Botanical Garden at Sibpore was vacant. Seeing that as an opportunity, and of course with a strong recommendation by Captain Christmas, Carey hurriedly went to Calcutta in need of the post but to his disappointment, Dr. Roxburgh was appointed a few days ahead of him. That disappointed him much at first but later he developed a good friendship with Roxburgh, paving the way for better opportunities in the future.

Although he didn't get the job at Sibpore, Carey was always willing to work with others for the well-being of the nature. Under the care of Roxburgh as the Superintendent of the Sibpore Royal Botanical Garden (1793-1815), Carey had planned to edit and publish *Hortus Bengalensis*, a document cataloguing 3500 species, but it was published only in 1844, ten years after his death. About the work, Chatterjee writes,

> Carey had the uncanny ability of a practical field-botanist. His idea of editing and publishing *Hortus Bengalensis*, cataloguing 3500 species in cultivation in the Sibpore Royal Botanical Garden, under the care of Dr. Roxburgh (Suptd.1793-1815) was an excellent idea. *Hortus Bengalensis* provided an excellent document of exotic flora many of those introduced by William Carey from different ecological areas, like Sundarban mangrove forest, sub-Himalayan areas of Terai and Bhutan as well as those from Europe, Africa, North America, the Middle East, neighboring Burma, and China. His publication of *Roxburgh's Flora Indica* is an outstanding work. Roxburgh, who had included 2200 species, acknowledged his debt to Carey for 80 of these.[7]

Carey also did other works. Five years after Roxburgh's death in 1820, under the new Superintendent of the Botanical Garden, Dr. Nathaniel Wallich, Carey edited and published the first volume of *Roxburgh's Flora Indica*, a description of Indian plants. In 1824, he edited and published the second volume of *Roxburgh's Flora Indica* which included a considerable contribution by Dr. Nathaniel Wallich himself. The publication of the second volume was delayed as Carey was deputed on a botanical mission to Nepal for one year but ended up working for eighteen months until he returned in the beginning of 1822.[8] The friendship between Carey and Wallich continued long after these two publications to the extent of joining hands together in contributing botanical specimens to the Royal Society of Agriculture and Botany's Show in Ghent, Belgium.[9]

When it comes to practical involvement in the actual work of horticulture, Carey had the opportunity to develop his knowledge and skill while working in Malda Indigo Factory, a factory owned by a private company. It was through his work there that Carey was able not only develop his skills in the fields of botany and horticulture but also to support his family and ministry in the first few years of his time in India. Carey had an opportunity to pursue and develop into a full scope of his talents in botany and horticulture when moved to Serampore in 1800, the interests that he had from his young age. Carey saw clearly in his mind the needs of India. In 1811, he published his finding of agricultural poverty and the condition of peasants in the district of Dinajpore. He laments:

> . . . in one of the finest countries in the world, the state of agriculture is so abject and degraded and the people's food so poor and their comforts are so meager. India seems to have almost everything to learn about the clearing of jungles, the tillage of wastes, the draining of marshes, the driving of river courses, the irrigation of large areas, the mixing of compost and manure, rotation of crops, betterment of tools, and transport, of stocks, culture of new vegetables and herbs, planting of orchards, budding, grafting, pruning of fruit trees, forestation of timbers.[10]

It was because of these concerns, and of course to professionally sustain his project, that Carey formed 'Agri-Horticultural Society of India' on September 14, 1820[11] with himself as its president. The society later was changed to 'Royal Agri-Horticultural Society,' ahead of many such a society.

Carey also established a five-acre botanical garden that attracted professionals from around the world. The garden became the source of origin of many plants that later spread across Bengal as the seeds were dispersed by birds and wind. Carey imported seeds from other countries; for instance, sugarcane from Mauritius, tobaccos and cotton from USA; initiated experimentations on several plants for instance, the culture of coffee, cotton, tobacco, sugarcane, cereals, and other economic crops. Besides, fruit trees including those brought from England and other countries such as English apples, Mozambique oranges, Cape figs, Canton litchis, Manila guava and others were also experimented with. It is said that many of these endemic or Indian plants were introduced by Carey and his son, Felix Carey, from different regions of India including Bhutan.[12]

In 1824, Carey's garden was badly affected by a devastating flood that destroyed many of his plants and again in 1831 a cyclone destroyed whatever was left by the flood. In the two natural calamities, all of Carey's correspondence with various people both in India and abroad including dried specimens were lost and cannot be traced anywhere in India. Thankfully, some of Carey's herbarium sheets are preserved in the UK: Kew Botanical Garden, London; Liverpool City Museum; and Fielding Herbarium and Druce Herbarium, Oxford.[13] His garden served Carey not only for the purpose of intellectual recreation but also for spiritual life and growth because it was there where he spent time for prayer and meditation. Mukherjee describes:

> Eminent Botanist and Naturalist as Carey was, his horticultural activities and love of nature were satisfied when he laid out a 'well-planned garden' (five-acre garden) in Serampore . . . . The garden did not only serve the purpose of intellectual recreation for him but was also a place of prayer and meditation.[14]

Besides his work through his own initiatives, Carey also made an impact in a wider society. To safeguard the forest wealth, the Government of India appointed the Plantation Committee with Carey as one of the members to take measures for the improvement of forest wealth.[15] *The Plantation Committee Report* shows that they [the committee] outlined plans for new forests and preservation of old ones. This shows that Carey was a person ahead of his time. In fact, some even suggest that Carey's plan for forestry might be the earliest known plan in India for afforestation.[16]

Based on his knowledge and contribution, William Carey was elected as a fellow of the *Linnean Society of London* in 1823, a member of the *Geological Society of London*, a member of *Horticultural Society of London* and was an active member of the *Asiatic Society of Bengal* until he died. As a mark of respect for Carey for his contribution in creation care, the Superintendent of the Botanic Garden (1793-1815) Roxburgh named the Sal tree after William Carey and called it *Careya aborea.*[17] Apart from this, there are other plants that carry Carey's name, for instance, *Cenus Careya, Careya herbacea* and *Careya sphoerica.*[18] *Carey herbacea* is one of the three varieties of eucalyptus found only in India.[19]

Having described the developments in the areas of Horticultural Crops, Animal Husbandry, afforestation and the like under the able leadership of

Carey, Ghosh writes, "All these events, 157 years after the death of William Carey owe their debts to the concepts that Carey first initiated in colonial India—but fully purposed at least 120 years after his death."[20] The contribution of Carey in creation care, particularly in the fields of Botany and Horticulture is truly remarkable and that raises a question, "what made him do what he did?" In a similar way, biologist George Michael rightly comments on Carey's farsighted recommendation for the management of forest and wastelands and writes, "One cannot but marvel at his [Carey's] foresight! Even two hundred years ago he thought of greening the earth—a concept we would consider as belonging to our times."[21] This leads us to explore the theology of Carey on creation care, the basis of his work.

Engaging with Carey's Theology of Creation Care

Why did Carey do what he did? For Carey, the purpose of collecting different plants was both religious and missional. His writings on the title page of his *Flora Indica* "All thy works praise Thee O Lord" and "The natural history of Bengal would furnish innumerable novelties to a curious inquirer"[22] reflect Carey's theology of creation care. Further indications of his theological conviction can be found in his writing in 1825, "The great Author of Nature has filled the world with so great variety of objects that something presents itself, at every step to the view of the most incurious observer, and either from its utility, its beauty, its singularity, or some other obvious property, forces itself upon his notice."[23] From these writings, it is clear that Carey's concern for creation care was connected with his understanding of God. For him, God being its creator, the natural world reflected God's rich wisdom and beauty. As such, he was amazed at the variety of tropical plants, species and animals in India which are different from the world that he was familiar with before. His writing in 'Friend of India' spells out some of his theological convictions more clearly:

> The works of God are confessedly calculated to raise the mind to sublime meditation upon and admiration of their Maker; and the works of Creation, especially will convince us that every part of them is the work of the Being who spake and it was done, who commanded and it stood fast; and the admirable adaptation of every animal and vegetable to the station it is intended to occupy, proves incontestably the wisdom and goodness the universal Parent of all creatures, who openeth his hand and filleth every living creature with plenteousness.[24]

Viewing from an evangelical point of view, Vishal Mangalwadi argues that Carey's work on creation care was based on his evangelical theological conviction. He writes, "If the Gospel flourishes in India, the wilderness will in every respect, become a fruitful field" and hence his main theological basis for this as Mangalwadi puts it, "He became the first person in India to write essays on forestry, almost fifty years before the government made its very first attempt at forest conservation, in Malabar. Carey both practiced and vigorously advocated the cultivation of timber, giving practical advice on how to plant trees for environmental, agricultural, and commercial purposes. His motivation came from his belief that God has made man responsible for the earth."[25] Then Mangalwadi continues, "Carey's deep and dogged interest in nature—in stones (geology), in insects (biology), in plants and flowers (botany and agriculture), in trees (forestry), and in the stars (astronomy)—was rooted in his understanding that this world was his Father's creation."[26] According to Mangalwadi's observation, for Carey, God has created us with a special responsibility to care for nature and we should care for nature because it belongs to God. This view is shared by Michael when he writes,

> In all his undertaking, whether it was his attempts to introduce novel agricultural practices; in forestry or horticulture; establishment of schools and colleges; setting up a printing press; or in social work for the abolition of Sati and upliftment of women, Carey worked with a clarity of mind that was rooted in his strong conviction of the benevolence and love of his Creator.[27]

Similarly, in his search for evangelical ecological consciousness among early evangelicals, Dave Bookless took Carey as one example. First, he observed Carey's early life and his theological background that sustained him throughout his life, arguing, "Carey's ecological interests were no mere hobbies, but a practical outworking of his evangelical faith. Carey's evangelicalism made him passionate about evangelism but, equally, it convinced him that all truth was God's truth and that scientific, linguistic, and literary studies could only enhance the self-evident truths of the Gospel of Jesus Christ."[28] The point here is the inseparable connection between Carey's theological conviction and his work. In this, it is also reflected, human knowledge including science and technology were considered as means that enhance God's truth. In other words, the place of scientific knowledge was elevated as part of the message of Christ making his approach more of an anthropocentric. This is evident in the way Carey managed his botanical garden using Linnaean classification system.[29]

Second, Bookless explores to find where Carey's theological influences might have come from. He suggests that as a nonconformist, Carey would have learnt the hymnody of Isaac Watts (1674-1748), a hymnody based on the Psalmist's celebration of God's glory in nature in the light of Christocentric New Testament theology.[30] He further suggests that Watts' effective way of combining personal evangelical spirituality with earthly imagery must have influenced Carey's theology. One example of Watts' creative work was 'Let heaven and nature sing . . .' in his Christmas song 'Joy to the World the Lord has come.' In Bookless' view,

> The words express the joy that all creation ('fields and floods, rocks, hills and plains') experiences at Christ's coming and the reversal of creation's curse ('Nor thorns infest the ground'). 'Joy to the World,' with its references to Psalm 98, Romans 8:19-22 and Colossians 1:15-20, predates some evangelicals' understanding of the cosmic scope of Christ's redemptive work by almost three centuries.[31]

Third, Bookless identifies the incorporation of non-human creatures in the concerns of the evangelical tradition that influenced famous preachers like John Wesley. He observes that Carey as a 13-year old was inspired by listening to John Wesley (1703-1791), the foremost preacher of the evangelical revival of his time, saying, "Wesley's theology included reference to animal welfare and an eschatology affirming the renewal of all creation."[32] He goes even further to explore the background of Wesley and Watts and writes, "Carey's, Watts's and Wesley's breadth of evangelical passion drew on a tradition of evangelical concern for non-human creatures that arose with the seventeenth-century Puritans and Dissenters, and later spread into Methodism and evangelical Anglicanism."[33] With this, Bookless also observes that the early evangelicals also welcomed scientific discoveries, seeing them as evidence of the scope of God's work in nature. He cited John Ray (1627-1705), who sought to combine scientific discovery and biblical foundations in a comprehensive nature theology as a good example.[34]

From the above discussions, it can be concluded that Carey was a product of his time; shaped, motivated and enabled by the evangelical theological conviction of his time. His holistic understanding of mission was connected with the evangelical understanding of God that includes the concerns of creation care. In Carey's understanding, although nature was included in the concerns of God's mission, the approach to creation care was anthropocentric. Human intellectual ability was given a special place to 'manage' nature and makes nature more of a therapeutic depending on its usefulness to human beings. It was with such a conviction that Carey brought exotics from Europe, Africa, North America, Middle East and neighboring Burma and China to increase production of better varieties of vegetables and fruits by hybridizing seeds. Carey was not only excellent in his knowledge of species but was also interested in maximizing the utilization of nature. For him, nature belongs to God but at the same time, it is human beings who need to manage and maximize its utility. Accordingly, Carey advocated the need for the establishment of a 'regional' botanical garden, an agricultural society and an experimental farm.[35] He also wrote about some animals saying, "It is thus with the elephant and the buffalo, so mischievous in state of Nature, have been made highly useful in carrying heavy burdens, or ploughing the soil."[36] From the above discussion, we can safely conclude that although Carey gave an important place to creation and creation care in his missionary work, his main concern was to maximize the utility of nature for human needs.

Dare to Ask Questions

The question for us is "how do we view nature today?" Alfred beautifully puts it, "Is the only value of plants and animals their value to us? Have they no value in themselves for themselves and for God?"[37] The question here is about the place and role of nature in the plan of God. We have seen that the work of the Serampore Mission was broad and integral in its scope. It has included concerns for the wellbeing of creation in the mission. We also observed that the missionaries, Carey in particular, were influenced by a theology of their time. Now we need to ask, 'how far does Carey's theology of creation care help our understanding of and response to global ecological crises today?'

In 1967, by highlighting the narrow understandings of biblical concepts like 'dominion,' 'Image of God,' and the like, Lynn White accused Judeo-Christianity of being the historical roots of the present-day ecological crises.[38] It was only five decades after his publication that evangelicals have taken the issue of ecology with more seriousness. In 2000, John Jefferson Davis in his timely article "Ecological 'Blind Spots' in Evangelical theologies" made a survey of recent theological text books written by evangelical scholars, including Charismatics and Pentecostals and suggests that there are certain blind spots in the structure and content of recent evangelical systematic theologies. These blind spots were, for instance, in the doctrine of creation and atonement and that has contributed to the neglect of environmental issues and creation care. He argues that texts like Col. 1:20 must be integrated into the doctrine of atonement.[39]

This raises the need to rethink, even when we think we include creation care in our mission, the place and role of creation in our understanding and vision of the world God is creating. The issue is the level at which we place nature in our theology and mission. The question is "do we care for nature because we love it, or are we to care for it because it is part of that God is going to save through the death and resurrection of Christ?" What would have been in Carey's mind when he writes in the title page of his *Flora Indica*, "All thy works praise Thee O Lord?" What would have been in Carey's mind when he writes, "The natural history of Bengal would furnish innumerable novelties to a curious inquirer?" Would Carey include nature in the plan of God's salvation through Christ? In light of the materials available at hand, it is possible to say that although Carey includes creation care as a part of his missionary duty, his approach was still more of an anthropocentric, giving human a special place to 'manage' and maximize the utility of nature.

Endnotes

1 Quoted in Subhro Sekhar Sircar, "William Carey: God's making a Versatile genius," 31-40, in Subhro Sekhar Sircar and Sanjoy Mukherjee, eds., *William Carey: The Multifaceted Genius* (Serampore: Council of Serampore College, 2018), 31.

2 Subhro Sekhar Sircar and Sanjoy Mukherjee, eds., *William Carey: The Multifaceted Genius* (Serampore: Council of Serampore College, 2018).

3 Scott Hummel, "The Legacy of William Carey at the Bicentennial of the Founding of Serampore College," 15- 30, in Subhro Sekhar Sircar and Sanjoy Mukherjee, eds., *William Carey: The Multifaceted Genius* (Serampore: Council of Serampore College, 2018), 15.

4 Quoted in Sircar, "William Carey," 35. Sircar provides helpful information on Carey's background in this article.

5 Sircar, "William Carey," 32.

6 Sanjoy Mukherjee, "Carey—The Multifaceted Genius and an Undiscovered Correspondence," 41-51, in Subhro Sekhar Sircar and Sanjoy Mukherjee, eds., *William Carey: The Multifaceted Genius* (Serampore: Council of Serampore College, 2018), 43.

[7] Mukherjee, "Carey," 44.

[8] William Carey, ed., *Flora Indica*, Vol. 2 (Serampore: The Mission Press, 1824), 11.

[9] https://www.wmcarey.edu/carey/flora/flora-indica.htm, accessed on 29th October 2018.

[10] Quoted in Mukherjee, "Carey," 45.

[11] A. K. Ghosh puts 1824 as the year of establishment.

[12] A. K. Ghosh, "William Carey: The Botanist," 257-260, in J. T. K Daniel and R. E. Hedlund, eds., *Carey's Obligation and India's Renaissance* (Serampore: Council of Serampore College, 1993), 258.

[13] A. R. Das, "Carey as Superintendent of the Botanical Garden," 276-280, in J. T. K Daniel and R. E. Hedlund, eds., *Carey's Obligation and India's Renaissance* (Serampore: Council of Serampore College, 1993), 280.

[14] Mukherjee, "Carey," 42.

[15] Mukherjee, "Carey," 45

[16] Ghosh, "William Carey," 259.

[17] According to John Overton Choules, Christ's Messager or the Missionary Memorial (New York: E. Walker, 1845), 335, cited in https://www.wmcarey.edu/carey/flora/flora-indica.htm, accessed on 29th October 2018. Some records this as "Careya Saula." Mukherjee, "Carey," 117.

[18] Ghosh, "William Carey," 258.

[19] Vishal Mangalwadi and Ruth Mangalwadi, *The Legacy of William Carey: A Model for the Transformation of Culture* (Wheaton: Crossway Books, 1999), 1.

[20] Ghosh, "William Carey," 260.

[21] George Michael, "Carey the Natural Historian," 261-267, in J. T. K Daniel and R. E. Hedlund, eds., *Carey's Obligation and India's Renaissance* (Serampore: Council of Serampore College, 1993), 262-263.

[22] Quoted in Ghosh, "William Carey," 257.

[23] From his article 'On the study of Nature' quoted in George Michael, "Carey the Natural Historian," 261-267, in J. T. K Daniel and R. E. Hedlund, eds., *Carey's Obligation and India's Renaissance* (Serampore: Council of Serampore College, 1993), 265.

[24] Quoted in Michael, "Carey the Natural Historian," 261-267, in J. T. K Daniel and R. E. Hedlund, eds., *Carey's Obligation and India's Renaissance*, 265.

[25] Mangalwadi, *The Legacy of William Carey*, 22.

[26] Mangalwadi, *The Legacy of William Carey*, 104.

[27] Michael, "Carey the Natural Historian," 261-267, in J. T. K Daniel and R. E. Hedlund, eds., *Carey's Obligation and India's Renaissance*, 266.

[28] Dave Bookless, "Jesus is Lord . . . of All? Evangelicals, Earth Care and the Scope of the Gospel," 105-120, in Kapya J. Kaoma, ed., *Creation Care in Christian Mission*,

Regnum Edinburgh Centenary Series 29 (Oxford: Regnum Books International, 2015), 106.

[29] Linnaean classification system is a scientific way of classifying organism in a hierarchy of grouping based on similarities and physical traits developed by a Swedish botanist Carolus Linnaeus in the 1700s.

[30] Bookless, "Jesus is Lord," 106. Watts' divine songs were so popular that it went through over a thousand editions and was constantly in print for over two centuries.

[31] Bookless, "Jesus is Lord," 107.

[32] Bookless, "Jesus is Lord," 107. Wesley's reputation was such that a man hearing his message was said to have risen and opened the window to let out a moth.

[33] Bookless, "Jesus is Lord," 107. For better explanation, Bookless quoted here Thomas Edwards (1640s) who wrote "God loves the creatures that creep on the ground as well as the best saint; and there is no difference between the flesh of man and the flesh of a toad."

[34] Bookless, "Jesus is Lord," 108.

[35] Here, the description of Carey's work by Ghosh is paraphrased to show his [Carey's] deeper and wider missional vision.

[36] Michael, "Carey the Natural Historian," 261-267, in J. T. K Daniel and R. E. Hedlund, eds., *Carey's Obligation and India's Renaissance*, 265.

[37] J. R. B. Alfred, "Carey and Ecological Conservation," 287-292, in J. T. K Daniel and R. E. Hedlund, eds., *Carey's Obligation and India's Renaissance* (Serampore: Council of Serampore College, 1993), 290.

[38] Lynn White, "The Historical Roots of Our Ecological Crisis," *Science* 155 (1967).

[39] John Jefferson Davis, "Ecological 'Blind Spots' in the structure and content of recent evangelical systematic theologies," in *JETS* 43/2 (June 2000): 273-286.

Bibliography

Alfred, J. R. B. "Carey and Ecological Conservation." *Carey's Obligation and India's Renaissance*. Eds. J. T. K Daniel and R. E. Hedlund. Serampore: Council of Serampore College, 1993: 287-292.

Bookless, D. "Jesus is Lord . . . of All? Evangelicals, Earth Care and the Scope of the Gospel." *Creation Care in Christian Mission, Regnum Edinburgh Centenary Series*. Ed. Kapya J. Kaoma. Vol. 29. Oxford: Regnum Books International, 2015: 105-120.

Carey, W., ed. *Flora Indica*. Vol. 2. Serampore: The Mission Press, 1824. https://www.wmcarey.edu/carey/flora/flora-indica.htm. Accessed on 29th October 2018.

Choules, J. O. *Christ's Messenger or the Missionary Memorial*. New York: E. Walker, 1845, 335. Cited in https://www.wmcarey.edu/carey/flora/flora-indica.htm. Accessed on 29th October 2018.

Das, A. R. "Carey as Superintendent of the Botanical Garden." *Carey's Obligation and India's Renaissance.* Eds. J. T. K Daniel and R. E. Hedlund. Serampore: Council of Serampore College, 1993: 276-280.

Ghosh, A. K. "William Carey: The Botanist." *Carey's Obligation and India's Renaissance.* Eds. J. T. K Daniel and R. E. Hedlund. Serampore: Council of Serampore College, 1993: 257-260.

Hummel, S. "The Legacy of William Carey at the Bicentennial of the Founding of Serampore College." *William Carey: The Multifaceted Genius.* Eds. Subhro Sekhar Sircar and Sanjoy Mukherjee. Serampore: Council of Serampore College, 2018: 15-30.

Mangalwadi, V. and Ruth Mangalwadi. *The Legacy of William Carey: A Model for the Transformation of Culture.* Wheaton: Crossway Books, 1999.

Michael, G. "Carey the Natural Historian." *Carey's Obligation and India's Renaissance.* Eds. J. T. K Daniel and R. E. Hedlund. Serampore: Council of Serampore College, 1993: 261-267.

Mukherjee, S. "Carey—The Multifaceted Genius and an Undiscovered Correspondence." *William Carey: The Multifaceted Genius.* Eds. Subhro Sekhar Sircar and Sanjoy Mukherjee. Serampore: Council of Serampore College, 2018: 41-51.

Sircar, S. S. "William Carey: God's Making a Versatile Genius." *William Carey: The Multifaceted Genius.* Eds. Subhro Sekhar Sircar and Sanjoy Mukherjee. Serampore: Council of Serampore College, 2018: 31-40.

11

Serampore Mission and Dalit Theology

Viju Wilson

Introduction

The Indian sub-continent witnessed the work of many mission movements/organizations which belonged to different Christian traditions/denominations in 19th century. Each mission movement is known for its unique contributions to the transformation of the society and the development of Christian community in India. While focusing on particular mission goals, almost all mission movements have directly or indirectly touched all dimensions of social life in India. The Serampore Mission was one of the mission movements which contributed to the holistic development of the church and society. Though it contributed to the progress of different realms of Indian social life in a limited way, it has been known for its mission of education. In that mission, theological education was one of the major contributions of the Serampore Mission, even though it was fully developed, as we see today, through the Senate of Serampore College. As we stand today and attempt to reflect upon the mission of Serampore, its task of promoting contextual theological thinking also has to be reckoned with. It has played a key role in promoting contextual theologies. This is one of the contributions of its mission of transforming education. This article is an attempt to reflect on the contributions of the Senate of Serampore College, the child of Serampore Mission, to the development of Dalit theological thinking in the Indian context.

Theology of the Serampore Mission and Contextual Theology

William Carey articulated his theology of mission within the framework of the Great Commission in the Bible.[1] His limited writings, particularly his famous pamphlet, *An Enquiry into the Obligations of Christians* and family letters, help us understand his missional thrust and perspective. His missional theology was Christ-centric. The belief in the divinity and atonement of Christ was central to his theology of mission. The promotion of this faith was the general aim of the college started by him and his colleagues. It is interesting to note that one of the criteria for professorship or membership to the Council of Serampore College was the confession of faith in Jesus' atonement.[2] Carey had a clear outlook about a Christian minister. For him, a Christian missionary/minister is primarily a servant of God. His/her 'person' completely belongs to the Lord. In other words, s/he is a slave of Christ. The ministry, which s/he involves, is essentially a 'sacred office.' When a person enters into it, s/he is expected to engage in Lord's work even at the cost of personal comforts and pleasures of this world. Moreover, a missionary must maintain piety, prudence and courage in carrying out the obligation that came upon him/her from God. He also believed that the Great Commission was a 'sufficient call' for every Christian to preach the Gospel. The salvation of humanity is the purpose of God's call through great commission.[3]

For Carey, the propagation of the Gospel was the main objective of Christian mission. He preached the Gospel in public places and distributed literatures to people who belonged to different religious traditions. He strongly believed that it was not the political kingdoms/situations which decided the course of God's mission. He objected to the idea that worldly blessings and respectabilities were the reward for believing in Christ in this world. He exhorted his colleagues and children to aim for heavenly life and develop 'spiritual prosperity' in personal and ministerial life. For him, material prosperity without 'spiritual prosperity' was worthless and futile. This outlook led him to identify spiritual values in the physical, mental and familial sufferings of the believers. He maintained the theological position that affiliations were means of sanctification, and they would take us closer to God.[4] He even interpreted his wife's (i.e., Charlotte's) illness as "a sore chastisement from God."[5] If we analyze his theological thinking on mission and Christian life within the contextual theological framework, we are informed that he maintained an 'otherworldly' theological perspective which mainly focused on the personal piety and eternal life. But, if we look at his missional and theological views "from the standpoint of time (Frantz Fanon),"[6] the standpoint of Carey's time, particularly in the light of his passion for mission and general evangelistic enthusiasm existed in Europe, his theological orientation and missional outlook stand validated. At the same time, one can sense Carey's theological link with contextual theologies and liberative missional praxis in his letters. Once he advised his son to live "to the glory of God and for the good of men, everything short of this is an inferior object which we should hold with a loose hand."[7] The expression, 'for the good of men/women' can be meant of his emphasis to engage with the issues of people in society. For him and his associates, mission was not limited to the propagation of the Gospel alone, but a vocation to address the wretched life realities of people too.[8] It was practically reflected in their interventions to combat the social evils of that time in India. Though they did not interpret faith contextually, their actions such as Bible translations in the languages of common people, educational and social reform initiatives, concern for nature were loaded with 'contextual interpretations of faith' today. It brings Carey and his associates closer to the mission of contextual theologies.

William Carey, William Ward, and Joshua Marshman (The Serampore Trio) were born in humble social status in terms of their parents' occupations. In Indian social setting, they were born to the parents of 'lower caste origin.' While the caste system created the walls of separation among the people in 19th century India, the class system divided the people in the native context of the Serampore Trio. William Carey was born as a son of a weaver who was later promoted to be a village school master. He was trained as a shoe-maker, and worked as a cobbler, *mochi*,[9] whose social position is very low in India. He was born in a family which even could not afford the education of children. William Ward was a son of a carpenter and builder. Joshua Marshman, son of a weaver, had to work as a weaver from his childhood days. He continued this profession for many years before coming to India.[10] Socially and occupationally, the weavers and the carpenters in India belong to the social category of 'Other Backward Classes' (OBC), the oppressed communities other than Dalits. The missionaries who were born and lived in humble socio-economic conditions actually shared the life of Dalits and other marginalized communities. This shared social experience is the connecting point of the Serampore Trio and marginal communities in

India. Perhaps, it even worked as a point of departure for their evangelistic activities among the lower castes and shaped their attitude against caste discrimination in society.

The Serampore missionaries, as part of evangelization, took a strong stand against the evil practices that existed in the society. William Carey and his associates raised their voice against the inhuman practices like *sati* and throwing babies into the river as propitiation to the deity. However, what brings the Serampore missionaries so closer to the Dalits and other oppressed communities and their efforts of theologizing is the stand taken by them against the practice of casteism. The college and schools established by the missionaries were open to all irrespective of caste and creed.[11] Beyond caste identities, every student was allowed to study Hindu Scriptures even though it was opposed by the pundits.[12] It was actually a sign of breaking the barrier of caste in education. The missionaries' stand against caste was also reflected in the faith community. They strongly discouraged the new converts to maintain their caste identity and mindset. They taught that caste basically stood against the values of the Christian faith. For them, Christianity was one 'caste.' It does not imply that they attempted to strengthen the caste system by introducing one more 'caste' into the cluster of castes in India. But they wanted to build up a Christian community beyond 'caste' lines, a community of equals. In their attempt to counter caste system, they promoted and conducted inter-caste marriages in their congregation. The marriage of a Brahmin convert with the daughter of a carpenter[13] is a case in point. For Carey and his associates, it was a victory over the powers of caste.[14]

Though the process of the annihilation of caste started with education, it touched every aspects of their mission. The native Christian community also followed Carey and his associates in their approach towards caste. A public display of the negation of caste occurred when a converted Brahmin and a converted Muslim along with Marshman and Felix Carey carried the dead body of a Shudra Christian. It happened in the social context where a Brahmin would never touch the dead body of a Shudra and vice versa.[15] The Serampore missionaries, particularly William Carey, opposed any kind of oppressive system in society even before they encountered caste system in India. He opposed class system and slave trade, particularly racism in it, and even refused to buy the goods such as sugar produced through slave labor. Whenever a lower caste was baptized, he and his associates used to celebrate the event by arranging fellowship meals which would be attended by the converts from all castes and the Europeans.[16] Perhaps, this was an empowering gesture for the lower caste people of his time. Indeed, it is also an act of life-affirming mission. The strong anti-caste attitude and inclusive community approach which embraced everyone irrespective of caste takes the Serampore missionaries closer to the yearning of present marginalized communities and the goal of their theologizing ventures. Every step taken by Serampore Missionaries primarily attempted to affirm the life of people, particularly the margins of the time. The life-affirming mission of the Serampore missionaries is reflected in the theological education promoted by the Senate of Serampore College.

Theological Education as Life-Affirming Mission

A discourse on Serampore Mission will be incomplete without theological education which has been instrumental in equipping men and women for building up faith communities in India. In fact, catering quality theological education is the mission of the Senate of Serampore College, the child of Serampore Mission.[17] The theological education under Senate of Serampore College (SSC) is life-affirming and missional in nature. It engages with every aspect of church and society, particularly encourages to stand with the marginal communities for their holistic empowerment. According to Felix Wilfred, "A good education is one in which the students are the active subjects, and the best in them is brought out."[18] If we appraise theological education within the framework of life-affirming mission, theological education under the SSC enables the students to actualize their agency to affirm life by participating in the life-realties of people groups, particularly the margins. It empowers them to be 'active subjects' with a different voice, a different perspective, and a different thinking in church and society. A praxis-oriented theological education is primarily a mission par-excellence. This mission "is not the transmission of information, but building the capacity to invent, discover and create."[19] It qualifies theological education of the SSC to be called as life-affirming mission. Theological education becomes life-affirming mission when it strengthens Christian mission and ministry in terms of the holistic empowerment of communities.[20] In the case of margins, they cease to be margins when they are brought forth into the mainstream of church and society. Theological education supplies methods and perspectives to come out of the periphery experiences.

Theological education under the SSC provides space for plurality of perspectives. Perspectival reading is an enabling and empowering activity. Theological perspectives from the margins enable respective communities "in developing new self-understanding and in their identity formation."[21] For the margins, a perspective is an embodiment of their aspirations, resistance and subjectivity to assert their life in society. Providing space for the articulation of different perspectives is actually a life-affirming missional endeavor because it helps in bringing the pertinent issues of people, particularly the margins into the centre of theologizing.

As a mission, theological education/research has liberative elements in it. It liberates the margins from the captivity of ignorance and strengthens them to defy the unawareness of the liberative potential of their agency that blocks their upward social mobility. Theological education also helps them how to look at the realities and the scripture through their eyes. Re-reading the scripture and interpreting the faith in context basically empower the life of the margins. It has the power to initiate the process of holistic liberation of the margins. This is possible when the margins become subjects and agents of theological education/research rather than objects.[22] The agency and subjecthood of margins in theological education lead them to enlarge their space of progression in church and society. This is the outcome of the life-affirming mission of theological education. Theological education is life-affirming mission because it attempts to transform 'passive subjects' into 'active subjects' and 'disempowered communities' into 'empowered communities.' One of the attempts in doing life-affirming mission initiated by the SSC was the promotion of Dalit theological thinking. It began with the entry of Dalit Theology into the curriculum of the SSC.

Serampore Mission and Dalit Theology

The Senate of Serampore College, the product of Serampore Mission, has contributed to the emergence of contextual theological thinking and its development in India. The contextual theologies have influenced Indian missional perspectives and challenged the faith communities/churches to address the issues of marginalized communities. Theological education of the SSC has given adequate space for different theological perspectives to develop contextual expressions of Christian faith. Today, it is known for promoting plurality of perspectives in theological thinking. The principle "difference-in-equality"[23] is evident in endorsing different perspectives in the theological education of the SSC. This is to achieve the larger aim of equipping future generation of Christian ministers and congregations "to live out the doxological, koinonial, reflective, diaconal and missional dimensions of their existence, with a strong commitment to the liberation of the down-trodden: Dalits, Adivasis, Tribals, Women, the disabled, persons infected and affected by HIV and AIDS and the like.[24] The plurality of perspectives reflects the ecumenical character of the theological education under the SSC.[25] As far as the Dalits and other marginalized communities are concerned, the acceptance and promotion of different perspectives is life-affirming mission. It provides them tools and resources for articulating their faith in the light of their life realities where Dalit theology is a case in point. By introducing Dalit theology as a subject into its curriculum, the SSC has contributed to the development of Dalit Theology. It has produced many theses/dissertations and resource materials; conducted consultations and seminars and facilitated the emergence of potential scholars in the area of Dalit theological thinking. This is not without resistance within the Senate family. Dr. James Massey, under whom I did my doctoral studies, once told me that when the proposal for incorporating Dalit perspective, particularly promoting Dalit theology as a subject, into the curriculum of the SSC was made there were many opposing voices in respective forums which discussed the curriculum revision.

The seeds of Dalit theology were sown in the address given by Rev. John Subhan, a convert from Islam, in All Religions Conference for Dalit leaders held in Lucknow in May 1936. His speech was on 'The Goodnews of Christ for the Depressed Classes' that was influenced by the theology of the social gospel.[26] However, the development of present Dalit Theology begins with 'Towards a Shudra Theology,' an address delivered by A. P. Nirmal at the United Theological College, Bangalore, in April, 1981.[27] According to James Massey, the first phase of Dalit theology was developed in 1980's. In this period, pioneers of Dalit theology movement articulated the vision, need, and goal of Dalit Theology. In the second phase (1990's), debate and discussions were concentrated on the role and sources of Dalit Theology. The attention was also given to reflect on Dalit identity, Dalit history, and Dalit solidarity. CISRS played an important role in this period to organize consultations and initiate studies in developing Dalit theologizing. The third phase, started from 2000, has witnessed new developments such as emergence of more Dalit theological literature, developing Dalit theology departments and establishing research institutes such as Centre for Dalit/ Subaltern Studies in New Delhi.[28] Gurukul Lutheran Theological College and Research Institute, Chennai, was the first theological college which established a full-fledged department of Dalit Theology in India. Through its academic initiatives, Dalit theology was recognized as an optional subject both in the B.D. and M.Th. programs under the SSC.[29]

The entry of Dalit Theology/Reading into Serampore theological curriculum was a gradual process. According to the B.D. Syllabus 1991, in the branch of Theology and Ethics, there was a course called *Introduction to Christian Theology*,[30] which explained the traditional/classical doctrinal formulations. There was no space for contextual theologizing in the syllabus. But in the end of the syllabus, there was a call for re-interpretations, re-formulations, and re-making of Christian doctrines. Dalit Theology appeared first in the Serampore curriculum as a sub-section under 'Action-Oriented Theological Formulations' in the course named *Indian Christian Theologians*. In the *Person and Work of Christ*, 'Dalit Christ' became part of the section, 'Selected Perspectives.' Dalit theology was introduced as one of the 'New Theologies' in *Contemporary Trends in Christian Theology*. In *Responses to Jesus of Nazareth*, 'Dalit Response' was given as one of the theological responses. In the branch of History of Christianity, 'Dalit Theology' was introduced as one of the recent developments in the subjects: *General Introduction to the History of Christianity* and *History of Christianity among Dalits and Tribal Peoples in India*.[31] Though Dalit Theology/Reading was included in the course outline of different subjects under theology and other branches of the B.D. program, there was no direct bibliographical reference related to Dalit Theology in the syllabus. During this period, there were some pioneer literatures on Dalit theology/reading. Was the absence of the bibliographical references in the syllabus an outcome of apathy towards Dalit reading? Was the inclusion of Dalit Theology a hypocritical exercise? Was it because of the lack of materials? Though these questions can be answered affirmatively and negatively, the revised syllabus of 2010 tells us a different story. The space of Dalit theology/Reading was enlarged in the revised curriculum of the B.D. program. This is very much evident if we look at the space given to it in the Theology Cluster alone.

In the Theology Cluster, *Theological Methodologies: Perspectives from the Margins* (TC 203) provided sufficient space for Dalit theological thinking. Though Dalit perspective was included in the subject, *Introduction to Christian*

Doctrines (TC 205), no bibliography directly related to the Dalit theological reading was given. Dalit Theological perspective was incorporated into *Introduction to Christian Theologies in India* (TC 206). Dalit perspective on Jesus Christ was given a small section in *Person and Work of Jesus, the Christ* (TC 207). While Dalit Theology/Reading/Perspective was introduced as one of the sub-sections/units in 1991 syllabus, Dalit Theology was offered as a separate subject (Optional) in 2010 syllabus (TC 209 a).[32] This has actually changed the status of Dalit Theology from a 'perspectival reading/response' to a 'fully developed' subject in the curriculum of the SSC.

In the current BD syllabus of 2014 (revised), in the Theology Cluster, Dalit perspective is included in the subject, *Discerning the Signs of the Times: Theological Methodologies from the Margins* (BTT 01). Dalit theology is included as one of the sections in *Introduction to Christian Theology* (BOS 17). The space for Dalit perspective is also given in *Introduction to Christian Social Ethics* (BTE 01). Though Dalit reading is incorporated in *Introduction to Christian Doctrines* (BTT 02), proper bibliography for the Dalit reading is not given. Dalit Christology is given as a sub-unit of 'Christological Reflections from Asia' in *Person and Work of Jesus, the Christ* (BTT 11). 'Dalit Christ' becomes one of sub-units in *Introduction to Christian Theologies in India* (BTT 12). In the new syllabus, *Dalit Theology* (BTT 13) is retained as one of the optional subjects.[33] Dalit theological resources are also added in to the subjects like *Third World Liberation Theologies* (BTT 52) and *Contemporary Trends in Theology* (BTT 51).[34] Apart from the Theology Cluster, Dalit Reading/Perspective is incorporated into the syllabi of the subjects in other clusters too. In fact, Dalit Theology/Reading has enlarged its space more in terms of content in the courses offered in 2014 (revised) syllabus.

The inclusion of Dalit Theology/Reading into M.Th. (Master of Theology) curriculum is another milestone in the development of Dalit theological thinking. 'Arvind P. Nirmal' and 'Kavi Joshua' were included in the *Major Figures in Christian Thought* (CT 14) in the revised syllabus of M.Th. in Christian Theology in 2007. *Major Figures in Indian Thought* (CT 15) provided space for the study of B. R. Ambedkar and Jyothirao Phule. In *Contemporary Theologies and Issues* (CT 18), Dalit Theology was offered as an optional subject. Dalit theological thinking/response was included in the subjects like *Theology and Concern for Justice and Peace* (CT 30) and *Christian Faith and Caste* (CT 32). *Integrated Paper* in the M.Th. curriculum also gives room for discussing the issues of Dalits and developing relevant theological reflections.[35] Also Dalit theology/theologians/scholars find/s place in recently revised M.Th. syllabus. *Indian Christian Contextual Theologies* (MCT014), *Study of Texts:* James Massey, B. R. Ambedkar, and Jyotirao Phule, *Dalit Theology* (MCT 009 ii) and *Theology from the Margins*[36] are the subjects which fully or partially provide the content of Dalit Theology. Theological education as mission informs that promoting a perspective or a theology, particularly contextual and liberating theology, is a life-affirming missional action. In this venture, the SSC facilitates the marginalized communities to express their faith through their eyes and body-mediated experiences, which is an empowering action for the margins like Dalits. In fact, Dalit theology provides resources and a liberating perspective for the marginal communities to affirm their lives in society. It also advocates solidarity approach than advocacy approach in theological education to accomplish the life-affirming mission.

Solidarity Approach in Theological Education

A look at the theological education in India from the perspective of advocacy approach informs that it does not create much impact in the life of Dalits and other marginalized communities (Dalit Bahujans). One of the factors which make theological education less successful in empowering the Dalit Bahujans is its dependency on traditional theological expressions, Euro-centric (pietistic) and classical Indian Christian theologies, which are not the theologies of majority Indian Christians who come from Dalit, Tribal, and Other Backward Class communities. Their life experiences and issues are not adequately acknowledged and addressed in those theological expressions.[37] The concerns and aims of the pioneers of Indian Christian theology were also entirely different from the majority Indian Christians. The upper caste Indian theologians attempted to interpret their new faith experiences in the light of Brahmanic Hindu thought forms. They were aiming for the indigenization of Christian faith in India. They interpreted the Christian faith in Indian thought forms which were completely ignorant to the majority Christians.[38]

Moreover, Indian Christian theological expressions primarily addressed the spiritual quest of upper caste Christians than the life issues of majority Christians. For them, the survival of their lives in oppressive conditions was the major concern. Even after they became Christians, they continued to face poverty, suffering, injustice, illiteracy and denial of identity. The situation has not completely changed even today. In fact, Indian Christian Theology failed to address their issues in church and society.[39] Therefore, the theological education influenced by traditional theological expressions remains 'disconnected' to the majority of the Indian Christians. It neither encourages them to stand on behalf of others nor prompt them to participate in the struggles of the oppressed communities. Even after the emergence of liberation theologies the influence of classical theological expressions continues to hold on to the outlook of many theological educators and scholars. Though the contextual understanding of faith has positively influenced the approach of theological education towards the concerns of marginalized communities, it is limited to advocacy programs. Therefore, a new approach is necessitated.

In the context of the growing awareness of rights and the emergence of new movements among the Dalits and other oppressed communities, theological education should promote solidarity approach than advocacy approach. It is easy to raise voice by developing theological reflections on the issues of Dalits, Tribals and Backward Communities. But we need theological education which leads theologically educated people to intentionally participate in the struggles of the marginalized in society. The solidarity approach helps a person to 'become' one among the suffering people.[40] The problem with present theological education is not the lack of vision but the absence of translating vision into action. The solidarity approach in theological education entails the theological educators and scholars to express their solidarity by standing with the oppressed in the locations of 'life-negation.' It needs strong commitment to stand for the cause of their salvation/liberation. In order to translate the vision into action, there has to be radical changes in the entire theological education—its structure, content, methodology in terms of solidarity approach.[41] The solidarity approach, in fact, redefines the role of the theological education: enabling the scholars to participate in the struggles of the oppressed than limiting their activities to advocacy. It makes theological education a life-affirming mission. The SCC has taken some bold steps in this direction by promoting Indian contextual theological methodologies in its curriculum. It has to promote solidarity approach which will certainly contribute to the process of empowering the life of Dalits and other marginalized communities in the society.

Conclusion

The theological education of the SSC is missional in nature. It is a mission which aims to affirm life and enables the marginal communities to celebrate the life in its fullness. By promoting different perspectival readings, the SSC has contributed to the development of contextual theological expressions. This is a part of life-affirming mission. While SSC has provided space for Dalit theology to grow as one of the contextual theologies in India, Dalit theology has become a channel of the life-affirming mission of the SSC. As a subaltern faith/mission movement, Dalit theology has developed a new mission and faith narrative among the Dalits and other marginalized communities within Christianity. It has encouraged them to assert their subjecthood in faith communities. The caste which has crept into the church/ Christian community influenced the outlook of majority Indian Christians. The Dalits, even after their conversion, were/are addressed and treated by the non-Dalit Christians within the caste framework of the social relations inside and outside the faith communities. It often forced them to cover up their identity to save themselves from impending caste humiliation. Dalit theology taught them the value of their subjecthood and encouraged them to assert their subjective experience in interpreting the faith. In fact, for the Dalits, Dalit theology has provided them new energy and space to reclaim their subjecthood within the faith communities.

Now, majority of the Dalits are emboldened to express their Dalit identity in church. Once they were ashamed to assert their identity; but now Dalit theology empowered them to assert it. It also encouraged them to fight for their rights and equality within the faith community and enlarge their space. Once their ministerial space in the church was restricted or negated, Dalit theology motivated them to question the negation of space and claim the deserved ministerial and administrative space. It also reminded the faith communities to reclaim the values of the Christian faith: justice, equality, freedom and acceptance. The idea of 'casteless' church articulated by the Dalit theology has, to an extent, influenced the Indian church to redefine its nature and mission. Dalit theology envisioned a new Christian community, a 'community of equals' in India. There is no doubt; Dalit theological thinking has brought at least some changes in the outlook of the Indian Christians for both Dalits and non-Dalits in terms of their faith/community life in church and society. The SSC has played an important role in it. It substantiates the argument that the theological education of the SCC is life-affirming mission, and it has to contribute to the further development and praxis of Dalit Theology for building up just and humane communities in Indian society.

Endnotes

[1] The theology of original Serampore Mission was centered on William Carey's theology of mission.

[2] Woba James, *Revisiting Ecumenical Theological Education in India* (New Delhi: CWI, 2016), 254.

[3] William Carey, *An Enquiry into the Obligations of Christians, to use means for the Conversion of the Heathens* (Leicester: Ann Ireland, 1792; London: Hodder and Stoughton, 1891 Reprint), 72-76.

[4] Sunil Kumar Chatterjee, Comp. *Family Letters of Dr. William Carey* (Serampore: The Author, 2007), 28, 31, 75-76, 120; John William Kaye, *Christianity in India: A Historical Narrative* (London: Smith, Elder and Co., 1859), 235.

[5] Chatterjee, *Family Letters of Dr. William Carey*, 61.

[6] Homi K. Bhabha, *The Location of Culture* (London and New York: Routledge Classics, 2004 Special Indian Edition), xxxii.

[7] Chatterjee, *Family Letters of Dr. William Carey*, 51.

[8] John Clark Marshman, *The Life and Times of Carey, Marshman and Ward: Embracing the History of the Serampore Mission*, Vol. 2 (London: Longmans & Roberts, 1859), 486.

[9] Hindi word for cobbler, but often it is used with stigma.

[10] Kaye, *Christianity in India: A Historical Narrative*, 218-219, 230-233; Chatterjee, *Family Letters of Dr. William Carey*, 1.

[11] James, *Revisiting Ecumenical Theological Education in India*, 255.

[12] Marshman, *The Life and Times of Carey, Marshman and Ward*, 486.

[13] Krishna Pal, the first convert of the Serampore Mission, whose social rank in the caste hierarchy was low.

[14] Kaye, *Christianity in India: A Historical Narrative*, 235-238; F. Deaville Walker, *William Carey: Missionary Pioneer and Statesman* (London: SCM, 1926), 226.

[15] Walker, *William Carey: Missionary Pioneer and Statesman*, 226; Marshman, *The Life and Times of Carey, Marshman and Ward*, 186.

[16] Mangalwadi, *The Legacy of William Carey* (Illinois: Crossway Books, 1999 reprint), 123.

[17] Serampore mission is not limited to the life and work of Carey, Marshman and Ward alone. It continues through the Serampore College, particularly its Senate which promotes life-affirming theological education.

[18] Wilfred, *Asian Public Theology* (New Delhi: ISPCK, 2010), 259.

[19] Wilfred, "Every Theologian A Researcher," *Theological Research in the Global South*, ed. P. G. George (Serampore: SATHRI, 2015), 20.

[20] John S. Sadananda, "Foreword," *Theological Research in the Global South*, ed. P. G. George (Serampore: SATHRI, 2015), 7-9.

[21] Isaac Mar Philoxenos, "Silver Jubilee of SATHRI: Where Do We Go From Here?" *Theological Research in the Global South*, ed. P. G. George (Serampore: SATHRI, 2015), 157.

[22] Wilfred, "Every Theologian A Researcher," 22-26.

[23] Bhabha, *The Location of Culture*, xvii.

[24] *Regulations and Syllabus 2010*, Bachelor of Divinity, Senate of Serampore College (Serampore: Senate of Serampore College, 2010), 11.

[25] James, *Revisiting Ecumenical Theological Education in India*, 217.

[26] John C.B. Webster, *The Dalit Christians: A History* (New Delhi: ISPCK, Revised and Enlarged Version 2009), 275.

[27] Arvind P. Nirmal, "Introduction," *A Reader in Dalit Theology*, ed. Arvind P. Nirmal (Chennai: GLTC & RC, 2007), iii.

[28] James Massey, "A Review of Dalit Theology," *Dalit and Minjung Theologies: A Dialogue*, eds. Samson Prabhakar and Jinkwan Kwon (Bangalore: BTESSC/SATHRI, 2006), 3, 6-10; James Massey, "Vision and Role of Dalit Theology," *A Theology from Dalit Perspective*, eds. James Massey and S. Lourduswamy (New Delhi: CDS, 2001), 69.

[29] Nirmal, "Introduction," iii.

[30] Italicized expressions are the names of different courses in the syllabus. How 'Dalit theology' was/is accommodated in different syllabi is narrated in this section.

[31] *Syllabus*, Bachelor of Divinity, Senate of Serampore College (Serampore: Senate of Serampore College, 1991, Reprint 2005), 70-78, 93-97, 102, 124.

[32] *Regulations and Syllabus 2010*, Bachelor of Divinity, 83-86, 122-125, 128-130, 131-134, 135-138, 145-149.

[33] *Regulations and Syllabus (Revised Edition) 2014*, Volume 1, Bachelor of Divinity, Senate of Serampore College (Serampore: Senate of Serampore College, 2015), 48-49, 106-109, 115-117, 118-121, 145-148, 149-152, 153-156.

[34] *Regulations and Syllabus (Revised Edition) 2014*, Volume 2, Bachelor of Divinity, Senate of Serampore College (Serampore: Senate of Serampore College, 2014), 74-77.

[35] *Master of Theology (M.Th.) Regulations, Senate of Serampore College* (Serampore: Senate of Serampore College, 1998, Revised 2007, Reprint 2011), 11, 39-41.

[36] New M.Th. syllabus received by the Registrar, UBS, from the Senate of Serampore College.

[37] James Massey, "Present State of Theological Education in South Asia: Response of SSC and BTESSC," *Partnership between Churches and Theological Institutions*, Ed. James Massey (Bangalore: BTESSC/SATHRI, 2010), 16.

[38] Deepak Seth, ed., *From Truth to Truth, A Journey through Faiths: A Selection of Representative Essays by Dr. James Massey* (New Delhi: CDS, 2008), 88.

[39] Massey, "Present State of Theological Education in South Asia: Response of SSC and BTESSC," 17.

[40] James Massey, *Dalit Theology: History, Context, Text and Whole Salvation* (New Delhi: Manohar, 2014), 230.

[41] Seth, *From Truth to Truth, A Journey through Faiths*, 90-92.

Bibliography

Bhabha, H. K. *The Location of Culture*. London and New York: Routledge Classics, 2004.

Carey, W. *An Enquiry into the Obligations of Christians, to use means for the Conversion of the Heathens*. Leicester: Ann Ireland, 1792; London: Hodder and Stoughton, 1891.

Chatterjee, S. K. Comp. *Family Letters of Dr. William Carey*. Serampore: The Author, 2007.

James, W. *Revisiting Ecumenical Theological Education in India*. New Delhi: CWI, 2016.

Kaye, J. W. *Christianity in India: A Historical Narrative*. London: Smith, Elder and Company, 1859.

Mangalwadi, V. R. *The Legacy of William Carey*. Illinois: Crossway Books, 1999.

Marshman, J. C. *The Life and Times of Carey, Marshman and Ward: Embracing the History of the Serampore Mission*. Vols. 1 & 2. London: Longmans and Roberts, 1859.

Massey, J. "A Review of Dalit Theology." *Dalit and Minjung Theologies: A Dialogue*. Eds. Samson Prabhakar and Jinkwan Kwon. Bangalore: BTESSC/SATHRI, 2006.

Massey, J. *Dalit Theology: History, Context, Text and Whole Salvation*. New Delhi: Manohar, 2014.

Massey, J. "Present State of Theological Education in South Asia: Response of SSC and BTESSC." *Partnership between Churches and Theological Institutions*. Ed. James Massey. Bangalore: BTESSC/SATHRI, 2010.

Massey, J. "Vision and Role of Dalit Theology." *A Theology from Dalit Perspective*. Eds. James Massey and S. Lourduswamy. New Delhi: CDS, 2001.

Master of Theology (M.Th.) Regulations, Senate of Serampore College. Serampore: Senate of Serampore College, 1998. Revised 2007. Reprinted 2011.

Nirmal, A. P. "Introduction." *A Reader in Dalit Theology*. Ed. Arvind P. Nirmal. Chennai: GLTC & RC, 2007.

Philoxenos, I. M. "Silver Jubilee of SATHRI: Where Do We Go From Here?" *Theological Research in the Global South*. Ed. P. G. George. Serampore: SATHRI, 2015.

Regulations and Syllabus 2010. Bachelor of Divinity. Senate of Serampore College. Serampore: Senate of Serampore College, 2010.

Regulations and Syllabus (Revised Edition) 2014. Vols 1 & 2. Bachelor of Divinity. Senate of Serampore College. Serampore: Senate of Serampore College, 2015.

Sadananda, J. S. "Foreword." *Theological Research in the Global South*. Ed. P. G. George. Serampore: SATHRI, 2015.

Seth, D., ed. *From Truth to Truth, A Journey through Faiths: A Selection of Representative Essays by Dr. James Massey*. New Delhi: CDS, 2008.

Syllabus. Bachelor of Divinity. Senate of Serampore College. Serampore: Senate of Serampore College, 1991. Reprinted 2005.

Walker, F. D. *William Carey: Missionary Pioneer and Statesman*. London: SCM, 1926.

Webster, J. C. B. *The Dalit Christians: A History*. New Delhi: ISPCK, Revised and Enlarged Version 2009.

Wilfred, F. *Asian Public Theology*. New Delhi: ISPCK, 2010.

Wilfred, F. "Every Theologian A Researcher." *Theological Research in the Global South*. Ed. P. G. George. Serampore: SATHRI, 2015.

12

Revisiting the Serampore Mission and the Tribal Worldviews: A Postcolonial Reading

Mayang Longkumer

Introduction

The eighteenth and nineteenth centuries are considered as a highly competitive and 'collecting' era; that means, it was regarded as an era when the colonizers collected resources from the colonized lands. In fact, from the perspective of a native, it can be more appropriate to be addressed as an era of 'stealing' native resources by the colonizers. Well hovered with the colonial cloud of domination, manipulation, and the imposition of their ideologies on the colonized inhabitants, the life situation was shattered by creating difficulties for the natives to relocate. This is true to many people groups who were either directly or indirectly under the control or influence of the colonial agents. Perhaps this thought paves a path to uncover the experiences of the people under the colonial regimes. Beyond such a period is still critical when it comes to the pertinent issues and challenges that continue in their lives for those living in the hangovers of radical destruction. A majority of the missionary activities took place in India fall under the colonial period and left with a vacuum to restore.[1] Those contextual realities persuade us for a critical analysis and a careful synopsis of both the Serampore missions and the tribal contexts in order to envision appropriate postcolonial perspectives for Christian missions.

As a site of missionary venture during the colonial period, William Carey a 'consecrated cobbler' turned 'legacy maker' declared: "Expect great things, Attempt great things." His early Christian ministry has impacted theoretically and practically in terms of expecting and attempting great things from/for God. In its generality, this six-word dictum remains undisputed as a mission paradigm for all ages. But how far these watchwords in particularity have impacted the Serampore Missions is one of the inquiries of this essay.

It is important to realize that the contemporary tribal context is fashioned by a collection of colonial effects. The colonial discourses exhibit visible truth in the postcolonial environment. This essay emerges out of my astonishments and concerns while engaging with the tribal worldviews. The protuberant colonial agents present in Serampore and in the tribal world, the foreign missionary activities, and the influences and alterations that have brought in the *Sitz-im-Leben* of the communities are some of the interests of this study. One of the significant questions to be answered is: 'Can something good come out of the Serampore Missions lensing through the tribal worldview?' Consideration is given to the socio-cultural and religious life experiences of the tribals while reading the Serampore Missions from a postcolonial lens.

Rise from Scratches to Legacy Makers

Biographically stating that Carey was a person who did not give up what he has already begun. A determination was instilled in him right from his childhood. He was also a person who was fond of nature, i.e., closely knitted to the mother earth.[2] He rose from an ordinary family to become an extraordinary bench maker in Christian socio-religious missions. The "Deathless Sermon" based on Isa. 54:2-3 preached in the year 1792[3] during the Baptist Association Meeting in Northampton with the watch-words—"Expect great things, Attempt great things" (in addition: . . . from God and . . . for God)—continue to challenge the present century missions. In his venture of missions in India, some of his contributions are worth noting—translating the Bible into various languages, abolition of infanticide (1802) and *sati* (1829),[4] and the establishment of the Serampore College.

The second person among the outstanding missionaries is William Ward whose family background is debatable in the views of historical observations. He is introduced, on the one hand, as a person hailed from a 'carpenter and builder' family, and on the other hand, as a person from 'a well to do family with skilled and cabinet maker.' No doubt, he was well known for his skills in editing and printing professions right from his young age. As such, he has contributed much in promoting printed materials for the Serampore mission works including the publication of the first Bengali New Testament in 1801.[5]

Joshua Marshman is another figure who also came from an ordinary family. One of the remarkable aspects about his childhood is that 'he is a good reader of books.' Though his schooling was not sound, yet he became a seeker of knowledge. In Serampore, he along with his wife Hannah Marshman had contributed immensely to the establishment of schools which later have provided financial support to meet the expenses of the mission activities.[6]

Witnessing such tremendous contributions and legacy has been left behind for the Indian missions through the Serampore Trio. However, it is also at risk to be conformist if the Serampore mission is being left without uncritical observations. Thus, under whose shadow were the missionaries able to do such great benchmarks become the scope of this essay.

Then British Colonial Outlooks

Every colonial agents work with their own ideologies and interests for attaining and gaining their own empire's wellbeing. In such a context, T. Katherine and John Thomas in their work state,

> The British East India Company established in 1600, the company was a private-trade enterprise, giving charter (monopoly of trading rights) by the British government. It opened up India and the Far East to commerce by making a trade agreement with the Mogul Empire that ruled India. The company eventually took control of the country. A governor was installed as representative of the British government. And this eventually brought India under the British crown. In 1784[7] further limitations were placed on the company, and its monopoly on trade was terminated in 1813. But its administrative role in India did not cease until its dissolution in 1874.[8]

During the many years of domination by the Company, the peasants lost their age-old rights over the land and in turn had to respond to the land revenue system introduced against their rights. The British intention was to put firm roots for them in the Indian soil to administer the natives they colonized. On the other hand, the manufacturing of silk fabrics by the native weavers was discouraged by regulations passed by the Company (Regulation 31 of 1793). In this sense, the natives should work for the interest of the British industries and promote products at the expense of Indian industries and resources. This impaired the natives tremendously and they suffered from repeated famine as a result of the Company's monopoly and coercion policy.[9]

Subsequently, the traditional learning and values of the natives faded away as the time passed by. At the same time, the colonists controlled all the available resources toward their own ends. This is the time when Carey arrived in India to fulfill God's mission in the land of the distressed inhabitants.

Until the arrival of Lord William Bentinck, the then Governor General, the British colonial attitudes towards colonized India was kept at minimum level. Three major influences have been maintained in this context as stated by Ruth and Vishal Mangalwadi:

> For *the Directors of The East India Company*, India was simply a trading base. Most of them did not even want to govern India, let alone assume the responsibility of reforming it. Their simple commercial minds, for example, found Lord Wellesley's empire-building military successes too much for their ledgers; the reason that Wellesley was recalled.
>
> The Company's greed was a major factor which, within the first fifty years of its power, helped destroy India's two thousand-year-old economic strength. This strength was built on trading and industry, like weaving. Unfortunately, casteism had ensured that the benefits of the economy did not percolate down to the average person, who therefore had little interest in defending the socio-economic system when it was attacked by foreigners.
>
> For *the British military men*, such as Clive and Wellesley, India was primarily so much "territory to be conquered." That attitude, for instance, ensured that even though Lord Wellesley was convinced of the rightness of Carey's campaign against *Sati* in 1806, he did not issue an edict against it, as Bentinck did later in 1829.
>
> *The British intellectuals and humanitarians* in India, such as Sir Thomas Munro and Sir John Malcolm, tended merely to respect and romanticize the "customs and wisdom of the natives." The *British Orientalists* patronized Sanskrit and rediscovered the greatness of the ancient Indian literature, which helped to revive the self-respect of the Indian elite. Their efforts, however, could do nothing to reform the populace of India. On the contrary, it appeared that they were reinforcing the religious basis for some of the social evils. Therefore, Raja Ram Mohan Roy—himself a great Sanskrit Scholar—severely condemned the attempt of the British Orientalists to start a Sanskrit College in Calcutta, which would have further solidified the existing class distinctions.[10]

Such was the stage set by the British colonizers by manipulating and negating the native Indians. In the midst of these scenarios, there were minorities among the British pupil who not only had visions for missionary activities but also had opened their eyes toward social evils that were existing in India. Ruth and Vishal Mangalwadi state,

> It took twenty years of successful field work by Carey in India, lobbying within the East India Company by Charles Grant, and magnificent political work by Wilberforce in England, which persuaded the Parliament in1813 (when the Charter came up for renewal) to begin to assume its moral obligation to India.[11]

Perhaps, during his lifespan in India, Carey had numerous opponents.[12] Nevertheless, amidst the oppositions, his immortal spirit of expecting and doing great things pressed him forward.

Stepping into Colonized India

Perhaps, when the East India Company had a policy of not engaging with Christian missionary activities in India, it was against their trade interest, Carey and his companions failed in attempting to get voyage pass.[13] Yet, through a Danish ship named *Kron Princessa Maria* and its Captain, they could reach India without a license.[14] In the process of his family's struggle and missionary venture, he got an opportunity to work as a manager at an indigo factory which also provided a license to stay in India for five-years.[15] While expanding the missionary excavations, one of the major steps initiated was the establishment of a printing press by William Ward who was recruited and sent from England. During these years, Carey did not give up his love for nature that took him to another level of contributions in maintaining a Botanical Garden. His interest in the physical universe was through the conception that God had blessed it for humankind.

Now, along the river Hooghly, there were a number of traders belonging to Portuguese, Dutch, French, English, and Danish who often saw Serampore as a prospective center. Indeed, "The Serampore Trio saw Serampore as a strategic center for the evangelism of India as a whole and for the eastern regions beyond."[16] During the times of Carey's missionary journey, he had encountered the plural Indian contexts when it comes to faiths, traditions, and practices. The 'social evils' like *sati* was considered as a great act of holiness that grieved Carey. As such, Carey only hoped for greater things. Further, even Ram Boshu who sacrificed for the benefit of Carey in teaching Bengali, assisting in the translation of the Bible, and missionary activities, was not willing to be baptized. This incident posed a question to the watchwords "Expect great things, Attempt great things." Carey strongly believed that God's Word alone could transform people who were in hopeless conditions, bound by the devil.[17] This leads to yet another question: Is God's Word enough for transforming the people or is encountering God important for transformation?

Seven years after Carey's arrival in India, the first person named Krishna Pal was converted and baptized who later became a local missionary in Calcutta and Assam. Pal also became the first Bengali hymn-writer.[18] There were also a handful of converts in the later part of the missionary venture and by the end of his missionary journey there were about 600 converts. Then with his abilities in language, Carey also became a Tutor in Fort William College, Calcutta. Then an opportunity came for Carey to oppose and share the practices of social evils to Lord Wellesley.[19] This incident resulted in the abolition of child infanticide.[20] But the practice of *Sati* was not abolished with immediate effect because it was related to Hindu religious acts and was a very sensitive issue. Furthermore, in 1803, on the occasion of Gokul's (i.e., one of the converts) death, the spectators (local people) have recognized the nature of Christian love. The pallbearers were three missionaries and three local converts. Indeed, this astonished the crowd in witnessing what real love was even in a bereaving situation.[21] However, almost all the achievements became a heap of ashes in 1812 when a great calamity (burned down the paper store) took place. It was reported that,

> Initially, Carey was of the belief that if he could give Bible in the language of the people, then the Bible itself would influence the people and transform them. But this was not to be. He learned from experience that the translated word has to be preached regularly to the people if their message was to be fully understood.[22]

Apart from the major translation of the Bible and other missionary activities, one of the benchmarks that resulted in a greater influence of the Serampore missions was the establishment of the Serampore College in 1821.[23] During Carey's lifetime, the practice of *Sati* was declared illegal and was considered as a criminal act in 1829 through the order of Lord William Bentinck.[24]

Tribal Environment before Colonialism

Tribal communities belong to the 'native' minority groups of the people in India who are designated as Scheduled Castes and Scheduled Tribes[25] in the constitution. Here it should be noted that every tribal society has its own framework and existence which can be identified as tribal worldviews. In a nutshell, to deal with the tribal worldviews, it requires the knowledge of all aspects of the tribal life such as people, culture, traditions, history, society, polity, customs, economy, psyche, and the like. Roger Gaikwad stated that "Life is not lived in a vacuum; rather life has meaning because it is lived in a context."[26] By understanding and experiencing the attachment of the tribals in terms of humankind, nature, and the supernatural beings in a given context will provide the environment of the tribal features. All the three—god, human, and nature possess life. Tribal people belong to relational beings who keep close attachment with the community members. Their social setting depends on an individual with the rest of the members of a family, clan, Khel,[27] or a village. This provides a sense of belongingness in maintaining identity and participation and contribution in a given society. It is not only about the social relations, but they maintain serenity similar to the nature in and around them. Considering the trees and forests, rivers and lakes, mountains and hills, birds and animals, winds and sun, water and earth, all of these elements are considered to be sacred and embodied with life that need to be accepted and respected.

Moreover, tribal existence itself is holistic in nature. The aspects of being political, cultural, religious, social, and others are based on the thought patterns of being a tribal that every experience and awareness perceived in her/his mind represents the relational reality. It is also noted that the tribal communities regardless of ethnicity and geography have distinctive features, besides the similar connotations for a general tribal understanding and implication regarding the community life. Indeed, every tribal community is independent and self-sufficient in their existence.

Tribal Encounters with the Colonial Powers

Everyone has her/his freedom to live a life! Before experiencing the total humanity, many people are faced with brutality through colonial ideologies and become victims of their domination and oppression. In a massive scale, the population, in general, becomes victims due to the imposition of colonial ideologies in varied aspects of their survival—economy, physical and emotional aspects, and psychological and the overall development as a being. Asoso Yonou in his essay *The Rising Nagas: A Historical and Political Study* records the first encounter of the Nagas with the British in January 1832, when Captain Jenkins and Lieutenant Pemberton along with Raja Gumbeer Singh's troops happened to pass through Mao Naga and Angami Naga areas on their way to the Assam Valley. Their encounter led to combat where the Nagas fought courageously to preserve their identity, land, and protect their fellow communities.[28] This encounter between the Britishers and the Nagas soon became quite different both politically and socially in later years. There were several raids with the Nagas by the British army beginning from 1832 until they took over Khonoma village in 1879. As such, the imperialists control over the then Naga Hills District took place. In this setting, the question of the "struggle for existence"[29] was raised, like any society that longed for their free existence and they worked hard to attain it. For their own convenience, the British divided the Naga lands into different geographical locations in India and Burma (now Myanmar). In India alone, they divided the four states (Nagaland, Manipur, Arunachal Pradesh, and Assam) without the Naga consent. In this sense, the Naga people were once ruled by British colonizers[30] under the 'divide and rule' policy.

In such a context, the inception of the colonial powers in the form of the British Raj brought chaos to the natives. A. Lanunungsang asserts that due to British colonialism in the Naga Hills, it has cost the total existence heavily. In the process, colonizers have forcefully occupied the tribal land and imposed their destructive ideology at their interest. At the same time, they discouraged higher education, imposed military power, exploited resources, crippled the social system, forced labor without rewards, and left India without any compensation. In this way, the tribal experiences of life were human handled and manipulated. There has been bombardment with western culture and religious ideas where the tribals were imprinted that western culture was better/acceptable much more than their own. This is where the statement of Zhodi Angami fits in, "Tribal hermeneutics has to begin by breaking the colonial mentality and undoing the western influences in the academic and socio-cultural life of the people."[31] This would restore the distinctive identity of the tribal being.

Mission Scenario in the Tribal Land

India is a land with 'multi-level' features and opportunities and also a land with a lot of challenges for co-existence. In a land beyond the colonial era, diversity continues to distinguish the inhabitants in faith, ethnicity, caste, class, gender, and geography. In a land such as this, can something promising come out of the tribal worldviews and in the context of the Serampore missions remain a pertinent thought to ponder deep into. It is appropriate to explore and relate a fraction of tribal worldviews to ponder into the contextual approaches of the Serampore Missions. However, to tackle all the tribal setting in this essay is not feasible. Therefore, the watchwords of Carey in the context of the colonial environment are considered.

The Gospel of Jesus Christ to the Nagas first came through the American Baptist Mission, which was the extension of the Burma Baptist Mission under Adoniram Judson. In 1839, the first contact was made with the Namsang Nagas (presently settled in Arunachal Pradesh), but it did not go well[32] despite of establishing a Namsang Naga Mission. The zeal for the Naga Mission did not fade away despite the fact that Mr. Miles Bronson and his family abandoned the Namsang Naga Mission field in 1841 due to health reasons. There are records about the first two Nagas[33] who were baptized during the missionary period. There was a gap in the mission to the Nagas for about thirty years until after E. W. Clark[34] arrived in Sibsagar (1869), who started the Naga Mission from a different location.

Godhula Rufus Brown, an Assamese evangelist first took the Gospel of Jesus to the Naga Hills and later took his wife Lucy to teach the villagers. Nine villagers were converted and were taken down to Clark and received baptism on 11th November 1871. In the following month, Clark himself went up to the Naga Hills and fifteen new converts were baptized and celebrated the Lord's Supper on 22nd December 1871 at Dekahaimong (Molungkimong) village. Thus, the first church to be established in the Naga soil was marked and the Mission to the Nagas advanced thereafter.

One of the important mission priorities for Clark was to build up bridges among the Naga villages for peace and prosperity, keeping in mind the 'permanent and systematic' ministry for the whole of Nagas. The plantation of churches grew fast as a result of lay native evangelists who visited along with Clark to near and far.[35] Impur,[36] a place on the hillock of Naga Hills was approved to be the mission center for the Nagas, from where wider visions and missions began among them. Education to Nagas was also an impact of Christianity; Clark and his wife Mary initiated to open schools to impart education for both boys and girls. Clark served among the Nagas for thirty-seven years and had firmly established the churches in the Naga Hills.

Although the Good News was sown in the Head-hunters' land, yet, it was mostly taught through the Western lenses of Christianity. The missionaries did not consider or understand the tribal worldviews of total existence while they were engaged in missions. As a result, they failed to relate themselves to the tribal thinking patterns. Tribal people considered space and time to relate their realities by means of experiencing the *Sitz-im-Leben*. All the belief systems, cultural practices, political functions, social engagements, and the like were related to their thinking patterns. In fact, tribal civilization progressed due to the activeness of recognizing their thinking capacities to relate to both visible and invisible features of life. As stated, the missionaries did not consider the thought patterns but rather imposed what they thought right. It can be stated as a stereotype of subjection and domination over tribal thoughts. Though the tribals confessed Christianity, yet it is simply the Western Christianity rather than Christianity with tribal environments and epistemological outlook. One of the simplest reasons is that the Good News did not germinate in tribal culture, society, economy, polity, belief systems, and thought patterns. Consequently, almost all the tribal practices discouraged in public were returning to the daily living.

Postcolonial Hermeneutics at a Glance

The rise of various postcolonial theories in the recent decades has provided a space for margins at all levels of the contexts to analyze and critique colonial ideologies and alter them towards alternate means of interpretation of history and issues related to imperialism. The approaches include—decolonizing, resistance, colonial discourses, ethnicity, feminist postcolonial studies, liberationism, primitivism, social justice, cultural identity, and the like. The context is the space where human domination continues to exist over against others through ideologies and praxes that hamper the peaceful existence of individuals and societies. The Nagas have been under colonial domination for more than a century which resulted in distorting their very identity from a humanitarian perspective. Considering such an environment in context, it is appropriate to deal with issues that demoralize the traditional setting of life. In this process, implementing the tribal postcolonial hermeneutics comes to the fore.

Tribal postcolonial hermeneutics seeks to analyze any given issue from factual experiences rather than literary history. The "questions about subjectivity, identity, agency and the status of the reverse-discourse as an oppositional practice, posing problems about the appropriate models for contemporary counter-hegemonic work"[37] are also raised. In other words, it deals with the resistance over against the colonial subject of predetermined political ends which limits the margins under their aspired ideologies. At the same time, this tool also investigates the activities of the missionaries who executed their missions under the shadow of the Empire. Regardless of any foreign elements that have impacted a particular region, this tool uncovers those negatives and decentralized forms in its original setting.

A tribal cultural identity that belongs to a tradition and history requires a place and time to promote itself with rightful exercise and co-existence. Stuart Hall held that cultural identity exists in the midst of many others; however, it should take place with space to produce 'one true self' in the light of ancestral sacred identity.[38] In other words, cultural identity depicts the group of people representing the same cultural practices, belief norms, cultural positions, experiences, factual past, ethics and ethos, refinement, and the knowledge of internal and external horizons of existence. Postcolonial reading attempts to view the experiences of the tribal people. Richard Kroner asserts, "Experience may be described as the procedure of becoming directly, i.e., by an immediate contact, acquainted with the object of knowledge . . . . What we experience is in some way given to us; we do not produce it . . . .We cannot do without experience."[39] This would mean that experience is an inevitable factor for human existence. In the northeastern tribal context, the colonists have executed their interest by overriding experiences and ideologies directly or indirectly at the cost of the natives. The following discussion will read the Serampore mission from a postcolonial perspective.

Serampore Missions in the Lens of Tribal Worldviews: A Postcolonial Reading

There are volumes of biographical, missional, and historical approaches that have been centered on Serampore Missions. Perhaps, this is the right moment to investigate the tribal perspectives of the Serampore missions. Simone Weil writes, "The need of truth is more sacred than any other need. Yet it is never mentioned."[40] Well in the context of North East India it is quite different. The anthropologist did not consider the thinking patterns of the tribal environment and the tribal settings were projected with more negative lenses rather than from a holistic approach. There has been unveiling of knowledge banks from those observers and commentators for their own cause but not for the tribals as such, since the whole concept of their knowledge was that the tribals were uncivilized, savage, backward, animistic, and the like. At the same time, the colonial agents in the form of British Raj also devalued and branded the tribals in the same line of thought. Hence, looking from the lenses of tribals' own location would make a difference to perceive the Serampore Missions in a new perspective. It would guide in leading towards redemptive denotation of tribal community and Serampore missions.

Based on the watchwords of Carey, it is important to uncover some of the relevant critiques that can be made through a tribal postcolonial lens. Both in terms of how Carey executed his visions from a humanitarian as well as from a Christian perspective need to be considered. As highlighted in the early part of this essay, the Serampore Trio envisioned Serampore to be a strategic location to evangelize India and beyond. This projects the similar ideology as any colonial agents would attempt to implement their interest. The point is that the missionaries did not enter into the foreign land legally but under the protection of the Danish kingdom they landed and settled. Almost all the excavations were initiated taking the advantage of political powers of the Empire at first. Nevertheless, to fulfill their aspiration to evangelize the Indian continent, they pitched their tents with many struggles. Not only did they risk their lives throughout their missionary activities but also relied on God to fulfill unseen challenges. In this context, colonial agents in the form of trade and commerce paved a way for the missionaries to continue their activities.

In both the contexts of Serampore and the tribals of the NEI, the commonality was the presence of the colonial powers, which became the channel towards free movement of the missionaries. A postcolonist would perceive that the strategies employed by the missionaries did not go well while imparting the Good News of Jesus. The strategies applied by Carey and Clark were similar as they ultimately attempted to bring people to the tent of Christ. They introduced Christianity in a foreign land from the perspective of the western world. They attempted to Christianize the natives with western flavor rather than emphasizing the nativity aspects. In this sense, contextual roots were not considered while evangelism was initiated. They attempted great things by spiritualizing all things in all forms. As a result, the new faith was not sown into the socio-cultural lives of the people. In fact, they were proclaimng a Jesus with foreign tenets rather than sowing the seed in the Indian ethos and pathos. Rather the missionaries were attempting great things in their own terms under the colonial powers.

The questions remain are: 'who attempts on whom?' and 'who can expect and from whom?' Since the attempts were made prominently through literature (Bible translation) in order to impose foreign faith and culture, it remained sometimes biased in results. It can also be noted that the attempts of the missionaries were mostly for the elite or high-class people, which sometimes did not impact the rest of the society. The margins (victims) who were illiterate could not access those Bibles. The ministry of Bible translation was sometimes considered as a means to extend imperial mentality and through literature they attempted to colonize the natives. It shows that the missionaries mostly wanted to transform the highest strata rather than the lowest in the society. As a result, the transformation cost the natives (margins) at the most. In this context, it is evident that the colonial mentality of the watchwords did not suit the real experiences of the natives in both the context of Serampore and of the tribal contexts.

One also cannot deny that Carey depended on human and material resources to progress the missions he ventured apart from God's providence. Human relations and supports were important for the missionaries. For this reason, Carey too even engaged in teaching activities, working in indigo industries, and relied on his friends and BMS for financial assistance. Moreover, he expected human assistance from the native Christians in evangelism, sharing concerns with the authorities of the land for eradicating social evils, seeking protection from the Empire, and the like. Carey knew that humans were created by God and in the image of God. This means that humans were also capable to do what they ought to do. While emphasizing on the human efforts, one can critique that Carey did not attempt as much as he did for translation works to eradicate the caste system. It reflects that human efforts have limitations. As acknowledged, every context is different. Christianity as a religious manifestation came through the western missionaries should not have been implanted as it existed in a foreign land. The sentiments, rich traditions and practices could have been considered while evangelism was initiated. This may be one of the reasons why Indian Christianity continues to struggle to locate Christ in their holistic environment.

Humayun Kabir observes, "I would like to point out that British political ideas have profoundly influenced India and the impact of the British Industrial Revolution shattered her ancient economy."[41] The colonizers imposed their culture on the Indian natives who were but shunned their rights and culture for the benefit of the British Raj. This does not leave behind the activities of the missionaries as well. In habitual impositions of foreign culture, they portrayed that theirs was superior to that of the natives' culture. As a result, the helpless natives were left with no choice but to accept[42] the superior and to abandon their distinctive cultures. In this context, a postcolonial approach counters the activities of those dominant agents by stating that great attempts to exploit and cripple the oneness of a community become insensible. Especially it is obvious in the context of any mission fields where colonial powers are present alongside the missionary activities. In that sense, Postcolonial studies attempt to locate a space within the exploited cultures in order to create an environment through which a community can yet again experience a total humanitarian socio-cultural *Sitz-im-Leben*.

Further, 'expect' and 'attempt' are the key words that Carey had focused in order to progress missionary activities. His strategies were not exclusive when it comes to evangelism, conversion, and other missional strategies as stated above. Even he encountered with tribal people like "the Khasis . . . the Santals, the Lushais, Konds, and others."[43] All these communities were welcomed into the greater mission of Serampore. However, when people experienced negation and de-centering from their original settings of life, it becomes critical as to whether their 'one true self' could be holistically realized or not. On the other hand, when the colonial ideologies were implemented by the missionaries, they also would have perceived the experiences and practices of the natives as inferior. It would have taken place both in Serampore and in the tribal contexts when Christianity was spread over the territories. This further leads to the concern of the land. For tribals, the land is life. When the colonial agents have forcefully occupied their land for their benefits, it became a matter of life being ceased. This is same with the Serampore context where the peasants lost their rights to their land and had to pay huge amounts of land revenues to the colonizers. The natives were even forced to abandon their traditional occupations like weaving that risked their very livelihood. It is well acknowledged that Carey was a missionary who runned his mission works in self-support. Yet the question is: 'did he encourage the natives for survival when it comes to economic stability?' Such kind of approaches were lacking both in the Serampore and in the tribal contexts. This may be one of the main reasons that the Good News of Jesus was sidelined from the roots of the Serampore natives and the tribal contexts. What the missionaries expected and attempted was to transform the natives into their fold.

Expecting and attempting great things from/for God does not mean that all things will be fulfilled. Many things are accomplished for humankind by the initiative of God and through human companionships. When the missionaries attempted to evangelize the maximum, they used several methods to fulfill their targets. Perhaps this could also be termed as yet another colonial strategy imposed in foreign contexts. The interest of the missionaries was to see the fruits (expect great things) of their endeavors (attempt great things) through spreading Christianity. However, as cautioned earlier, it was, sometimes and mostly, not executed through the means of transformative efforts. A postcolonial reading or approach seems mutual while interacting with missionary and colonial activities. Only then, the approaches can be realized and experienced toward the existence of life in totality.

Conclusion

Every community has its own unique framework of life existence in totality. At the same time, one can acknowledge that the contexts in which Carey and Clark worked are different from that of the *Sitz-im-Leben* in which we live today. In today's context, there are many constructive features that resulted into a better living situation. Therefore, the perspectives that can be developed through a tribal postcolonial approach to the Serampore missions and the tribal worldviews can be summed up with three points to ponder:

First, the Gospel of Jesus should be sown and germinated from within the socio-cultural environment and experiences of each context. Christian missionaries should not repeat the mistake of bombarding the teachings of Jesus with a colonial dictum of "Expect great things, Attempt great things." Rather, there should be an approach considering the mutuality in existence where every human being is considered. Since human beings are part of the socio-cultural setting, the socio-cultural factors should be taken into consideration with respect, dignity, sensitivity, and holistic life existence. The devalued socio-cultural elements should be resurrected in the light of Christian perspectives and at the same time the church need to develop inclusive strategy.

Second, the future of the Serampore missions in contexts is possible through following the constructive legacy left behind by the pioneers. When we are engaged in missions, it is important to remember that holistic transformation of individuals and communities is not possible through the means of colonial attitudes and practices. Therefore, the 'time' and 'space' aspects of the target persons and communities should be prioritized with constructive brainstorming and endeavors. Third, contemporary issues and challenges in Christian missions include problems related to sexuality, minority concerns, Hindutva agenda, illegal migration and immigration, and the like. Christianity or Hindutva 'can' be termed as neo-colonial agents in today's mission scenario. Then what can we take back from this critique? Christian missions or Serampore missions or tribal missions belong to the Savior. We, the human beings, are shouldering the task on behalf of God. In that sense, Christian missions should be approached in a holistic sense in order to experience life without domination that degrades and devalues humanity and natural world around us. The bottom-line is that, the watchwords of Carey should not be taken literally like how the colonial agents would enforce; missions should be 'approached' as the springboard to transform individuals and societies with a consideration of the *Sitz-im-Leben*.

Endnotes

[1] Here few questions can be raised: When did it happen? Where was it taken place? Who were the victims? How far the victims were victimized? What did they experience? Why the natives were subjects? The discussion on this essay would be reflected based on these inquiries in order to locate space for the colonized inhabitants.

[2] J. B. Middlebrook, *William Carey* (London: The Carey Kingsgate Press Limited, 1961), 11-13.

[3] Middlebrook, *William Carey*, 21; cf. Sunil Kumar Chatterjee, "William Carey: Missionary Sermon," *Indian Journal of Theology* 35/1 (1993): 38-40.

[4] Andrew Lalhmangaiha, *Holistic Mission and the Serampore Trio* (Delhi: ISPCK, 2010), 36; cf. Sunil Kumar Chatterjee, *William Carey and Serampore*, second edition (Serampore: By the Author, 2004), 65; Mary Drewery, *William Carey: A Biography* (Grand Rapids: Zondervan Publishing House, 1979), 192.

[5] Drewery, *William Carey: A Biography*, 124.

[6] Lalhmangaiha, *Holistic Mission and the Serampore Trio*, 50.

[7] "In 1784 the British Parliament passed an Act requiring the Directors of the East India Company to make permanent rules for the collection of land revenue. The Directors asked Lord Cornwallis to make a settlement with the *zamindars* for ten years and if it was found satisfying it was to be made permanent. From 1786-

1989, Sir John Shore carried out an inquiry in the question of revenue collection and then in 1791 a settlement was made for ten years with the *zamindars*. Sir John Shore wanted to wait for full data on the working of the system before taking the irrevocable step to making a settlement permanent. However, Lord Cornwallis the Governor-General overruled him and the Code of Permanent Settlement of Bengal was passed in 1793. That was the year that William Carey came to India." See Malay Dewanji, *William Carey and the Indian Renaissance* (Delhi: ISPCK, 1996), 7.

[8] T. Katherine and John Thomas, *William Carey: The Man Who Loved India* (Bangalore: New Life Literature, 2001), 16.

[9] Dewanji, *William Carey and the Indian Renaissance*, 9-12.

[10] Ruth and Vishal Mangalwadi, *William Carey: A Tribute by an Indian Woman* (New Delhi: Nivedit Good Books Distributers Private Limited, 1993), 32-33. Even for decades, the colonizers' policy did not allow the colonized people to be employed with respectable administrative status, due to fear that they might also reform and possibly might become upright morally. This includes the payment where par was sliced off for native elite people.

[11] Ruth and Mangalwadi, *William Carey: A Tribute by an Indian Woman*, 43.

[12] "It came from the British Parliament, from the Company, from Military, from the Oriental scholars, from his own Mission board, and also from the very people he was seeking service – the Indian themselves." See Ruth and Mangalwadi, *William Carey: A Tribute by an Indian Woman*, 47.

[13] Middlebrook, *William Carey*, 7-9.

[14] Dewanji, *William Carey and the Indian Renaissance*, 16.

[15] Dewanji, *William Carey and the Indian Renaissance*, 18.

[16] Middlebrook, *William Carey*, 43.

[17] Further, there were new missionaries that were sent by the Baptist Missionary Society (BMS) who landed in the Indian soil without a permit. They could not settle and have to flee since they were not permitted to stay in India without any permit. This was the time when the missionary families found refuge in Serampore, a place under the Danish Empire. The British could not lay hands on them to remove from Serampore since the land was not under their control. The then Governor of the Danish Empire permitted the missionaries to settle in Serampore to do missionary works. Meanwhile, the movements of the missionaries in Serampore were closely watched by the British authorities. However, on the ground that the missionaries were safe under the shadow of the Danish government, Carey decided to shift his base to Serampore instead of Kidderpore. This is how the stage was set for Serampore missions during this yet another crucial time of growing missionary activities. See Katherine and Thomas, *William Carey: The Man Who Loved India*, 29-30.

[18] Middlebrook, *William Carey*, 57.

[19] Middlebrook, *William Carey*, 74; Ruth and Mangalwadi, *William Carey: A Tribute by an Indian Woman*, 46.

[20] See, Ruth and Mangalwadi, *William Carey: A Tribute by an Indian Woman*, 17-18.

[21] Katherine and Thomas, *William Carey: The Man Who Loved India*, 35-36.

[22] Katherine and Thomas, *William Carey: The Man Who Loved India*, 40.

[23] Katherine and Thomas, *William Carey: The Man Who Loved India*, 42.

[24] Ruth and Mangalwadi, *William Carey: A Tribute by an Indian Woman*, 21.

[25] With regard to Scheduled Tribes, Thanzauva argues that it is difficult to decide who belongs to tribals and who are not according to the classified criteria since it mentions that they should belong to a homogeneous community who do not belong to either Hindu or Muslim; at the same time should be economically poor and socially marginalized. He writes, "The criteria used for determining which groups constitute Scheduled Tribes are religious identity on the one hand and social and economic status on the other." Furthermore, he argues that the term tribe has been branded by anthropologists and later imposed by the Indian government. Prior to this, the tribes in India did not identify in any means as this except by their own community names. Nonetheless, the term tribe also affirms that tribals are the primal people. Thanzauva, "Is 'Tribal' A Redeemable Term?" *Journal of Tribal Studies* 1/1 (1997): 3, 8, 10.

[26] Roger Gaikwad, "Equipping the Church for its Witness vis-à-vis Religious Pluralism and Fundamentalism and Increasing Marginalization of the Poor," *Journal of Tribal Studies* 5/2 (2001): 34.

[27] Khel is a unit division within a village. They administer and function with a separate social and political objective. It could be formed either by three or more clans or through the division unit within a village.

[28] Asoso Yonou, *The Rising Nagas: A Historical and Political Study* (Delhi: Vivek Publishing House, 1974), 72; cf. Luingam Luithui and Nandita Haksar, *Nagaland File: A Question of Human Rights* (New Delhi: Lancer International, 1894), 16. In another narration, it is also mentioned that "The British, along with the Ahom and Meitei Kingdoms, invaded the Naga villages beginning in 1832." Further in 1833, the British allowed Raja Gambir Singh of Manipur to annex a large area of Naga inhabited areas so as to dominate; however, it was fiercely resisted by the Nagas to defend their freedom. See E. Deenadayalan, *Naga Resistance and Peace Process: A Dossier* (Bangalore: Other Media Communications Pvt. Ltd., 2001), 7. It also depicts the praxis of colonial ideologies to erase an identity using local resources and gain power and dominate. It has to be noted here that the British did not take control over all the Naga inhabited during their reign. See Yonou, *The Rising Nagas: A Historical and Political Study*, 106-108. In another case, the British colonial laid their hands beyond Bengal to North East India simply with their justification as for economic interests. However, their ideology was not limited to the claim as such but their ideologies totally had the intention for total control over the region which could be understood as political aspiration through imperialism. See Frederick S. Downs, *History of Christianity in India: North East India in the Nineteenth and Twentieth Centuries* (Bangalore: The Church History Association of India, 1992), 16-17.

[29] John Woodroffe, *Is India Civilized? Essays on Indian Culture* (Madras: Ganesh and Co. Publishers, 1919), 3.

[30] For details see "The Naga Problem: An Account," Presented by The Naga Student's Federation at the Seminar Jointly Sponsored by Citizens for Democracy and The Naga Students' Federation in New Delhi, December 14, 1995, 3-4; cf. Mangyang Imsong, *Trapped! Indo-Naga Conflict and the Psychosocial Effect on Naga Youth* (Dimapur: By the Author, 2000), 17-23; V. K. Anand, *Nagaland in Transition* (New Delhi: Associated Publishing House, 1967; reprinted 1968), 18.

[31] Zhodi Angami, "Tribal Biblical Interpretation," *Journal of Tribal Studies* 18/1 (2013): 38.

[32] Mr. Miles Bronson along with his wife and his younger sister moved to the Namsang Naga Mission and started a school. It was very unfortunate for the missionaries as well as for the Nagas that they have to stop their mission. The reason was that Bronson's sister Ms. Rhoda lost her life due to malaria sickness. Namsang area was known for its malaria borne-zone, which it is said to be even today. The missionary family with tears left the new mission field for their physical recovery. Thus, the Namsang Naga Mission field was abandoned for nearly three decades until E. W. Clark arrived. One of the reasons for the failure of the Naga Mission at Namsang may be due to the missionaries giving more priority to the Assamese Mission or not enough missionaries. The hope was that the neighboring Christians would be able to evangelize the hill people. The loss of two first Naga converts could have been another reason for the failure.

[33] In 1847 the first Naga person to be baptized was Hubi by Nathan Brown at Sibsagar Mission field, Assam; unfortunately, he died of cholera the following month. The second person to be baptized was an Ao Naga named Longjanglepzük from Merangkong village. He also did not live long, because he was killed by his village while he visited about three years after baptism.

[34] Clark was sent to Sibsagar, Assam for the Assamese Mission and not for the Nagas, yet, during the year of the Lord 1871, some Ao Nagas came down to the Assam valley for trading where the missionaries interacted with them. The visitors from the hills were amazed by the printing machine and the classrooms the missionaries were working on. The missionaries asked them whether they could teach their children. The chief of the group accepted but warned them about the headhunting in the hills. From then on Clark was challenged to do Mission work with the Nagas and settle among them; his target was changed from the Assamese to the Nagas. In October 1871, Godhula along with the villagers from Dekahaimong (Molungkimong) went up to the Naga Hills for evangelizing them. For certain days he was not permitted to stay inside the village though those traders with whom he went informed that he was harmless. No stranger was allowed to stay within the village boundary during those days because of fear for the British East India Company conquest. He was kept with sharp observation outside the village; but he wisely used his time by trying to communicate with the broken Ao language and sing gospel songs in Ao language

that fascinated the local village people. Later he was permitted to enter into the village without any hesitation to preach and teach.

[35] O. Alem, "From Darkness to Light," *From Darkness to Light* (Kohima: NBCC, 1997), 47-49. Further, on Clark's request to the Home Board in America, Rev. C. D. King, and his family were sent to the Angami Nagas in 1881 and Mr. and Mrs. Witter to the Lotha Nagas in 1885 to expand their missions. Rev. S. W. Rivenburg and his wife were transferred from Molung to Kohima in 1887 as reinforcement towards wider Naga Mission.

[36] Before Impur, Molongyimsen village was the mission center for the Nagas. Molungyimsen was established on 1876, just some distance down from Molongkimong by those earliest converts along with Clark in order to establish a Christian village as well as for a new beginning of mission works among the Naga Hills. Impur at present is the Mission Center for the Ao Baptist Church Association (Ao Baptist Arogo Mungdang).

[37] Benita Parry, "Resistance Theory/Theorizing Resistance or Two Cheers for Nativism," *Colonial Discourse/Postcolonial Theory*, eds. Francis Barker, Peter Hulme and Margaret Iversen (New Delhi: Viva Books, 2012), 172.

[38] Stuart Hall, "Cultural Identity and Diaspora," *Contemporary Postcolonial Theory: A Reader*, ed. Padmini Mongia (Delhi: Oxford University Press, 1997), 110-111.

[39] Richard Kroner, *Culture and Faith* (Chicago: The University of Chicago Press, 1951), 13.

[40] Simone Weil, *The Need for Roots: Prelude to a Declaration of Duties towards Mankind*, tran. Arthur Wills (New York: Routledge, 2002), 36.

[41] Humayun Kabir, *Britain and India* (Calcutta: Orient Longmans Private Ltd., 1960), 5.

[42] V. V. Thomas, *Understanding Subaltern History: Theoretical Tools* (Bangalore: BTESSC, 2006), 49.

[43] Middlebrook, *William Carey*, 51.

Bibliography

Alem, O. "From Darkness to Light." *From Darkness to Light*. Kohima: NBCC, 1997.

Anand, V. K. *Nagaland in Transition*. New Delhi: Associated Publishing House, 1967; reprinted 1968.

Angami, Z. "Tribal Biblical Interpretation." *Journal of Tribal Studies* 18/1 (2013): 25-43.

Chatterjee, S. K. *William Carey and Serampore*. Second edition. Serampore: By the Author, 2004.

Chatterjee, S. K. "William Carey: Missionary Sermon." *Indian Journal of Theology* 35/1 (1993): 38-40.

Deenadayalan, E. *Naga Resistance and Peace Process: A Dossier*. Bangalore: Other Media Communications Pvt. Ltd., 2001.

Dewanji, M. *William Carey and the Indian Renaissance*. Delhi: ISPCK, 1996.

Downs, F. S. *History of Christianity in India: North East India in the Nineteenth and Twentieth Centuries*. Bangalore: The Church History Association of India, 1992.

Drewery, M. *William Carey: A Biography*. Grand Rapids, Michigan: Zondervan Publishing House, 1979.

Gaikwad, R. "Equipping the Church for its Witness vis-à-vis Religious Pluralism and Fundamentalism and Increasing Marginalization of the Poor." *Journal of Tribal Studies* 5/2 (2001): 34.

Hall, S. "Cultural Identity and Diaspora." *Contemporary Postcolonial Theory: A Reader*. Ed. Padmini Mongia. Delhi: Oxford University Press, 1997.

Imsong, M. *Trapped! Indo-Naga Conflict and the Psychosocial Effect on Naga Youth*. Dimapur: By the Author, 2000.

Kabir, H. *Britian and India*. Calcutta: Orient Longmans Private Ltd., 1960.

Katherine, T. and John Thomas. *William Carey: The Man Who Loved India*. Bangalore: New Life Literature, 2001.

Kroner, R. *Culture and Faith*. Chicago: The University of Chicago Press, 1951.

Lalhmangaiha, A. *Holistic Mission and the Serampore Trio*. Delhi: ISPCK, 2010.

Luithui, L. and Nandita Haksar. *Nagaland File: A Question of Human Rights*. New Delhi: Lancer International, 1894.

Mangalwadi, R and V. *William Carey: A Tribute by an Indian Woman*. New Delhi: Nivedit Good Books Distributors Private Limited, 1993.

Middlebrook, J. B. *William Carey*. London: The Carey Kingsgate Press Limited, 1961.

Parry, B. "Resistance theory/theorizing resistance or Two cheers for Nativism." *Colonial Discourse/Postcolonial Theory*. Eds. Francis Barker, Peter Hulme and Margaret Iversen. New Delhi: Viva Books, 2012.

Thanzauva. "Is 'Tribal' A Redeemable Term?" *Journal of Tribal Studies* 1/1 (1997): 3, 8, 10.

"The Naga Problem: An Account." Presented by The Naga Student's Federation at the Seminar, Jointly Sponsored by Citizens for Democracy and The Naga Students' Federation in New Delhi, December 14, 1995.

Thomas, V. V. *Understanding Subaltern History: Theoretical Tools*. Bangalore: BTESSC, 2006.

Weil, S. *The Need for Roots: Prelude to a Declaration of Duties towards Mankind*. Tran. Arthur Wills. New York: Routledge, 2002.

Woodroffe, J. *Is India Civilized? Essays on Indian Culture*. Madras: Ganesh and Co. Publishers, 1919.

Yonou, A. *The Rising Nagas: A Historical and Political Study*. Delhi: Vivek Publishing House, 1974.

13

The Modern Missionary Movement of the Serampore Trio: A Missiological Perspective

James Patole

Introduction

The missionary endeavor of the Serampore Trio undoubtedly occupies a significant place in the history of modern missionary enterprise in India and beyond. This paper looks at the historical aspects of the Serampore Trio[1] and their selected missionary works from a missiological perspective and also in the light of contemporary Protestant concept of mission. The Trio perhaps epitomizes the modern Christian movement that has brought about significant and all-inclusive socio-cultural, economic, and missional transformation through their holistic ministry and initiatives.

It will be an enormous task to cover all their missionary experiences and initiatives; thus, we concentrate on a few modes and approaches of their missionary work that has insights and implications for contemporary missional endeavor, particularly, with regard to their pioneering missionary movement, centrality of scriptures, Jesus and the Great Commission, holistic approach with a broader scope of evangelism, multilingual educational and literature ministry, contextualization of the gospel and native leadership development, missiological research and importance of statistics, and Bi-vocational mission and 'all inclusive' biblical paradigm. These are a few aspects that have significant missional insights and implications for the contemporary missional endeavor which provides important perceptions, approaches and practical insights.

The Serampore Trio

William Carey instituted the Baptist Missionary Society (BMS) in 1793 and undertook the Indian missions, beginning at the State of Bengal. According to Christopher Smith, such volunteer missionary societies were the driving force of the modern missionary movement.[2] In a broader sense, the Serampore Trio's history commences in the year 1799 when Charles Grant, Joshua Marshman, and William Ward arrived in India and joined hands with William Carey and his ongoing missionary work. The new co-workers were exceptionally intellectual and were wholly devoted to the service of God.[3] By then Carey had already begun his Bengali translation, preaching the gospel, and learning new languages. On 10th January 1800, Carey left Madnabati, Bengal, area under British India and moved to Serampore. It was Ward who proposed and convinced Carey for this move as he felt "There was no hope for the immediate furtherance of the gospel in British India, he argued, but in Serampore they could preach and teach freely and could print the Bengali Bible. Besides, the area around Serampore was densely populated and the Danes were anxious that more missionaries should join them."[4] As a result, the Trio established a center of operations to the Danish ruled Serampore, situated on the Hooghly River, south of Calcutta. Later, they expanded the mission slowly in the British ruled regions even during oppositions. They were incredibly a close-knit leadership team that worked together for several decades while complementing each other in an intricate manner.

The Serampore Trio and Their Missionary Endeavor

According to the mission tradition, the Serampore Trio had much in common and they functioned together as a remarkable team. As Carey started early, he visited two hundred villages in the district and preached the gospel who had never heard of Christ. However, as Ward and Marshman joined him, the mission works started growing though slowly but steadily.[5]

Pioneering Missionary Movement: Centrality of the Scriptures, Jesus and the Great Commission

Carey and his colleagues undeniably believed that salvation of humankind is a universal call of God to the church and an individual believer. The Great Commission of Matthew 28:18-20 is an obligatory mandate for every generation of followers of Jesus Christ. Bruce Nichols notes that Carey did not leave much as far as his mission theology is concerned except few of his letters, the booklet, *An Enquiry into the Obligations upon Christians to Use Means for the Conversion of the Heathen*, published in early 1792 and articles in the *Friend of India* and *Samachar Darpan*. However, Carey's "understanding of the 'Great Commission' was a radical break from the history of interpretation of the passage from the Patristics through the Reformation . . . He made a radical departure from the traditional ways in which Matthew 29:18-20 was understood. It was frequently used either to support the deity of Christ or to support a Trinitarian baptismal formula."[6] The text was seldom used in a missiological context; however, it is remarkable how Carey and his colleagues understood this text in its own biblical context of missions to the nations. Nichols further notes that the Bible was the mutual manifesto of the Evangelical Movement and it became the leading factor in Carey's and Serampore Trio's life and mission works. Nichols states:

> William Carey's theology was clearly Christocentric. Jesus Christ was the centre of his spiritual pilgrimage and the only hope for the salvation of the world . . . Carey sought to bring every thought captive to Christ and he refused to speculate beyond the revelations of scripture . . . the cross was the centre of his preaching . . . Christ's death was a substitutionary atonement for sin . . . Carey called upon his hearers to repent of their sins and put their trust in Christ for salvation alone.[7]

As observed, the Serampore Trio's mission theology was not only Christ-centered but also church-centered which followed the 'primitive' New Testament model. They always stressed "preaching, spontaneous spirituality in worship, prominence on fellowship, and the ordinances of believers' baptism and the Lord's Supper and on independency in church organization."[8] It clearly indicates a biblical underpinning for demonstrating God's love and preaching of the gospel.

Pioneering a Holistic Movement with Broader Scope of Mission Praxis

The Serampore Trio was holistic in their missionary vision and praxis. In 1802, Marshman led the first trip to Jessore, about ninety-five kilometres to the northeast of Serampore in what Bangladesh is now. Again, in 1803, the Trio continued regular preaching in Calcutta that resulted in the formation of a church at Lal Bazaar. In 1807, they crossed over to Burma, and in 1808, a mission team was sent to Bhutan. Later in 1812, an expedition was sent to Agra in North India. In further expansion, in 1812, at the beginning there were not much productive efforts were made in Java. In 1813, along with Carey's son Jabez, they established the Java station while in 1814 with John Chamberlain, a missionary who joined Serampore mission after Ward and Marshman, made a productive trip to Delhi. The ministries of preaching, teaching, discipleship, and church planting were close to the hearts of the Serampore Trio for which they toiled for years.

William Ward and Joshua Marshman produced some significant writings better known as *The Form of Agreement*[9] that has earned attention from mission scholars and practitioners. Ward framed the Serampore mission's "theology of evangelism" that consisted many experiences from evangelistic ventures and engagements with various types of "Hindoos" in Bengal. These literatures continue to offer in-depth contextual understanding for the effective cross-cultural missions. Furthermore, Carey's *An Enquiry* ultimately became the manifesto of the modern missionary movement.[10] Moreover, by the time of Carey's death in 1834, there were 50 missionaries ministering in 18 mission stations in India.[11]

The Serampore Trio equally co-focused on several civilization reforms, social justice, equality and environmental concerns. Their contribution in abolition of the practice of *sati*[12] and other social reforms were transformational. It was nothing less than a socio-cultural transformation in a few important areas of the Indian society that helped countless others who perhaps did not come to an encounter with Jesus. In addition, the Trio's contribution in issues related to ecology, establishment of the Agri-Horticultural Society in 1820, helping with forestation programs, initiating banking program for the poor, providing education for the poor children, creating job opportunities for unemployed are worth mentioning.

Multilingual Educational and Literature Mission

For the Serampore Trio, Christian mission and education were intrinsically woven together. Carey noticeably desired more than converts and reckoned that education is a sure means to develop respective government, arts and laws.[13] Furthermore, teaching was a central aspect of the missionary method. Christian values and morals articulated through education were "freedom from infanticide, the caste system, and *sati*, yet freedom to learn, freedom to read, freedom to read the Bible in own language, and freedom to come to a saving knowledge of God in Christ through such reading."[14] In further development, the Serampore missionaries were the pioneers of the very first women schools, "where female education was practically unknown because of the superstition that a literate girl would be widowed shortly after marriage,' such a legacy can be seen in Serampore's deliberate encouragement of women theologians."[15] According to Brian Pennington, Ward was exceptionally good and today remembered essentially for his groundbreaking work in printing in colonial Bengal that included supervising the making of the first typefaces for several Asian languages.[16] For decades, he managed "the most important printing and publishing house in the world for books in the Oriental languages."[17] Ward was also known for his assessment of the Hindoos that is said to be among the first English-language efforts at a wide-ranging distinct study of Hinduism.[18] Eventually, he achieved a great celebrity standing in England and in America when in 1819, he turned out to be the leading missionary to return from the East to the English-speaking world and lecturing them for two years on Hinduism and the great need "for a concerted evangelical effort to subvert what he described as its sanguinary and stultifying effect on India."[19] In further attempt to arouse the consciences of educated national leaders and their people, and the political authorities on issues of social injustice, Ward and Marshman started *Samachar Darpan* and *Friend of India*, where they exposed certain social evils such as infanticide, *sati*, the ill treatment of lepers, and occurrences of slavery.[20]

William Carey with the help of various learned Indians and Europeans translated the entire Bible in several languages. Similarly, in 1822, Joshua Marshman completed the translation of the Bible into the Chinese language, the first complete Bible to be published in that language. Later, the very first printing press where the first ever "complete set of metal types of the Chinese language was developed by John Lawson in Serampore."[21] The Serampore mission was successful in carrying out the educational and literature advancement. It was nothing less than a cultural transformation that made a lasting impact.

Re-emergence of Sodality and Modality Paradigm

In 1792, Carey had urged the leaders of the Northampton Baptist Association to establish a "society for propagating the gospel among the heathen . . . Thus, a particular Baptist voluntary society was born in 1792 that became to be known as the Baptist Missionary Society (BMS)."[22] It is interesting to see Carey's attempt to look beyond the existing structures of the local churches that seemed to be reluctant to engage in global mission. Ralph Winter, while differentiating the subject of church and mission structures and their continual appearance across the centuries in mission movements names these two structures as: Modalities and Sodalities.[23] Modalities are structures primarily focused on nurture and fellowship of the local church and a network of such groups. Paul Pierson calls it as 'congregational structures' and states that "these structures are local and inclusive of fervent as well as nominal believers, youths and the elderly, new Christians, and mature disciples."[24] While, Sodality structures, "are structures primarily focused on missionary task, beyond the church's existing scope, formation of groups, societies or structures that takes into consideration the broader scope of missions."[25] Although there are detractors and advocates to such missional approaches, Ralph Winter establishes his exegetical stance through the Scriptures and Jewish history. He insists that both the early church and contemporary missionary endeavors employed modalities and sodalities on a varied degree which were and are validated expressions of the church of Jesus Christ. Winter remarks in his concluding inference that these two models of missions are essential to fulfill God's redemptive purpose and *missio dei* on the earth.[26]

Carey was convinced about "the necessity of taking specific steps to take the Gospel to the rest of the world. Specifically, Carey proposed the formation of a mission structure . . . ."[27] Carey came from a Baptist church, which was hyper-Calvinist and believed that "If God wants to bring the people of other nations and lands to himself, he will do it in his own time and in his own way." Of course, "that rationalization relieved the church of all responsibility to evangelize or engage in missions beyond its shores. It left mission totally up to God with no human responsibility."[28] William Carey "later discovered he had to break from his Baptist Missionary Society in order to have enough flexibility of action in India."[29] Carey's formation of BMS demonstrates "remarkable ability to move from the *Missio Dei* to a positive plan of action in setting up a Protestant sodality in the form of a mission society . . . that would end up fuelling the entire "Great Century" of Protestant missions."[30] Bruce Nichols further elaborates Serampore Trio's pioneering efforts in this regard:

> Part of the Serampore Mission's unique contribution to missions was their ability to develop structures and institutions to carry through the functional programmes they initiated. For example, William Ward pioneered the printing

> press as a vehicle to publish Carey's biblical translations and as a means of self-support for the Serampore Mission. Carey and Marshman opened numerous schools to give education to the poor. Again, Carey and Marshman established Serampore College to provide training for Indian pastors and teachers for the schools. Carey started a Savings Bank to enable the poor to provide for the education of their children and to assist the unemployed.[31]

With all that, the Trio continued to partner with their local church/es and other missionary friends and agencies that significantly contributed in several pioneering missionary initiatives and movements.

Contextualization of the Gospel and Native Leadership Development

Culture is one of the most important and integral part of people's worldviews, beliefs, and way of life and is very crucial for any communication. How, then, did the Serampore Trio look at Indian culture and respond? It is important to mention here that for William Carey and others:

> The Christian faith and Indian culture were not irreconcilable. He strove to affirm Bengali culture where it did not conflict with the gospel so that converts could retain their cultural self-identity and give leadership in evangelism and to the emerging church. He resisted attempts to replace Indian culture by the so-called Christian culture of the West.[32]

Furthermore, the Trio symbolized respect for Indian language, literature and culture without disregarding the values of Western science and knowledge. In doing so, they remained steadfast to the message of the Bible and to Christian moral lifestyle.[33] However, according to Brian Pennington, Ward produced significant materials that initially countered what he viewed as Indology's own misrepresentations of Hinduism, some of which could have shaped the Hindus. Pennington further notes:

> Indologists concerned with religion favored textual sources over the study of rites in practice, seeing in popular Hinduism a decayed and compromised form of the pure religion found in its ancient texts. Shaped by his early experience in journalism, Ward was among the first authors to address this vacuum and take seriously the daily religious exercises and ejaculations of the people he knew. He regularly attended Hindu festivals and temples, and comprehended quite fully the rhythm and texture of local ritual life.[34]

Ward's twenty years in India contributed significantly in several areas, however, the four-volume *Account of the Writings, Religion and Manner of the Hindoos* (1807-1811) and *A View of the History, Literature, and Mythology of the Hindoos* (1815) were significant in Serampore Trio's missionary endeavors as well as mission enterprises in several parts of the world. These masterworks were exceedingly persuasive and were widely cited throughout the century, to an extent that they appeared in several editions throughout the first quarter of the nineteenth century.

Moreover, the recipients were not only Orientalist scholars and missionary reformists but also politicians and policy-makers.[35] Ward's study of Hindu ideologies and teachings was the outcome of his and other's day-to-day life and their personal observations, interactions and ministry to the Hindu people—their ceremonies surrounding birth, marriage, death and various festivals and rituals. Furthermore, what Ward contributed had its foremost and direct influence on denominational Christianity in Britain and India. It became the standard work on Hindu beliefs and practices for those interested in the spread of missionary work and vocation itself. "It offered a hybrid of academic description and evangelical invective against 'heathen' religion."[36] Pennington notes that "missionaries carefully followed the lives of individuals out of both genuine biblical compassion and an eagerness for converts. These certainly contributed then and now in understanding Indian culture and religion with a detailed account of beliefs and practices along with testimonies of those who embraced Christ and His teachings."[37]

Similarly, Marshman with his profound and practical missional involvement challenged the British-based BMS to become "less metropolitan in outlook, to make space for creative decentralization and to foster operational flexibility on the mission field."[38] The Serampore Trio's cultural understanding of Bengal and India was not flawless, but they were sensible, discerning and biblical. They learned how to contextualize their mission in a better way while not compromising with the Biblical truth. Bruce Nichols further provides Serampore Trio's cultural sensitivity towards native missionaries. He notes that the Serampore Trio did not compel their converts to change their names to anglicized or western even though they carried the name of a Hindu god. Besides, Carey and his colleagues supported new believers to retain their traditional costumes and even the sacred thread of the higher castes.[39] However, Carey and his colleagues though respected Bengali cultural practices, at times rejected certain evil traditions that opposed the biblical standards, and equality and social justice. For instance, they opposed "idolatrous practices such as the Jagannath festival in which worshippers lost their lives, but he did not attack idolatry as such in public."[40] As seen earlier, they sought to eradicate certain practices associated with religious and cultural beliefs that were socially unjust and unacceptable.

Regarding native leadership, John Clark Marshman details the experiences of the Serampore Trio, in particular, their efforts in advancing vernacular education. It is important to note that in addition to training Christians as teachers and evangelists they opened the Serampore College in 1818 for youths from all parts of India 'without distinction in caste or creed' that seen eleven Brahmin students registered in the first session.[41] They believed that Indians could be profoundly evangelized only by their own countrymen and was principally the task of the national Christians.[42] Their decisive determination was to prepare Indians to substitute the European missionaries and thus develop an entirely indigenous church.[43] It is interesting that by the end of 1802, they witnessed at least thirteen native communicants in the church and eight inquirers.[44] But by 1807, they could account that they had baptized one hundred converts, including 12 Brahmins, 16 of the writer class, and 5 Muslims.[45] In further growth, in 1813 alone they baptized one hundred and sixteen converts,[46] and by 1821, their ministry resulted into baptizing nearly 1400 converts.[47] The Serampore Trio was much more committed to the principle of establishing indigenous churches than were the Calcutta and General Baptist missionaries. It is important to note here that the *Enquiry* shows how Carey argued for native leadership,[48] on which the work of the Serampore Trio rested.[49]

Missiological Research and Importance of Statistics

The significance of the statistic survey in *An Enquiry* is generally ignored. However, the statistics and the geographical material take up most of the book.[50] W. Bieder notes that "Carey challenged Christianity to accept its responsibility to become familiar with the world's religious condition. No missions without enough information! With astonishing accuracy, Carey drew up a sound statistic on world religion, thus recognizing the importance of statistics for mission activity."[51] On the other hand, William Ward, known as a missionary ethnographer contributed through printing materials related to missions. He also penned his own books on Hindu culture and history that significantly enhanced missionary work.[52] His writings and researched materials on Hinduism spread beyond India and in most of the English-speaking world in the early nineteenth century.

In 1803, the Serampore missionaries delegated some Indians to collect data about *Sati* from the neighborhood of Calcutta. According to the information collected, the number of *Satis* exceeded four hundred in one year. Later, in 1804 the Serampore missionaries again stationed ten agents at different places in the same area for six months in order to obtain more precise data. At this time, the number of *Satis* found to be about three hundred. During the same time, Carey gathered data from the *Pandits* of the Fort William College and the numerous texts of the Hindu *Shastras* on which the practice of *Sati* was constructed. All these resources were placed at the disposal of G. Udney who was then a member of the Governor General's Council. The statistics collected by the Serampore missionaries were used often in missionary writings and publications in India and England."[53] Here, we find, a remarkable commitment of the Serampore missionaries for the accurate information and data for the strategic mission work and literature ministry.

Furthermore, the British government hesitantly accepted the fact that social evils such as polygamy, female infanticide, child marriage, widow-burning, euthanasia, and forced female illiteracy "as being an irreversible and intrinsic part of India's religious mores. Carey began to conduct systematic sociological and scriptural research on these issues. He published his reports in order to raise public opinion and protest both in Bengal and in England."[54] These efforts indeed resulted in socio-cultural transformation, for instance, Lord Wellesley passed a Regulation in 1802 prohibiting infanticide.[55] The Serampore Trio organized several other social attempts and brought a transformation in the society.

Bi-vocational Mission Paradigm

Carey, Ward, and Marshman as well as a few other missionaries had commenced their missionary service after some occupational/professional work experience. In the case of Carey, he had previously worked as a grammar school teacher and a cobbler.[56] Whereas, Ward developed the printing press that published Carey's biblical translations and other mission related literatures. These enterprises were helpful as a means of self-support for the various Missions initiatives in Serampore.[57] Marshman complemented through overseeing various educational institutions, some of which generated some proceeds.

George Ella records developments when Carey pursued employment at Indigo factories in Mahipal and Madnabati to self-sustain Serampore mission and his family. In due course, Carey's salary increased substantially and besides earned additional commission on all sales. He started believing that his initial aim to be economically independent of any home support was now realized. Carey therefore wrote to BMS, to Fuller and Ryland, "I now inform the Society that I can subsist without any further monetary assistance from them. I sincerely thank them for the exertions they have made, and hope that what was intended to supply my wants may be appropriated to some other mission."[58] Carey along with others was even confident of the providence of God and they were hoping to offer "employment to those Indians who lost their cast through coming under the gospel. So now, Carey was an independent missionary, able like Paul, to earn his own keep and still minister to others."[59] However, the Serampore mission had to seek reunion with BMS in December 1837 due to financial crisis so that the work would not be halted.[60]

In such a scenario, Carey's employments and schools run by Hannah and Joshua Marshman provided for the Serampore missions for a longer period. In such a bi-vocational mission model, Carey and others made themselves useful enough to Bengal's British authorities and gained a considerable measure of immunity from official opposition to the mission's work.[61] Carey was later invited to teach there. During Carey's professorship, lasting thirty years, he significantly influenced "the ethos of the British administration from indifferent imperial exploitation to 'civil' service."[62] This further resulted in securing printing contracts from the government for the Serampore Mission Press. They also recognized that native pastors needed to be self-supporting and that the churches must be self-governing. Their first step in this policy was to establish as many schools as possible giving a general education in the Bengali language and seeking to make the schools self-supporting. [63]

All Inclusive Missiology

The Serampore Trio, while fostering inclusiveness in their approach to missions, persistently focused on all the caste groups and opposed the existing caste system. They even restrained new converts from displaying the caste superiority as they held that there is a principal antithesis between caste and Christianity. However, "the insistence on the renunciation of caste undoubtedly hindered conversions but some thought this as an excellent method for a convert to display his sincerity"[64] It is interesting to know that Carey's first convert was a *Sudra* by the name Krishna Pal (a carpenter), however, the second one was a young man called Krishna Prasad, a high caste, Kulin Brahmin. In due course, the number of converts increased, majority of them were Hindu converts.[65] All of them were accommodated together where the Serampore Trio was very vigilant to see that these newly added understand and follow casteless and inclusive Christianity. Further, crossing the Bengal region, the Serampore mission strived to conduct their ministry on broader lines embracing the whole of India, even the whole of Southern Asia.[66]

In the field of educational ministry, once again the Serampore Trio set a trend. Marshman, together with his wife, Hannah, founded a school for the children of both sexes, educated parents while equally focusing on poor, middle and upper class families even though the response from the affluent was not very positive.[67] Their literature work too focused on all people groups, as much as possible, including all caste groups and both educated and uneducated. With all this background, although the Serampore Trio lived almost more than two centuries before, they continue to provide missiological insights, practical guidance and inspiration to stimulate the ongoing wave of missionary movement around the globe.

Insights and Implications for the Contemporary Missions

The significant task that the Serampore Trio accomplished was to awaken the obligation of believers to fulfill the Great Commission. If not all, most of the churches in India and elsewhere are plagued with nominalism and even the ministers serving in various set ups are not significantly engaging in direct or indirect evangelistic and social justice pursuits; however, fulfilling their given responsibilities which are commendable, it is inadequate to impact the hurting and lost humanity surrounding us.

The Holistic Vision and Contemporary Missional Praxis

The church has overcome, to an extent, the dichotomy between social justice and evangelism, as they must go together. Several scholars and practitioners have deliberated and assessed this, both for and against. John Stott argues that most people failed to understand the biblical truth and tried to make social justice either superior or supplementary to evangelism.

The superior stance diminishes the importance of witnessing and salvation in Jesus Christ—something Stott observed absolutely incongruent with the New Testament teachings. On the other hand, the subordinate position, he finds as equally flawed. It somehow made social action, a means to gain favor in order to lead to conversions, a mere means to an end. Stott notes, "In its most blatant form this makes social work the sugar on the pill, the bait on the hook, while in its best forms it gives the gospel credibility it would otherwise lack. In either case the smell of hypocrisy hangs round our philanthropy."[68] In addition, the ecological concerns, issues and challenges[69] are real and demands urgent attention and more thoughtful response from the church, Christian NGOs, and theological institutions.

It is of great importance to balance social justice and evangelism focus knowing that they "belong to each other and yet are independent of each other. Each stand on its own feet alongside the other. Neither is a means to the other, or even a manifestation of the other. For each is an end in itself."[70] In the contemporary context, such biblical and balanced approach towards holistic mission is vital for a healthy and Christ centered Christianity. In recent times, the amount of civilization or social work among various segments of society has drastically increased. K. Rajendran, a noted mission's leader for more than three decades, remarks that "in the future, social work might grow more than direct evangelism. This change in focus is related to the holistic approach to evangelism. The increase in social work needs to be watched and a balance maintained, or else missions could become merely social organizations."[71] He further notes that the undue emphasis on tribals who constitute 8-10% of the total population was and is due to "the fact that these people are generally open to the gospel and it is economically easier to support missionaries who live among them. It also comes from a 'win the winnable' philosophy. This strategy needs to be positively and intentionally revised so that 'all inclusive' focus is sustained."[72] It is important to remember that the Serampore Trio's holistic approach and efforts not only resulted in enhancing trans-cultural exchanges and socio-cultural and education transformations, but also resulted in an increased church growth and gospel initiatives by the twentieth century.

Bible Literature, Translations and the Educational Model of Missions

As seen earlier, the education and literature model of mission was productive to a certain extent and for a period. However, most of the schools were not able to retain for long and the whole venture proved to be not a very effective method for mission's expansion. The high optimism of the Serampore Trio and the subsequent missionaries that modern western education would undermine Hinduism and expose several beliefs and ritualistic views as erroneous proved greatly overstated and did not accomplish much as expected. It is important to note here that "in as much as missionary educational activities are regarded as a means of conversion, they may indeed be adjudged to have failed in India, but this is not their only possible justification, as the missionaries themselves realized."[73] Today, educational model continues to exist in different forms and purposes, however, with mission focus, one will make wise and more strategic decisions whether to follow such models or how differently they can be pursued for better results for the Kingdom.

In the area of literature missions, eradicating Bible poverty is still a huge challenge before the Indian and global church. "Over 4,000 people groups in Africa, America and Pacific, and Asia and Middle East are in bible poverty with little to no scripture in their language . . . the need is urgent." [74] The followers of Christ, all over the world, are indebted to the role of Scripture in their own spiritual lives and growth. We can "scarcely imagine what it would be like to not to have the Bible in our own language. Yet, 1 billion people in the world today do not have a completed Bible in their own language; 165 million people do not have a single verse of scripture in their own language."[75] As we further study the mission history on a deeper level it is a crucial reminder of the fact that all mission works and theological educations are deeply rooted in the translatability of the Gospel which has made Christianity so remarkably different from other world religions.[76] As far as theological education is concerned, the indigenization of theology making gospel relevant to culture and breaking away from the dominance of Western theology and academicians on the whole is still a great task before the Indian church. The western influence has crippled the Indian theology to a great extent. There exists an urgency to construct a contextually balanced, biblical theology for the Indian church, and pluralistic Indian society.

Re-emphasizing Sodality and Modality Models

The Serampore Trio was prominent catalysts in the creation of 'sodality' model societies in Europe and in the United States and they led to what has been called "the great century" of the missions.[77] Consequently, many non-western churches started establishing their own mission organizations.[78] To mention a few societies that started in such a scenario are: a student movement that launched in 1810 as the overseas mission that facilitated the formation of the American Board of Commissioners for Foreign Missions; the Triennial Convention of the Baptist Denomination for Foreign Missions was organized in 1814; and followed in 1816 by the United Foreign Missionary Society. The new societies and boards began their work with the strategic presuppositions and methods inherited from the American Indian Missions and the Danish-Halle Mission.[79] The emphasis here is that, both 'modality' or 'congregational' structures and 'sodality' mission structures are vital for the fulfillment of the great commission "both are equally the Church, the People of God."[80] The Serampore Trio functioned as a combination of both structures: church and mission while remaining committed to the Great Commission.

Contextualization in Ever Changing Context and Native Leadership Development

Timothy Tennent emphasizes that, Carey was an Orientalist and not an Anglicist. Anglicists were those who mostly embraced a "superior West, inferior East" mindset. Here, it's imperative to emphasize "the importance of learning from the host culture and, as far as possible, indigenizing the gospel message into native soil, rather than extracting the people group out of their culture into a foreign system of thought and language . . . the contextual translatability of the Christian gospel has become one of the hallmarks of both modern Protestant missions and the field of missiology."[81] In the area of contextualization, Paul Hiebert notes that, "roughly from 1800 to 1950 most Protestant missionaries in India, and later in Africa, rejected the beliefs and practices of the people they served as "pagan."[82] John Pobee writes that ". . . to the present time all the historical churches by and large implemented the doctrine of the tabula rasa, i.e., the missionary doctrine that there is nothing in the non-Christian culture on which the Christian missionary can build and, therefore, every aspect of the traditional non-Christian culture had to be destroyed before Christianity could be built up."[83] Such understanding and complete denunciation of host cultural norms and values did not help much to the overall missionary endeavor.

However, in critical contextualization, according to Hiebert, we understand the importance of each culture, phenomenologically, while following exegesis of the Scripture and the Hermeneutical Bridge. In the second step, the pastor or missionary leads the church in a study of the Scripture related to the question at hand and offers a critical and balanced response. Lastly, the people are encouraged to corporately evaluate their own past customs and traditions according to their new biblical understandings, and make their choices and responses.[84] Thus, critically and biblically engaging with context is necessary and should be followed without cultural superiority and biased approach or attitude. As seen earlier, the Trio resisted idolatrous practices such as the 'Jagannath festival' in which the devotees lost their lives, but they did not condemn idolatry in public spaces.[85] The Trios strived to understand the socio-cultural and religious context of their time and engaged with people of other faiths sensitively and appropriately while utilizing diverse approaches and communication means.

As far as native and lay leadership development is concerned, the Indian church and missions have made significant progress, but much remain undone. The call of God, faithfulness, Christian witness, commitment for the Lord's work, gifting and grace are at times disregarded over theological and secular education, financial status, regionalism, race or caste dynamics and the like. Moreover, the insecurity among the senior leaders, lack of equipping and training ministry at the local church, lack or restricted acceptance of women's and lay leadership, dearth of theological and leadership resources are some of the hindrances for the indigenized lay and native leadership. It is noteworthy to recollect that irrespective of the confines of Serampore Trio's mission "the principles for indigenous self-supporting churches are standard practices today."[86] The Trio's hearts, as seen earlier, was in evangelizing the natives and then develop their leadership skills and education to help the local church grow and missionaries to spread the good tidings in other areas.

The Significance of Scientific and Missiological Research

The Indian church and missions face a huge task of developing creative and innovative approaches to engage with various tribal, rural, and urban groups, their issues and challenges that requires in-depth research and cutting-edge data. It was not an "accident that Carey's knowledge was almost unrivaled in his time, just as the ethnologists of Wycliffe Bible Translators know more than others about the languages of the present."[87] Carey's statistics, as well as those of Theodor Christlieb (1879)[88] and Patrick Johnstone's Operation World [89] have been and still are outstanding reference materials for 'secular' interests as well as mission's enterprise. It is important that the Indian church and missions give adequate time, finances and importance to scientific research. The important advantages of scientific research are: it improves decision making; it reduces uncertainty; it enables adopting new strategies; it helps in planning for the future; and it helps in ascertaining trends.[90] Such statistics are important as they serve as the basis for prayer, strategic planning, and appropriate orientation. The Trio precisely gave importance to research and gathering various geographical, socio-cultural and other needed data to evaluate the contextual reality and develop their missional strategies and approaches.

Re-visioning Mission: 'Inclusive' Paradigm of Missions

The 'inclusive' paradigm demands no predisposition based on gender, race, color, caste, class and tribe. The fact that thousands of Indian Christians and missionaries are serving "the Dalits, the Adivasis and the destitute, handicaps and poor should not be discouraged or dismissed as following outdated mission paradigm."[91] However, Mark Laing, while suggesting a more balanced approach in our mission endeavour notes that, "traditional mission models initially evolving out of existing missionary methods had their own repercussions both for good and bad . . . . In today's context, striking the balance between poor and non-poor as well as various other castes/classes is essential to widen the approach and better response to the gospel."[92]

In the further assessment of Indian church and missions, a lopsided approach in thinking and strategizing for Indian missions and evangelism, IMA (Indian Missions Association), the national federation of Missions in India notes that:

> The Gospel came to India in the first century. But the mission work has had many twists and turns, and the reality is that the job is not done. The Christian percentage remains the same. Moreover, we have failed to concentrate in all clusters of people. Our focus, our definition/understanding and our initiatives have been only around the 1/3rd of the people called marginalized. Although we do not minimize the focus on the marginalized as they too are human being created in the image of God yet all people (all clusters) have to be reached by us—the Indian Church.[93]

As God's community, the Indian church and missions must affirm and live-out the central message of the Bible that all humans are created in the image of God and He loves them all equally and concerned for their wellbeing. There are still "nearly three thousand people groups in India with little or no access to the gospel. Thousands of other ethnic groups have been identified around the world with either no Christian residents within the group or so few that there is no viable gospel witness. This great burden must lie at the heart of our understanding of missions."[94] It was significant and intentional missional praxis of the Serampore Trio that notably contributed in demonstrating an all-inclusive approach as much as possible that positively resulted in beneficial outcomes but were not without challenges and resistance. In our present context, it is high time that Indian church/missions take serious efforts to re-define the "all inclusive" and holistic missiology that has focus on all clusters of the society.

Conclusion

The Serampore movement was and is God's movement that continues to give a clarion call to engage with our world and share the love and power of Jesus Christ in a meaningful way. The modern missionary movement owes a lot to the pioneering efforts of the Serampore Trio and their sacrificial life and path breaking missionary work. It has incredibly enriched the holistic understanding of missions, reiterated the importance of centrality of the Scriptures, Jesus Christ and the Great Commission in the missions and the church ministry. The Trio through their socio-cultural engagement and reforms, literature and translation works, theological education, adequate contextualization, and native leadership development, and missional research continues to inspire and enhance the missional thinking and praxis. The Serampore Trio's life, vision and ministry have incredible insights and implications for the Indian church and missions. It also has great lessons to rediscover the prophetic thought and re-visioning *Missio Dei* for the global church.

The Serampore Trio's contribution with regard to missionary endeavor significantly enhanced the campaign to advance the Gospel. They not only established significant models of missions in the 18th century India but initiated a new era in modern Protestant missions throughout the world. The Serampore Trio significantly contributed in the ongoing Protestant mission works that were undertaken by various societies that proved to be catalysts for the revitalization of Christian missions in the modern era. The movement that began to grow so rapidly with the Serampore Trio continues to inspire and rekindle a passion for the worldwide Great Commission initiatives, networking, and strategic mission movements.

Endnotes

[1] The 'Serampore Trio' "is the popular, shorthand term used by mission promoters and historians to refer to the close partnership of William Carey, William Ward, and Joshua Marshman, who co-directed the Serampore Mission in Bengal between 1800 and 1823." A. Christopher Smith, "The Legacy of William Ward and Joshua and Hannah Marshman," *International Bulletin of Missionary Research* 23/3 (July 1999): 128.

[2] Christopher Smith, "William Carey 1761–1834: Protestant Pioneer of the Modern Mission Era," *Mission Legacies: Biographical Studies of Leaders of the Modern Missionary Movement*, ed. Gerald H. Anderson (Maryknoll: Orbis, 1994), 245–254.

[3] E. L. Wenger, *The Story of Serampore at Its College*, Fourth Edition (Serampore: The Council of Serampore College, 1918), 4.

[4] George Ella, "William Carey: Using God's Means to Convert the People of India," *William Carey Theologian—Linguist—Social Reformer*, ed. Thomas Schirrmacher, The Theological Commission of the World Evangelical Alliance 4 (Bonn, Germany: Verlag für Kultur und Wissenschaft Culture and Science Publ., 2013), 62.

[5] Basil Miller, *10 Boys Who Become Famous Missionaries* (Grand Rapids: Zondervan Publishing House, 1991), 9.

[6] Timothy C. Tennent, "William Carey as Missiologist: An Assessment," *Expect Great Things, Attempt Great Things: William Carey and Adoniram Judson, Missionary Pioneers*, eds. Allen Yeh and Chris Chun (Eugene: Wipf and Stock Publishers, 2013), 17.

[7] Bruce J. Nichols, "The Theology of William Carey," *William Carey Theologian -Linguist–Social Reformer*, The Theological Commission of the World Evangelical Alliance 4 (Bonn, Germany: Verlag für Kultur und Wissenschaft Culture and Science Publ., 2013), 93.

[8] Nichols, "The Theology of William Carey," 101.

[9] George Smith, *The Life of William Carey: Shoemaker and Missionary* (Edinburgh/ London: John Murray, 1885), 441-450; A. H. Oussoren, *William Carey: Especially His Missionary Principles* (Leiden: A. W. Sijthoff, 1945), 274-284.

[10] Timothy George, *Faithful Witness: The Life and Mission of William Carey* (Birmingham, Alabama: New Hope, 1991), 21-22.

[11] "Expect Great Things, Attempt Great Things: The Life and Ministry of William Carey" (Granbury, Texas: Grace Bible Church, n.d.), http://www.gracebiblegranbury.

com/home/398/398/docs/William%20Carey%20biography.pdf?sec_id=398, accessed on 21st November 2018.

[12] "The practice of widows burning themselves upon their late husbands' funeral pyres-a dreadful custom that was often imposed upon widows who had little voice in Indian culture." Nathan Finn, "Missionaries You Should Know: William Carey," *International Mission Board* (July 31, 2018), https://www.imb.org/2018/07/31/missionaries-you-should-know-william-carey/, accessed on 14th October 2018.

[13] Alexander Walton, "A Christian Republic on the Hooghly: A Contextualization of William Carey's Missionary Vision" (Thesis, Master of Philosophy, School of Philosophy and Religion College of Arts and Law University of Birmingham, 2014), 125.

[14] Bennie Crockett, "An English Garden in India: William Carey's Integrated Christian Vision," *News Journal of the International Association of Baptist Colleges and Universities* 76/2 (August 2012): 7, https://www.wmcarey.edu/carey/j-term/eng-gard-0712.pdf, accessed on 20th October 2018.

[15] Potts, *British Baptist Missionaries in India, 1793-1837: The History of Serampore and Its Missions,* 122.

[16] Sunil Chatterjee, "Reverend William Ward, 1769-1823," *Serampore College Students' Magazine*, 1972, 86–97.

[17] David Kopf, *British Orientalism and the Bengal Renaissance: The Dynamics of Indian Modernization, 1773-1833* (Berkeley and Los Angeles: University of California Press, 1969), 72.

[18] Brian K. Pennington, "Reverend William Ward and His Legacy for Christian (Mis)Perception of Hinduism," *The Society for Hindu-Christian Studies and Butler University* 13/6 (January 2000): 6.

[19] Pennington, "Reverend William Ward and His Legacy," 7.

[20] Nichols, "The Theology of William Carey," 108-109.

[21] Potts, *British Baptist Missionaries in India, 1793-1837: The History of Serampore and Its Missions*, 89,111.

[22] Smith, "Carey, William (1761-1834): History of Missiology," 115.

[23] Ralph Winter, "The Two Structures of God's Redemptive Mission," *Perspectives: On the World Christian Movement*, eds. Ralph Winter and Steven C Hawthorne, Third Edition (CA: William Carey Library, 1999), 220-230.

[24] Paul Everett Pierson, *The Dynamics of Christian Mission: History Through a Missiological Perspective* (Pasadena: WCIU Press, 2009), 6.

[25] Pierson, *The Dynamics of Christian Mission*, 6.

[26] Winter, "The Two Structures of God's Redemptive Mission"; Pierson, *The Dynamics of Christian Mission*, 6-7, 30, 82-83.

[27] Pierson, *The Dynamics of Christian Mission*, 30.

[28] Pierson, *The Dynamics of Christian Mission*, 30.

[29] Pierson, *The Dynamics of Christian Mission*, 83.

[30] Tennent, "William Carey as Missiologist: An Assessment," 20.

[31] Nichols, "The Theology of William Carey," 107.

[32] Nichols, "The Theology of William Carey," 103-104.

[33] Nichols, "The Theology of William Carey," 104.

[34] Pennington, "Reverend William Ward and His Legacy for Christian (Mis) Perception of Hinduism," 7.

[35] Phil Hine, "Lecture Notes: On William Ward," April 12, 2012, http://enfolding.org/lecture-notes-on-william-ward/, accessed on 23rd November 2018.

[36] Pennington, "Reverend William Ward and His Legacy for Christian (Mis) Perception of Hinduism," 6.

[37] Pennington, "Reverend William Ward and His Legacy for Christian (Mis) Perception of Hinduism," 8; also see Brian K. Pennington, *Was Hinduism Invented? Britons, Indians, and the Colonial Construction of Religion* (Oxford; New York: Oxford University Press, 2005).

[38] Smith, "The Legacy of William Ward and Joshua and Hannah Marshman," 128.

[39] Nichols, "The Theology of William Carey," 104.

[40] Nichols, "The Theology of William Carey," 104.

[41] Nichols, "The Theology of William Carey," 103-104.

[42] Brian Stanley, *The History of the Baptist Missionary Society 1792-1992* (Edinburgh: T&T Clark, 1992), 51-52.

[43] Potts, *British Baptist Missionaries in India, 1793-1837: The History of Serampore and Its Missions*, 89, 129.

[44] John Clark Marshman, *The Life and Times of Carey, Marshman, and Ward: Embracing the History of the Serampore Mission*, Vol. 1 (London: Longman, Brown, Green, Longmans & Roberts, 1859), 174.

[45] Marshman, *The Life and Times of Carey, Marshman, and Ward*, 1:324.

[46] Marshman, *The Life and Times of Carey, Marshman, and Ward*, 2:76.

[47] Potts, *British Baptist Missionaries in India, 1793-1837: The History of Serampore and Its Missions*, 89, 36.

[48] Stanley, *The History of the Baptist Missionary Society 1792-1992*, 47-57.

[49] Stanley, *The History of the Baptist Missionary Society 1792-1992*, 36-47.

[50] An exception is Jim Montgomery, Eine ganze Nation gewinnen: Die DAWN Strategie (Lörrach: Wolfgang Simson Verlag, 1990), 101-103.

[51] W. Bieder, "William Carey 1761-1834," *Evangelisches Missions-Magazin*, 1961, 161.

[52] William Ward, *A View of the History, Literature and Mythology of the Hindoos*, Serampore Edition (Courtesy Derby Local Studies Library, 1814).

[53] Kanti Prasanna Sen Gupta, *The Christian Missionaries in Bengal:1793-1833* (Calcutta: Pinna K. L. Mukhuopdhyay, 1971), 169.

[54] Vishal and Ruth Mangalwadi, *The Legacy of William Carey* (Wheaton: Crossway Books, 1999), 17-21.

[55] A. Jayakumar, *History of Christianity in India* (Kolkata: SCEPTRE, 2013), 65.

[56] Nathan A. Finn, "Missionaries You Should Know: William Carey," *International Mission Board* (July 31, 2018), 1, https://www.imb.org/2018/07/31/missionaries-you-should-know-william-carey/, accessed on 14th October 2018.

[57] Nichols, "The Theology of William Carey," 108.

[58] Ella, "William Carey: Using God's Means to Convert the People of India," 53.

[59] Ella, "William Carey: Using God's Means to Convert the People of India," 53.

[60] M. A. Laird, "The Contribution of the Serampore Missionaries to Education in Bengal, 1793-1837," *Bulletin of the School of Oriental and African Studies, University of London* 31/1 (1968): 98-112.

[61] A. Christopher Smith, "The Legacy of William Carey" 16/1 (January 1992): 4-5.

[62] Mangalwadi, *The Legacy of William Carey*, 17-25.

[63] Nichols, "The Theology of William Carey," 103-104.

[64] Potts, *British Baptist Missionaries in India, 1793-1837: The History of Serampore and Its Missions*, 89, 158.

[65] Ajith George, "Serampore Mission-History of Christianity in India," 2, https://www.academia.edu/22904952/Serampore_Mission-History_of_Christianity_in_India, accessed on 18th October 2018.

[66] Julius Richter, *A History of Missions in India*, tran. Sydney H. Moore (New York, Chicago: Fleming H. Revell company, 1908), 139, http://archive.org/details/historyofmission00rich, accessed on 18th October 2018.

[67] Firoj High Sarwar, "Christian Missionaries and Female Education in Bengal during East India Company's Rule: A Discourse between Christianized Colonial Domination versus Women Emancipation," *IOSR Journal of Humanities and Social Science* 4/1 (2012): 41.

[68] John R. W Stott, *Christian Mission in the Modern World* (Downers Grove: IVP Classics, 1975).

[69] Between 1850 and 1950 one animal species vanished every year; in the 1980s one animal species vanished per day; today, one animal species vanishes per hour

and within 50 years, 25% of the animal and plant species will have vanished due to global warming. (Won-Seong Park, *Towards Life Enhancing Civilization in Asia*, eds. Melisande Lorke and Dietrich Werner, Ecumenical Visions for the 21st Century, GETI Reader, Geneva, 2013, 74).

[70] Stott, *Christian Mission in the Modern World*, 43.

[71] K. Rajendran, "Evangelical Missiology from India," *Global Missiology for the 21st Century: The Iguassu Dialogue*, ed. William David Taylor (Grand Rapids: Baker Academic, 2000), 312.

[72] K. Rajendran, "Evangelical Missiology from India," 312; IMA, "IMA Goals 2013" (Hyderabad: India Mission Association, 2013).

[73] "The Serampore Missionaries as Educationists 1794–1824," *Baptist Quarterly* 22/6 (January 1, 1968): 325.

[74] The New York City Leadership Center, "Eradicating Bible Poverty," https://lead.nyc/eradicating-bible-poverty/, accessed on 31st October 2018.

[75] The New York City Leadership Center, "Eradicating Bible Poverty," https://lead.nyc/eradicating-bible-poverty/, accessed on 31st October 2018.

[76] Lamin Sanneh, *Translating the Message: The Missionary Impact on Culture* (NY: Maryknoll, 1989).

[77] Paul Pierson, "A History of Transformation," Ralph D. Winter, ed., *Perspectives on the World Christian Movement* (Pasadena, California: William Carey Library, 1981), 265.

[78] Pierson, *The Dynamics of Christian Mission*, 12.

[79] R. Pierce Beaver, "The History of Mission Strategy," *Perspectives on the World Christian Movement*, ed. Ralph D. Winter (Pasadena, California: William Carey Library, 1981), 246, 247.

[80] Pierson, *The Dynamics of Christian Mission*, 6.

[81] Tennent, "William Carey as Missiologist: An Assessment," 23.

[82] Paul G. Hiebert, "Critical Contextualization" 11/ 3 (July 1987): 104.

[83] Paul G. Hiebert, "Critical Contextualization" 11/3 (July 1987): 104.

[84] Hiebert, "Critical Contextualization," 109-111.

[85] Nichols, "The Theology of William Carey," 104.

[86] Nichols, "The Theology of William Carey," 108.

[87] Schirrmacher, "Be Keen to Get Going," 153

[88] Theodor Christlieb, *Protestant Missions to the Heathen: A General Survey of Their Recent Progress and Present State throughout the World*. Tran. W. Hastie (Edinburgh: T. Spink and Company, 1882).

[89] Patrick J. G. Johnstone, *Operation World: A Day-by-Day Guide to Praying for the World* (Kent, England: STL Publications, 1979).

[90] Ram Ahuja, *Research Methods* (Jaipur; New Delhi: Rawat, 2001).

[91] F. Hrangkhuma, "A Review of The Statement of International Conference on Mission" 37/1 (1995): 68-69.

[92] Mark T. B. Laing, "Top Down and Bottom Up: Two Examples of Protestant Mission in 19th Century India," *The Indian Church in Context*, ed. Mark T. B. Laing (Delhi/Pune: ISPCK/UBS, 2002), 132-133.

[93] IMA, "IMA Goals 2013."

[94] Tennent, "William Carey as Missiologist: An Assessment," 25.

Bibliography

Beaver, R. P. "The History of Mission Strategy." *Perspectives on the World Christian Movement*. Ed. Ralph D. Winter. Pasadena, California: William Carey Library, 1981.

Bieder, W. "William Carey 1761-1834." *Evangelisches Missions-Magazin*. 1961.

Carey, W. *An Enquiry into the Obligations Upon Christians to Use Means for the Conversion of the Heathen*. Leicester, UK: Ann Ireland, 1792.

Chatterjee, S. "Reverend William Ward, 1769-1823." *Serampore College Students' Magazine*. Serampore: Serampore College, 1972.

Christlieb, T. *Protestant Missions to the Heathen: A General Survey of Their Recent Progress & Present State throughout the World*. Tran. W. Hastie. Edinburgh: T. Spink & Company, 1882.

Crockett, B. "An English Garden in India: William Carey's Integrated Christian Vision." *News Journal of the International Association of Baptist Colleges and Universities* 76/2 (August 2012). https://www.wmcarey.edu/carey/j-term/eng-gard-0712.pdf. Accessed on 20th October 2018.

Ella, G. "William Carey: Using God's Means to Convert the People of India." William Carey Theologian—Linguist—Social Reformer." Ed. Thomas Schirrmacher. "World of Theology Series." *Theological Commission of the World Evangelical Alliance* 4. Bonn, Germany: Verlag für Kultur und Wissenschaft Culture and Science Publ., 2013: 43-66.

"Expect Great Things, Attempt Great Things: The Life and Ministry of William Carey." Granbury, Texas: Grace Bible Church, n.d, http://www.gracebiblegranbury.com/home/398/398/docs/William%20Carey%20biography.pdf?sec_id=398. Accessed 21st November 2018

Finn, N. A. "Missionaries You Should Know: William Carey." *International Mission Board* (July 31, 2018), https://www.imb.org/2018/07/31/missionaries-you-should-know-william-carey/. Accessed on 14th October 2018.

George, A. "Serampore Mission-History of Christianity in India" (January 30, 2016), https://www.academia.edu/22904952/Serampore_Mission-History_of_Christianity_in_India. Accessed on 18th October 2018.

George, T. *Faithful Witness: The Life and Mission of William Carey*. Birmingham, Alabama: New Hope, 1991.

Gupta, K. P. S. *The Christian Missionaries in Bengal :1793-1833*. Calcutta: Pinna K. L. Mukhuopdhyay, 1971.

Hiebert, P. D. "Critical Contextualization" 11/3 (July 1987): 104-112.

Hine, P. "Lecture Notes: On William Ward," http://enfolding.org/lecture-notes-on-william-ward/. Accessed on 23rd November 2018.

Hrangkhuma, F. "A Review of The Statement of International Conference on Mission" 37/1 (1995): 68-75.

IMA. "IMA Goals 2013." *India Mission Association*. Hyderabad, 2013.

Jayakumar, A. *History of Christianity in India*. Kolkata: SCEPTRE, 2013.

Johnstone, P. J. *Operation World: A Day-by-Day Guide to Praying for the World*. Kent, England: STL Publications, 1979.

Kopf, D. *British Orientalism and the Bengal Renaissance: The Dynamics of Indian Modernization, 1773-1835*. Berkeley and Los Angeles: University of California Press, 1969.

Laing, M. T. B. "Top Down and Bottom Up: Two Examples of Protestant Mission in 19th Century India." *The Indian Church in Context*. Ed. Mark T. B. Laing. Delhi/Pune: ISPCK/UBS, 2002: 110-31.

Laird, M. A. "The Contribution of the Serampore Missionaries to Education in Bengal, 1793–1837" 30/1 (February 1968): 92-112.

Mangalwadi, V and R. *The Legacy of William Carey*. Wheaton, IL: Crossway Books, 1999.

Marshman, J. C. *The Life and Times of Carey, Marshman, and Ward: Embracing the History of the Serampore Mission*. Vol. 1. London: Longman, Brown, Green, Longmans, and Roberts, 1859.

Marshman, J. *A Defense of the Deity and Atonement of Jesus Christ, in Reply to Ram-Mohun Roy, of Calcutta*. London: Kingsbury, Parbury, and Allen, 1822.

Miller, B. *10 Boys Who Become Famous Missionaries*. Grand Rapids: Zondervan Publishing House, 1991.

Nichols, B. J. "The Theology of William Carey." William Carey Theologian—Linguist—Social Reformer." *The Theological Commission of the World Evangelical Alliance* 4. Bonn, Germany: Verlag für Kultur und Wissenschaft Culture and Science Publ., 2013: 97-106.

Oussoren, A. H. *William Carey: Especially His Missionary Principles*. Leiden, Netherlands: A. W. Sijthoff, 1945.

Pennington, B. K. "Reverend William Ward and His Legacy for Christian (Mis) Perception of Hinduism." *The Society for Hindu-Christian Studies and Butler University* 13/6 (January 2000): 5-11.

Pennington, B. K. *Was Hinduism Invented? Britons, Indians, and the Colonial Construction of Religion*. Oxford/New York: Oxford University Press, 2005.

Pierson, P. "A History of Transformation." *Perspectives on the World Christian Movement*. Ed. Ralph Winter. Pasadena, CA: William Carey Library, 1981.

Pierson, P. E. *The Dynamics of Christian Mission: History through a Missiological Perspective*. Pasadena: WCIU Press, 2009.

Potts, D. *British Baptist Missionaries in India, 1793-1837: The History of Serampore and Its Missions*. Cambridge: Cambridge University Press, 1967.

Rajendran, K. "Evangelical Missiology from India." *Global Missiology for the 21st Century: The Iguassu Dialogue*. Ed. William David Taylor. Grand Rapids: Baker Academic, 2000: 307-332.

Richter, J. *A History of Missions in India*. Tran. Sydney H. Moore. New York/ Chicago: Fleming H. Revell company, 1908, http://archive.org/details/ historyofmission00rich. Accessed on 18th October 2018.

Rouse, R. *William Carey's 'Pleasing Dream'* (1949).

Sanneh, L. *Translating the Message: The Missionary Impact on Culture*. Maryknoll, 1989.

Sarwar, F. H. "Christian Missionaries and Female Education in Bengal during East India Company's Rule: A Discourse between Christianised Colonial Domination versus Women Emancipation." *IOSR Journal of Humanities and Social Science* 4/1 (2012): 37-47.

Schirrmacher, T. "Be Keen to Get Going." William Carey Theologian—Linguist—Social Reformer." Ed. Thomas Schirrmacher. *The Theological Commission of the World Evangelical Alliance 4*. Bonn, Germany: Verlag für Kultur und Wissenschaft Culture and Science Publ., 2013: 109-152.

Schirrmacher, T. "William Carey, Postmillennialism and the Theology of World Missions." *Contra Mundum Publications*, http://contra-mundum.org/ schirrmacher/careypostmil.html. Accessed on 14th October 2018.

Smith, A. C. "Carey, William (1761-1834): History of Missiology." Ed. H. Gerald Anderson. *Biographical Dictionary of Christian Missions*. Grand Rapids: Eerdmans Publishing, 1999.

Smith, A. C. "The Legacy of William Carey" 16/1 (January 1992): 2-8.

Smith, A. C. "The Legacy of William Ward and Joshua and Hannah Marshman." *International Bulletin of Missionary Research* 23/3 (July 1999): 120-126.

Smith, A. C. "William Carey 1761–1834: Protestant Pioneer of the Modern Mission Era." *Mission Legacies: Biographical Studies of Leaders of the Modern Missionary Movement*. Ed. Gerald H. Anderson. Maryknoll: Orbis, 1994: 245-254.

Smith, G. *The Life of William Carey: Shoemaker and Missionary*. Edinburgh/London: John Murray, 1885.

Stanley, B. *The History of the Baptist Missionary Society 1792-1992*. Edinburgh: T&T Clark, 1992.

Stott, J. R. W. *Christian Mission in the Modern World*. Downers Grove: IVP Classics, 1975.

Tennent, T. C. "William Carey as Missiologist: An Assessment." *Expect Great Things, Attempt Great Things: William Carey and Adoniram Judson, Missionary Pioneers*. Eds. Allen Yeh and Chris Chun. Eugene: Wipf and Stock Publishers, 2013: 15-26.

The New York City Leadership Center. "Eradicating Bible Poverty," https://lead.nyc/eradicating-bible-poverty/. Accessed on 31st October 2018.

"The Serampore Missionaries as Educationists 1794–1824." *Baptist Quarterly* 22/6 (January 1, 1968): 320-325.

Walton, A. "A Christian Republic on the Hooghly: A Contextualization of William Carey's Missionary Vision." Thesis, Master of Philosophy, School of Philosophy and Religion College of Arts and Law University of Birmingham, 2014.

Ward, W. *A View of the History, Literature and Mythology of the Hindoos*. Serampore Edition. Courtesy Derby Local Studies Library, 1814.

Ward, W. *Account of the Writings, Religion, and Manners of the Hindoos: Including Translations from Their Principal Works*. Serampore Edition. Vol. 4. Serampore: Mission Press, 1811.

Wenger, E. L. *The Story of Serampore at Its College*. Fourth Edition. Serampore: The Council of Serampore College, 1918.

Werner, D. "Expect Great Things from God – Attempt Great Things for God: The Serampore Vision for Integral Education, the Ecumenical Search for a Theology of Life and the Future of Theological Education in World Christianity." *World Council of Churches* 2014, https://www.oikoumene.org/en/press-centre/news/SeramporeConvocationadressfinal3Jan2014.pdf. Accessed on 31st October 2018.

Winter, R. "The Two Structures of God's Redemptive Mission." *Perspectives: On the World Christian Movement*. Eds. Ralph Winter and Steven C. Hawthorne. Third Edition. CA: William Carey Library, 1999: 220-230.

14

Beyond the Serampore Mission Historiography: Re-defining Ecumenism from the Context

Kaholi Zhimomi

Introduction

Investigation into the mammoth records of the Serampore Mission affirms that the mission underwent an extended and tumultuous evolution since its inception. However, the number of memoirs and historical studies over the centuries were inadequate to quench the thirst of many curious researchers and this mission continues to provoke diverse imaginations. William Carey, a Baptist, and his friends, William Ward, Joshua Marshman and Hannah Marshman, and their animating seminal movement in the nineteenth century pioneered myriad of missionary strategies and methodologies. This cohort from the locale of the evangelical Edwardsian[1] and Calvinistic Baptist and pragmatically colonial outlook crossed the national and religious boundaries to establish a Christian religion in Bengal's religious and cultural context. The Indo-European Serampore Mission and their strategic methodologies in engaging in the cross-cultural evangelism did not gain significant impetus. Therefore, they began a series of cross-cultural interpretations and observations in order to develop a practically significant approach to the Indian realties. They initiated a multi-dimensional and holistic approach from the underside in an attempt to address the multi-faceted social-cultural and religious issues of the Indian society. The Serampore Mission came under the critical lens of many scholars and an appraisal of it is imperative from the perspective of the context. It is therefore appropriate to re-examine the various historical dimensions in order to understand the modern missionary movement and the historical contributions to the contemporary discourse on ecumenism. The Serampore missionaries' active enterprises can be a vantage point for a renewed strategy in the discourse of ecumenical engagement. However, in the milieu of changing issues can we move from the Serampore Mission historiography, challenge the various qualified ecumenical studies, and begin to re-define ecumenism according to the need of the Indian context?

The Baptist "Evangelical" Tradition versus the Ecumenical "Evangelicals"

The Orientalists[2] and their concept of orientalism gained impetus during the nineteenth century influencing many missionaries that sailed to India. Orientalists such as Sir William Jones and William Robertson studied the oriental languages and esteemed Indian religions and cultures. Sir Jones attempted to master Sanskrit and transmitted the literature and learning of India to the West, he explored into the lost knowledge of Indian science, philosophy, history and theologies of the Hindus. Out of his research work, he wrote a comprehensive treatise on Hindu and Mohammedan Law, founded the Royal Asiatic Society of Bengal (1784), a platform to encourage British and Indians for research into the Indian heritage.[3] Indian poetry and drama were appreciated as the highest quality and Indian architecture sublime. Indian astronomy was found to be accurate and Indian scientific methods correct. He stated that the protestant missionaries should, "correct their error of considering Indian theology and ethics as vastly inferior to Christianity."[4] Some Evangelicals with missionary spirit were associated with these Orientalists. Chief among them were Charles Grant, William Wilberforce and Claudius Buchanan. But they were also on the other hand spokespersons for the promotion of Christianity and asserted that the ultimate purpose of the empire was to spread Christianity.

James Mill presented the superiority of medieval European society to Indian culture, art, intellectual and moral qualities of the native people. He stated, "India experienced the worst forms of priestly superstition and despotism . . . India's future lay in Westernization."[5] Alexander Duff in, *India and Indian Missions*, remarked, "though Hinduism possesses very lofty terms in its religious vocabulary what they covey are 'vain and foolish,' and wicked conceptional." Therefore, the Westerners felt it their great responsibility, "to demolish so gigantic fabric of idolatry and superstition."[6] This feeling of cultural superiority was a by-product of the political supremacy and economy which reflected itself in the missionary attitude as well. It was in this earlier atmosphere of the assumption of racial and cultural superiority that the Serampore Mission commenced. It would be surprising, therefore, if the feeling of superiority, so general in the west, had not been reflected in certain missionary attitudes. Here and there it crept into the literature of early missions, taking it for granted that just as the west had the only worthy culture, so their religion also was the only faith embodying any truth.[7] In this context it was demanding to be the voice of the opposition. The Serampore missionaries were aware of the dissension in going away from the traditional evangelical Baptist beliefs but if they were to establish their religion in a culturally and religiously diverse context, they have to go ecumenical in their stance.

Establishment of the Reconciled Socio-Cultural Diversity

No doubt the Serampore missionaries were the product of the nineteenth century evangelicalism but in many ways their ideas differed from the established ideology. They were of course not far removed from their contemporaries but they also on the other hand had pushed forward ideas that none of the Westerners were thinking of during those centuries, for example, the well-being of the native people. Joshua Marshman stated that their duty was to, "take an active interest in every measure calculated to relieve the wretchedness of the people and to promote their temporal well-being."[8] For the Serampore missionaries, it was the conversion of the Indians into Christianity and their temporal well-being that they were called for. To this aim they lived amongst the Indian people, preached in the villages and cross-roads and learned a great deal about the country. In *an Enquiry into the obligation of Christians to use means for Conversion of the Heathens,* Carey indicated two main principles namely: missionaries must live among the people in the simplest manner possible and missionaries must support themselves by agriculture, industry or some other work.[9]

The evangelicals during the eighteenth and nineteenth centuries advocated for the rejection of Indian culture and the promotion of Westernization to the Indian mass. However, the Serampore missionaries were interested in introducing Western improvements to the Indians rather than completely rejecting their culture. Carey and his associates stood between the 'Orientalists' and the 'Liberals.' Although the missionaries could not appreciate all that is within Hinduism, yet they realized that Hinduism like Christianity was meant to be monotheistic. They tolerated many of the Hindu rites and festivals. They knew that an attack on the religious ceremonies and doctrines of the country was unacceptable. Unfortunately, they were not well equipped to probe deep within the concept of Hinduism and continued to emphasize on the drawbacks of Hinduism then their positivity which were points of contentions for many contemporary scholars. Nevertheless, they were curious about all the aspects of Indian life, studied Hindustani in order to converse with the people, admired the handicrafts of India, familiarized themselves with the local people, and demonstrated kindness and humanity towards the people of other faiths. Theirs was an important service to the Christian and humanitarian cause.

Ecumenical Pragmatism of the Serampore Mission

In an attempt for a missionary co-operation, Carey wrote a letter from Kolkata on May 5, 1806 to Andrew Fuller which read as follows: "The Cape of Good Hope is now in the hands of the English; should it continue so, would it not be possible to have a general association of all denominations of Christians, from the four quarters of the world, held there once in about ten years? I earnestly recommend this plan; let the first meeting be in the year 1810 or 1812 at farthest. I have no doubt, but it would be attended with every important effects; we could understand one another better and more entirely enter into one another's views by two hours' conversation than two or three years' epistolary correspondence."[10] Carey knowing of the practical experience in the mission field, realized the urge for Christian unity at that time of church history. This makes Carey a pioneer of the twentieth century Ecumenical Movement and was once again found expression when the Serampore College was founded.

In *An Enquiry into the Obligation of Christians*, published in 1792, Carey stated, "prayer is perhaps the only thing in which Christians of all denominations can cordially and unreservedly unite; but in this we may all be one, and in this the strictest unanimity ought to prevail."[11] Indeed, the missionary activities of the Serampore missionaries were reinforced by a Serampore Covenant[12] or Form of Agreement which they adopted in 1805 with eleven statements of purpose. They read the covenant publicly at least three times a year in their corporate worship on the first Lord's day in

January, May and October in order to renew their vows to God and their commitment to one another which helped them to uphold "honesty, intimacy and equality" in the community.[13] In such corporate prayer meetings, the Serampore missionaries were convinced to move beyond their particular Baptist tradition which had kept the non-Baptists away from the Lord's Table originally. Ward reminded Fuller on December 15, 1807, the importance of all Christians participating in the Lord's Table together overcoming all denominational differences. He further remarked, "If this is not the spirit of the whole New Testament, I was never in anything more . . . mistaken."[14] With this growing spirit of ecumenism among Ward, Marshman and other missionaries representing different branches of the church, Carey was outnumbered and complied to the other traditions.

William Carey and the Serampore missionaries were inventive pragmatic ecumenicists who emphasized learning from the 'other' particularly the languages of the land. Carey preached in Bengali, became a Bengali professor at Kolkata, and taught Sanskrit.[15] F. Deaville Walker stated that Carey was, "far too practical to take a text and break it up in the usual pulpit style, he would talk to such an audience of their own Shastras, or the nine incarnation of Vishnu, lead them on to the message of salvation through Christ." Carey also inferred that mission among the Indian women must be done entirely by the wives of the missionaries or unmarried Christian women. Later, the Serampore Mission also established subordinate missionary stations in Bengali for the native people to take their place at the leadership and commence their own missionary works.[16] The missionaries aim to train Indian leaders to replace them and create a truly indigenous church. They established schools in connection with each mission stations, educated gifted young people from India as the missionaries were convinced that only native people can speak effectively to their own people about Christ. They also planned for a college for spiritual and intellectual improvement of the country.

On July 15, 1818, they issued the prospectus of a, "College for the instruction of Asiatic Christian and other youth in Eastern literature and European Science."[17] It was drawn up by Marshman propagating the idea of Christian engagement through native excellence. Those who were to be employed in propagating the gospel should be familiar with the doctrine which was then held sacred in the country and this could not be attained without knowledge of the language. The necessity for a college like Serampore College was to train the Christian workers with full instruction on the doctrines and to equip in a complete knowledge both of the sacred Scriptures and those of the philosophical and mythological dogmas which formed the soul of the Hindu and Buddhist systems.[18] Students were admitted at the direction of the Council from any Christian background whether Protestant, Roman Catholic, the Greek or the Armenian Church and for the purpose of study even from the Muslim and Hindu backgrounds.[19] It was proposed to impart a thorough knowledge of Sanskrit, Arabic and canonical language of the Muslims to the students to enable them to understand the tenets and principles of the prevailing system.

The Serampore missionaries received numerous criticisms both from the Evangelicals and the Indian high caste people. Creating an Indian college for the teaching of Indian classics generated debates and reproach from the Baptist Missionary Society on the other hand the Pandits were disgruntled with the missionaries for teaching the sacred scriptures to the Sudras. However, these challenges where by no means a barrier for the missionaries to continue with their visions of inclusive mission. They established a new Christian national system without caste differences and other structures. The caste system was also broken when Krishna Pal and his friend Gokool ate together with the missionaries and their wives sitting at the communion table. Brahmins and Sudras were treated as equals and family.[20] The Serampore missionaries believed in the basic antithesis between caste and Christianity and did not allow the converts to keep their caste. They firmly believed that there should not be any caste distinction in the Christian community.

Because of their surge into different ideological terrain, the Serampore missionaries had to sever ties with their parent body the BMS. When a breach was seen to be inevitable with reluctance and grief an Agreement of Separation was signed between the Serampore missionaries and the BMS lead by Marshman and Secretary Dyer. According to the terms of the Agreement the Serampore missionaries were given the College and the grounds attached to it, and all the older mission properties were to be vacated and left in the hands of the committee. This meant complete severance from the Missionary Society which Carey himself had founded and sadly never in his life time was the breach healed.[21] In many ways this was indispensable because the Serampore missionaries became ever more convinced through their experience in India that there was no missionary way which could be forced on India. Further, the Serampore College was founded mainly to raise indigenous leadership by training and equipping Asians for the future of the Asian church and Society and not for the continuation of the parent mission establishment. Through their ecumenical vision for theological education, the missionaries left a permanent mark by initiating the process of development of an ethos of Indian culture by their creative participation in the struggles of the people. They were able to shape the people's thought with new values which made an impact on the national renaissance even as it is acknowledged by the secular Asiatic Journal (1938) which reads: "Their educational exertions were such as no preceding gentlemen had made nor have any hope that men with equal knowledge and benevolence will again be born and impart such benefits to us."[22] They emphasized on the self-supportive indigenous Christian leadership, vision for common theological education for the whole church, and the holistic mission to humankind. The Serampore Mission had pragmatically planned for an ecumenical body of theology students residing, worshipping and studying together in the College. How true it is to note that ecumenism became a visible reality in our time because of the deep concern for world evangelism by visionaries like the Serampore Missionaries.

Ecumenical Future: After Serampore Missionaries

The Senate of Serampore College has undoubtedly carried out the ecumenical vision of the Serampore Mission by bringing the Protestant, Orthodox and some Pentecostal seminaries together under the same evaluating criteria of theological education. But there is a serious need to move forward beyond the Serampore Mission and create a history unique to its own in the third millennium. This is important not only for strengthening our witness as Christians in this country where Christians make a small minority, but for the enlargement of our vision for a meaningful experience of being Christians in a multi-faith context.

At the heart of ecumenical movement was the impulse for the unity of the church, with an acknowledged appropriate diversity. Konrad Raiser[23] remarked that the ecumenical movement during the 1970s was characterized by a significant widening of scope and agenda that includes: inter-religious dialogue, racism and ethnicity, science, technology and ecology, the Bible, spirituality, ecumenical formation and women.[24] There is an ambivalence of ecumenical experience in the churches and societies amidst conflicting contexts. Walter Kasper[25] therefore stated that the ecumenical movement is today clearly in a transitional period and ecumenical dialogues have yielded good fruits, but one cannot overlook the theological, political and institutional critique of the ecumenical movement. He stated that there are two sides of ecumenical movement at the global level, "on the one side unions and alliances, a huge number of bilateral and multilateral ecumenical consensus or convergence documents are being observed while on the other side, tensions and even new divisions, often because of ethical questions, are being witnessed." Therefore, for many, ecumenism has become a negative term, equivalent to syncretism, doctrinal relativism and indifferentism.[26]Among other defects, there is a fear of losing their own Christian identity therefore, from this locale what becomes of the present ecumenical ecclesiology response? Across diverse attempts of ecumenical discussions in the recent past it can be determined that the true vision of ecumenism is yet to be fully achieved. Obviously, this does not mean that ecumenical endeavors per se were a complete failure but the questions that need to be addressed are: Is ecumenism trapped in the past visions? Is ecumenism limited only to a certain context? How can ecumenism be refined in the contemporary multiplicities? The call is to de-politization of ecumenical unity going beyond Christianity and contesting the Christian consciousness by re-examining the former methods and working on new models of ecumenism.

Beyond Unity: Receptive Ecumenism

The Edinburgh World Missionary Conference in 1910 inspired the birth of the modern ecumenical movement and this was probably one of the first unofficial contacts between the Catholic church and the early beginnings of the ecumenical movement. The fundamental ecumenical concern was to seek for ways to move from mutual hostility and mistrust to recognition and effective collaboration in worship, work, and mission.[27] The Second Vatican Council created an atmosphere which led the Catholic church to enter into the mainstream of modern ecumenism. Kasper remarked that the, "Catholic Church and the WCC are two quite different entities, one a worldwide Church with a universal mission and structure of teaching and governance; the other a council of churches, which understands itself as a fellowship of churches. However, when one reads again the numerous statements and eight reports of the JWG (Joint Working Group) one immediately becomes aware of the engagement with which it has carried out its ecumenical vocation and has sought to bring together the theological, social and pastoral dimensions of ecumenism. One is also led to reflect on the rich common experience it has offered its members and the progress towards full visible communion, which, with God's help, was made possible in this period."[28] But Kasper builds further on the notion of an ecumenical winter. He made reference to 'a spirit of resignation' or 'a phase of hibernation' in current ecumenism. Both the Roman Catholic church and the Protestant churches concentrated on understanding the different concepts of church and unity and the role of the ecumenical movement which felt like an "unrealistic dream and a useless utopia." Hans Küng, another ecumenist, was also skeptical about the progress of ecumenical discourses. He expressed what he believed was a widely held growing impatience with the lack of real change in the church in spite of the work of the ecumenical movement. To this end Kasper believes that Receptive Ecumenism (RE) and the call to Catholic learning will contribute to a new start and hopefully also a new spring within the ecumenical movement.[29]

Reception as a concept is not a new idea but has always been part of the Christian witness. But Receptivity was further improved by twenty-first century ecumenists for deliberating on renewed ecumenical discourses. This Receptive Ecumenism came out of a series of Catholic Learning research project devoted to developing and modeling a fresh new strategy in Christian ecumenism at the Centre for Catholic Studies within the Department of Theology and Religion at Durham University, United Kingdom. This initiative constitutes a fresh approach in methodology to ecumenical theology and practice. According to Paul Murray, Receptive Ecumenism is to re-emphasize into 'reality of the contemporary ecumenical moment' and 'find an appropriate means of continuing to walk the way of conversion towards more visible structural and sacramental unity.'[30] The core theological principles of Receptive Ecumenism include among others the following:

> First, the churches are called by the Triune God to grow ever more visibly together in order to express this union-in-relation in appropriate structural and sacramental unity;
>
> Second, 'Life and Works' ecumenism—doing things together—is vitally necessary but insufficient alone;
>
> Third, authentic Christian ecumenism can never be a matter either of simply bearing with communion-dividing differences or of collapsing and eradicating such differences; it must rather be a matter of learning from and across such differences that they can with integrity be brought into configured, mutually enriching communion;
>
> Fourth, the primary aim of ecclesial learning is not the promotion of increased mutual understanding and appreciation between traditions but continuing

ecclesial conversion, deepening and expanding growth within traditions by receptive learning from and across traditions; the conviction is that pursuing this primary aim will in time move each tradition, with integrity, to a new place and so open up fresh possibilities for overcoming currently communion-dividing differences between traditions; this emphasis on the ecclesial dimension of conversion needs to extend beyond the doctrinal-theoretical to include also the organizational, the structural, the cultural and the broadly practical;

Fifth, Receptive Ecumenical learning, when pursued with dynamic integrity, is not about becoming less but about becoming more deeply, more richly, more fully, more freely what we already are: about our becoming all that we are called to be; rather than worrying unduly about what others may need to learn, each should take responsibility for their own learning, mindful that 'We cannot change others, we can only change ourselves but doing so can also promote change in others'; with this, receptive ecumenical learning requires a move away from the presupposition of mutuality—'we'll move if you move'—to the embrace of a certain unilateral willingness to walk the path of ecclesial conversion for the sake of the greater flourishing of one's own tradition and regardless, to some extent, of whether others are currently prepared to do likewise;

Sixth, exclusively past-oriented views of tradition and associated problem-solving understandings of the ecumenical task and engage also future-oriented understandings of the Christian tradition as all it is and might be relative to the saving purposes of God in Christ and the Spirit should be resisted.[31]

The main aim of RE is to find an appropriate ecumenical ethic and strategy for living between the times which is orientated upon the promise of and calling to being made one in the Trinitarian life of God. It hopes for the theological principle by pragmatic insight. The ecumenical drawback is the fragmentation among the Christian churches and the failure to fulfill their dream of full and visible structural, sacramental, and ministerial communion. RE can progress towards its fulfillment if only the Christians shift the question from, "What do our various others first need to learn from us?" to "What is that we need to learn and can learn, or receive, with integrity from our others?" Relevantly Paul notes that, "this reflects a move away from ideal theorized, purely doctrinally driven ecclesiological constructs in ecumenical dialogue and a definite move towards taking the lived reality of traditions absolutely seriously, together with the difficulties and problems, tensions and contradictions to be found there." This ecumenism is not just to theorize about the church but to diagnose and address problems in its actual lived structures, systems, and practices, alongside the predictable mix of theologians, ecumenists, and ecclesiastics. It seeks to engage in the exercise of self-critical, receptive, and ecclesial learning or receiving, examples of 'best practice' in the other traditions.[32]

Receptive ecumenism should move the churches forward by developing on the theoretical results which should be reflected in their own church life. RE can be a helpful tool for the church to re-view their own circumstantial situation as they struggle amidst the on-going questions like the demographic changes, the challenge we face to retain our young people and difficult questions about gender and sexuality. Receptive Ecumenism may offer a way to learn from others in facing up to these challenges. From this vantage point RE as rightly perceived by Gerard Kelly, can help Christians in, "examining themselves to discover their own limitations and incompleteness; and on the other hand, we are speaking about churches looking outwards towards other churches, ready to find gifts and insights about the faith and how it is lived."[33]

Because of the fear of losing one's own identity while receiving the 'other' RE is viewed with apprehensions but receptivity does not mean diluting or abandoning one's identity. This new idea does not destroy what has been fundamental to a particular idea or identity. It is the blending of the old traditions and new which results in the synthesis of the two. It is a continuity between the old and the new which heralds in innovative vivacity and dynamism to the community. It is in receiving from others, one is enriched. For example, Catholics can become more fully Catholic as they become appropriately Anglican, Lutheran, Methodist, and Orthodox. Listening to each other's question like, "What can we learn, or receive, with integrity from our various others in order to facilitate our own growth together into deepened communion in Christ and the Spirit?" can be fulfilling.[34]

In evaluating the current situation, diverse twentieth century ecumenical methodologies have failed unsuccessfully and RE comes as a revitalized suggestion to a positive way forward. Ultimately this Receptive Ecumenism leads towards the church's own restoration and enhanced development and to realize itself in the other, the other, and both would be merged in the fullness of Christ and the Spirit. Despite apparently opposing variances the churches should be committed to unify for God's work and receive 'others' as their own 'others' with a willingness to be self-critical and open to grow through learning from others. Receptive Ecumenism is after all not only about learning from other traditions by exchanging gifts, but also about applying these gifts in one's own tradition for the enlightenment of the Church of Jesus Christ.

Beyond Classical: Transformative Ecumenism

Transformative Ecumenism (TE)[35] seeks to re-look into the concept of *diakonia* in the context of the changing contemporary world and its wide-ranging challenges. Ecumenism should move away from the classical understanding of *Oikoumene* to *Diakonia*, from 'visible Christian unity' to 'unity in ministry, service, relief and support.'[36] Transformative Ecumenism is preconditioned to rationally assess and encounter the prevailing social and economic directives and not confine to the ecclesial orders of pyramid. It ought to enter into a communion with the other civil progressive groups and engage in transformative pro-active initiatives for achieving a just socio-political world. Transformative Ecumenism makes an attempt to celebrate life at the grass-roots. For this reason, the criterion for the third millennia Christians is to be based on their theology/ies on a life-centered vision. A life-centered understanding of the *Oikoumene*, which embraces all of God's creation, is inevitable.

The Korea Institute for Future Ecumenism (KIFE) states that, "the ecumenical movement is no longer strongly rooted in the people and it does not speak a prophetic voice which echoes in the realities of people's struggles for life; the ecumenical movement no longer produces a new and heart-beating vision for the church and the world that are deeply divided and wounded; the ecumenical leadership has suffered from patriarchal, bureaucratic and business-oriented mindedness that lacks the sense of calling and devotion."[37] Transformative Ecumenism is therefore a call to be rooted in people's struggle for justice and life, an ecumenism that envisions not only the unity of the church but an ecumenism focused on the unity of whole humanity and the creation.

At the first International Theological Colloquium for Transformative Ecumenism, Seoul, Korea, from 15 to 17 July 2013, TE emphasized on three areas that will give shape to an alternative and transformative ecumenism that is life-giving and justice-centered: First, how to rejuvenate the movement out of prophetic bankruptcy of ecumenism; the ecumenical movement is no longer strongly rooted in the people and it does not speak a prophetic voice which echoes in the realities of people's struggles for life? Second, how to redefine ecumenism itself out of intellectual bankruptcy of ecumenical spirituality and vision; the ecumenical movement no longer produces a new and heart-beating vision for the church and the world that are deeply divided and wounded. There should be a basic vision and ethos behind transformative ecumenism. And third, how to re-shape the leadership out of moral bankruptcy of ecclesiastical leadership? The ecumenical leadership has suffered from patriarchal, bureaucratic and business- oriented mindedness that lacks the sense of calling and devotion?[38] The second colloquium, held in Manila in 2014, which provided a road map for how Transformative Ecumenism can serve as an alternative paradigm for the ecumenical movement in the twenty-first century. The following objectives of TE had been indicated at the Manila Colloquium: first, to develop transformative ecumenism as an alternative to conciliar ecumenism; second, to deepen and consolidate agenda, concept and participation of transformative ecumenism; third, to critically reflect on the Busan Assembly[39] and to envision the Pilgrimage of Justice and Peace in the light of transformative ecumenism; and fourth, to strengthen and expand the network of transformative ecumenism.[40]

The Third International Theological Colloquium for Transformative Ecumenism took place from 11 to 16 January 2016 in Moshi, Tanzania. The aim of the colloquium was to extend the vision of TE into the African context in order to rejuvenate the movement, to redefine ecumenism and to reshape leadership in the continent. Transformative Ecumenism has to do with: first, an ecumenism that is rooted in the people's struggle for justice and life; second, an ecumenism that envisions not only the unity of the church but also the unity of the whole humanity and creation; and third, an ecumenism that is led by passionate and issue-oriented leaders who can clearly stand with the suffering and struggling people.[41] To situate TE into substantial Indian perspective, Christopher Rajkumar proposed a workable framework for Indian contextual standards:

> First, must continue to network and form alliances in order to work together and add value to the transformative diaconal work in rapidly changing development contexts in which the private sector and new actors are increasingly playing a role in the development and in times where migration is changing the global demographics.

> Second, must respond to the shrinking political space even where it may be a new role for churches. We must claim our space through and for common action, advocacy and building awareness together with other faith and ideologies in civil society.
>
> Third, must respond to the signs of the times by developing a common diaconal language. We are faith based and rights based, and we need to identify what this means in practice including defining our mandate, our core values and to map our diaconal assets.
>
> Fourth, must be in closer contacts with local congregations and support diaconal work at the grass-root level.
>
> Fifth, must respond to the social impact of gender, economic and climate injustice through networking, developing the capacity for policy analysis and transnational advocacy in order to promote equitable and sustainable development.[42]

Human beings are surrounded by the cultural and historical confusions. Christian communities especially the theological fellowships are persuaded by and seek to introduce many ideas but there are in fact less reflective or transformative thoughts that make one critically review self and the world passionately. There is therefore the exploration for theologically jargonized alternatives which deviates the people more towards confusion rather than being the road maps. Ecumenism should extend to all the world wide community because of its unique cosmic nature. It should seek to be a *Diaconal* element which is reflected in the Transformative Ecumenism. Developing a methodology for fostering TE is a challenge as transformation cannot be scripted but be understood as an ongoing discourse. Transformative Ecumenism is a process of change and challenge in one's old worldview, yet it is not unachievable because change is integral to all.

Transformative Receptive Ecumenism for a Contextual Experiential Ecumenism

The heart of the church's universality is undeniably moving to the global South and Receptive Ecumenism can be a notable approach towards ushering in Transformative form of ecumenism in this locale. However, Receptive Transformative Ecumenism will have to take into consideration the grass-roots or learn from below for which a contextual Experiential Ecumenism becomes imperative. Ecumenical movement in the twenty-first century should wrestle with the critical questions and problems germinating from the day-to-day encounters of the global South, such as all dimensions of justice, holistic peace, ecological justice, and life together. Ecumenism needs to be understood as people's encounter and lived experiences of various spiritualities, communities and cultures. It cannot be a mechanically narrated content; it should as a matter of fact be an engaging Experiential Ecumenism in context. It should move beyond the tables and seminar halls and challenge the exclusivist tendencies.

It is a shift from foundational to conversational model of ecumenical learning to understand the different traditional contexts. This model introduces transformed methods for witnessing to Christ collectively.[43] Theology should be more local and attached to the experiences and circumstances of the community giving voices to the living local theologies.[44] Dietrich Werner stated that ecumenical learning is part of theology and theological education which is to be experienced parallel to the other Christian confessions and the diverse religious traditions.[45] The traditional binaries between a *guru* and *shishya*, conventional and circumstantial, instruction and learning, from above to below, and from passive to active have reduced to mutuality and co-learning in a post-colonial era. But the vividness of the same is yet to be realized.[46] Santanu K. Patro commented that the ideals of pluralism and universalism have remained stagnant because of the overtly academic and theoretical approaches discussed within the elitist intellectual community. He further stated that human beings are of the communities based on culture, religion and social identities and an infringement of it leads to anarchy.[47] There is also an increase of sectarian fundamentalism that has crept in almost all the sections of the society from the government, political, economic to the religious institutions that threaten the co-existence of the different citizens in a multi-civilized world.[48]

Ecumenism should not be limited only to the union of the churches but a union of minds to extend our boundaries even to the people of other faiths. Building a structural empire should not be the goal of the ecumenism rather it should be building people from all sections of the society. Instead of some Western philosophical approaches to understand reality in its sameness and universality, we must listen to the ruptures, irregularities and inconsistencies in existence in a particular context.[49] The church offers an unlimited unit of exploration which needs to be understood by the Christians; the church also needs to be understood for the comprehensive world-historical context. The church is a church in world history and not only limited to the sacred history and isolation of itself from the world.[50] Unfortunately, Christians have quarantined themselves from the civic societies and focused mainly on the spiritual facets of the church's need. There is a fear of involving in the political affairs of the state and people's movement for peace and justice. It is observed that this apprehension might be a residue from the agitated sagas of Cold War between the various superpowers and the pietistic Christian traditional characteristic of emphasizing on spiritual matters.[51] The church is 'finite, fallible and sinful' however the humanness of the church should not be seen as a problem and limited. Church is a human community in a sense that the full participation of the church in the humanizing work of God in the world gives shape to human possibilities and hopes. Karl Barth argues that the basic form of community is based on 'self' as 'social being.' Human beings can never exist in isolation but co-human beings, 'for life not shared in community is not human,' and 'being human is being in community.'[52]

Experiential Ecumenism provides a chance to share experiences with Christians as well as people of other faiths, experiences will include both positive and negative, but this helps in confronting stereotypes about the other and reflects theologically on those experiences. For Experiential Ecumenism theology/ies should engage in experiential education and field studies for a process of spiritual, academic, personal, and professional formation while simultaneously developing, practicing, and refining the arts and skills of ministry. Move beyond the intellectual learning of the 'inform' stage to a level of experiential education characterized by relationship and encounter. Move beyond the learning outside of oneself, connect ecumenism deeply with an individual's life and faith systems leading to transformation of the community as well and develop a cultural and socialization approach of the community of learning. We must transform one's original perspectives to accommodate a new perspective and be willing to integrate into a new self and reinforce theology and social system through ecumenical encounters. It should not focus on differences or on maintaining borders with other cultures. It should rather be open to share values and dialogue.

An Indian Transformative Receptive Ecumenism should recognize socio-cultural identities, such as national, ethnic and tribal identity, at the same time confirming the unity of the church for gathering people from many different traditions, communities and even religions to work together for justice and peace. All ecumenists along with other Christians and adherents of other faiths and contemporary ideologies should search anew for God and truth for the church and the world today. In a collaborative way, account should be taken of the various traditions and theologies in order to embark on new and practical ways in which a local parish, Christian agency or governing body may carry out Transformative Receptive Ecumenism. Transformative Receptive Ecumenism is certainly not a one-way approach but an active interaction between two frequencies. It also does not occur in a vacuum but in a certain context requires a pragmatic approach to it therefore it necessitates Experiential Ecumenism. Transformative Receptive Ecumenism requires Experiential Ecumenism as it gives importance to the context, culture, history, religious demography and popular piety of the community into which the vision of visible unity is to be received.

Conclusion

The international Christian community had affirmed mission to be of concern to the whole church; and there can be no church without mission. T. K. Daniel remarked, "Christian mission has to be carefully contextualized with the spirit of ecumenism rather than by any divisive ethos of denominationalism."[53] Yakob Mar Irenaios further stated that, "A mission that does not care for human dignity and integrity of creation will not thrive, however much money is spent on it. This is to say that the strict purpose of mission is not to increase the number of converts, but to take care of the whole individual as a creation of God, irrespective of color, faith and language."[54] So the challenge upon the worldwide church is to understand Ecumenical mission from the perspective of 'Life-centered' than church-centered, human-centered or nation-centered. The Serampore missionaries sought for the breaking of the socio-cultural monopoly and prerogative of the Brahmins who socially ostracized the lower caste Indians subjecting them to mental disfranchisement and bondage throughout their lifetime. They emphasized that every Indian including the children of the poorest should have the access to learn Sanskrit and to study Indian philosophy and religion and they should become "the leaven in the lump" to bring about renewal in the society.

When the Indo-European Serampore Missionaries began their work in India, they were inherently trained to win souls and convert people of other faiths regardless of the native peoples' contexts and realities but their strategic methodologies in a cross-cultural milieu like India needed massive changes. Basing on their experiences with the Indian realities they developed new approaches which suited the India minds. They initiated a multi-cultural and religious dialogue with people of other faiths, established their ecumenical relationships with Christians from other denominations and mission societies. The Serampore missionaries began the Serampore University to train Indian leaders for Indian society and churches which was ecumenical in its nature. This University has accommodated thousands of Indians since its inception. However, today after two hundred years of its commencement we have been little successful in moving beyond the Serampore Mission success stories. Our ecumenical endeavors are the hangovers of the Serampore mission methods. The Serampore College has progressed in its curriculum by the extensive inclusion of diverse contemporary ecumenical issues but the uncertainty of ecumenical understandings at the grassroots continues. Undoubtedly the ecumenical discourse goes through transitional phases but the ecumenical undertakings of the past few centuries were deemed unproductive in-terms of fully determining the true ecumenical vision. Therefore, catering to the twenty-first century Christian demography and its populace, indicators germinating from the contextual experiences and encounters cannot be undermined.

Life is common to all and affects the whole of creation. How to retain the quality as well as the fullness of life must be the concern of ecumenical movement. But we continue to retain the church-centric ecumenism hence ecumenism remains idealistic even today. From church-centric (concern for unity of the church) to anthropo-centric (concern for unity and well-being of humanity), we need to move towards a life-centric ecumenism (concern for the welfare of the whole life on earth). Theology/ies can degenerate into a nationalist, rightist, leftist ideology and no Christian movements are immune to such tendencies therefore a self-critical theological reflection is imperative for addressing the many issues in the twenty-first century. Ecumenism will reduce itself to a functional presidency if it focuses only on the fundamental campaign moreover insignificant ecumenical theoretical contests deficient of the grassroots and the undersides are deemed futile. If the worldwide church looks for a possibility for ecumenical identity, it first has to dismantle the ingrained hierarchies and create space for the other in the society.

Now the questions that arise are: Can the Christians worldwide overcome the inherent binaries of 'self and other,' Christian communities and the 'other' communities and redefine the theology of ecumenism from the perspective of the excluded and the otherized? Can we seek for a Reflective,

Transformative and Experiential Ecumenism today? Centering on this can Christians committed to ecumenical identity challenge the contemporary discourses on ecumenism? Embodying its true essence ecumenism in reality should test whether the church does not only *preach* the 'Universal Church,' but *lives as part* of the church Universal. To act *for* or *with* and *of* the 'other' is our renewed challenge for an "imaged communities" or a "transcultural Christians."

Endnotes

[1] These Evangelicals are those who followed the teachings of Jonathan Edwards an influential American revivalist preacher, philosopher and Congregationalist Protestant theologian.

[2] The Orientalists' understanding of the Indian religious and cultural society marked the beginning of many scholarly researches for the Indian society from the context of the Indian people rather than from the perspective of the privileged colonial scholars. However, this in any way does not outweigh the presence of subjective and bias reading of the overwhelming Indian milieu.

[3] George D. Bearce, *British Attitudes Towards Indian 1784-1858* (London: Oxford University Press, 1961), 21.

[4] Bearce, *British Attitudes Towards Indian*, 24.

[5] Bearce, *British Attitudes Towards Indian*, 71-76.

[6] Alexender Duff, *India and Indian Missions* (Edinburgh: John Johnstone, 1839), 187-192.

[7] Daniel J. Fleming, *Wither Bound in Missions* (New York: 1925), 3.

[8] John Clarke Marshman, *Life and Times of Carey, Marshman and Ward*, Vol. 2 (London: Longman, 1859), 486.

[9] William Carey, *An Enquiry into the Obligation of Christians to use means for Conversion of the Heathens,* New facsimile Edition (London: Carey Kingsgate Press, 1961), 73-75.

[10] L. G. Champion, "William Carey a pioneer of Ecumenical Movement," *Indian Journal of Theology,* Vol. 11 (April-June 1962): 55.

[11] T. K. Daniel, "Ecumenical Pragmatism of the Serampore Mission," *Indian Journal Theology*, Vol. 42/2 (2000): 172.

[12] Serampore Covenant or Form of Agreement was signed on October 6, 1805 by nine missionaries of the Baptist Missionary Society which consist of eleven clauses. The nine missionaries were William Carey, William Ward, Joshua Marshman, Felix Carey, John Chamberlian, Richard Mardon, John Biss, William Moore and Joshua Rowe. See "The Serampore Form of Agreement" *The Baptist Quarterly*. https://biblicalstudies.org.uk/pdf/bq/12-05_125.pdf, accessed on 13th October 2018.

[13] Timothy George, *Faithful Witness; The Life and Mission of William Carey* (Birmingham: New Hope Publishers, 1991), 123

[14] Daniel, "Ecumenical Pragmatism of the Serampore Mission," 172.

[15] J. N. Ogilvie, *The Apostles of India* (London: Hodder and Stoughton, 1915), 154.

[16] F. Deaville Walker, *William Carey Missionary Pioneer and Statesman* (London: Church Missionary Society, 1926), 178-195.

[17] Walker, *William Carey: Missionary Pioneer and Statesman*, 293.

[18] Walker, *William Carey: Missionary Pioneer and Statement*, 292.

[19] Champion, "William Carey a pioneer of Ecumenical Movement," 57.

[20] Marshman, *Life and Times of Carey, Marshman and Ward*, 354.

[21] Walker, *William Carey: Missionary Pioneer and Statesman*, 301.

[22] Daniel, "Ecumenical Pragmatism of the Serampore Mission," 177.

[23] Konrad Raiser was the General Secretary (1993-2003) of the World Council of Churches.

[24] John Briggs, Mercy Amba Oduyoye, eds., *A History of the Ecumenical Movement,1968-2000*, Vol. 3 (Geneva: WCC Publication, 2000), xiv.

[25] Walter Kasper was the President of the Pontifical Council for Promoting Church Unity (2001-2010).

[26] Walter Kasper, *The Ecumenical Movement in the 21st Century,* Presentation at the event marking the 40th anniversary of the Joint Working Group between the Roman Catholic Church and the WCC on 18 November 2005. https://www.oikoumene.org/en/resources/documents/commissions/jwg-rcc-wcc/the-ecumenical-movement-in-the-21st-century, accessed on 20th October 2018.

[27] Paul D. Murray, "Introducing Receptive Ecumenism," *The Ecumenist*, Vol. 51/2 (Spring 2014): 2.

[28] Kasper, *The Ecumenical Movement in the 21st Century.*

[29] Mary-Anne Plaatjies van Huffel, "From Conciliar Ecumenism to Transformative Receptive Ecumenism," HTS Teologiese Studies/Theological Studies. https://hts.org.za/index.php/hts/article/view/4353, accessed on 20th October 2018.

[30] Paul D. Murray, "Introducing Receptive Ecumenism," *The Ecumenist*, Vol. 51/2 (Spring 2014): 1-2.

[31] Mary-Anne Plaatjies van Huffel, "From Conciliar Ecumenism to Transformative Receptive Ecumenism."

[32] Murray, "Introducing Receptive Ecumenism," 2-5.

[33] Gerard Kelly, "A New Ecumenical Wave," *A Public Lecture at the National Council of Churches Forum, Canberra, 12 July 2010.* https://www.ncca.org.au/faith-and-unity/46-a-new-ecumenical-wave/file, accessed on 23rd October 2018.

[34] Peter J. Leithart, "Receptive Ecumenism." https://www.firstthings.com/web-exclusives/2015/02/receptive-ecumenism, accessed on 21st October 2018.

[35] During July 2012, a group of Korean ecumenical theologians, activists and pastors who have been deeply involved in the local and global ecumenical movement and who are deeply committed to building a new, transformative ecumenism in the twenty first century organized the Korea Institute for Future Ecumenism (KIFE), see Mary-Anne Plaatjies van Huffel, "From Conciliar Ecumenism to Transformative Receptive Ecumenism."

[36] Huang Po Ho, "A Paradigm Shift in Theology: A Holistic Redemption to God's Creation," *Green Theology*, ed. Wati Longchar (Kolkota: SCEPTRE, 2014), 180.

[37] van Huffel, "From Conciliar Ecumenism to Transformative Receptive Ecumenism."

[38] van Huffel, "From Conciliar Ecumenism to Transformative Receptive Ecumenism."

[39] The tenth WCC Assembly was held in Busan, the Republic of Korea from October 30 to November 8, 2013.

[40] van Huffel, "From Conciliar Ecumenism to Transformative Receptive Ecumenism."

[41] van Huffel, "From Conciliar Ecumenism to Transformative Receptive Ecumenism."

[42] Christopher Rajkumar, "Towards a Transformative Ecumenism," *Religion and Society*, Vol. 59/ 3 (September 2014): 74.

[43] Paul F. Knitter, "Beyond a Mono-Religious Theological Education," *Shifting Boundaries: Contextual Approaches to the Structure of Theological Education*, eds. Barbara G. Wheeler and Edward Farley (Louisville: John Knox Press, 1991), 159.

[44] Wati Longchar, *Doing Contextual Theologies in Asia* (Kolkata: SCEPTRE, 2014), 31.

[45] David Suh, "An Ethos for Teaching Theology Ecumenically in Asia," *Asian Handbook for Theological Education and Ecumenism*, eds. Hope S. Antone, Wati Longchar, Hyunju Bae, Huang Po Ho and Dietrich Werner (Oxford: Regnum Books International, 2013), 643.

[46] Namsoong Kang, "Envisioning Postcolonial Theological Education: Dilemmas and Possibilities," *Handbook of Theological Education in World Christianity*, eds. Dietrich Werner, David Esterline, Namsoong Kang, and Joshva Raja (Oxford: Regnum Books International, 2010), 32-33.

[47] Santanu K. Patro, "Democracy, Secularism and Understanding of Religion—A Social Perspective," *Religion and Society* 51/1 (March 2006): 23-24.

[48] Cynthia Stephen, "Religion and Civil Society: Its Role in Social Change and Transformation," *Religion and Society* 57/4 (December 2012): 80-82.

[49] Antony Kalliath, ed., *Christian Leadership: The Shifting Focus in Theological Education* (Bangalore: Dharmaram Publications, 2001), x.

[50] Joseph C. Hough and John B. Cobb, *Christian Identity and Theological Education* (California: Scholars Press, 1958), 19-20.

[51] Hope S. Antone, "Models of Teaching-Learning Ecumenism in Asia," *Asian Handbook for Theological Education and Ecumenism*, eds. Hope S. Antone, Wati Longchar, Hyunju Bae, Huang Po Ho, and Dietrich Werner (Oxford: Regnum Books International, 2013), 636.

52 Hough and Cobb, *Christian Identity and Theological Education*, 50-51.

53 Daniel, "Ecumenical Pragmatism of the Serampore Mission," 171.

54 Yakob Mar Irenaios, "Forward," *Mission and Local Congregations: Essay in Honor of William Carey's 250th Birth Anniversary*, ed. Solomon Rongpi (Delhi: ISPCK/ NCCI, 2011), xii.

Bibliography

Antone, H. S. "Models of Teaching-Learning Ecumenism in Asia." *Asian Handbook for Theological Education and Ecumenism*. Eds. Hope S. Antone, Wati Longchar, Hyunju Bae, Huang Po Ho, and Dietrich Werner. Oxford: Regnum Books International, 2013, 634-648.

Bearce, G. D. *British Attitudes Towards Indian 1784-1858*. London: Oxford University Press, 1961.

Briggs, J. and Mercy Amba Oduyoye, eds. *A History of the Ecumenical Movement, 1968-2000*. Vol. 3. Geneva: WCC Publication, 2000.

Carey, W. *An Enquiry into the Obligation of Christians to use means for Conversion of the Heathens*. New facsimile Edition. London: Carey Kingsgate Press, 1961.

Champion, L. G. "William Carey a pioneer of Ecumenical Movement." *Indian Journal of Theology*, Vol. 11 (April-June 1962): 54-59.

Daniel, T. K. "Ecumenical Pragmatism of the Serampore Mission." *Indian Journal Theology* 42/2 (2000): 171-177.

Duff, A. *India and Indian Missions*. Edinburgh: John Johnstone, 1839.

Fleming, D. J. *Wither Bound in Missions*. New York: 1925.

George, T. *Faithful Witness: The Life and Mission of William Carey*. Birmingham: New Hope Publishers, 1991.

Ho, H. P. "A Paradigm Shift in Theology: A Holistic Redemption to God's Creation." *Green Theology*. Ed. Wati Longchar. Kolkota: SCEPTRE, 2014: 170-185.

Hough, J. C. and John B. Cobb. *Christian Identity and Theological Education*. California: Scholars Press, 1958.

Irenaios, Y. M. "Forward." *Mission and Local Congregations: Essay in Honour of William Carey's 250th Birth Anniversary*. Ed. Solomon Rongpi. Delhi: ISPCK/ NCCI, 2011: ix-xii.

Kalliath, A., ed. *Christian Leadership: The Shifting Focus in Theological Education*. Bangalore: Dharmaram Publications, 2001.

Kang, N. "Envisioning Postcolonial Theological Education: Dilemmas and Possibilities." *Handbook of Theological Education in World Christianity*. Eds. Dietrich Werner, David Esterline, Namsoong Kang, and Joshva Raja. Oxford: Regnum Books International, 2010: 30-41.

Kasper, W. *The Ecumenical Movement in the 21st Century*. Presentation at the event marking the 40th anniversary of the Joint Working Group between the Roman

Catholic Church and the WCC on 18 November 2005. https://www.oikoumene.org/en/resources/documents/commissions/jwg-rcc-wcc/the-ecumenical-movement-in-the-21st-century. Accessed on 20th October 2018.

Kelly, G. "A New Ecumenical Wave." *A Public Lecture at the National Council of Churches Forum, Canberra, 12 July 2010*. https://www.ncca.org.au/faith-and-unity/46-a-new-ecumenical-wave/file. Accessed on 23rd October 2018.

Knitter, P. F. "Beyond a Mono-Religious Theological Education." *Shifting Boundaries: Contextual Approaches to the Structure of Theological Education*. Eds. Barbara G. Wheeler and Edward Farley. Louisville: John Knox Press, 199: 151-180.

Leithart, P. J. "Receptive Ecumenism." https://www.firstthings.com/web-exclusives/2015/02/receptive-ecumenism. Accessed on 21st October 2018.

Longchar, W. *Doing Contextual Theologies in Asia*. Kolkata: SCEPTRE, 2014.

Marshman, J. C. *Life and Times of Carey, Marshman and Ward*. Vol. 2. London: Longman, 1859.

Murray, P. D. "Introducing Receptive Ecumenism." *The Ecumenist* 51/2 (Spring 2014): 1-8.

Ogilvie, J. N. *The Apostles of India*. London: Hodder and Stoughton, 1915.

Patro, S. K. "Democracy, Secularism and Understanding of Religion- A Social Perspective." *Religion and Society* 51/1 (March 2006): 23-24.

Rajkumar, C. "Towards a Transformative Ecumenism." *Religion and Society* 59/3 (September 2014): 72-79.

Stephen, C. "Religion and Civil Society: Its Role in Social Change and Transformation." *Religion and Society* 57/ 4 (December 2012): 74-82.

Suh, D. "An Ethos for Teaching Theology Ecumenically in Asia." *Asian Handbook for Theological Education and Ecumenism*. Eds. Hope S. Antone, Wati Longchar, Hyunju Bae, Huang Po Ho, and Dietrich Werner. Oxford: Regnum Books International, 2013: 642-648.

"The Serampore Form of Agreement" *The Baptist Quarterly*. https://biblicalstudies.org.uk/pdf/bq/12-05_125.pdf. Accessed on 13th October 2018.

Van Huffel, M-A. P. "From Conciliar Ecumenism to Transformative Receptive Ecumenism." HTS Teologiese Studies/Theological Studies. https://hts.org.za/index.php/hts/article/view/4353. Accessed on 20th October 2018.

Walker, F. D. *William Carey Missionary Pioneer and Statesman*. London: Church Missionary Society, 1926.

15

William Carey's Approach to the People of other Faiths, Religious Practices, Caste System, and Conversion

Giri K.

Introduction

As the Serampore family celebrates the bicentenary of the foundation of the Serampore College, it is appropriate for us to revisit the Serampore Mission and see what it means for us in the 21st century. Even after two hundred years, the legacy of the Serampore Mission continues in the form of education and various other Christian ministries in India. Here in this paper an attempt is made to look at the Serampore Mission and the Indian Religions to understand William Carey's approach to the people of other faiths, religious practices of India, caste system and conversion. The paper is mainly divided into two broad sections. The first section takes a journey through the life of Carey to know his approach to other faiths and their adherents while engaging in Christian mission in India. The second section analyzes the significance of his approaches in the contemporary context, thereby attempting to bring the perspective in contexts.

Carey's Approach to Other Faiths and their Adherents

In understanding William Carey's approach to the people of other faiths and his views on other religions, various aspects of his life are significant. Here this paper tries to find answer to the following questions: How did Carey develop the concern for the Christian mission, especially among the people of other faiths in an alien and far away continent? What was his approach towards the people of other faiths? As a Christian missionary, what was his experience with the people and their religions in his early years in India? What was his attitude towards the scriptures of other faiths? How did he conceive the concept of conversion and what was the thrust in carrying out conversion activities? While engaging in mission in India, what was his attitude towards the casteism and other evil practices like *sati* and infanticide?

Development of Carey's Concern for the Mission

William Carey, in his childhood, is said to have had aversion towards books on religion.[1] In one of his letters, he notes, "I chose books of science, history, voyages, [and the like] more than any others. Novels and plays always disgusted me, and I avoided them as much as I did books of religion, perhaps from the same motive."[2] But by 1st August 1787, this village shoemaker became an ordained minister of the Baptist church.[3] It was the reading of the *Journal of Captain Cook's Last Voyage* that became the turning point in Carey's life to focus on the Missions. He writes, ". . . reading Cook's voyages was the first thing that engaged my mind to think of missions."[4] Ironically Cook was not concerned of religion rather was an extraordinary sailor and an explorer of hidden lands. However, Cook's journal that discusses the details of his voyage, description on 'strange people' and 'tattooed natives' became, for Carey, "a call to missionary effort . . . [and] a revelation of human need."[5] With the inspiration he received from Cook's book, Carey gathered all the information available from books on world including India, China, Africa, America and Europe and concluded that Christ is the greatest need of the people in the world. He also marked with a pen in a home-made world map the population and religions of each known nation.[6] As he acquired more information, he became more and more aware of the problems, such as slave trade, that exist in the world.[7] It prompted him to set his heart on the Christian mission in distant lands as he continued in pastoral ministry in his home land. Thus, in spite of the opposition he had from his senior colleagues and friends on his view of Christian mission, he went on to write a small book titled *Enquiry* that surveyed the whole world.[8] The *Enquiry* is said to be the first great achievement of Carey for the conversion of the 'heathens' with the appeal for mission works.[9]

Approach towards the People of Other Faiths

William Carey and the founders of the Serampore Mission were passionate about the distant lands as they prepared to arrive in India. Carey seemed to be very much concerned of people of India from various religious backgrounds whom he called 'heathens.' Such expressions on the people of other faiths were not in terms of diminishing their value. It was the expression about the 'other', the people of other faith, by the European Christians in general therefore one may conclude that Carey was the product of his own time.

Carey's attention fell on the religious conditions of the inhabitants of various regions of the world, while he was instructing geography to his people during his pastoral ministry. He suggested his fellow-ministers to discuss in a meeting on "the duty of Christians to attempt the spread of the gospel among heathen nations."[10] However, it was in 1792 he strongly felt the need of becoming a missionary to 'Hindostan,' i.e., India. Eventually Carey ventured for a 'mission to Bengal' by joining hands with Mr. John Mathew.[11] Conversion was the sole motive behind his concern towards the people of other faiths. The famous book *Enquiry* published in 1788, before he ventured for his missionary expeditions, was originally titled as *An Enquiry into the Obligations of Christians, to Use Means for the Conversion of the Heathens.*[12] The very title reveals his intention. While spreading the gospel, he writes, ". . . it is necessary that we should become, in some measure acquainted with the religious state of the world . . . ."[13] He thus brought out some guidelines with the clear purpose worded as 'to use the means for the heathens.'

From *Enquiry* it is evident that Carey wanted to follow the 'successful'[14] ministries of apostles who proclaimed the gospel to the 'lost world'—the 'civilized Greeks' and 'uncivilized barbarians' who are involved in 'all the darkness of heathenism.'[15] Hence he cried out, "Alas! the far greater part of the world, as we shall see presently, are still covered with heathen darkness!"[16] In his survey on the Christian missionary activities in the world, he made remarks on John Eliot (1632), David Brainerd (1743), and Ziegenbalg (1706), who had great success in making many of the 'heathens' turn to the Lord.[17] In one of the letters, Mary Carey, sister of William Carey, noted about her brother that he had been very thoughtful and impressed about the heathen lands and the slave trade. Mary wrote: "I never remember his engaging prayer, in his family or in public, without praying for those poor creatures."[18] So it is obvious that his concern for the poor is evident even in every prayer he offered.

In his survey on the present state of the world, which contains 23 pages (39-61) in *Enquiry*, Carey brings out statistical tables with five columns, stating name of each country or island, length, breach, number of inhabitants and religions, respectively.[19] Carey divides the population into Christians, Jews, Mahometan [Muslims] and pagans. It would imply that, for Carey, all religious groups other than Judeo-Christian and Muslims are 'pagans.' He records that 50,00,000 inhabitants live in India beyond the Ganges and 1,10,00,000 in 'Indostan', i.e., Hindustan, comprised of 'Mahometans' or Muslims and pagans.[20] Thus he estimated that one hundred and sixty million people in India alone.[21] Carey had a very positive and realistic estimate about the Hindus in India. In one of his letters to his father Carey writes, "They are the most mild and inoffensive people in all the world, but are enveloped in the greatest superstition, and in the grossest ignorance."[22] Having completed the list of the entire population of the world in religious categories, Carey remarks in *Enquiry*, ". . . a vast proportion of the sons of Adam there are, who yet remain in the most deplorable state of heathen darkness, without any means of knowing the true God, except what are afforded them by the works of nature; and utterly destitute of the knowledge of the gospel of Christ . . . only led by the most childish customs and traditions."[23] Carey was concerned of the conversion of the 'heathens' from their 'barbarious and savage manner of living.'[24] He considered that the spread of the gospel is the effective means of their 'civilization' and to make them "useful members of the society."[25] He insisted that the missionaries who work among these people should not think 'high' of themselves and despise the 'poor heathens.'[26] In his case, he worked hard for the conversion of the people of other faiths in India but without despising them till he died at the age 72.[27]

Early Encounters with the People of India and Their Religions

On 17th January 1793, Carey wrote to his father, "I am appointed to go to Bengal in the East Indies, a missionary to the Hindoos."[28] Although he was prevented from travelling by an English Vessel *Oxford*, it was on Thursday, 13th June 1793 , he along with his family and friends sailed to India by the *Kron Princessa Maria*, a Danish Vessel commanded by an English captain J. Christmas.[29] They arrived in the Balasure Road in Bengal on 7th November 1793. After two days, Carey was able to see for the first time the people of Bengal while some from fishing boats which came along side of the vessel attempted to sell fish.[30] With much enthusiasm Carey along with his friend Thomas went to see an Indian village. When the people gathered around them to see the strangers, Thomas could address the crowd in native language in the market place.[31] Regarding the people Carey wrote: "They left their merchandise, and listened for three hours with great enthusiasm."[32] After landing in Calcutta, in the following day on 11th November 1793,[33] his visit to the famous Kali Temple gave him vivid picture of Hindu religious life. Walker writes, ". . . he visited the famous temple of Kali from which the city had taken its name and (he had) the sight of the crowding worshippers bathing upon the adjacent *ghat* (bathing place) and then going to the temple to sacrifice their goats."[34] Thus Carey came across for the first time the Indian religiosity and had first impression of Indian life as he visited the Kali temple.

When Carey wrote a letter from Bandel to his sisters in England on 4th December 1793, his initial impression about the people and their religiosity in Bengal are made evident in his words:

> The country is amazingly populous, and the inhabitants are very attractive . . . . They are remarkably talkative and curious; but, go where you will, you are sure to see something of an idolatrous kind; flowers, trees, or little temples by the way-side, consecrated to religious uses; and I have seen two or three who have swung by flesh-hooks, with the mark in their backs; yet they are very willing to hear . . . .[35]

One of the early occasions, while Carey had a good rapport with the people of other faiths, he arrived at Deharta[36] on the Jubano river bank where he set up a temporary small bamboo house for living. The people who abandoned their houses due to the constant tiger attack began to return as Carey set up the house with the view that he must be having a gun to protect them from tiger attack. Five or six Brahmins came to him and expressed their gratefulness to him for deciding to live among them. Carey was impressed by their gestures and saw a kind of breakthrough for his mission in India, though they had to soon leave Deharta as per the advice of John Thomas.[37]

The zeal of a European missionary is seen in Carey as one analyzes his early days in his journal. He attempted to preach the gospel with the help of a Munshi to almost two hundred people at temple premises on 26th May 1794. He discussed with them ". . . the vanity of idols, the folly and wickedness of idolatry, the nature and attributes of God, and the way of salvation by Christ."[38] While undertaking the work as the manager of an Indigo factory in June 1794 at Madnabaty, thirty-two miles north of Malda,

Carey anticipated that he would be an effective witness of the gospel to the employees to form a Christian congregation. He wrote on 28th June 1794 in his journal, ". . . having about ninety people under my management; these will furnish a congregation immediately, and . . . will open a wide door for activity."[39] On 4th July 1794, he noted in the journal, that Munshi with whom he had spiritual conversation that day would soon lose caste for the gospel.[40]

Carey began to slowly understand the dark side of the realities of Indian religions as he continued as the manager at Madnabaty. During the monsoon in 1794, some of the workers of the Indigo factory approached Carey with a request to make an offering to goddess Kali for his own success as the manager in the factory. Carey in turn made use of the opportunity to preach to those factory workers, urging them to turn to the true God. His preaching and effort went in vain as he came to realize to his dismay that the workers went on to offer a child to the goddess Kali on the following day.[41] On August 1794, at least a thousand people from the Muslim Community gathered for two days and two nights to display festivity with pipes, tom-toms and symbols as they celebrated the Islamic festival Muharram, which became a new experience for Carey in India.[42] He observed, "Their zeal on these occasions is very great; everything is sacrificed to their religion, and every Mussulman, rich or poor, joins in the ceremony."[43] Carey learned about Indian thought and Indian beliefs through personal conversations with the workers from Hindu and Islamic backgrounds. He directly witnessed one of his workers who made an image of the goddess of learning. Therefore, he tried to convince them to turn away from such ways of life with the view that idolatry is sinful and foolishness.

Although the primary purpose of Carey was conversion of the Hindus, he was repeatedly unsuccessful as the people were not accepting the gospel in spite of readily listening to the gospel. He wrote about the reason behind his futile efforts as follows: "The Brahmuns [Brahmins] fear to lose their gain; the higher caste their honor; and the poor tremble at the vengeance of their debtors. Thus, we have been unsuccessful."[44] Therefore, he planned to establish two colleges where he wanted to introduce Sanskrit and Persian languages, and the study of the Holy Scriptures. He also learned various words and terms from the Indian languages. In the matters of religion, he realized that the Indian words and terms are different from the English and from the Christian concepts of sin, salvation and holiness.[45] Having completed almost two years in India, Carey began to understand various festivals and the rituals attached to them. Before the hook swinging festival season, Carey preached in the factory against the gruesome practices of self-torture, swinging in the air suspended by hooks, and splints of bamboos pierced of their bodies; but unfortunately, he had to directly witness them a week later as the people continued to celebrate the festival.[46]

Having spent six years in Madnabaty, attached to an Indigo factory, Carey moved to Serampore in January 1800 to join the missionaries who were sent by the Baptist Mission. On the following day of his arrival in the city, he went out to address the Indians on a Sunday afternoon for the first time in Serampore. Thus, Baptist Mission was established in Serampore, in a Danish Colony, by William Carey, William Ward, a printer, and Joshua Marshman, a school teacher, along with their families, comprised of twelve members including four children.[47]

After setting up the Press, they employed Ram Ram Boshu,[48] a Bengali Scholar from Hindu background, to write tracts for the propagation of the gospel. Besides printing a tract with the title 'The Gospel Messenger,' a tract that dealt on the folly of idolatry was also printed and circulated among the natives. Carey regularly engaged in open-air preaching to the Hindus in the market place. He often met the Brahmins who had white mark on their forehead at the temple gateway and enquired about the mark on the forehead to start the conversation. When they explain that the mark is based on the Indian sastras they believe, he usually asked them if they ever have seen Christian Sastra and introduced the printed gospel to them. While walking beside the Hooghly River, often he noticed the worshipers were bathing and he enquired how sin is forgiven. The usual response would be by bathing in the holy river. Then Carey engaged in conversation with them on sin and its remedy. However, Brahmins usually disliked their preaching and printing works.[49]

Attitude towards Other Scriptures

In regard to the scriptures of other faith traditions, unlike many other missionaries, Carey was not narrow-minded. When he began to learn Sanskrit, he stated, "that I may be able to read their *Shastras* for myself."[50] He began to read the Vedas, the Puranas, and Mahabharata to familiarize with the Hindu Scriptures as he continued Sanskrit learning. While Carey was serving in the College in Calcutta, he submitted a proposal to the college authorities to publish a series of Sanskrit classics with English translations, but the response was so cold. But in two years, Carey and Marshman undertook a project for translating some of the most important Sanskrit works under the patronage of the Government. They also obtained a stipend of three hundred rupees per month from the College as well as from Asiatic Society for this project. Carey began the translation of the great Indian epic *Ramayana*, which he considered as the *Iliad* of India, with the view to have the access for the English readers. Between 1806 and 1810, the first three books of the translated Ramayana were printed at the mission press. Carey also edited the Sanskrit text of the *Hitopadesa*[51] for the College and printed *The Sanskrit Dictionary of Amara Sinha*[52] with English interpretation and annotations. Unfortunately, the translation of *Ramayana* and other valuable literary works were completely destroyed due to fire in the press and they were never resumed.[53]

Views on Conversion, and Conversion Activities

Conversion of the Indians to Christian faith was the main purpose of the establishment of the Baptist Mission Society and the Serampore Mission. Carey also believed that even the Christians surely require conversion at different points in history just as the people of other faiths. He says, "But blind zeal, gross superstition, and infamous cruelties, so marked the appearances of religion all this time that the professors of Christianity needed conversion, as much as the heathen world."[54] Thus he wished for the conversion of both Christians and non-Christians.

Seven years of Carey's hard labor in India in the form of evangelistic preaching, translations, establishment of press and schools did not yield any result to that end. Though many Hindus and Muslims received the Gospel, they never accepted it to the extent of receiving baptism.[55] But the end of the year 1800 became an eventful one because of the first conversion of the Serampore Mission. In October 1800, a poor carpenter from the Hindu background, namely Krishna Pal, met with an accident, dislocating his shoulder. Dr. John Thomas along with Carey and Marshman went to help him. Krishna Pal cried out with pain saying, "I am a sinner . . . save me . . . ." While Dr. Thomas was trying to put back his bone into the socket, he urged Krishna Pal to repeat the following ten times, "He that covereth his sins shall not prosper, but who so confesseth and forsaketh them shall find mercy," which he introduced as the true *gayatri*. While he was recovering, Krishna Pal along with his friend Goluk began to visit the Mission House to receive further Christian teachings.[56]

Krishna Pal and Goluk openly renounced their caste and joined the Serampore missionaries for a meal on 22nd December and in the same evening along with Krishna's wife and daughter confessed the Christian faith. Although breaking off their caste led to a riot kind of a situation which was promptly intervened by the magistrate, their baptism was fixed for Sunday, 28th December 1800. By Saturday, Goluk and two women backed off from the decision. On Sunday, Krishna Pal and Felix Carey took baptism officiated by William Carey, witnessed by the multitude of natives from Hindu and Muslim background along with Danish and Portuguese Christians. Thus, the first conversion brought enough joy to the Serampore Missionaries, although it had its own ill effects on their personal lives and the mission works.[57] Followed by, Krishna Pal's sister-in-law, the first Hindu woman, was baptized along with Mr. Fernandez early in 1801. Krishna's wife and another woman received baptism in the following month. The same year in August, Goluk, and in November Goluk's wife embraced Christian faith in baptism. In 1802, on the first Sunday, a sixty-year old highly intelligent man from Kayust or Writer caste renounced caste and received baptism to join the Christian fold. After a month, two others from Writer caste and a Kulin embraced Christianity. In early 1803, the first person from the Brahmin community received baptism as a result of reading the mission tract. Thus, there were thirteen baptized Bengali converts into Christian faith by 1803.[58] As the work of the Serampore Mission was expanded to other parts of Upper India, Bengal, Orissa, Burma, Java and Mauritius, about 420 adults were converted between 1815 and 1818. However, it is estimated that more than 1000 converts were baptized by the Serampore Mission till 1818.[59]

Attitude to Caste System

Within a couple of weeks after his arrival, Carey had a very realistic understanding on the caste system that was practiced among the people of Bengal. It is evident from his letter to his sisters, ". . . their superstitions are very numerous, and their attachments to their caste so strong, that they would rather die than lose it upon any account."[60] He wrote an incident on 5th July 1794 in his journal that a very poor boy from a shoemaker caste refused to become a servant on account of loosing caste practices.[61] In yet another occasion, while he was at Madnabaty, the natives did not even carry the dead body of his five year old son as they had aversion to corps based on rigid caste practices. Yet he was never judgmental but noted, "This was not owing to any disrespect in the natives towards us, but only to the cursed caste."[62] It was their religion that prevented them from helping at the time of death in the family.

When the new Christians from other religious background joined the church, it raised a couple of issues to grapple with by the missionaries. First is on the name of the Converts. Some had the opinion that they should be given new Christian names instead of continuing with the old Hindu or Muslim names in order to proclaim the fact of embracing Christian faith. Carey however opposed such a move and resolved rather to allow the new converts to retain the old names. Second is on the attitude towards caste. Carey and his friends were against the danger of social distinctions the caste system imposed in the society that might also creep into the church. They were well aware of the practice of caste distinction that was allowed in the church by the Danish missionaries in South India. But Serampore missionaries were convinced that "caste system is contrary to the spirit of Christ."[63] Therefore they insisted right from the beginning that the Bengali Missions must be 'one' in Christ once they are baptized, irrespective of their caste background. It was in this context, in the very year of Carey's arrival in Bengal, he applied to the governor to grant an uncultivated land to settle upon, which ". . . will be an asylum for those who loose caste for the gospel sake."[64]

As if to vindicate this notion against the practices of caste, they celebrated Holy Communion, made marriage alliances, and even conducted funeral services without following the traditional caste practices. When the first Bengali Christian marriage was conducted in 1803, it was a Brahmin convert who married Krishna Pal's daughter. Thus, a Brahmin joining in Christian marriage with a Sudra that Ward calls it "a glorious triumph over caste."[65] Similarly, after six months in the same year, Christians demonstrated their oneness and casteless character during the first funeral service of Goluk, a Bengali Christian who was led to Christian faith by Krishna Pal. The Serampore missionary Marshman did not employ the low class Portuguese who are usually drunk on such a duty to carry the dead body as per the customary practice of the day. Rather Marshman along with Felix Carey, Bhyrub—a Christian convert from Hindu Brahmin background, and Piru—a Christian convert from Muslim background together carried the coffin of a low caste Christian Bengali upon their shoulders to the graveyard through the streets of Serampore. It was to the utter amazement of the onlookers Marshman set an illustrious example for the Christian brotherhood that broke all the caste barriers at the funeral. Walker writes, "Thus was proclaimed the unity of all Christians at Holy Communion, at the marriage alter, and at the graveside."[66] These incidents ideally and practically broke all the caste rigidity and set an example of Christian community as one unit in the world.

Humanitarian Concerns

There were occasions when Carey directly witnessed the religious practices of *sati* and *infanticide* in Bengal. In 1794, while he was at the Indigo factory managed by John Thomas, he found the remains of an infant hanged on the branch of a tree. Carey wrote in his journal, ". . . we saw a basket hung in a tree, in which an infant had been exposed; the skull remained, the rest having been devoured by ants."[67] It was customary that during Hindu festivals the children were offered to the river goddess at Gunga Sangor, where the river joins the sea, for some sections of the Hindu community. Therefore, Carey's friend George Udney appealed against the practice of infanticide to the Lord Wellesley in 180. Carey was asked by the government to investigate to see if it had any scriptural sanction. His study revealed that the practice had no sanction from the scripture, and he urged the government to prohibit it. Immediately the Government issued an edict, counting infanticide as murder and a punishable crime.[68]

The prohibition of infanticide motivated Carey to fight against the practice of *sati* as well. In 1799, while Carey was an Indigo planter, he witnessed for the first time a case of widow-burning. In 1803, Ward also recorded about the burning of three women together with their husbands in a funeral pyre. This triple burning prompted the missionaries to survey on the practice of *sati* with the help of some trustworthy individuals. They concluded that every year over four hundred women in around Calcutta and not less than five thousand in the whole of Bengal province become the victims of *Sati*. With the help of Mr. Udney, they appealed to Wellesley and he in turn approached the Judges. However, the Government was urged to refrain from any action on the religious affairs of the natives. As Wellesley returned to England at the completion of his term, the matter was put to rest for a while.[69] But 5th December 1829, happened to be one of the joyful days for Carey as he received an edict of abolishing *sati* in India from Lord

Bentinck to translate into Bengali. Without even attending the church on that Sunday he immediately got into his work, saying, "If I delay an hour to translate and publish this, many widows' life may be sacrificed."[70] Such was the enthusiasm and concern of Carey to eradicate the inhuman practice of *Sati*.

In all his work the very attitude of him was more than a mere narrow minded missionary. He undertook all works physically or intellectually beneficial to the natives. It was his persistence that led to the formation of Asiatic Agricultural Society in which he was the President and active member for years.[71] Francis Wayland comments, "he considered himself not merely a missionary, and a translator of the Scriptures, but also a man and a citizen of India."[72] Thus Carey was a man for others to whom he devoted to serve.

Relevance of Carey's Approach in Contemporary Context

William Carey's approaches towards the people of other faiths and his attitude to the religiosities of different faith traditions are the matters under review in this section. No doubt, there is a universal significance of Carey, as Roger Hedlund would portray,[73] as we analyze his contributions in various realms in India. However, a lot of water has flowed under the bridge since Carey's missionary adventures in India. Nationalism gained momentum and India has been freed from the colonial powers and consequently she turned to be an independent secular democratic country. Hindutva elements have come to play, and political power is wheeled by fundamentalists and communalists today. Unlike Carey's time, Christian mission in its theology and expressions faces challenges from various quarters—religious, communal, political, and institutional—to name a few in general. Therefore, the questions naturally arise: Is Carey still relevant? How far his attitude towards the people of other faiths with whom he came to serve is significant in the 21st century? How do we need to perceive his mission in an era when religious fundamentalism and communalism fabricate the Indian society? In other words, how far Carey's approach is relevant in the context of contemporary views on theology of religions and Indian renaissance? How significant is the approach of Carey in the contemporary context of various religious superstitions, practice of casteism and conversion?

From the Perspective of Theology of Religions

Theology of religions is understood as the theological view of other faiths from one's own faith perspective. In other words, as K. P. Aleaz puts it, "From the perspective of one's own religious faith how a person should conceive other faiths theologically . . . ."[74] Christian theological views on other faiths are mainly *exclusivism*, *inclusivism*, *pluralism*, and others. For an exclusivist, salvation is only through Christ and the revelation in Christ is the sole criterion to assess other religions. Christ-event is the only revelatory activity of God for an exclusivist; hence Christ is normative, and all other religions are erroneous.[75] Whereas the basic character of *inclusivism* is to have openness towards other faith traditions while maintaining commitment to one's own. Although *inclusivism* acknowledges the divine presence in other religions, it affirms that Christ is the authoritative revelation of God and the fulfillment of all other religions. Thus, it tries to hold together, as Aleaz puts it, "the axioms of the 'universal salvific will of God' and 'salvation comes through God in Christ alone.'"[76] In *inclusivism*, hence we see both openness and commitment, and also acceptance and rejection, simultaneously. Whereas *pluralism* holds that the world religions are true and equally valid in their communication of the truth about God, the world, and salvation. In one sense 'respecting the otherness of others' is pluralism and it affirms the universal will of God for human salvation. The chief expounder of this view is John Hick, who first propounded it in his book *God and the Universe of Faiths (1973).*

In view of theology of religions, the beginning of Carey's mission activities are viewed as based on the category of exclusive religious position. This is the traditional missionary view of the past. His *Enquiry* and various early correspondences support this position. However, when Carey began to learn other religions, his viewpoints slowly changed, appropriating to the pluralistic context of India. Tapan Kumar Banerjee, former Professor of Mathematics at Serampore College, states:

> It may be noticed that Carey and his missionary brethren wanted to learn oriental languages for grasping the knowledge of religion, loop holes in them and to point out those faults at the time of bandy arguments for establishing the superiority of Christianity. But Carey, after going through the Bhagavad Gita, Mahabharata, Ramayan, Upanishad abandoned their malicious motives against the native religions. The use of the examples from those epic or from

> translations of Dharmapustaka in the chapters of his Sanskrit Grammar established his secular character.[77]

It may be viable that one can be more aware of the significance of other religions and give due respect to the views of the people of other faiths. Carey had more openness towards other religious texts and the people of other faiths in his later missionary endeavors. But at the same time, he was vocal about the evil practices prevalent in other religions. Therefore, his approach, as the present essay prefers to call it, can be termed, as 'Dialectic Dialogical Exclusivism' as a theological position which was rather radical in the missionary era.

'Dialectical dialogue' involves "the battle for recognition, the ethics of giving recognition, and the multiplicity of conversation."[78] It paves the way for the evolution of ideas, the process through which the truth is evolved. But in the contemporary religiously pluralistic world, where various faiths can be viewed as part of God's general or natural revelation, it requires a radical shift from *exclusivism* to *inclusivism*, and therefore it necessitates dialogue, having a scope for mutual enrichment.[79] In the dialogue, however, "both sides must be ready to be 'questioned,' 'purified,' thoroughly 'challenged' . . . . In other words, to be shaken up."[80] It may be true when we consider the attitude of Carey towards other traditions that he questioned the validity of 'Sati' and 'infanticide' or child sacrifices. Inhuman tenets need to be questioned in dialogical engagements. Therefore, for meaningful mission engagements today, one has to move ahead of narrow and extreme *exclusivism* to take a theological position of 'dialectic dialogical inclusivism,' in which elements of truth from other faiths are acknowledged in a dialectical manner, and simultaneously critiquing the dehumanizing tenets of any faiths as a responsible partner of dialogue process.

From the Perspective of Indian Renaissance

Renaissance that began in Europe could germinate in India in 19th and 20th centuries as a result of the spread of English Education, British supremacy, efforts of the Christian missionaries and works of the Oriental Scholars.[81] As an Indian historian Nemai Sadhan Bose notes, "The decay of knowledge and learning coupled with social degeneration helped the extensive spread of blind superstition and inhuman social customs. Polygamy, early marriage, sati rites, killing female children, throwing the first born into the holy rivers were some of the most dreadful and inhuman practices performed in different parts of the country in varying degrees."[82] Tapan Kumar Banerjee notes that although the English came first as merchants to gain wealth, then as warriors to gain land, ". . . the work of William Carey was for the benefit of the native society, not always aiming to fulfill their ardent desire of propagating Christianity."[83] In fact, Carey arrived in a transitory period of India when she was braving for a modern phase, therefore he was rightly called as "the forerunner of Indian Renaissance."[84] The educational institutions in the form of schools and a college began by the missionaries ignited the renaissance in India. Education of girls undertaken by Carey and colleagues was primarily intended ". . . to free from ignorance and degradation . . . ."[85] Carey's translation of Indian literatures and the Bible along with the establishment of printing press could further spread the renaissance in India. The renaissance in India gave education to the girls, oppressed classes and to the poor who were otherwise deprived of basic and higher education. However, the women of menstrual age are deprived even today from entering certain worship places due to the stigma associated with puritan codes prevalent in Indian religions. 'Woman's Wall' (*vanitha mathil*) that was built on the streets throughout Kerala on 1st January 2019 was an attempt to continue spreading the values of renaissance (*navodhana mulyam*) in order to create awareness against such discrimination to women. The works of Carey that paved the way for the renaissance in India and transformation of India's culture[86] still has the relevance as India requires miles to go for attaining gender equality and education to the poor and deprived classes.

From the Perspective of Overcoming Superstitions

Carey was vocal against inhuman and superstitious activities in India in the name of religion. He pleaded against infanticide[87] and sati practices[88] and it was further taken up as a crusade by the Indian reformers like Raja Ram Mohan Roy.[89] Such interventions in the history were necessary as India was gripped under superstitious beliefs of various kinds. Probably by acknowledging the importance of scripture among the Hindus in their religious life, he verified with the Pundits and made sure those evil practices had no scriptural sanctions and whatever is contrary to the scriptures of other faith he questioned too. Even after more than two centuries, many Indians are in the grip of superstitions and inhuman practices in the name of religion. Torturing the children by way of hanging on hooked skin and pierced cheek in the name of oaths or penance by parents is one of the superstitious practices prevalent in different parts of India today. The mythical elevation of cow as 'Goumata,' the mother or divine cow, [90] often lead to lynching minorities.[91] Many of these are not sanctioned by the religion per se but crept in over the period of time leading to dehumanizing tendencies in India. Riya Oli Roy comments, "Carey was the man to understand that the people with superstitions are sinking into oblivion very fast even without the torch of truth. He was so keen . . . to spread literacy and to bring people to the light of education."[92] Although Carey was not convinced of the spiritual content of the Sanskrit literature, it is argued, "Yet paradoxically Carey spent a great deal of time collecting, translating and printing these same classics . . . ."[93] By introducing the learning of Sanskrit in the College he established, Carey helped the native Hindus to properly understand the religious idealism which can remove the superstitious beliefs.[94] Voicing against the superstitions and eradicating social and religious evils through education are necessary even today in India as it was practiced in the time of Carey.[95]

From the Perspectives of Casteism and Conversion

The practice of caste system[96] is one of the evils that have existed in the Indian society from the time immemorial. While accepting the people of other faiths in the Christian fold, Carey made sure that the converts give up their caste first and foremost in order to embrace Christian faith. They were not aggressive to add the number of converts to the Christian fold. They made sure the converts have changed their way of life and given up their caste affinities. Conversion is understood as a dynamic and multifaceted process of change. Conversion in its practical form allies with personal as well as communal metamorphosis.[97] Unlike their counterparts in the South, Serampore Missionaries wanted to resist the caste system in the church. This is one of the most difficult criteria to be followed by any Indian especially for those belong to the high castes.

Many reformists like Sri Narayana Guru fought against the evils of casteism in India but in vain. B. R. Ambedkar along with several lakhs of followers from Mahar community went on to convert to Buddhism from Hinduism so as to get rid of it; but the caste stigma still follows the community even after six decades of that event. Carey could foresee the need of getting rid of the evil of casteism for the Christians in India. Ideally Christian church is a casteless community. But over a period of time, casteism crept in within the church and she turned out to be a caste-ridden institution. Churches are divided on caste ground and silently it ruins the integrity and unity of the Christians in India. Therefore, Carey's vision on the Christians without caste identity is highly commendable and still relevant in the 21st century to envision church as a casteless community in India.

Conclusion

Based on the discussion above, William Carey can be looked up as a man of all times. Although Carey's original understanding of the other religions were lopsided, his attitudes towards other people, faiths and religious practices, caste system and conversion are seen unique. Carey also fought against the social evils such as infanticide and *sati*. In view of his theological position, it may be termed as a 'dialectical dialogic exclusivism,' but requires a change into inclusivism in order to be relevant in the contemporary world. His disapproval to the social evils that threatened the very life and dignity of the human beings is very relevant even today as India still battles with the superstitious beliefs and practices in the name of religion. His stand on the caste system is a real inspiration today for developing church as a casteless community in the contemporary Indian scenario.

Endnotes

[1] F. Deaville Walker, *William Carey: Missionary Pioneer and Statesman* (London: SCM, 1926), 26.

[2] Eustace Carey, *Memoir of William Carey, D.D.* (Boston: Gould, Kendall and Lincoln, 1836), 5.

[3] Walker, *William Carey: Missionary Pioneer and Statesman*, 54.

[4] Eustace Carey, *Memoir of William Carey*, 12.

[5] Walker, *William Carey: Missionary Pioneer and Statesman*, 57-58.

[6] Cf. Eustace Carey, *Memoir of William Carey*, 45-46.

[7] Walker, *William Carey: Missionary Pioneer and Statesman*, 58-60.

[8] Walker, *William Carey: Missionary Pioneer and Statesman*, 63-65.

[9] Walker, *William Carey: Missionary Pioneer and Statesman*, 78.

[10] Eustace Carey, *Memoir of William Carey*, 35.

[11] Eustace Carey, *Memoir of William Carey*, 49-51.

[12] William Carey, *An Enquiry into the Obligations of Christians, to use means for the Conversion of the Heathens*, Leicester: Ann Ireland, 1792.

[13] Carey, *Enquiry*, 3.

[14] Carey, *Enquiry*, 15.

[15] Carey, *Enquiry*, 5.

[16] Carey, *Enquiry*, 10.

[17] Carey, *Enquiry*, 36.

[18] William Carey, *Memoir of William Carey*, 26. This letter was written on 17th January 1793 from Leicester.

[19] Walker, *William Carey: Missionary Pioneer and Statesman*, 85.

[20] Carey, *Enquiry*, 62.

[21] Walker, *William Carey: Missionary Pioneer and Statesman*, 85.

[22] Eustace Carey, *Memoir of William Carey*, 43.

[23] Carey, *Enquiry*, 62-63.

[24] Carey, *Enquiry*, 67.

[25] Carey, *Enquiry*, 70.

[26] Carey, *Enquiry*, 75.

[27] Francis Wayland, "Introductory Essay," *Memoir of William Carey*, xiii.

[28] Walker, *William Carey: Missionary Pioneer and Statesman*, 112.

[29] Eustace Carey, *Memoir of William Carey*, 72.

[30] Walker, *William Carey: Missionary Pioneer and Statesman*, 143.

[31] Walker, *William Carey: Missionary Pioneer and Statesman*, 146. The villagers' reception seemed to be very cordial and one man brought food for them and Carey for the first time sat on ground and took the food from plantain leaves using his fingers.

[32] Eustace Carey, *Memoir of William Carey*, 80.

[33] Their voyage took all five months but two days to arrive in Calcutta on 11th November 1793.

[34] Walker, *William Carey: Missionary Pioneer and Statesman*, 147.

[35] Eustace Carey, *Memoir of William Carey*, 82-83.

[36] As Carey journeyed along with his family by a boat with the help of a native Mounshi reached Dehrata on the bank of Jubona River on 6th February 1794. Seeing an English built house Carey mistook it as Company's dark bungalow. He stepped ashore with his family but realized that it belonged to Mr. Charles Short, an Englishman. It was because of Short's cordial welcome and generosity Carey decided to build a temporary house there. Cf. Eustace Carey, *Memoir of William Carey*, 101-102.

[37] Walker, *William Carey: Missionary Pioneer and Statesman*, 156-160.

[38] Eustace Carey, *Memoir of William Carey*, 118.

[39] Eustace Carey, *Memoir of William Carey*, 124.

[40] Eustace Carey, *Memoir of William Carey*, 125.

[41] Walker, *William Carey: Missionary Pioneer and Statesman*, 165-171.

[42] Walker, *William Carey: Missionary Pioneer and Statesman*, 172.

[43] Eustace Carey, *Memoir of William Carey*, 127.

[44] Cited in Walker, *William Carey: Missionary Pioneer and Statesman*, 175.

[45] Walker, *William Carey: Missionary Pioneer and Statesman*, 176-177.

[46] Walker, *William Carey: Missionary Pioneer and Statesman*, 177.

[47] Walker, *William Carey: Missionary Pioneer and Statesman*, 204-212.

[48] Carey had the friendship with Ram Ram Boshu right from the time of his arrival in India to learn Bengali language. Though Carey persuaded him to be baptized, Boshu was repeatedly reluctant.

[49] Walker, *William Carey: Missionary Pioneer and Statesman*, 213-215.

[50] Walker, *William Carey: Missionary Pioneer and Statesman*, 277.

[51] The Collection of Aryan folk-tales.

[52] The oldest Indian lexicographer.

[53] Walker, *William Carey: Missionary Pioneer and Statesman*, 276-277, 284.

[54] Carey, *Enquiry*, 35.

[55] In one of such incidents, John Thomas brought Fukeer, a Sugar-boiler from Islamic faith, to the missionaries in Serampore as he has reached to the point of a decision to embrace Christian faith. The missionaries listened to his simple confession of faith and received him as a brother in Christ. All of them were delighted. When the question on baptism was discussed Fukeer sought the permission to visit home and take leave of his family probably forever. He went home, but to the utter disappointment of the missionaries Fakur never returned. Cf. Walker, *William Carey: Missionary Pioneer and Statesman*, 221.

[56] Walker, *William Carey: Missionary Pioneer and Statesman*, 220-223.

[57] The following day of Conversion and baptism of Krishna Pal, the vernacular school was empty without students as they feared of conversion to Christianity. The sudden joy caused by the conversion of Krishna Pal led John Thomas to develop 'religious mania', becoming insane and so violent, and at last had to be admitted in Calcutta lunatic asylum on New Year's day. Cf. Walker, *William Carey: Missionary Pioneer and Statesman*, 224.

[58] Walker, *William Carey: Missionary Pioneer and Statesman*, 224-225.

[59] Walker, *William Carey: Missionary Pioneer and Statesman*, 287-288.

[60] Eustace Carey, *Memoir of William Carey*, 83.

[61] Eustace Carey, *Memoir of William Carey*, 125-26.

[62] Eustace Carey, *Memoir of William Carey*, 134.

[63] Walker, *William Carey: Missionary Pioneer and Statesman*, 226.

[64] Eustace Carey, *Memoir of William Carey*, 81.

[65] Walker, *William Carey: Missionary Pioneer and Statesman*, 226.

[66] Walker, *William Carey: Missionary Pioneer and Statesman*, 227.

[67] This not found in his journal written, dated between July 9 and August 4. See Eustace Carey, *Memoir of William Carey*, 126.

[68] Walker, *William Carey: Missionary Pioneer and Statesman*, 242-244.

[69] Walker, *William Carey: Missionary Pioneer and Statesman*, 244-247.

[70] Walker, *William Carey: Missionary Pioneer and Statesman*, 310.

[71] Wayland, "Introductory Essay," *Memoir of William Carey*, xviii.

[72] Wayland, "Introductory Essay," *Memoir of William Carey*, xviii.

[73] Roger E. Hedlund, "William Carey's Universal Significance," *Carey's Obligations and India's Renaissance*, eds. J. T. K. Daniel and R. E. Hedlund (Serampore: Council of Serampore College, 1993), 96-113.

[74] K. P. Aleaz, *Theology of Religions: Birmingham Papers and Other Essays* (Calcutta: Moumita Publishers and Distributers, 1998), 1.

[75] K. P. Aleaz, *Dimensions of Indian Religion: Study, Experience and Interaction* (Calcutta: Punthi Pusthak, 1995), 260.

[76] Aleaz, *Dimensions of Indian Religion*, 260-261.

[77] Tapan Kumar Banerjee, "William Carey and National Harmony," *William Carey and National Harmony*, eds. Pratap Chandra Gine and Ratna Dutta (Serampore: Serampore College, 2012), 94.

[78] Gurevitch Z, "Dialectical Dialogue: the struggle for speech, repressive silence, and the shift to multiplicity," https://www.ncbi.nlm.nih.gov, accessed on 16th January 2019.

[79] Paul F. Knitter, *Introducing Theologies of Religions* (New York: Orbis Books, 2008 [2002]), 83.

[80] Knitter, *Introducing Theologies of Religions*, 83.

[81] Aleyamma Zachariah, *Modern Religious and Secular Movements in India* (Bangalore: Theological Book Trust, 1992), 11-14.

[82] Cited in Ashish Kumar Massey and June Hedlund, "William Carey and the Emergence of Modern India," *Carey's Obligation and India's Renaissance*, eds. J. T. K. Daniel and R. E. Hedlund (Serampore: Council of Serampore College, 1993), 299.

[83] Banerjee, "William Carey and National Harmony," 95.

[84] Ashish Kumar Massey and June Hedlund, "William Carey and the Emergence of Modern India," *Carey's Obligation and India's Renaissance*, 300.

[85] M. A. Laird, "William Carey and the Education of India," *The Indian Journal of Theology* 10/3 (July-September 1961), 103.

[86] Cf. Vishal and Ruth Mangalwadi, *The Legacy of William Carey: A Model for the Transformation of a Culture*, Illinoise: Crossway Books, 1999 [1993].

[87] Ruth Mangalwadi, "William Carey and Emancipation of Women," *Carey's Obligations and Indian Renaissance, eds.* J. T. K. Daniel and R. E. Hedlund (Serampore: Council of Serampore College, 1993), 337-338.

[88] Ruth Mangalwadi, "William Carey and Emancipation of Women," 338-341.

[89] D. S. Sarma, *Studies in the Renaissance of Hinduism in the Nineteenth and Twentieth Centuries* (Benarus: Benarus Hindu University, 1944), 71-11; Kalidas Nag, "The Brahmo Samaj", *The Cultural Heritage of India* Vol. IV, ed. Haridas Bhattacharyya (Calcutta: Ramakrishna Mission Institute of Culture, 2001 [1956]), 613-633.

[90] Dwijendra Narayan Jha, *The Myth of the Holy Cow* (New Delhi: Navayana Publishing Pvt. Ltd., 2009).

[91] Giri K., Yoga, "*Ghar Wapsi* and Beef Politics: Dance of Pseudo-Democracy in India." *Bethany Journal of Theology* VIII/1 (April 2016): 9-30.

[92] Riya Oli Roy, "Eulogy to the Magnanimous," *William Carey and National Harmony*, eds. Pratap Chandra Gine and Ratna Dutta (Serampore: Serampore College, 2012), 55.

[93] Laird, "William Carey and the Education of India," 101.

[94] Bikash Paul, "Tribute to the Elevator—William Carey," *William Carey and National Harmony*, eds. Pratap Chandra Gine and Ratna Dutta (Serampore: Serampore College, 2012), 57.

[95] Cf. Roy, "Eulogy to the Magnanimous," 56.

[96] B. R. Ambedkar, *Annihilation of Caste, 1936* (New Delhi: Critical Quest, 2007).

[97] Lewis R. Rambo, "Conversion," *The Encyclopedia of Religion*, Vol. 4, ed. Mircea Eliade (New York: MacMillan Publication Co., 1984), 73.

Bibliography

Aleaz, K. P. *Dimensions of Indian Religion: Study, Experience and Interaction.* Calcutta: Punthi Pusthak, 1995.

Aleaz, K. P. *Theology of Religions: Birmingham Papers and Other Essays.* Calcutta: Moumita Publishers and Distributers, 1998.

Ambedkar, B. R. *Annihilation of Caste, 1936*, New Delhi: Critical Quest, 2007.

Banerjee, T. K. "William Carey and National Harmony." *William Carey and National Harmony.* Eds. Pratap Chandra Gine and Ratna Dutta. Serampore: Serampore College, 2012.

Carey, E. *Memoir of William Carey, D.D.* Boston: Gould, Kendall and Lincoln, 1836.

Carey, W. *An Enquiry into the Obligations of Christians, to use means for the Conversion of the Heathens*, 1792.

Giri, K. "Yoga, *Ghar Wapsi* and Beef Politics: Dance of Pseudo-Democracy in India." *Bethany Journal of Theology* 8/1 (April 2016): 9-30.

Gurevitch, Z. "Dialectical Dialogue: The struggle for speech, repressive silence, and the shift to multiplicity." https://www.ncbi.nlm.nih.gov. Accessed on 16th January 2019.

Jha, D. N. *The Myth of the Holy Cow*, New Delhi: Navayana Publishing Pvt. Ltd., 2009.

Knitter, P. F. *Introducing Theologies of Religions.* New York: Orbis Books, 2008 [2002].

Laird, M. A. "William Carey and the Education of India," *The Indian Journal of Theology* 10/3 (July-September 1961): 97-104.

Mangalwadi, R. "William Carey and Emancipation of Women." *Carey's Obligations and Indian Renaissance.* Eds. J. T. K. Daniel and R. E. Hedlund. Serampore: Council of Serampore College, 1993: 334-345.

Mangalwadi, V and R. *The Legacy of William Carey: A Model for the Transformation of a Culture.* Illinoise: Crossway Books, 1999 [1993].

Massey, A. K. and June Hedlund. "William Carey and the Emergence of Modern India." *Carey's Obligation and India's Renaissance.* Eds. J. T. K. Daniel and R. E. Hedlund. Serampore: Council of Serampore College: 1993, 299-308.

Nag, K. "The Brahmo Samaj." *The Cultural Heritage of India* Vol. IV. Ed. Haridas Bhattacharyya. Calcutta: Ramakrishna Mission Institute of Culture, 2001 [1956]: 613-633.

Paul, B. "Tribute to the Elevator—William Carey." *William Carey and National Harmony.* Eds. Pratap Chandra Gine and Ratna Dutta. Serampore: Serampore College, 2012: 57.

Rambo, L. R. "Conversion." *The Encyclopedia of Religion.* Vol. 4. Ed. Mircea Eliade. New York: MacMillan Publication Co., 1984: 73-74.

Roy, R. O. "Eulogy to the Magnanimous." *William Carey and National Harmony.* Eds. Pratap Chandra Gine and Ratna Dutta. Serampore: Serampore College, 2012: 55-56.

Sarma, D. S. *Studies in the Renaissance of Hinduism in the Nineteenth and Twentieth Centuries* Benarus: Benarus Hindu University, 1944.

Walker, F. D. *William Carey: Missionary Pioneer and Statesman.* London: SCM, 1926.

Wayland, F. "Introductory Essay." *Memoir of William Carey, D.D.* Boston: Gould, Kendall and Lincoln, 1836.

Zachariah, A. *Modern Religious and Secular Movements in India.* Bangalore: Theological Book Trust, 1992.

Author Index

C

D

E

F

G

H

I

J

K

L

M

S

T

U

V

W

Y

Z

www.ingramcontent.com/pod-product-compliance
Lightning Source LLC
Chambersburg PA
CBHW030403030726
47497CB00002B/465